DANGER AT DARKMOOR PARK

THE AUDACIOUS SISTERHOOD OF SMOKE & FIRE
BOOK 3

SYRIE JAMES

ARE YOU SIGNED UP FOR DRAGONBLADE'S BLOG?

You'll get the latest news and information on exclusive giveaways, exclusive excerpts, coming releases, sales, free books, cover reveals and more.

Check out our complete list of authors, too!

No spam, no junk. That's a promise!

Sign Up Here

www.dragonbladepublishing.com

Dearest Reader;

Thank you for your support of a small press. At Dragonblade Publishing, we strive to bring you the highest quality Historical Romance from some of the best authors in the business. Without your support, there is no 'us', so we sincerely hope you adore these stories and find some new favorite authors along the way.

Happy Reading!

CEO, Dragonblade Publishing

Dedication

I dedicate this novel to the memory of my dear and loving parents, Morton and Joann Astrahan, who encouraged my love of books and reading from an early age. You live on in my mind and heart forever.

*"He who learns but does not think, is lost!
He who thinks but does not learn is in great danger."*

Confucius

*"Three things cannot long stay hidden:
the sun, the moon, and the truth."*

The Buddha

*"He who learns but does not think, is lost!
He who thinks but does not learn is in great danger."*

Confucius

*"Three things cannot long stay hidden:
the sun, the moon, and the truth."*

The Buddha

CHAPTER ONE

Yorkshire, England
December 23rd, 1852

I T WAS GOING to be the most wonderful Christmas house party that Darkmoor Park had ever seen. Ten days of holiday cheer with festive Christmas traditions, delicious food, lovely walks on the grounds, and fine evening entertainments.

Best of all, it would be an opportunity for Selena Taylor to meet new people and make new friends, a pleasant diversion from her duties as a schoolteacher. She looked forward to every minute—even though, for the past few days, she had been troubled by a vague feeling of foreboding that *something* would go wrong.

"I thought we'd let everyone settle in when they arrive and get reacquainted over dinner tonight," Selena told her dear friend Mrs. Rose Hillman, who sat in the green velvet wingback chair across from her, beside the front parlor fire. "Tomorrow night is tree decorating. On Christmas morning, we can gather in the drawing room for—"

"Selena! Stop." Mrs. Hillman waved a silencing hand. "Your students have left for the holidays, my dear. For the next ten days, you don't have to organize every single minute."

"I just want everything to go perfectly." Despite herself, another inexplicable ripple of anxiety raced down Selena's spine.

"And it *will* go perfectly," Mrs. Hillman insisted. "My house parties always do. I would rather you sit back and enjoy yourself, along with all the other guests."

"But I'm not a guest. I live here." Selena not only lived at Darkmoor Park, but she was also the heir to the magnificent, ancient estate. A fact that surprised and thrilled her every time she thought about it. Her good fortune was not due to birth or rank, but to the generosity of the genteel widow seated across from her.

When Selena and her sister Athena had moved to the neighborhood over two years ago, they had become such close friends that Mrs. Hillman, who had no natural heirs, had named Selena as her successor to Darkmoor Park. The older woman had invited Selena to move in at once, for she was tired of living alone—a request which Selena had been only too happy to oblige.

"We have six guests coming, and ever so many meals and activities ahead," Selena continued. "It is too much for you to manage on your own, ma'am." Although Mrs. Hillman, with her perfectly coiffed copper-and-grey curls, looked a decade younger than her sixty-five years, she had suffered a mild stroke a few years ago, and Selena didn't want to risk endangering the woman's health. "Please allow me to join you in serving as a second hostess of your party."

Mrs. Hillman's face creased in a warm smile. "Very well, if that's what you truly wish."

"Thank you." Selena exhaled with satisfaction.

"I hope you know how grateful I am, Selena, that you decided to stay home for the holidays instead of going down south," Mrs. Hillman said as she smoothed out the skirts of her purple brocade satin gown.

"I do."

Selena's sister Athena; Athena's husband, Ian; and their nine-month-old son, Henry, had left several days ago to spend Christmas with their older sister, Diana, and her family at Pendowar Hall in Cornwall. Their brother, Damon, a clergyman, had to officiate at the Christmas services for his congregation in a poor parish in London, but he planned to join the family in

Cornwall later in the week.

Selena had been invited, of course, and she had wanted very much to go. She and her sisters had been close since childhood, when they had solved many small mysteries together. They had been such avid sleuths that they had called themselves "The Audacious Sisterhood of Smoke and Fire," after a saying of their late mother's—"*Where there's smoke, there's fire*"—a reminder to not always accept things at face value, but to seek the truth that may lie beneath.

They had never been parted from each other until, when Selena had been sixteen years of age, their father had lost his fortune in a bad investment. Diana and Athena had immediately found positions as governesses to earn to their keep, and Selena had soon followed in their footsteps. They had all served in that capacity for nearly a decade.

Three years ago, Diana had become embroiled in a dangerous mystery at Pendowar Hall that had nearly ended her life—but she had identified the culprit and married her Prince Charming, the wealthy baronet and Royal Navy Captain William Fallbrook. That good man had purchased Thorndale Manor, an ancient property about a mile away from Darkmoor Park, to enable Selena and Athena to achieve their lifelong dream to open a school for girls.

After weathering some dire difficulties—including several near-death experiences and the solving of two murders—Selena and Athena had successfully run the Darkmoor Bridge School for Girls at Thorndale Manor for two years. This past fall, however, at Mrs. Hillman's invitation, they had moved the school to Darkmoor Park. The stunning estate, with its many dozens of elegantly furnished rooms and thousands of acres of gardens and woods, had proven to be an ideal location for their growing band of pupils, and the move had given Athena and her husband and son more privacy at Thorndale Manor. It had all worked out perfectly.

"I feel a little guilty, though." Mrs. Hillman twisted her pale, freckled hands in her lap. "I know I'm stealing you away from your family."

Selena brushed back a stray, blonde curl from her forehead and gave Mrs. Hillman a reassuring smile. "Don't be silly. I'm glad to be here." In truth, she *was* a bit regretful to be missing the holiday season in Cornwall with her family. Selena would have loved to have seen William's cousin, Emma, who had been Diana's pupil when she'd first gone to Pendowar Hall as a governess, and who continued to benefit from Diana's tutelage. And it had been a year since Selena had seen Diana and William's daughter, Charlotte, who now was nearly two. She adored children of all ages and wished she could be more present in little Charlotte's life. But she had sensed that Mrs. Hillman was going to need her over the coming weeks, and that it would be better if she stayed.

Besides, Selena told herself, had she gone to Pendowar Hall, every day in her family's company would have just been a vivid reminder that, at age thirty, she was the only unmarried—and the least accomplished—sister.

Diana and Athena were both so talented and adept. They had both solved real-life murders. They had married well, had children, helped to run large estates, and still managed to teach. Selena felt so inadequate in comparison. She had only served as Athena's confidante when her sister had uncovered the deadly secrets at Thorndale Manor. Selena had never solved a murder by herself.

Not that she *wanted* a murder to occur in her vicinity! But she couldn't deny it ... when she and Athena had been embroiled in those mysterious circumstances two years ago, it *had* been a thrill.

Mrs. Hillman was slowly teaching Selena how to manage Darkmoor Park, but the property would not be under her direction, hopefully, for many decades. She had recently taken over as headmistress of the school so that Athena could spend more time with her young son, but Selena was still new in the position and unsure of herself. And as for marriage ... she had no prospects of a suitor on the horizon.

Selena had become accustomed to her unmarried state. She was devoted to her occupation. She adored teaching and believed she was good at it. She earned a good income from her work and in addition, Mrs. Hillman was treating her to an allowance, which meant that Selena was financially independent. Darkmoor Park would one distant day be hers. She didn't *need* to marry.

Not so long ago, Selena had harbored the same worries that had plagued Athena at one time: that as long as they remained unwed, they retained control of their money, their property, and their person. But if they married, under law, all that control would go to their husband.

After seeing how happy her sisters were, though, Selena was no longer concerned about that. Diana and Athena had married wonderful men. In her secret soul, Selena dreamed of making a similar match—of finding and falling in love with an intelligent, kind, caring, supportive, and *honest* man. A man who understood and valued her and honored her desire to work. A man she could both love *and trust*.

Because people were not always trustworthy. They did not always have your best interests at heart and could betray you in an instant. She had learned *that* the hard way.

"I realize this party was all my idea, my dear, and that you won't know a single soul." Mrs. Hillman's voice pulled Selena from her thoughts. "The guests are all *my* friends from various parts of England."

"I look forward to meeting them," Selena assured her.

"They'll be happy to meet you as well. I have been looking forward to this reunion for such a long time. Everything that *can* be done *has* been done." Mrs. Hillman raised a finger and ticked things off on an invisible list. "My six best guest rooms are ready. The house is beautifully decorated. The Yule log is in place. An exquisite evergreen has been brought in and set up in the great hall. The table is set for tonight's dinner. And we have drawn up a fine list of activities to occupy everyone all the way through New

Year's Day, have we not?"

"Indeed, we have."

"Well, then, we can both relax. We have nothing to worry about."

Selena nodded uneasily. Although a fire blazed in the hearth, a chill ran up her spine and she was glad she had worn a warm shawl over her blue-and-white-striped woolen dress. "I hope we will have clear weather this week."

Mrs. Hillman glanced out the front casement windows, where the late-afternoon sky had dulled to a misty grey and a few snowflakes danced on the breeze. "It does look as though it might snow. I pray that it holds off for another few hours at least, until Manfred returns from the train station with our two sets of arrivals."

"So do I." Selena bit her lip.

Mrs. Hillman turned her gaze back to Selena. "My dear. Something else is on your mind. What is it?"

Selena hesitated, then took a deep breath. "You'll think this is mad, Mrs. Hillman, but I have a strange premonition that something … *unexpected* is going to happen at this party."

"'Unexpected'?" Mrs. Hillman's pale-blue eyes narrowed. "What do you mean?"

"I don't know. I've never had a feeling like this before."

"You've never helped host a house party like this one before, either, have you?"

"No," Selena conceded.

The older woman shrugged. "It's probably just nerves. But then, to be fair, I haven't seen these people in a long while."

Selena knew that Mrs. Hillman had met this small group of friends four years ago, when they had spent a month in residence at the Worthing Seaside Hotel in West Sussex. "It's the first time the four of you have been together since that summer at the hotel, isn't it?"

"Yes." Mrs. Hillman's eyes crinkled as if in fond remembrance. "They are lovely people. I am not acquainted with everyone who's coming, though. One of the guests is a new lady's companion, and there's also a young couple whom I've never met."

"I remember."

Mrs. Hillman frowned, her gaze focusing on some distant point. "I do hope we won't have any more unpleasantness, like we did at the hotel that summer."

Selena looked at her sharply. "What unpleasantness?"

Mrs. Hillman hesitated and then shook her head. "Never mind. I don't know why I even mentioned it. It is all the past."

The sound of distant hoofbeats and jangling harnesses rent the air. Through the window, Selena caught sight of Mrs. Hillman's gleaming, black carriage pulled by four matching black horses rounding the bend at the far end of the long dirt lane.

"Here they are now." Mrs. Hillman grabbed her cane from beside her chair. "Let us go out and greet them."

A BRISK WIND flirted with the branches of the few prized evergreens that bordered the front lane and an occasional snowflake drifted by. Selena wrapped her woolen shawl more tightly around her as she and Mrs. Hillman stood on the roofed front porch of the manor house watching the unhurried progress of the arriving carriage. Mrs. Hillman eschewed the practice of obliging every upper servant to stand on ceremony outside to meet arriving guests, so they were accompanied only by the head footman, George, a tall, strapping young man with coal-black hair.

While she waited, Selena couldn't help but glance up at the building behind them. Darkmoor Park, a former abbey that had undergone a multitude of additions and renovations, was an immense, three-story structure of weathered, grey stone, with two broad wings, a steeply gabled roofline, and three rows of tall casement windows that reached up to the attics.

Selena shook her head in wonder. Residing in this magnificent place and being allowed to run her school for girls here with Athena was such an honor. But never in her wildest dreams could Selena have ever imagined that she would be named the *heir* to a house like this. Although she was the daughter of a gentleman and had grown up comfortably, her family's old country house was a mere cottage in comparison to the splendor of Darkmoor Park, not to mention all the lands attached to it.

She didn't know what she had done to deserve such munificence, other than to be Mrs. Hillman's friend—a relationship that Selena treasured. She had lost her mother at a young age, and in many ways, Mrs. Hillman had come to fulfill that role in Selena's life. Every morning, Selena woke up wondering what service she could perform for Mrs. Hillman, to help herself feel more worthy of the gift she'd been given.

Mrs. Hillman's coach reached the curved gravel drive and with a gentle crunching of hooves, it stopped before them. The tall, sandy-haired footman leaped down from the carriage, opened the door, and let down the steps. Selena had spoken no more than a few words to Sam, a handsome, reserved young man who had been hired for a few weeks only to help with the holiday house party.

The first passenger to descend from the vehicle was a short, apple-shaped woman of perhaps sixty years of age. Her sumptuous-looking black velvet coat was trimmed in white fur and a massive matching hat with several tall ostrich plumes crowned her dark curls, which were streaked with white, as if designed by nature to match her ensemble.

"That is Mrs. Opal Whitlock," Mrs. Hillman explained quietly to Selena. "The widow I told you about from Hertfordshire."

"You said she adores knitting and playing parlor games and cards?" Selena asked, attempting to keep the details fresh in her mind.

"That's right."

"She looks very well-to-do," Selena observed, taking in the

woman's stunning attire.

"I believe she *was*. Although ever since her husband passed away, I understand her circumstances are somewhat reduced." Mrs. Hillman paused. "At times, she can be a bit, how shall I say it, finicky and exacting? But deep down, she's a dear."

"Where is my brown case with the blue strap?" Mrs. Whitlock snapped at Sam. "The one I expressly asked to hold on my lap? I hope you didn't leave it at the station!"

"We brought everything, ma'am," Sam replied. "I can show you what's tied on back, after I help the other passengers down."

"They can take care of themselves." Mrs. Whitlock's eyes blazed. "This cannot wait. Show me at once!"

Sam nodded in acquiescence. A dark-haired young woman who looked to be in her mid-twenties and was clad in a black hat and cloak, grey frock, and sensible, black boots emerged from the vehicle and hurried after Mrs. Whitlock towards the rear of the coach.

"*That* must be Mrs. Whitlock's new companion, Miss Maud Thompson. She also serves as her lady's maid."

"Mrs. Whitlock is the only person who brought a servant, I believe?" Selena asked.

"She is. At Mrs. Whitlock's request, I arranged for Miss Thompson to be accommodated in the same wing as us and the other guests. Apparently, Mrs. Whitlock prefers to have her companion close by in case she needs anything during the night."

A barrel-chested gentleman of medium height appeared in the coach doorway. His charcoal-grey overcoat seemed to be stretched to the limit over his bulky frame, and his short, silvery hair was neatly combed over an attractive, ruddy-cheeked face.

"And here is Jack Clarke. He's a successful businessman." At the sight of him, Mrs. Hillman's cheeks, which were already rosy from the cold, grew an even deeper shade of pink.

Selena studied her friend with surprise. "Are you *blushing*, Mrs. Hillman?"

With a demure smile, the good woman lowered her voice to

a whisper. "He and I had what you might call … a *little holiday romance* the summer we met."

"A romance!" Selena whispered with delight. "You are a dark horse, Mrs. Hillman. You never mentioned anything about that."

Mrs. Hillman shrugged. "A woman has to keep *some* secrets."

The new arrival caught sight of Mrs. Hillman, and a wide grin split his face. "Well, as I live and breathe, if it isn't my little Rosie!" he boomed, his voice deep and hearty.

"'Rosie'?" Selena couldn't hold back her own smile.

Mr. Clarke briskly crossed the drive, bounded up the steps, and held out a broad hand to Mrs. Hillman. "How wonderful to see you!"

"And you, Mr. Clarke." Mrs. Hillman placed her gloved hand in his, and he kissed it.

Selena thought she detected a shadow pass over the gentleman's features, but the look vanished as quickly as it had appeared, and she wondered if she had imagined it.

"How I've missed you, my Rosie," Mr. Clarke said as he released her hand. "Can it really have been four years? You haven't aged a minute."

"Flattery will get you everywhere." Mrs. Hillman's eyes twinkled. "But, sir, may I remind you that we are no longer at the Worthing Seaside Hotel, and I am not 'your Rosie.' Here, you must address me as 'Mrs. Hillman.'"

"'Mrs. Hillman'?" He scoffed. "That won't do for me, Rosie darling. But if you insist on formalities, I'll settle for 'Mrs. H.'"

Mrs. Hillman laughed. "You are incorrigible, Mr. Clarke."

"*Incorrigible* is my middle name." His gaze rose to the building behind them. "My goodness. Every time you described Dark-moor Park, I thought you must have been overstating things. But I see the opposite is true. It is truly magnificent."

"Thank you." Mrs. Hillman gave a modest nod.

Turning to Selena now, Mr. Clarke said, "And who is this pretty, young thing?"

"Mr. Clarke, may I present my dear friend, Miss Selena Taylor. I wrote to you about her. Selena, this is Mr. Jack Clarke."

"A pleasure to meet you, Miss Taylor." He took Selena's gloved hand in the same gallant manner as he had taken Mrs. Hillman's and impressed it with a kiss.

"The pleasure is mine, sir." The gentleman had such a larger-than-life presence and exuded such charm, it was impossible for Selena to look away.

"As I recall, Mrs. H said you're a schoolteacher? And heir to the kingdom?" He winked at Selena as he released her hand.

His comment, and the cheeky expression that accompanied it, made Selena's face grow warm. She struggled for a reply.

"You are quite right, Mr. Clarke," Mrs. Hillman interjected, taking Selena's arm in the crook of her own and giving her an affectionate smile. "Selena and I get along like two peas in a pod. I'm fortunate to have her living here with me and thrilled to know that she will one day be the new caretaker of Darkmoor Park."

"I'm sure she'll do a fine job and make you proud." Mr. Clarke's smile was kind and encouraging. Lowering his voice, he added to Selena, "Did you know I asked this good woman to marry me four years ago? And she turned me down?"

Selena felt her brows raise. "Is that so?" It seemed that the day was to be full of surprises.

Mrs. Hillman shrugged. "I have no need to marry, and I told him so."

"I intend to impress her with my charms and try again," Mr. Clarke told Selena, which made Mrs. Hillman roll her eyes.

At that moment, Mrs. Whitlock and her companion, lifting up their long skirts, mounted the front steps and joined them on the front porch. "My dear Mrs. Hillman! What an extraordinary house! I have no words to express my delight!" Mrs. Whitlock held out her arms.

"Mrs. Whitlock! You look marvelous, my dear," Mrs. Hillman said as the two women embraced.

Mrs. Whitlock's companion was clutching a small, brown

case with a blue strap. It seemed that the missing piece of luggage had been found.

"As do you." Mrs. Whitlock exhaled in a huff. "However, this has been the longest two days of my life. I cannot tell you how glad I am to be here. I had to rise in freezing darkness yesterday to catch the 8:16 train from Exeter. There were delays everywhere and ever so many changes! Last night, we had to stay at the most dismal inn in Warwick."

"Have you forgotten?" put in Mr. Clarke. "It used to take three or four days by coach to cover the same distance. This new age of the railway is a like a miracle."

"I do hope you'll think the trip was worth it, Mrs. Whitlock," Mrs. Hillman replied dryly. "I, for one, am glad to see you after all these years."

Mrs. Whitlock's frown turned upside down and she let out an unfettered laugh. "Oh, listen to me, going on and on. Yes, yes. The feeling is mutual."

"Allow me to introduce Miss Selena Taylor." Mrs. Hillman gestured to Selena.

"Mrs. Hillman has spoken of you endlessly in her letters, Miss Taylor," returned Mrs. Whitlock, holding out her hand. "I am pleased to make your acquaintance."

"The pleasure is all mine, Mrs. Whitlock." Selena greeted Mrs. Whitlock with a handshake and then extended her hand to the woman's companion, thinking it rude that she had not been introduced. "I am Selena Taylor. And you must be Maud Thompson?"

"Yes," replied Miss Thompson quietly, her grip tentative and brief.

"I am so happy to meet you." Selena gave her a cordial nod.

Before Miss Thompson could respond, Mrs. Whitlock announced with a scowl, "Miss Thompson has only been a few months in my employ and has yet to prove herself." Gesturing to the case Miss Thompson was carrying, Mrs. Whitlock added, "I told her to make sure that bag was brought to me inside the carriage, but was it? No! I was sick with worry all the way from the station!"

"I'm so sorry, Mrs. Whitlock." Miss Thompson spoke just above a whisper. "It will never happen again."

"See that it doesn't!" Mrs. Whitlock shot back.

Selena felt sorry for the young woman. Having served many years as a governess, Selena knew from personal experience how difficult and demeaning it could be to work for people who didn't value you in any way other than the manner in which you could be of use to them. Thinking it best to change the subject, she glanced at Mr. Clarke and said, "I presume the three of you met up on the train today?"

"In fact," replied he, "we met up by chance yesterday in Warwick at the White Hart Inn, where we all stayed the night en route."

"What a horrid excuse for a lodging house that was!" Mrs. Whitlock grimaced. "The bedding was unclean, and I am sure there were rats in the walls."

"Ah, but they had excellent meat pie and the best ale I have tasted in many a month," Mr. Clarke put in with a smile. "And how nice it was to see a familiar face. I had dinner there with these two ladies and what a jolly evening it was."

Mrs. Whitlock's eyes narrowed as she glanced at Mr. Clarke. "Running into you, sir, *did* add some levity to the evening. Although I fear you may have had a bit too much to drink last night."

Mr. Clarke waved away this remark with a chuckle. "A man is always more congenial when he is in his cups, Mrs. Whitlock." A comment that made that lady frown and shake her head.

The footmen had been busy all this time bringing in the luggage. Mrs. Hillman led the new arrivals into the house, where an exhibition of ancient weaponry was displayed above the polished black-and-white marble floor of the spacious entrance hall. Beyond, a wide central oak staircase, whose elaborately carved handrails were intertwined with holiday greenery, led to the upper floors.

Mrs. Hillman introduced the two head servants who stood waiting at attention. "Wells is a treasure," she said of the white-haired butler, who was clad in a traditional black tailcoat. "He has been with me since I came to Darkmoor Park as a bride. Mrs. Middleton, my housekeeper, has also been here for many years and is a wealth of knowledge."

Mrs. Middleton wore a high-necked, long-sleeved, black woolen gown beneath an immaculate white apron, and her light-brown hair was tucked up neatly beneath a white cap.

"Feel free to ask either of them any questions you have," Selena added. "Mrs. Middleton will oversee all your needs."

"Since the other guests won't be arriving for another couple of hours, we'll wait to give you all a house tour until tomorrow," Mrs. Hillman said. "But everyone always wants to see the great hall, so let's take a quick peek in there before you go up to your rooms."

The immense great hall, which opened off to one side of the entry hall, was paneled in dark oak and featured a high ceiling carved with elaborate scrollwork, a marble parquet floor, and more displays of weaponry above two gleaming ancestral suits of armor.

Selena had overseen the arrangement of the Christmas decorations and was pleased to see how pretty it looked and how good it smelled. Boughs of evergreens, ivy, and holly, entwined with red ribbons, decked the mantel of the enormous marble fireplace and were draped in garlands around the pillars, entrances, doors, and sideboards, which held an array of silver and pewter objects. A tall evergreen tree, as yet devoid of any Christmas ornaments, stood in one corner and imbued the room with its fresh piney scent.

"I've made many improvements to Darkmoor Park over the years," Mrs. Hillman explained as the three guests took in the vast space with open-mouthed admiration, "but the great hall is the one room that my late husband didn't want to change, so it remains as it has been for many a century."

"Marvelous," Mr. Clarke said with an appreciative nod.

"It's so festive," Miss Thompson said quietly.

Mrs. Whitlock merely stared in silence, her jaw and shoulders tense. Selena couldn't tell if the woman was envious or merely in an eternally bad mood.

"Roger and I held many a ball in this chamber." Mrs. Hillman seemed to be lost in memory for a moment, which she shook off with a little sigh. "But that was ages ago. I'm sure you are all tired after two long days of traveling. Mrs. Middleton will show you to your rooms."

"This house functions as a school now," Selena put in as the group headed back towards the entry hall and main stairs. "Our pupils occupy the bedchambers in the south wing on the first floor. Although they've all gone home for the holidays, we didn't wish to disturb their rooms, so we have placed you all in the guest rooms in the north wing, not far from Mrs. Hillman's and my own rooms."

"Please take all the time you need to settle in," Mrs. Hillman said. "Dinner is at eight. We'll meet for drinks before dinner in the drawing room at seven."

"A staff member will meet you at the foot of the stairs to show you the way," Selena added. "We'll see you then."

CHAPTER TWO

"J ACK CLARKE! HOW wonderful to see you again."

The cheerful greeting was pronounced by Colonel Arthur Blackwood, a tall, broad-shouldered widower in his early fifties who had recently retired from the Royal Army, and whose thinning, auburn hair was peppered with grey. Selena had briefly made his acquaintance when he had arrived with the second group of guests.

The grandfather clock in the hall had just struck seven and most of the party were assembled in the elegant, spacious drawing room, Selena's favorite room in the house.

Ancestral portraits and landscapes adorned the sage-green walls. A multitude of mirrors in gilded frames reflected the flickering candlelight from the ornate bronze-and-crystal chandeliers. Sofas and chairs upholstered in shades of blue and green faced each other in small groups and multi-colored Turkish carpets were scattered across the polished oak floor. The immense Yule log that burned in the carved marble hearth added a soft, warm glow to the room, which was as festively bedecked as the great hall with multitudes of holiday garlands.

The footmen circulated with drinks in crystal glasses on silver trays. The guests had dressed for dinner and the hum of conversation and gentle laughter filled the room.

"And what a pleasure to see you, sir," Mr. Clarke was saying, as he and Colonel Blackwood heartily shook hands.

Selena stood alongside the two gentlemen, warmed by her cocktail and by the obvious affection between the two. She felt pretty in the black velvet gown with silver trim that her benefactress had generously ordered from Paris. The gentlemen had both dressed for dinner in well-tailored black suits, white ties, and white satin waistcoats.

"I wasn't sure you'd be able to join us, Clarke," Colonel Blackwood remarked. "You're such a busy man."

"I wouldn't have missed this house party for the world." Mr. Clarke turned to Selena with a smile. "The last time I saw this man was in Dublin—what was it, eighteen months ago?"

"Indeed," the colonel replied. "We ran into each other by the purest chance."

Mr. Clarke shot the colonel a grin. "How can you cross Dublin without passing a pub?"

Colonel Blackwood raised his cocktail. "You must stop in at every single one."

The two men chuckled at the joke and clinked glasses. Selena laughed along with them.

"We certainly put that theory to the test, didn't we?" Mr. Clarke grinned.

"We did and yet lived to tell the tale," the colonel replied. "So, my friend, what have you been up to?"

"No good, as usual." Mr. Clarke waggled his eyebrows.

"But seriously." Colonel Blackwood gave him a direct look. "You always seem to have some new business venture or scheme in the works."

Mr. Clarke's smile faltered. "I *have* been working on something. But ..."

"I knew it," the colonel replied. "Do tell."

"I'm not at liberty to talk about it at present." Mr. Clarke lowered his gaze.

Selena sensed that Mr. Clarke was avoiding the colonel's gaze and wondered why.

A flash of impatience crossed Colonel Blackwood's features

and then it was gone. "You can tell me anything, old fellow."

Shaking his head, Mr. Clarke gave a sigh and said, "I've reached that age—like you, I'm thinking of retiring."

"I highly recommend retirement." Colonel Blackwood bobbed his head. "All the time in the world to see and do things."

"And to take holidays like this one." Mr. Clarke sipped his drink.

"We ought to meet again next summer," Colonel Blackwood suggested, "at the Worthing Seaside Hotel."

"Marvelous spot!" enthused Mr. Clarke. "I have such fond memories of the place."

"How did you pass your time there?" Selena asked, curious.

"Lots of long walks on the beach," Colonel Blackwood replied, "swapping stories and watching the boats sail by."

"Mrs. Goodwin ran that hotel like a tight ship," Mr. Clarke said. "She was a good soul. Served fine meals—and the best wine. How many nights did we end up drinking ourselves under the table?"

"Too many to count."

The two men exchanged another laugh.

"Speaking of which. Mrs. H!" Mr. Clarke called out to Mrs. Hillman, who stood nearby in conversation with Mrs. Whitlock. "Why isn't Flora Goodwin here? We all liked her so much. I thought you planned to invite her to this reunion?"

An awkward silence filled the room. Selena shifted her feet uneasily. She knew why Mrs. Goodwin was not here and judging from the uncomfortable expressions on the faces of everyone except Mr. Clarke, they did too.

Mrs. Hillman cleared her throat. "I'm sorry to say, Mr. Clarke, that Mrs. Goodwin passed away a few months ago. I'm sure I wrote to you about it?"

Mr. Clarke's eyes widened, and his cheeks grew pink. "Ah. I do seem to recall now that you mentioned something about that. Forgive me. Things seem to fall out of my head these days. I'm sorry that she is gone."

"So am I." Colonel Blackwood's brow wrinkled. "I was shocked, Mrs. Hillman, when you wrote with the news. Mrs. Goodwin couldn't have been more than fifty years old, am I right? And she seemed to be in perfect health."

Mrs. Hillman nodded. "It *is* very sad. I know we will all miss her."

"I suppose that hotel will go to rack and ruin now." Mrs. Whitlock heaved a sigh.

"I hope not," Mrs. Hillman retorted sharply. "Mrs. Goodwin's daughter, Nancy, has been helping to run the place the past couple of years, and she has now taken over. In fact, Miss Goodwin is here now, along with the man to whom she is engaged, and they will be staying for the holidays."

"What? You invited *the daughter*?" Mrs. Whitlock sounded aghast.

"I did," Mrs. Hillman answered.

"Why?" demanded Mrs. Whitlock.

Mrs. Hillman took a breath as if struggling to remain calm. "Because, my dear Mrs. Whitlock, when I sent Mrs. Goodwin the invitation, her daughter replied with the sad news of her mother's death and mentioned that she was newly betrothed. Knowing that the hotel would be closed for the winter and thinking it might cheer Miss Goodwin up to have a place to go for the holidays, I encouraged her to come in her mother's stead, and to bring her husband-to-be."

"But this is supposed to be a reunion!" Mrs. Whitlock exclaimed. "None of us know the daughter or this gentleman!"

"Miss Goodwin was away on holiday with friends, I believe, when we all stayed at the hotel that summer?" Colonel Blackwood asked.

"Yes, she was," Mrs. Hillman confirmed.

"It is most uncouth for an unmarried young woman to come unchaperoned with a man who is not yet her husband," decried Mrs. Whitlock with a frown.

"She's a working lady," Mr. Clarke pointed out, "and they do things differently than 'proper ladies' do. So, I say it's quite all right."

"I agree. And I think it was sweet of you to include them," Selena told Mrs. Hillman.

"I understand they came on the late-afternoon train?" Mrs. Hillman asked Selena.

"They did." Although Selena had greeted the young couple and the colonel upon arrival at the house, Mrs. Hillman had been napping, and the others had been sequestered in their rooms.

"Excellent," Mrs. Hillman said. "I look forward to meeting them."

As if on cue, a couple who appeared to be in their mid-twenties entered the drawing room and paused just inside the doorway.

"Here they are!" Selena beckoned to the pair to come forward. "Mrs. Hillman, everyone, allow me to introduce Miss Nancy Goodwin and Mr. Graham Davis."

Miss Goodwin was petite, svelte, and raven-haired with pleasant features and a pale complexion. Her high-necked, long-sleeved, black bombazine gown, an indication that she was in mourning, was devoid of any ornamentation. "How do you do?" She curtsied with her head held high.

The tall, slender young man at her side was attired in a plain, black suit. "Good evening." He bowed, ran a hand through his dark hair, and glanced around, wide-eyed. "What a lovely house."

Selena gestured to the lady of the house. "May I present our hostess, Mrs. Rose Hillman?"

Mrs. Hillman offered her hand to each of the newcomers in turn. "Miss Goodwin, how lovely to meet you. And Mr. Davis? This young lady spoke of you so fondly in her letters. Welcome to Darkmoor Park." In an earnest tone, she added quietly, "Pray accept my deepest condolences, Miss Goodwin, on the passing of your mother. She was a fine woman."

"Thank you." A tear sprouted in the corner of one of Miss Goodwin's eyes. "It has been a difficult time."

Mrs. Hillman tilted her head. "I thought you would resemble your mother, but you don't look a thing like her. She was so fair. You must take after your father?"

"I'm told that I do." Miss Goodwin nodded. "I don't remember him, though. He passed away when I was just a little girl."

"That's right. Your mother told me." Mrs. Hillman sighed. "I'm so sorry. And again, I'm sorry for your mother's loss. I can only imagine how much you must miss her."

"I know she would have loved to be here." Miss Goodwin withdrew a handkerchief from her handbag and used it to wipe her eyes. "But since she cannot ..."

"I admit, Nancy and I feel a bit like interlopers." Mr. Davis fidgeted with his hands. "We appreciate you including us in your holiday plans."

"I am delighted that you could come." Mrs. Hillman smiled warmly. "And now allow me to introduce you to those whom you've not met."

She presented the other guests in turn, who expressed their own words of sympathy on Mrs. Goodwin's passing. When Mr. Clarke shook the couple's hands, his brow creased. "Wait. You two look familiar. Were you at the White Hart Inn in Warwick last night?"

Miss Goodwin nodded. "Yes, sir."

"We were at the next table from where you were dining with Mrs. Whitlock and her companion," Mr. Davis put in.

"But we had no idea who you were at the time," Miss Goodwin said quickly.

"What a shame!" exclaimed Mr. Clarke with a grin. "Had I known, I would have invited you to join us at our table."

The bell rang, announcing dinner. Mrs. Hillman took Mr. Clarke's arm as the rest of the party assembled in pairs to make their way to the dining room, a splendid chamber where the candles in the gilt-brass chandelier and wall sconces cast shimmering beams of light upon the gold-flecked wallpaper and the white Wedgewood ceiling.

A bevy of servants, attired in their best uniforms and livery, stood at the ready to assist the diners to their seats around the linen-draped table, which was set with one of Mrs. Hillman's many sets of bone china dishware, crystal glassware, and silver cutlery. A holiday centerpiece of blazing candles, fragrant evergreens, holly, ivy, and apples added a festive look. Mrs. Hillman sat down at the head of the table, placing Mr. Clarke to her right, and Colonel Blackwood to her left. Selena took the chair at the foot of the table, and the other guests filled in on the sides.

"Oh, look, Graham!" Miss Goodwin exclaimed happily when they had all sat down, and the oyster soup had been served. "It's snowing."

All eyes turned to the tall casement windows. Although it was dark, Selena perceived a steady fall of snow without. Her stomach clenched. This was exactly what she'd been worried about.

"Looks like we got here just in time." Mr. Davis opened his white, linen napkin on his lap.

"And the snow is just in time for Christmas," remarked Colonel Blackwood, picking up his soup spoon.

"I love the snow," breathed Miss Thompson. It was one of the few times she had spoken all evening.

"That's because you have no sense," retorted Mrs. Whitlock, her tone disparaging. "None of you do. Snow clogs the roads and rails. It has to be shoveled. It becomes impossible to go out. And when it melts, it turns the roads and lanes to mud, and everything is mired in filth."

Miss Thompson's smile fled, and she turned her attention to her soup.

"Don't listen to the woman, Miss Thompson," Mr. Clarke said firmly. "There's nothing so charming as a white Christmas."

On the one hand, Selena agreed with Mr. Clarke. She loved the snow, and the way it changed the landscape into a wintry wonderland. On the other hand, although she felt that Mrs. Whitlock's words had been too harsh, Selena was concerned about what the change in weather might mean for their holiday plans. If this turned into a full-blown snowstorm, they could all be trapped inside the house for days.

"Thank goodness the food has all been delivered," Mrs. Hillman said, as if reading Selena's mind. "If perchance we should be snowed in, there is no cause for alarm. We have enough supplies to feed us all for a good ten days."

"Good to know. I say, what is on the agenda?" Colonel Blackwood took a spoonful of soup.

"That is Selena's department," Mrs. Hillman replied.

Selena sat up straighter in her chair, determined not to let the weather dampen her spirits. "Well, tomorrow is Christmas Eve, so we'll begin in the morning by trimming the tree. There will be Christmas carol singing and a festive dinner on Christmas day. We can take walks on the grounds—weather permitting—and I have several parlor games planned."

"I love parlor games." Mrs. Whitlock nodded with approval.

"I like the 'walks' idea." Mr. Clarke turned to their hostess. "Speaking of which, Mrs. H. I rise early every morning and like to take a good, long walk myself. Will breakfast be ready at six o'clock?"

Mrs. Hillman pursed her lips. "I recall your early-morning habits at the Worthing Seaside Hotel, Mr. Clarke. They are the opposite of mine. At Darkmoor Park, breakfast will be available in the morning room from nine A.M. to eleven A.M. And you will not see *me* any time before ten."

Mr. Clarke laughed. "Duly noted."

"However," Mrs. Hillman went on, "feel free to rise whenever you wish. Bread and butter, jam, and nuts will be available in the morning room all day and night, should any of you feel in need of an impromptu snack. And I will ask Mrs. Middleton to have hot coffee and tea available in the morning room at six."

"That would be lovely," Mr. Clarke replied. "Thank you."

Selena glanced out the window, where, as she'd feared, the wind had picked up and the flurries were growing stronger. "If it keeps snowing like this, tomorrow may not be the best day for a walk."

"It will be glorious," Mr. Clarke insisted. "Nothing beats a morning walk in freshly fallen snow." Raising his glass of wine to all assembled, he cried, "May the festivities begin!"

"Hear, hear!" proclaimed the others, and everyone took a drink.

As the footmen served the next course of boiled ham with mashed potatoes, Colonel Blackwood said, "Mrs. Hillman, didn't you tell me that Darkmoor Park used to be a friary?"

"It was," replied their hostess. "The original part of the building dates to 1170, when it served as a Cistercian abbey. During the reign of Henry VIII, the property was taken over by a nobleman who took the church and cloisters apart stone by stone and built this residence, which has been expanded over the centuries into what you see now."

"How did this place come to you?" asked Mr. Davis as he speared a slice of ham.

"I can answer that," Selena said. "The estate was not entailed to the male line. In time, it came to an earl's daughter who married a man named Hillman, and the title became extinct."

"I met that gentleman's grandson, Mr. Roger Hillman." Mrs. Hillman's eyes went misty. "We fell in love and were married. Do you see this brooch?" She gestured affectionately to the ornament pinned at the neckline of her midnight-blue satin gown. The gold brooch was in the shape of an iris and fitted with diamonds, sapphires, emeralds, and pearls. "Roger knew how much I love flowers, blue irises in particular, and he gave this to me as a wedding gift."

"It is stunning," observed Miss Goodwin.

"It reminds me of an antique jewelry collection I saw recently at an estate sale," commented Mrs. Whitlock with a wistful look. "I fell in love with it at first sight. There's a necklace, earrings, bracelet, ring, and the most stunning brooch set in gold and depicting pansies with diamonds and amethysts, and marquis-shaped emeralds for the leaves."

"My mother always says, 'If you love something as much as that, you should snap it up the moment you see it,'" remarked Colonel Blackwood. "You may not get a second chance."

"I'm afraid it's out of my reach, Colonel." Mrs. Whitlock shrugged and turned to admire Mrs. Hillman's brooch again, adding, "Your husband had excellent taste in jewelry."

"Yes, he did," Mrs. Hillman agreed.

"Where does your mother live, Colonel?" Selena asked.

"She's spent the past twenty years in London, ever since my father died," the colonel replied. "She's seventy-five now and I keep trying to persuade her to come back to our family seat in Warwickshire. A Blackwood has been in residence at Waverley House for over two hundred years. It's a lovely old place, if a bit moldy and desperately in need of repair. But Mother insists that she spent enough of her life 'buried in the countryside,' as she puts it. She prefers the excitement of Town—the theater, museums, galleries, and shops. That woman runs up such bills, she will drive me to the poorhouse." He chuckled and gave Mrs. Whitlock a hooded glance. "My mother's a magpie, Mrs. Whitlock. Last month, she bought a diamond pendant with her initial 'E' for Evelyn. I bet she'd buy that jewelry set you mentioned and not think twice about it."

"If she did, I'd be green with envy, Colonel." Mrs. Whitlock sighed.

"My mother was the opposite of yours, Colonel," Miss Goodwin said with a sniff. "She pinched every penny and didn't even like spending money on the hotel. I had to make over all my dresses year after year." She laid one hand over the simple bodice of her dress. "This is my first new gown in ages, and of course it had to be black."

"You are dressed with such dignity," Mrs. Hillman noted.

"Thank you." Miss Goodwin responded.

Conversation flowed smoothly throughout the rest of the meal, which ended with a sponge cake topped with whipped cream and preserved strawberries, reportedly a new favorite of Queen Victoria's.

The group returned to the drawing room afterwards for coffee and tea. When the clock struck eleven, Mrs. Hillman announced that it had been a long day for all, and they ought to turn in.

"You promised us a tour of the premises tomorrow," Mr. Clarke reminded her. "Can we put that on the schedule?"

"Of course," Mrs. Hillman assured him.

Selena asked everyone if they had what they needed and received affirmative replies from everyone except Mrs. Whitlock, who demanded that a hot toddy be sent up to her room.

"I cannot fall asleep without one," Mrs. Whitlock insisted.

"Certainly." Selena rang a bell to call the housekeeper. "Thank you so much everyone for coming. I wish you all a good night."

As the guests began exiting the room, Selena saw Mr. Clarke draw Mrs. Hillman to a quiet corner, where he unobtrusively handed her an envelope. Mrs. Hillman's smile upon receiving it was incandescent. Selena wondered what he had given her. She wondered, too, if he would indeed propose to Mrs. Hillman again over the coming days. Only time would tell.

It suddenly occurred to Selena that if Mrs. Hillman did remarry, all her property would come under her husband's control, which might well put an end to Selena's incumbency as heir to Darkmoor Park. *But c'est la vie*, Selena thought. She didn't truly consider herself worthy of inheriting this estate, anyway. The most important thing was for Mrs. Hillman to be happy. And if need be, Selena and Athena could always move the school back to Thorndale Manor.

Selena retired to her chamber, the first room off the central stairway in the first floor's north wing, where she undressed and fell into bed with relief. After all the stress of preparations for the house party and the excitement of the newly arrived guests, she was so tired that she fell asleep minutes after her head had hit the pillow.

She was wrapped in a dream in which she desperately needed to write down a lesson plan for her students, but there was no paper to be had anywhere, and not a single pen, when she was yanked from the depths of slumber by an earsplitting scream.

Selena lurched up in bed. *What on Earth was that?* It was dark as pitch, except for the embers that burned low and red in the hearth.

The shriek stopped, returning the house to silence except for the howl of the wind. Selena threw on her dressing gown and slippers, lit her bedside candle, and glanced at the clock on the mantel. It was five minutes past six.

Selena shivered as she left her room, heading for the main staircase, the direction from which the scream had seemed to come. Gladys, a freckled, red-haired chambermaid who had started at Darkmoor Park just a few months ago, barreled up the stairs with a look of horror on her face.

"Gladys! I heard a scream. Was that you?"

"Yes!" Gladys was trembling. "I'm so sorry, miss. I know I'm not supposed to use the main stairs, but I were coming up from the morning room with the firewood and it is so much quicker than the servants' stairs and I didn't think anybody would ever know!"

Selena's heart thudded with dread. "Never mind that, Gladys. What's wrong?"

"Oh miss! It's a gentleman, miss! Mr. Clarke, I think his name is? He's on the half-landing below, lying in a pool of blood!" Gladys wrung her hands. "I think he's dead!"

CHAPTER THREE

SELENA RUSHED DOWN the main staircase in the early morning darkness, shielding her candle with one hand as the wind whistled through the eaves and rattled the shutters.

On the half-landing below, where the steps turned in the opposite direction, Mr. Clarke, dressed in the same suit he'd worn upon arrival, lay face up and unmoving, his legs splayed in an ungainly manner, his feet angled towards the bottom of the stairs. Pieces of firewood and a wicker basket, which Selena guessed had tumbled from the chambermaid's hands, were scattered across the dark, floral carpet.

Selena, filled with trepidation, set her candlestick on the floor and knelt at Mr. Clarke's side. His eyes were closed. Beneath his head, blood had stained the carpet. She gently squeezed his shoulder. "Mr. Clarke? Mr. Clarke?"

He didn't answer.

Selena's mind was going a mile a minute. *What happened? Was he dead? Had he missed a step in the dark and fallen? Or ....*

Her thoughts darted to another time and place, more than three years before, when a man had been pushed to his death at Pendowar Hall—a crime that her sister Diana had solved, at the risk of her own life. *Surely, that's not what happened here. It couldn't be. This was just an accident. Wasn't it?*

Selena gently jostled his shoulder again. "Mr. Clarke?"

This time, his eyes blinked open. Selena gasped in consternation as Mr. Clarke gripped her arm and with labored but feverish intensity whispered, "I ... hid ... it!"

Selena was too startled to speak. He continued in the same frenzied, low tone, his eyes wild and staring. She had to lean closer to hear him.

"Under ... the ... dragon." Every word seemed to take great effort. "Four rows!" he added insistently. "In the ..." He blinked, his eyes glazed over and closed, and his head drooped to one side.

"Sir? What do you mean?" Selena asked, her stomach clenching.

He gave no reply.

"Mr. Clarke!" Selena rubbed his cheek, but he did not stir. *What did his strange words mean? Has he just expired? Please, please, don't let it be so.* She lay a hand on his chest and to her relief, she could detect a light rise and fall. *Thank goodness. He's still living.*

"What's going on?" Colonel Blackwood, clad in his nightshirt and dressing gown, his auburn-grey hair in disarray, stared down from the first-floor landing. "Merciful heavens!" he exclaimed.

"Is he dead?" cried Gladys, her eyes wide and staring.

"No, he's still breathing," Selena called up to them. "But I fear he is gravely injured. Gladys, did you see him fall?"

"No, miss. I just found him like that."

Mr. Davis, Miss Goodwin, and Miss Thompson, all dressed in their nightclothes and carrying candles, joined the other two on the landing.

"Did someone scream?" inquired Miss Goodwin.

"Mr. Clarke seems to have fallen down the stairs," the colonel answered, his features drawn.

Miss Thompson gasped in dismay. "Oh, no!"

"Don't move him," Colonel Blackwood warned as he descended the steps to join Selena on the half-landing. "He might have broken his neck or his back."

Selena nodded. She'd been thinking the same thing.

"Shall I waken Mrs. Hillman?" Gladys was wringing her hands.

"Not yet." Selena was reluctant to rouse Mrs. Hillman. The woman tended to get agitated in times of trouble and might be overcome by Mr. Clarke's present state.

"Is there a doctor in the village?" Colonel Blackwood asked.

"No, but we have an apothecary. It's so early, he won't be in the shop yet." Selena glanced out the half-landing window. It was snowing hard and must have been for some time, for although the sky was dark, she could perceive that the rear grounds around the abbey ruins and the distant parklands were all blanketed in frosty white. She hated to send out anyone in such conditions, but there was no alternative.

"Gladys, fetch Billy," she called up to the maid. Billy was the hall boy, a lad of thirteen and the son of the cook. He had lived at Darkmoor Park since he was an infant, slept on a cot in the servants' corridor, and did many odd jobs. "Tell him to dress warmly, go to Mr. Quince's house, and tell him we have an injured man who needs medical attention without delay. Mr. Quince lives just south of the village in a red brick house. Do you know the place?"

"I do, miss."

"Good. Tell Billy not to take *no* for an answer. He must bring the apothecary straight back here at once."

"Yes, miss. I'll tell him." Gladys vanished.

The colonel crouched down beside Mr. Clarke's prone form. "Clarke!" he cried, fear in his eyes. "Wake up, old man!" But Mr. Clarke remained immobile, and his eyes did not reopen. "What happened?" he asked Selena. "Did you see him fall?"

"No. Gladys found him like this. He must have been going down for his early morning coffee and missed a step."

"Poor devil. We need to stop the flow of blood from his head."

Selena called up to the group above. "Will someone please fetch some towels? You'll find a fresh stack in the first-floor linen closet, just south of the stairwell."

"I'll go." Miss Thompson hurried off.

"What can we do?" Mr. Davis called out.

"Thank you for offering to help, but please return to your rooms, both of you," Selena advised, "and go back to sleep if you can. I'll stay with Mr. Clarke until the apothecary arrives."

Miss Goodwin and Mr. Davis moved off, murmuring. A tense couple of hours followed. Colonel Blackwood, who had gained some medical experience during his years in the army, carefully laid a folded towel under Mr. Clarke's head and instructed Selena to press it firmly against the wound. She knelt in that position for quite some time, all the while keeping her eyes on Mr. Clarke's chest, grateful to see that he was still breathing. *Please wake up,* she chanted in her mind. *Please don't die.*

The colonel remained at Mr. Clarke's side, afraid to leave in case Selena should require assistance, or the wound should start bleeding again. Half a dozen servants appeared to gawk at the injured man but were shooed away by Wells. Later, the butler directed Mrs. Whitlock, who had slept through the disturbance, and the other guests to use the servants' stairwell to descend to the morning room for breakfast, where they were to wait for more information.

By now, the sun was fully up and beyond the half-landing window, Selena observed a full-blown snowstorm in progress. Speared by worry, she told Colonel Blackwood, "I hope the apothecary will come. And I pray Mrs. Hillman doesn't awaken until he has made his assessment, and we know Mr. Clarke's all right."

"I hope Clarke *is* all right," returned Colonel Blackwood, concern etching his face. "I don't like that he hasn't woken yet."

"His respiration has grown very shallow," Selena noted with concern. She was beginning to wonder if he was breathing at all when she heard some bustle downstairs. Mrs. Middleton appeared, leading a gentleman up the stairs. Selena stood in anticipation, expecting to greet Mr. Quince. But the man in the housekeeper's company was someone she had never seen before.

"Miss Taylor," said Mrs. Middleton as she and the stranger

halted several steps below the half-landing, "it seems Mr. Quince has gone away to spend Christmas with relatives in Scotland. At least that's what his housekeeper told Billy." The housekeeper's brow creased over a deep frown. "The boy said he didn't know what to do, so he went to the vicarage for help, but Mr. Johnson is also gone for the holidays. Billy has brought *this* gentleman in his stead. He says he's a doctor. He left his overcoat, hat, and luggage in the servants' hall, but he refused to remove his boots. I hope I did right to let him in."

"You did very well, Mrs. Middleton," Selena told her. "Thank you."

The housekeeper nodded and withdrew. Selena, her pulse racing with anxiety, took in the stranger who stood below.

He was tall and lean, perhaps six-foot-three, and clad in a black woolen suit. Sporting a head of wavy, light-brown hair, he appeared to be in his early thirties, perhaps a couple of years older than she was. A jagged scar on his forehead that bisected his right eyebrow only added to his roguish handsomeness and his well-shaped nose and clean-shaven cheeks were red, no doubt from the cold. His feet, encased in the damp and snow-encrusted boots which had so offended Mrs. Middleton, moved back and forth on the step as if he were struggling to regain the feeling in his toes. A black, leather medical bag hung from a strap over his shoulder.

All this Selena noticed in a flash. *He's so young*, was her next thought, followed by, *What a stroke of luck that in the middle of a snowstorm, Billy found a doctor.* She would have to thank Billy later.

"Thank you for coming, Doctor," she said quickly. "I'm Selena Taylor. This is Colonel Blackwood."

"Dr. Adrian Scott. How do you do." The doctor bowed. His voice was refined and deep.

"Please hurry," Selena rushed on. "We're so worried. My maid found this gentleman shortly after six this morning. We believe he fell down the stairs." Selena moved aside as the newcomer darted up the last few stairs to the half-landing.

"We haven't moved him, other than to staunch the bleeding

from his head," Colonel Blackwood added, stepping back. "Please do everything you can."

When the doctor reached the half-landing and took in the prone figure, his eyes widened, and his jaw dropped slightly. For an instant, he seemed incapable of speech. Selena had the strangest sense that he recognized the fallen man—but the doctor quickly put that theory to rest when he exclaimed, "What's the man's name?"

"Clarke. Jack Clarke," Selena told him.

"Mr. Clarke!" the doctor called out as, without wasting a second, he knelt down and set his black bag on the carpet. "Mr. Clarke!" He opened Mr. Clarke's frock coat, removed his tie, unbuttoned his shirt, and then used a stethoscope from his black bag to listen to the man's chest. At length, in a tone of regret, he sat back on his heels and said, "I'm sorry. I'm too late. I'm afraid your friend has passed away."

"Oh, no!" Selena's hand went to her mouth.

"It can't be." Colonel Blackwood's face crinkled with sorrow. "There must be something you can do."

"I wish there were. Again, I am so sorry."

A heaviness descended on Selena's limbs. She had only known Mr. Clarke less than a day, but she felt terrible that he'd lost his life and in such a dreadful way. She felt bad, too, for the colonel and for Mrs. Hillman, who had both clearly been fond of Mr. Clarke.

Dr. Scott glanced at the landing area around Mr. Clarke's body. "Do you know if he was carrying anything when he fell?"

It seemed an odd question. Selena noticed a candlestick and snuffed candle amidst the scattered pieces of firewood. "He may have been carrying that candle. Why?"

The doctor hesitated. "I was curious if he'd had something in his hands that might have prevented him from holding on to the rail."

"I don't know. The maid said she found him like this," Selena told him.

"Such a senseless accident." Colonel Blackwood shook his head. "It is too awful."

Dr. Scott glanced up at the staircase and then back to Mr. Clarke's prone form. His brows drew together as he said quietly, "Was it really an accident, I wonder?"

Selena's body tensed as she stared at him. "What do you mean? Are you saying that he might have been pushed?" The same thought had occurred to her at first, but she had rejected it. *For who would wish to harm Mr. Clarke?*

"Pushed?" exclaimed Colonel Blackwood, his eyes huge. "Whatever put that idea into your heads?"

The doctor paused again, then gave his head a shake. "Never mind. At first, I thought it might have been more likely, if he had fallen while walking down the stairs, that he would have landed face down instead of face up. But that's wrong. He might have tumbled head over heels or slid down on his back."

"Or rolled onto his back when he hit the landing," Selena pointed out.

"Very true." The doctor rebuttoned Mr. Clarke's shirt and frock coat. "As you said, he most likely took a misstep in the dark."

Selena wrung her hands. She had no clue what to do next. Her own life had been put in peril once when she'd lived at Thorndale Manor, but she had never had to deal with a dead body before. "Doctor. I have no experience with this sort of thing. Please tell me what to do."

He rose to his feet. "Are you a relation of the deceased?"

"No," Selena answered. "Mr. Clarke is—he *was* a guest here. I only met him yesterday afternoon when he arrived to attend our holiday house party."

"I see. Is this your house?"

"No," Selena said again. "I live here, but I am a friend of the mistress of Darkmoor Park, Mrs. Rose Hillman."

The doctor glanced away, his eyes narrowing as if he were having difficulty focusing on the task at hand. "Is there someone—a family member, perhaps—we should contact on Mr. Clarke's behalf?"

Selena frowned. "I have no idea."

"Clarke was unmarried," Colonel Blackwood interjected. "I don't know about any next of kin. Mrs. Hillman might know."

Dr. Scott gave a slight nod. "Normally, I'd have the body transferred to an undertaker. But that would prove impossible at present." He gestured towards the window, beyond which was a swirl of white. "Do you have an icehouse where we might move him for the time being? He will keep there until the storm passes and other arrangements can be made."

As Selena processed the idea of moving poor Mr. Clarke to the icehouse, an involuntary shiver ran down her spine. "Yes, we have an icehouse. It's about a five-minute walk from the kitchens. I could summon the footmen to help."

Dr. Scott held up a hand. "First, is there anyone here whom you think might like to see him before we move him?"

Selena hesitated. "Mrs. Hillman, I suppose. I believe she's still asleep." She sighed. "I had hoped we wouldn't have to disturb her until—until Mr. Clarke had recovered. But I see that I shall have to rouse her, after all."

"What can I do?" asked the colonel. "I want to be of help."

"Please inform the other guests as to what has happened, Colonel," Selena told him, "and keep them calm and away from here until all this is resolved."

"Very well, Miss Taylor. Dr. Scott," Colonel Blackwood added in parting, before proceeding down the stairs.

Despite the dreadfulness of the morning's events, it suddenly occurred to Selena that she was, most improperly, still in her nightclothes—in front of a complete stranger. And a handsome one, at that. Heat flooded her cheeks, and she wrapped her dressing gown more tightly about herself as she turned back to Dr. Scott. "Before I waken Mrs. Hillman—can you tell me what you think killed Mr. Clarke? Was it the injury to his head?"

The doctor didn't answer. He was staring out the window. A

scowl had taken over his face and once again, he appeared to be lost in thought.

"Dr. Scott?" Selena repeated. She was about to call his name again when he blinked and turned to her.

"I beg your pardon. I was wool-gathering. What did you say?"

"I only wondered what you think may have killed Mr. Clarke? Medically speaking?"

"I'm guessing there was internal bleeding in his body or his brain," Dr. Scott mused. "Are you certain he was alive when you found him and sent for help?"

"Yes. I saw him breathing. And ... he spoke to me." In the anxiety of the past hours, Selena had forgotten all about that.

The doctor's brows shot up. "What did he say?"

Selena paused, as Mr. Clarke's anxious but enigmatic last words came back to her. *"I hid it ... under the dragon. Four rows! In the ..."* There, he had broken off. He seemed to have been trying to tell her something of great import. But what? Had he truly hidden something? If so, had he wanted her to find it? Selena wished now that she hadn't mentioned it to the doctor. She wanted to give the matter more thought before sharing it with anyone—and she had only just met this man. "It was rather nonsensical," Selena said quickly. "I could make neither heads nor tails of it."

Just then, a shout rang out from above. Mrs. Hillman, clad in her red, silk dressing gown, her hair still covered by her frilly, white nightcap, burst into view at the top of the stairs, with Gladys at her heels.

"Where is he?" Mrs. Hillman's voice was filled with anguish. When she caught sight of Mr. Clarke lying on the half-landing below, her features contracted with horror. "Oh, no! Jack! No!" Her legs collapsed beneath her, and the chambermaid raced to prevent her fall.

Selena's gut constricted. She had worried that something might go wrong at this holiday party, but she could never have imagined *this*—that one of Mrs. Hillman's friends would die. It was too, too horrible.

CHAPTER FOUR

M R. CLARKE'S BODY was removed to the icehouse. The guests were ensconced in the morning room, awaiting further news. When Mrs. Hillman recovered from her fainting spell, she was taken to her front parlor, where Dr. Scott tended to her.

Selena got dressed and hurried down to the front parlor, where she found Mrs. Hillman lying on the sofa, still clad in her dressing gown, one arm draped dramatically across her eyes. Dr. Scott sat at her side, holding her hand, his medical bag on the floor beside him.

"Oh! My poor, dear Mr. Clarke—gone!" Mrs. Hillman cried tremulously. "I cannot believe it. What an awful state of affairs!"

"Again, I am so sorry for your loss," Dr. Scott was saying.

Selena silently crossed the room to them, filled with sadness for the man who had departed this life so suddenly. The doctor stood and greeted her with a nod. "Miss Taylor."

"Dr. Scott." Selena was reminded of how good-looking he was. His strong jaw and intelligent, blue eyes reminded her of the sea during a tempest. "How is she?" she inquired under her breath.

"She has suffered a great shock but otherwise seems to be in good health," he returned quietly.

"You needn't whisper," Mrs. Hillman declared authoritative-ly. "I'm right here and I can still hear perfectly well."

Selena felt an inward rush of relief. She had worried that Mrs. Hillman would be too overcome to cope with this tragedy, but she seemed to be her usual feisty self.

Dr. Scott turned back to the older woman. "Ma'am, if there is anything you need, please say the word. I have medications for pain and anxiety in my bag."

"I require no drugs at present, Doctor, but you may help me to sit up." Mrs. Hillman allowed the doctor to assist her to a seated position on the couch. Her eyes were sad, but she clasped her dressing gown closed around her neck as if determined to preserve an air of dignity and propriety. "It seems, however, that you have come at an opportune time. Thank you for all you've done to assist Selena through this ordeal. I will, of course, pay you for your services."

"I wouldn't think of accepting payment," Dr. Scott insisted. "I fear I have not done much. I'm sorry that I arrived too late to help Mr. Clarke."

"Such a terrible accident!" Mrs. Hillman's voice broke. From her pocket, she withdrew a linen handkerchief and dabbed at the moisture in her eyes. "I have always said it is dangerous to walk about a house in the dark. If only Mr. Clarke had slept in this morning, as anyone with sense would do."

Selena said gently, "Mrs. Hillman, do you know if Mr. Clarke has any family whom we should alert about his passing?"

"He had no family," Mrs. Hillman replied with a frown. "He never married nor had any children, and he was an only child."

"When the weather clears, I suggest you make inquiries on his behalf," Dr. Scott suggested, "and find out if he had a solicitor."

Selena nodded. "In the meantime, Mrs. Hillman, we have five guests in the drawing room, waiting for some word. What do you wish to do?"

"I don't know. I need a moment to think." Mrs. Hillman sighed. "Oh! To have this happen on Christmas Eve, of all times. Such an awful start to our holiday week." Her gaze went to the window, where a heavy snowfall was being buffeted by strong winds. "And such horrid weather!"

Selena frowned. All of her worries, she realized, had come to pass. The weather had turned for the worse, and something unexpected—and truly terrible—had indeed occurred. "I'm afraid there will be no walking out on the grounds today." It suddenly occurred to her that Dr. Scott had walked here in a snowstorm. "Doctor. I can't thank you enough for coming to us in our hour of need. But how is it that you happened to be in Darkmoor Bridge?"

"I was on my way to Edinburgh early this morning when my train was stopped south of the village due to snow on the tracks," he explained.

"Were you on your way to see your wife and children, or perhaps your sweetheart, for Christmas?" Mrs. Hillman inquired.

"I have no wife or children, ma'am. Nor any sweetheart."

Selena was glad to hear that, although she couldn't say why.

"I walked to Darkmoor Bridge and came upon your hall boy by chance outside the vicarage," Dr. Scott continued. "He said you had a man in need of medical attention, and he was told not to return unless he'd found help. I urged him to bring me here."

"I'm so grateful you came," Selena told him. "Where are you from?"

"I'm from Bath."

"It seems I must thank Billy for his presence of mind." Mrs. Hillman wiped her eyes again. "Where are you staying, Dr. Scott? At the inn in the village?"

"I had hoped to find an inn," he admitted, "but I'm afraid I never got that far. My bag is in the servants' hall."

"Well, now that you are here, it seems you will be obliged to stay the night at the very least, or a few days, perhaps." Mrs. Hillman pulled the bell rope to summon a servant. "There is no telling how long this storm will last."

Dr. Scott hesitated. "Are you certain, ma'am? As I understand it you have a house full of guests. Today is Christmas Eve. I wouldn't wish to intrude."

"You are not intruding, Doctor." Mrs. Hillman waved a hand, as if swatting away an invisible fly. "There is always room for one more at Darkmoor Park. And I would never turn a man out into the snow."

"Thank you, ma'am. I am most grateful."

Selena noted relief in the doctor's eyes. She wondered whom he had been planning to visit in Edinburgh. "I'm sorry you'll be stuck here and miss out on your own holiday plans, Doctor," she remarked, fishing gently.

He shrugged his broad shoulders. "My friends will understand that I was detained by the weather. And if I must be *stuck* somewhere, as you say, over Christmas, I'm sure I could wish for no more comfortable place than Darkmoor Park." He turned to Mrs. Hillman. "However, I must warn you, ma'am, I have no formal clothes with me, so I fear I won't be properly attired for the kind of evenings you most likely have in mind."

Mrs. Hillman studied the doctor with pursed lips. "Thank you for bringing that to my attention. I will take care of it."

Mrs. Middleton entered the room. "Ma'am? You rang?"

"Please make up a room for Dr. Scott in the south wing," Mrs. Hillman directed the housekeeper. "He will be staying with us until the weather clears. Have Sam bring up his bag. And tell Wells to take Dr. Scott's measurements and find him some evening wear."

"Yes, ma'am." Mrs. Middleton nodded.

Mrs. Hillman turned to Dr. Scott. "I keep an assortment of gentlemen's wear on hand for emergencies like this one. I'm sure my butler, Wells, can find you something suitable, and if it requires alteration, one of the maids will see to it."

"I am in your debt." Dr. Scott bowed.

"Ma'am," Mrs. Middleton inquired, "shall we proceed with all meals today as previously scheduled?"

Mrs. Hillman hesitated, then said, her voice breaking slightly, "Yes. I'm afraid I'm not up to seeing anyone just yet, and I couldn't eat a bite. I shall retire to my chamber for a couple of hours. But that is no reason for anyone else to suffer or go hungry."

"Yes, ma'am." The housekeeper curtsied and left the room.

Mrs. Hillman glanced at Selena and Dr. Scott. "Have either of you had breakfast?"

Selena shook her head.

"It is a long while since I had anything to eat," the doctor admitted.

"Well, then, the two of you must go in to breakfast. Please give everyone my apologies, Selena. What did we have planned for this morning again?"

"We were going to trim the Christmas tree."

"That's right." Mrs. Hillman sighed. "Poll the guests. If the majority are inclined to proceed with tree trimming, then do so— with or without me." She grabbed her cane and rose. "As for the days ahead, Selena—here's what I want you to say. Tell them that although the colonel and Mrs. Whitlock and I have just lost a good friend, I believe Mr. Clarke wouldn't want us to feel sorry for him. He would want us to go on and celebrate the holidays as planned."

"Very well." Selena nodded. It seemed a sensible plan. With this weather, their guests would be obliged to remain at Dark-moor Park for a while in any case, whether they wanted to or not.

As Mrs. Hillman headed upstairs and Selena led the doctor towards the morning room, he said, "It was kind of Mrs. Hillman to invite me to stay."

"She is a kind woman. But no one with any heart would turn away a traveler on a day like this."

"Still, I am grateful. It must have seemed like I came out of nowhere."

"In truth, you did." Selena smiled and thought he might return the gesture, but instead, he fell silent and glanced away.

As they walked along, Selena studied Dr. Scott. Her heart

began to beat to an unfamiliar rhythm—and her guard immediately went up. He was so handsome and charming. She had learned from personal experience that such men could not always be trusted. One only had to look to Jane Austen for further confirmation. Nearly all the gentleman described in Miss Austen's novels as handsome and charming—Willoughby, Wickham, and Henry Crawford, for example—turned out to be rascals and cads. Only one exception came to mind: her favorite Austen hero, Mr. Darcy. *He* had been introduced as a handsome, fine figure of a man. But on the other hand, he hadn't been charming. At the outset, he had been proud, arrogant, and aloof.

Selena gave herself a mental shake. Why on Earth was she thinking about Mr. Darcy?!

She wasn't looking for romance! She had more important things to consider. Mrs. Hillman had taken to her room. From the looks of it, this storm would not be ending any time soon. A member of their party had just unexpectedly died. They had a house full of guests who might be cooped up inside the manor house for days. Somehow, Selena had to keep everyone in good spirits and entertained.

At the moment, it seemed like a Herculean task.

OVER BREAKFAST, THE mood was somber. Colonel Blackwood kept sighing and shaking his head as if having difficulty accepting the morning's dreadful turn of events.

Mrs. Whitlock said, "It is just like that Jack Clarke to die today of all days and ruin Christmas for us." But her bitter tone was mitigated somewhat by her furrowed brow, and the manner in which she twisted her napkin in her hands.

The others spoke in hushed voices and, although they had only just met Mr. Clarke, they expressed their shock over what had happened. The entire party politely welcomed Dr. Scott, who focused his attention on his bacon and eggs and was even quieter than the rest.

Selena detected a hard, distant look in the doctor's blue eyes and sensed that he was still distracted. She could understand why. He had been on his way to Scotland, no doubt to enjoy a cheerful holiday with people of his acquaintance, and instead had been forced by foul weather to abandon his train, trudge miles through the freezing snow, and attend a death. On top of that, he was now obliged to spend Christmas Eve, and perhaps Christmas Day and longer, confined to this house with people he did not know. Anyone would be upset by the circumstances.

Once, she caught him studying her across the table, with an expression that seemed to reflect an awareness of her—a look that did strange things to Selena's inner equilibrium. The moment their gazes touched, however, he averted his eyes. She was grateful to him for the help he had provided in a difficult situation—but he was an enigma as of yet. *And I am not interested in him*, she sternly reminded herself.

As the meal proceeded, Selena's mind returned to the cryptic message Mr. Clarke had given her before he'd died. Instinct told her not to share that information with anyone else, at least not yet.

Recalling Mrs. Hillman's request, Selena cleared her throat and said, "As I mentioned, our hostess has taken to her room to deal with this unexpected loss. I know we are all shocked and grieved by what has happened. But Mrs. Hillman bade me to tell you that in spite of Mr. Clarke's tragic demise, she believes he would want us all to celebrate the holidays as planned."

"I agree." Mrs. Whitlock took a last sip of coffee. "We can't let a foolish accident stop us from enjoying ourselves."

What a callous remark, Selena thought. The accident had hardly been foolish.

But Colonel Blackwood seemed to agree with the assessment. He slapped the table and exclaimed, "You're absolutely right. Clarke didn't stand on ceremony, and he wasn't prone to sentiment. I'll bet he would say, 'Why are you all so down in the dumps? Carry on! It's Christmas! It's a party!'"

An uncertain laugh went around the table. Selena seized on the tentative change in mood. "What do you all think? Shall we follow the colonel's advice and Mrs. Hillman's wishes and proceed with our holiday activities?"

A brief pause ensued as glances were exchanged around the table; then everyone nodded in response. The only outlier was Dr. Scott, who continued to be wrapped in his own thoughts.

"We might as well," Miss Goodwin put in. "Judging by the weather, none of us are going anywhere."

"You said last night that you have enough food and firewood to last ten days?" asked Mr. Davis.

"We do," Selena assured everyone. "And now, I'd like the announce the first item on today's agenda: we are decorating the Christmas tree in the great hall. When you have all finished with breakfast, let us adjourn there."

THE TALL EVERGREEN that stood at attention in the great hall, a stepladder positioned beside it, filled the chamber with its fresh scent.

The evening before, the servants had wrapped the tree with popcorn garlands and attached a great number of candles, secured in brass *bobeches*—candleholders that Mrs. Hillman had ordered from France, designed to keep the candles upright on the branches and catch dripping wax. Baskets of ornaments and ribbons had been positioned near the tree. The footmen, George and Sam, stood at attention nearby, ready to assist if required.

"I have never understood the point of bringing a fresh evergreen tree into the house," Mrs. Whitlock complained. "Think how long it has taken this beautiful tree to reach this size, and now it will die in a matter of weeks."

Although Selena thought Mrs. Whitlock to be a curmudgeon in many respects, she couldn't disagree with her on this point. "That's true, ma'am. It is sad, when you think of it that way. But it *is* a lovely and festive new tradition."

"I had never heard of a 'Christmas tree' until four years ago, when that engraving of the Royal family appeared in the illustrated *London News*," Colonel Blackwood noted.

Selena picked up an ornament from a basket. "Neither had I. But Mrs. Hillman has been making and collecting Christmas ornaments for over thirty years, ever since she took a trip to Germany and saw the tradition practiced there."

"There are so many lovely decorations," Miss Thompson softly enthused.

Miss Goodwin clasped her hands in excitement. "We should put up a Christmas tree at the inn next year, for all the guests to enjoy," she told Mr. Davis.

Mr. Davis hesitated and darted her a look. "But the hotel closes in winter, dear. No one will see it but us."

"Oh … yes." Color rose to Miss Goodwin's cheeks. "Silly me, I'd forgotten." To the room at large, she added quickly, "Hotel management is still new to me, you understand. It is only a few months since my mother …" She broke off.

"Your mother was a dear soul." Mrs. Whitlock heaved a sigh. "It will be difficult to fill her shoes."

Miss Goodwin's blush deepened at this remark. "I know it will."

Mr. Davis put his arm around Miss Goodwin and said testily, "I assure you, Mrs. Whitlock, that Nancy and I will do our best to run the hotel as her mother would have done."

"It takes time to learn a new trade." Dr. Scott pressed his lips together and gave the young couple a compassionate glance. "You'll get there."

It was one of the few times the doctor had spoken since breakfast.

"And I'm sure you'll both do a fine job," Selena put in,

touched by the doctor's kind words, and her heart going out to the beleaguered Miss Goodwin.

A familiar voice rang out. "I hope I'm not too late?"

Selena turned with delight to find Mrs. Hillman entering the great hall. "You've come!"

"Decorating the tree is my favorite part of the Christmas tradition. I didn't want to miss it," Mrs. Hillman said as she crossed the chamber, accompanied by her cane.

Selena always thought of that lady's cane as an "accompaniment"—a show of grandness and authority, perhaps—rather than as a necessity, for as far as she could tell, Mrs. Hillman was able to walk perfectly well without it.

"I'm so glad," Selena said. "It felt wrong to do this without you."

Colonel Blackwood took Mrs. Hillman's hand and greeted her with a grave expression. "Madam. May I say on behalf of the entire party, how good it is to see you. We are all brokenhearted by what happened to Mr. Clarke."

"As am I." Mrs. Hillman gave a deep, sad sigh. "Under any other circumstances, I might have taken to my bed for a week. But it's Christmas. You have all come a long way to celebrate the season. I decided it would be wrong to hide away in my chamber and miss out on any Christmas fun. Mr. Clarke was very big on having fun."

"He was, indeed," the colonel agreed.

The other guests voiced their pleasure at their hostess's appearance, at which point Mrs. Hillman said, "Shall we get started, then?"

The party sprang into action, tying the handblown glass ornaments, porcelain animals and birds, pewter angels, and objects made from pinecones and straw to the tree. The footmen moved the ladder into position and held it whenever the gentlemen required it to hang ornaments at the highest places.

"This one is so sweet." From the basket, Miss Thompson pulled out a handblown glass ornament shaped like a sprig of bluebell. "It reminds me of your iris brooch, Mrs. Hillman."

"It does a bit." Mrs. Hillman smiled.

"I love flowers," Miss Thompson commented as she hung the ornament on the tree. "I've always longed to own a flower shop."

Selena smiled at her. "Maybe you shall, one day."

Mrs. Whitlock made a scoffing sound. "Don't go putting ideas into her head, Miss Taylor. It takes brains to run a flower shop and skills which *that one* does not possess."

Miss Thompson colored and ducked her head.

Selena winced at Mrs. Whitlock's harsh tone and cruel words. *It's a wonder*, she thought, *that Miss Thompson continues to work for this woman.* But then, it wasn't all that many years ago that Selena herself had been dependent on the meager income and housing provided by her governess positions, where she'd sometimes suffered similar verbal abuse from her employers.

"Where would I get the money, in any case?" Miss Thompson said quietly. "It's just a dream."

"Dreams can be achieved through hard work and determination," Mrs. Hillman assured the young lady. She shot a withering look at Mrs. Whitlock, who shrugged as if unconcerned by what she'd just said. "Just look at what Mr. Clarke achieved during his lifetime. Many of his business ventures were quite successful."

Dr. Scott paused, an ornament in hand. His scarred eyebrow arched. "What kinds of business ventures?"

"As I recall," Mrs. Hillman answered, "he once owned a hat factory in Bristol that gave employment to a great many people and made him a fortune. He said he had built an orphanage in Dublin—he was very proud of that. And there were several other things. I've forgotten what now."

Dr. Scott's jaw tightened as he took this in. Selena wondered why.

"It's strange to think that I only met Mr. Clarke less than twenty-four hours ago," Selena observed.

"It's hard to believe he's gone." Colonel Blackwood sighed. "I have such fond memories of the man."

"He was such a *good* fellow," Mrs. Hillman agreed, moisture gathering in her eyes.

"I'm sorry the man passed away," remarked Miss Goodwin. "And perhaps this isn't the right time to bring this up, but … now that he's gone, what will happen to all the money he had with him?"

A hush descended on the room. Seven pairs of questioning eyes turned to her.

"What money?" Selena asked.

"Why, the fifty-two hundred pounds that he claimed to have in his coat pocket," said Miss Goodwin.

Selena choked in surprise at this revelation and nearly dropped the ornament she was holding. *Fifty-two hundred pounds? It would take most men more than a lifetime to earn that sum. Why had Mr. Clarke been carrying so much money?*

CHAPTER FIVE

THE GREAT HALL was so silent that the howl of the wind that rattled the shutters seemed as loud as the roar of a locomotive. The members of the tree-trimming party paused in their labors and stared at the young lady who had just spoken.

"How do you know, Miss Goodwin, that Mr. Clarke was carrying such a huge sum of money?" Selena asked.

"Well. As you know, the night before last, Graham and I were dining at the White Hart Inn just a table away from where Mr. Clarke was seated with Mrs. Whitlock and her companion." Miss Goodwin toyed with a glass angel in her palm. "We had no idea who they were, but we couldn't help overhearing."

"Overhearing what?" asked Dr. Scott.

Miss Goodwin took a breath. "He said, rather proudly, 'I'll tell you a little secret. I'm a very rich man tonight.' Mrs. Whitlock said, 'Is that right, Mr. Clarke?' And Mr. Clarke said, 'I've got fifty-two hundred pounds in fifty-pound notes in my coat pocket.'"

Selena bit her lip, astonished. It was a king's ransom.

"What were you doing listening to a private conversation?" blustered Mrs. Whitlock. "That is so rude!"

"Forgive me." Miss Goodwin shrugged her shoulders. "We didn't mean to eavesdrop. But Mr. Clarke *was* drinking a lot, and he spoke rather loudly."

Colonel Blackwood's brow knit. "Clarke must have been joking. Or you heard wrong."

"No, that's what we heard," Mr. Davis interjected. "Mr. Clarke said he rescued the money to save it from a blackguard."

"What blackguard?" Selena asked.

"His business partner." Mr. Davis twiddled an ornament between his fingers as he addressed the group. "Mr. Clarke said they had spent more than half a year raising that money to build a new hospital in London. He didn't trust banks, so he'd kept the money in a safe at his house. But the day before Mr. Clarke left for Yorkshire, a barmaid told him she had overhead his partner declaring that he'd stolen the combination to the safe, and now he planned to steal the money and kill Mr. Clarke."

"*Kill* him?" repeated Mrs. Hillman with a gasp. "Good heavens!"

Mr. Davis nodded. "Mr. Clarke feared for both his life and the hospital fund. He knew he had to act fast, so he took the money and brought it with him. After the holidays, he said, he planned to open a proper bank account and report his partner to the London police."

"Good lord," Selena exclaimed, uncertain if Mr. Clarke's actions had been valiant or misguided. She turned to Mrs. Whitlock and her companion. "Ma'am, Miss Thompson, you were dining with Mr. Clarke. Is that truly what he said?"

Miss Thompson nodded. "It is."

"Oh, please!" Mrs. Whitlock flapped a hand. "If you think Mr. Clarke's life was really in danger, or that he was carrying a fortune upon his person, you are out of your minds. It was just the drink talking. Mr. Clarke was a boaster! From the day I met him, he was always making up things in an attempt to sound more important."

"I wouldn't say that," Mrs. Hillman began, but Mrs. Whitlock interrupted.

"My dear Mrs. Hillman, I know you cared for the man, and he *was* a charmer. But you don't honestly believe that Mr. Clarke built an orphanage in Dublin, do you?"

Mrs. Hillman hesitated. "W-Well," she spluttered, "I can't be absolutely certain, but—"

"The man was all talk!" Mrs. Whitlock insisted. "When he said all that about raising money to build a hospital, I knew there couldn't be an ounce of truth to it."

Colonel Blackwood's lips pulled downward. "Clarke did tend to blather when he was in his cups and go and on about his grandiose achievements. When we met up in Dublin a while back, he mentioned that orphanage, but when I expressed an interest in seeing the place, he became vague and changed the subject."

"That doesn't mean the orphanage didn't exist," Mrs. Hillman pointed out.

Miss Goodwin tilted her head. "What do you think, Colonel? Was everything Mr. Clarke said a lie?"

"It may have been," Colonel Blackwood admitted.

Mrs. Hillman let out a long sigh. "All right, look, I was aware of Mr. Clarke's tendency to brag. But he always had the best of intentions. And not *everything* he said was a lie. He did have a great deal of money with him. Not fifty-two hundred pounds, but two hundred pounds."

"How do you know?" asked Dr. Scott.

"Because he gave it to me last night, after dinner." Mrs. Hillman picked up a red, glass sphere from a basket and fiddled with it. "It was the repayment of a loan I gave Mr. Clarke the summer we met. Well, it wasn't really a loan, but more of an investment."

Aha, Selena thought, recalling the envelope she had seen Mr. Clarke handing to Mrs. Hillman the previous night. *So that's what that was about.*

"An investment in what?" Dr. Scott prodded, his lips thinning.

Mrs. Hillman held her chin high. "He was raising money to build a school for orphaned children. But he was defrauded by the builders, who ran off with all the money."

Mrs. Whitlock let out a snort of disbelief. "A likely story."

"Mr. Clarke promised to repay me when he was able," Mrs. Hillman asserted. "In his last letter, he wrote to say that he finally had the two hundred pounds and would bring it to me at Christmas. And he did—every penny of it!"

"Well, that was good of him." Mrs. Whitlock shrugged her shoulders. "But I suppose *that* story was too dull for a man with his inflated ego. So, he made up that ridiculous tale over dinner about having fifty-two hundred pounds and a killer on his tail."

"That would be just like him," Colonel Blackwood stated firmly. "Clarke became all the more effusive when he'd had too much to drink. But it was all part of his charm."

Miss Goodwin made an impish face. "Perhaps the threat on his life was an embellishment. But what if Mr. Clarke was telling the truth about the money? If so, after repaying Mrs. Hillman, there might be five thousand pounds lying around here some-where."

An awkward silence fell. For a moment, everyone seemed to be looking anywhere but at each other.

Mrs. Hillman crossed her arms over her chest. "Don't be ridiculous. You didn't know Mr. Clarke as I did. If he'd had a fortune of that size with him, he would have told me so that I could have put it in a safe place until it was time for him to return home."

"Good point," Colonel Blackwood declared.

Mrs. Hillman brought her hands together with a solid clap. "Now, I don't want to hear another word about this. If Mr. Clarke stretched the truth a bit the other night after imbibing too much ale, so be it. But I won't have any more talk that sullies his memory."

"Yes, ma'am." The colonel saluted their hostess, and gentle laughter erupted around the room.

"By the way," Mrs. Hillman added, "I always go to church after breakfast on Christmas Day. But if the weather tomorrow should make that impossible, I'd like to assemble in the Dark-moor Park chapel and share a moment in memory of Mr. Clarke."

"What a lovely idea," said Miss Thompson.

"If you don't mind a layman at the helm, ma'am," the colonel offered, "I'd be glad to offer my services. During my time in the army, I led my men in prayer many times."

"Thank you, Colonel. That would be wonderful." Mrs. Hillman gave him an appreciative nod.

"Speaking of Mr. Clarke," Mr. Davis said, blushing slightly, "last night, he asked if we could have a tour of the house today. Might we be afforded that pleasure?"

"You may. Selena, would you mind doing the honors after lunch, while I take my nap?" Mrs. Hillman asked.

"I'd be happy to," Selena agreed.

The party returned to tree-decorating. Although their attention seemed to be focused on the activity, Selena's thoughts drifted back to the conversation that had just ensued.

She knew that drink could loosen a person's tongue. Was it possible that Mr. Clarke hadn't just been boasting when he'd said that he had fifty-two hundred pounds in large notes in his coat pocket? If so, after repaying his two-hundred-pound debt to Mrs. Hillman, what had he done with the rest of the money?

Mr. Clarke's last words echoed in Selena's mind. *"I hid it … under … the dragon."*

A possible meaning for those words came to Selena in such a flash, it was all she could do not to gasp aloud. Had Mr. Clarke been talking about the money? *Five thousand pounds*—an immense sum that had been earmarked to build a hospital. Money that he may well have hidden and—afraid that he was dying—he wanted Selena to find.

The rest of the message, *"Four rows,"* might have been another clue as to where he had hidden the cash. She thought back to the events of the previous day. Mr. Clarke would have had several opportunities to hide the money—either during the quiet interval just after he had arrived, when he, Mrs. Whitlock, and Miss Thompson had gone up to their rooms, or later that night, after everyone had gone to bed.

Now Mr. Clarke was gone. If Selena was right about this, that money might remain hidden at Darkmoor Park forever if she didn't intervene. Her stomach tensed. *When the weather clears, I'll verify that the hospital foundation exists,* she vowed silently. *In the meantime, I'll search for whatever Mr. Clarke hid. If I find that money, I'll return it to the hospital fund, just as Mr. Clarke had intended.*

Selena briefly considered sharing this with Mrs. Hillman but thought better of it. Mrs. Hillman had made it clear that she didn't want to discuss the subject further. If Mr. Clarke's last words had indeed been about five thousand pounds in hidden cash, he'd had the opportunity to tell Mrs. Hillman about it before then, but he had chosen not to. Instead, he had apparently hidden it himself. He must have had a reason for that. Furthermore, Selena couldn't be sure she was right about any this. He might have hidden something else *under the dragon*—whatever that meant. She wouldn't know for sure unless she actually found the hidden cash. That would be the time to tell Mrs. Hillman.

Meanwhile, she needed to embark on a treasure hunt.

Selena's heart pounded with excitement as she glanced around the room. The assembled party was merrily decorating the tree, all apparently undisturbed by the ideas rattling around in her brain. All except for one person, that is.

Dr. Scott was leaning one arm on the mantelpiece, a distant stare on his face, seemingly as deep in thought as she was. He didn't know about Mr. Clarke's final message, though—but *something* was clearly bothering him.

Selena made a mental note to seek him out later to discuss the matter.

AFTER LUNCH, SELENA led the group on an excursion through the ground floor of the house.

"Last September, the Darkmoor Bridge School for Girls moved from Thorndale Manor to Darkmoor Park, and it has proved to be a most advantageous location," Selena explained as they glanced into the former gentleman's parlor and lady's parlor, which had been turned into schoolrooms. Each chamber was outfitted with a dozen student desks, a good-sized teacher's desk, a blackboard, a globe, and shelves full of books.

Selena showed them the small study that Mrs. Hillman had given over to Selena and Athena to conduct school business and prepare their lessons. As they moved on to the north wing of the manor house, Selena's thoughts wandered to the prospect of the hidden money. If Mr. Clarke really *had* stashed a huge sum of cash here, where was it? What had he meant by *"under the dragon"*? He'd also said, *"Four rows."* She couldn't think of any dragon images at Darkmoor Park, much less four rows of them.

She sternly reminded herself to stay focused on the tour she was conducting. Everyone seemed to be interested in what they were seeing. Although Dr. Scott's expression was reserved, he appeared to be taking in every detail with particular attention.

The moment they set foot inside the library, however, Dr. Scott's face lit up like a beacon—the first time, Selena realized, that she had seen him truly smile since they'd met that morning. And oh, how handsome he looked when he smiled.

Selena understood why he might like the library. She adored it herself. With its carved, vaulted ceiling, acres of books, and floors covered by lush Turkish carpets, the spacious chamber was an inviting and elegant space. Comfortable sofas and chairs stood beside low mahogany end tables and a writing desk. Tall casement windows with window seats, framed by velvet draperies, overlooked the swirling whiteness outside, and stuffed bookcases covered every other inch of available wall space.

"How splendid," Dr. Scott enthused, taking in the place.

Mrs. Whitlock made a face. "Books are generally dusty and moldy, which is very bad for one's health. And who could possibly have time to read all of these?"

Selena had patiently borne the woman's unpleasant attitude until now, but an attack on books was more than she could bear. "My dear Mrs. Whitlock, books contain all the knowledge of the universe. With mere marks of ink on a page, books can transport the reader to distant countries and worlds and teach us the most extraordinary things."

"Indeed." Dr. Scott gave Selena a nod. "Books allow us to enter the minds of people whom we would otherwise never have a chance to meet. They entertain us and challenge us, and they stir the heart. I, for one, cannot imagine a world without books—and one can never have too many."

Mrs. Whitlock cast her eyes heavenward. "To each his own."

Colonel Blackwood laughed. "I have never heard anyone express the purpose of books so eloquently as you two just did."

Selena was equally delighted by the doctor's words. "I have been a great reader since I was a child. Ever since I moved to Darkmoor Park two years ago, it has been my aim to read every book in this library."

"How are you progressing with that?" The doctor arched a brow.

"Very slowly," Selena admitted. "I'm afraid most of my time has been spent poring over science and mathematics textbooks and making lesson plans. But my goal lingers, and I have every belief that I shall achieve it by the time I reach the age of one hundred and seventy-three."

Everyone laughed at that, even Mrs. Whitlock.

Maybe, Selena thought, *the woman isn't a complete killjoy, after all.* "Feel free to spend time in the library whenever you like," she announced. "You are welcome to borrow any book that takes your fancy, as long as you replace it before you leave. I placed a fresh supply of note paper in the top drawer of the desk, along with pens and pencils, should any of you wish to write a letter."

Next, Selena led the party into the billiard room, where the men voiced their appreciation for the mahogany billiard table with its ornately carved legs and green felt surface.

"We'll have to play a game one of these nights, eh, Mr. Davis?" the colonel remarked.

"Love to," responded the gentleman.

"I play as well," Miss Goodwin declared. "I'd love to join you."

The comment caused Mrs. Whitlock to draw a shocked breath. "Billiards is a man's game!"

"*Public* billiard rooms might be for men," Miss Goodwin shot back, "but it is entirely acceptable for ladies to play billiards in private homes."

"Well!" Mrs. Whitlock replied with a tightened jaw. "I hope you don't intend to do so unchaperoned. You are not yet married, Miss Goodwin, and *that* would be unseemly."

Miss Goodwin pursed her lips and looked away but made no reply. Selena, who regarded the rules about chaperones for unmarried couples to be outdated—for how else were people to get to know each other, if someone else was always breathing down their necks?—felt bad for the young lady. Mrs. Whitlock seemed determined to make everyone in the house the object of her scorn.

They proceeded to the music room, a well-appointed chamber paneled in textured wood featuring floral designs. A grand pianoforte and a harp stood before more than a dozen plush chairs, as if in readiness for a concert.

"We are hoping to sing Christmas carols here this evening," Selena told the group. "Do any of you ladies play?" The room fell silent.

"What about you, Miss Goodwin?" Colonel Blackwood suggested.

Miss Goodwin's cheeks grew pink. "I'm afraid I don't play very well."

"Nor do I," Selena put in quickly, hoping to mitigate the young woman's embarrassment. "We have no music master at present, so I am obliged to teach the subject at school. I can stumble along at the keys if need be—although I would prefer someone else to do it."

Colonel Blackwood raised his hands as if warding off a blow. "I haven't touched the instrument in my life."

"I can play," offered Miss Thompson tentatively. "If you like."

Selena was struck once again by how quiet and withdrawn the young lady was, but the response from her employer reminded Selena of the reason behind it.

"*You* play?" Mrs. Whitlock's tone was as derisive as the look she gave her companion. "I've never heard you so much as *talk* about music, much less play it," she added with a disbelieving snort.

"That's because you don't own an instrument, ma'am," Miss Thompson responded softly. "But I *can* play, and would be happy to, tonight—should you wish it, Miss Taylor. Christmas carols are generally easy enough even for a novice musician."

"That would be lovely, thank you." Selena's heart again went out to the unfairly disparaged young woman. Changing the subject, she added, "And now, let us move on to the chapel, shall we?"

At the far end of the north hall, a studded, wooden door like something out of a castle stood beneath a stone archway in the plastered wall.

"It can be a bit cold in here, for it's an extension of the main house," Selena explained as she opened the heavy door and gestured for the others to precede her into the sanctuary.

The chapel walls were fashioned from the same grey stone as the exterior of the house. Two stained-glass windows in the side walls were flanked by clear glass, beyond which the snowstorm raged. Selena crossed her arms over her chest against the chill, taking in the high, open-beamed ceiling, the ancient floor of grey stone, and the dozen rows of brown, wooden pews that faced an altar made of the same wood, upon which rested two massive brass candlesticks. Along the walls stood several porcelain urns below niches holding statues of the saints and the Virgin Mary.

The humble beauty of the place seemed to inspire a sense of respect in the guests, except for the irrepressible Mrs. Whitlock. "It's very plain," she grumbled.

"True." Selena's voice echoed in the serene space. "The chapel was added on after the abbey was destroyed and it hasn't been updated since. It's simpler in design than the rest of the house, but I think equally beautiful in its own way."

A spark lit Miss Thompson's eyes and her mouth widened slightly. "You are fortunate to have a place of worship at Darkmoor Park."

Selena, hoping to prevent another cutting remark from Mrs. Whitlock, quickly replied, "We are, indeed. Mrs. Hillman often likes to start her days here with a few minutes of reflection. On a busy school day, I sometimes steal in here as well, to give myself a moment to ponder and give thanks."

Selena ended the tour with a peek into Mrs. Hillman's small front parlor, which she used as a private retreat, and then led the party back through the great hall to the main staircase.

"We will meet again for drinks before dinner at seven P.M.," Selena told the guests. "Please spend the interval at your leisure."

The group voiced their thanks for the tour and dispersed. Miss Goodwin and Mr. Davis directed a covert glance at Mrs. Whitlock and then hurried off together. Selena wondered with amusement if the couple was, in direct defiance of the older woman's warning about propriety, headed for the billiard room *unchaperoned.* Dr. Scott and Colonel Blackwood said they would return to the library. Mrs. Whitlock bade Miss Thompson to fetch her knitting.

Selena pounced on this opportunity to spend a bit of time on her own—and to follow her hunch that Mr. Clarke might have hidden a fortune somewhere in the house. She decided to start with the most obvious place: the chamber Mr. Clarke had occupied the night before. She hurried upstairs to that room near the end of the north wing and shut the door. The curtains were open. Outside, wind and snow gusted ferociously, lighting the room in a greyish glow.

A rush of nerves took hold of Selena, and she paused. What would she say if a servant were to walk in? She may have been the heir to Darkmoor Park and have the right to go anywhere and do just about anything she pleased, but servants gossiped. She didn't want anyone to know she was snooping.

It occurred to her that someone needed to pack up Mr. Clarke's belongings, a grim task that Mrs. Hillman would probably assign to a member of the staff. Selena decided to do the job herself—it was the perfect explanation for her presence here, should one be required, and she could search the room while she was at it.

"Under the dragon," she reminded herself. She made a quick survey of the chamber but found no image, statue, or other sign of a dragon. Had she misinterpreted the message? It was so cryptic, after all.

Selena opened the wardrobe and removed Mr. Clarke's clothing, methodically checking each coat, shirt, waistcoat, and pair of trousers to see if it might contain a billfold or a packet of money but finding none. She folded and placed each garment in the leather trunk by the window seat. There were two pairs of shoes. Nothing was concealed within them. When the wardrobe was empty, she searched for a hidden drawer or false bottom but found none.

She picked up the shaving kit and comb and brush set from the dresser and added them to the trunk, feeling a stab of sorrow for the gentleman who would have no more need of them. In the top drawer of the bureau, she discovered Mr. Clarke's billfold. It contained twenty-one pounds in cash. She scooped up a stack of stockings and underclothing, and her heart seemed to still.

An envelope lay at the bottom of the drawer.

Selena seized the envelope. It was letter-sized, of high-quality paper, and slight, as if it contained only a letter, not thousands of pounds in cash. Yet Mr. Clarke had deliberately hidden this envelope under his clothing. Why?

It was addressed to Mr. John Clarke at a London address. Why *John Clarke*, not Jack? John must have been the man's formal name and Jack a diminutive, Selena deduced.

She knew she ought to place the letter in the trunk with Mr.

Clarke's other possessions and walk away. But curiosity got the better of her. The envelope had been previously opened. Surely, no one would ever know if she took a peek. And she told herself, although they thought Mr. Clarke had no family, she ought to make sure there was no one who needed to be notified about his death.

Selena unfolded the letter within and read it.

> *December 18, 1852*
> *Hammersmith House, London*
>
> *My dear Mr. Clarke,*
>
> *I am so pleased to invest in your worthy project. Enclosed please find the sum we discussed.*
>
> *I do hope to live long enough to see the London General Hospital built and serving our great city.*
>
> *Cordially yours,*
> *Mrs. Evelyn Stout*

The letter had been folded around a cheque for the sum of a hundred and fifty pounds made out by the Bank of England to the bearer, meaning that whoever possessed it could cash it.

Selena stared at the letter and cheque, her pulse racing. These proved one aspect of what Mr. Clarke had told his listeners at the White Hart Inn—that he *had*, at least purportedly, been raising money to build a hospital. *The London General Hospital*. Mrs. Evelyn Stout, whoever she was, had invested a hundred and fifty pounds—a large sum of money.

Selena's gut told her that that the rest of Mr. Clarke's tale had also been true. He had taken the money he had raised to protect it from a business partner with malicious intent and had brought it to Darkmoor Park—and he had trusted her, with his dying words, to find it.

Now it was up to Selena to make good on that deathbed wish: to locate the money and return it to the hospital building fund. She began to doubt, though, that it was in this room—because it *was* the most obvious place to look. Still, she needed to make sure. She returned the letter and cheque to the envelope, tucked it in her skirt pocket for safekeeping, and made a thorough study of the rest of the room. She found no secret compartments, loose floorboards, or other places where one might conceal wads of cash. And no dragons.

She was about to leave when the chamber door creaked and then slowly opened.

Selena's heart leaped into her throat. She had every right to be here, she reminded herself, clearing out Mr. Clarke's things, but even so, she had hoped to not be discovered. She whirled to face the doorway, readying her explanation for whichever servant might have been coming in.

To her shock, it was Dr. Scott who quietly entered the room and shut the door behind him.

CHAPTER SIX

D R. SCOTT FROZE when he caught sight of Selena. His face turned pink as the two of them stared at each other in the quiet of Mr. Clarke's bedchamber.

"Miss Taylor." He seemed to be struggling for words.

Her own cheeks warmed. "Dr. Scott," she managed. "I have just been packing up Mr. Clarke's things."

"Yes. Er. Um." He glanced at the open trunk and then back at her. "I see. A grim duty. I'm sorry."

"It had to be done." Selena's heart began thundering in her breast. The man really was impossibly handsome. Not that it *mattered* that he was so good-looking. Honesty, good character, kindness, compassion—those were the qualities that mattered in a person. Why, then, were electric sparks rippling through her? Perhaps because she was alone in a bedroom with an unmarried gentleman, a circumstance which was entirely inappropriate? She swallowed hard, hoping he would leave before he noticed the effect he was having on her—or the guilt she felt for being here in the first place. "May I help you, Doctor?"

"Yes. No. Forgive me. I seem to have entered the wrong … I thought this was my chamber." His blush deepened. "The doors all look the same in this hallway and they're not marked."

"Oh! I can see where that might be confusing. But your room is in the south wing. This is the north wing."

"Is it?" His forehead creased.

"Yes. Mrs. Hillman and I housed all the guests here in the north wing with us, but there were no other vacant rooms when you arrived. We placed you in the largest room on the other side of the stairwell. I hope it suits?"

"I'm sure it will be fine," Dr. Scott replied quickly. "I've only seen it briefly. I trust I can find it again. Thank you." He opened the door, bowed, and left the room without another word.

Selena stood there for a long moment, willing her heart to resume its usual pace. Something about their encounter felt odd to her. She remembered the pensive look on the doctor's face earlier, during the tree-trimming, when it had come to light that Mr. Clarke may have brought a huge sum of money with him.

Was it possible, Selena wondered, that Dr. Scott had entered Mr. Clarke's chamber on the same errand that had brought her here? Was he, too, looking for Mr. Clarke's money?

SELENA RETURNED TO her room, planning to change into something more festive for their Christmas Eve celebrations, when a knock sounded at her door.

It was Miss Thompson. A frown marred her features. "Miss Taylor, I'm sorry to disturb you. But I need your help."

"Please come in." Selena ushered the young woman into her chamber and closed the door.

"I was writing a letter to my brother," Miss Thompson said without preamble, "and I spilled the bottle of ink." She was clad in the same frock she had worn since her arrival, a garment of pale-grey wool that seemed to have seen better days, and which now had a big black ink stain on the skirts. "I'm so embarrassed."

"Don't be. I've spilled more ink on myself over the years than I can count."

"I was planning to wear this to dinner tonight and on Christmas Day. Do you know of any way to remove ink from a gown?"

Selena bit her lip. "I do, but it can be a lengthy and not entirely reliable process. I'd be happy to have one of the servants attempt it."

"Thank you." Miss Thompson sighed. "I only have one other dress with me, and it's even plainer than this one."

Selena studied the young woman. "We look to be about the same size and height. I'll loan you one of my frocks."

Miss Thompson blushed and stammered. "I—I couldn't ask you to do that."

"It's no problem at all." Selena opened her wardrobe. "Since I came to live with Mrs. Hillman, she has treated me to so many lovely gowns. I'd be happy to lend you one." Selena pulled out an evening gown of teal-blue velvet, with a pleated bodice, full skirts, and matching bows on the short sleeves. "How about this?"

"Oh! That is much too fine for me, Miss Taylor. What would Mrs. Whitlock say?"

"Who cares what Mrs. Whitlock says?" Selena made a face. "She may be your employer, but she is not your ruler."

"Mrs. Whitlock made it clear when she hired me that I must dress plainly and simply and never outshine her in any way," Miss Thompson insisted. "She'd be angry if I wore a gown as lovely as that."

"All right, then," Selena capitulated. She withdrew another gown that she'd had made for evening events at school but had seldom worn. It was fashioned from navy-blue satin, and its high-necked bodice was unadorned by trimmings. "Will this do?"

"That is also lovely, but I will pray that Mrs. Whitlock approves."

"Try it on here," Selena encouraged. "That way, if it doesn't fit, we can try another. I'm going to change my frock as well. We'll be like sisters, getting ready for a ball."

Miss Thompson laughed at that. "I've never had a sister, but I always wished I had."

As they removed their frocks, Selena said, "I'm lucky. I have two sisters, and growing up, we always enjoyed getting dressed together."

"Where are your sisters now?"

"In Cornwall for Christmas. My oldest sister, Diana, lives there. She's married to a captain in the Royal Navy. My other sister, Athena, and I run the school here, but she and her husband and son went to Cornwall for the holidays. Our brother, Damon, is going to join them there in a few days."

"Yet you stayed here?" Miss Thompson's brow furrowed.

Selena felt a sudden pang of loss, and it hit her how much she missed her brother and her sisters and their families. Had she been wrong to stay? But no, she reminded herself. She'd made the right decision and was glad she was here to assist Mrs. Hillman, especially in light of Mr. Clarke's tragic death that morning, and Selena's important new quest to find the hidden money.

And, said a voice that piped up in her head, *if you hadn't stayed, you wouldn't have met Dr. Scott.*

A sudden blush heated Selena's face. Why was she thinking about Dr. Scott? They had only shared the briefest of conversations, most of which had related to a man who had died. "Mrs. Hillman asked me to help her host this house party," Selena responded quickly, "and I couldn't refuse. She is a dear friend."

"I can see that. You are fortunate to have such close relations and friends. I have no one other than my brother."

From the closet, Selena withdrew a new forest-green velvet gown, which she'd had made for the occasion. It featured long sleeves and gold beading at the V-necked ruched bodice. "Your parents are no longer living, then?" she asked.

"No. My father was a clergyman, but he passed away when I was twelve. We had to give up the rectory, of course, when Papa died." Miss Thompson stepped into the dark-blue gown and put her arms through the sleeves. "My mother found work for us at a great house in Surrey. She was a cook, and I was a chambermaid. We were ever so close. We'd meet in the kitchen late at night and tell stories. She used to say, 'Maud, you can do anything with your life. Don't let anybody tell you different.' She persuaded the mistress of the house to hire her daughter's music master to give me lessons, and I was allowed to play the pianoforte in my spare time."

"How wonderful!" Selena said as she put on her own dress.

"Yes, but …" Miss Thompson sighed. "My mother died six years later."

"I'm so sorry. I lost my mother when I was very young, and my father when I was only sixteen. I know how difficult that can be."

Miss Thompson's voice softened. "I'm sorry for your losses as well." She hesitated. "Shall I button you up?"

"Thank you, but I can do it. I have most of my gowns designed to fasten in the front. But for those that don't, like this one, my sisters and I developed a method, long ago, to enable us to dress ourselves without the need of a lady's maid."

"What method?" Miss Thompson asked with interest.

"I'll show you." Selena faced the back of her gown forward and buttoned it almost all the way, then slid it around before slipping her arms through the sleeves and, twisting her shoulders slightly, pulling the bodice into place. "Now it's just a simple matter of reaching back to fasten the top two buttons," she said as she demonstrated.

Miss Thompson's eyes widened. "That's ingenious."

"It's a useful trick, but it takes time to get the hang of it. I'm happy to button you up." Selena gestured for Miss Thompson to turn around. As the young lady complied, Selena added, "How did you go from being a chambermaid to a lady's companion?"

"It wasn't a direct path. In between, I worked as a governess."

"Oh?" Selena fastened Miss Thompson's dress, which seemed to be a good fit on her slender frame. "My sisters and I were governesses for years."

"Were you?" Miss Thompson sighed. "I trust you were better at it than I was. I found it to be a lonely profession. I love children, but my pupils were indulged by their parents and often took advantage of me."

"I had a similar experience," Selena admitted, "but I loved many of my charges and I loved teaching."

"The teaching was my favorite part. I miss that very much. I've often thought, if I can't open a flower shop, I'd like to teach at a school. Do you enjoy it?"

"I do. It is a most fulfilling occupation. I can't imagine doing anything else." Thinking about the joy she felt, every day, when interacting with a room full of students, made Selena glow with pleasure. She stepped back to survey Miss Thompson in the dark-blue gown. "It's about an inch too short, but I don't think anyone will notice. It looks wonderful on you. Take a look." She turned Miss Thompson towards the cheval glass.

"Oh!" Miss Thompson beamed, as if she were a girl who had always thought herself plain and had just discovered that she was a beauty. "It's beautiful. But … are you sure you want to lend it to me? What if I spill something on it at dinner?"

"Don't give that another thought. Keep this during your stay and wear it as often as you like."

"Thank you, Miss Taylor." Miss Thompson stole another look in the mirror and couldn't hide her smile. "I cannot tell you how much I appreciate this."

"It is my pleasure. We have both been governesses, after all. There is a kind of sisterhood in that. And sisters often share a great many things."

They exchanged a parting hug. How nice it was, Selena thought after Miss Thompson had left the room, to have such an amiable young woman in the house, one who had a similar history. It might help Selena to miss her sisters a *bit* less.

WHEN SELENA ENTERED the drawing room for before-dinner cocktails, everyone was already gathered except Miss Thompson.

Although the curtains were drawn, the storm audibly raged outside.

"Lovely weather," joked Mr. Davis, which elicited a laugh from Mrs. Hillman.

"How glad I am," proclaimed Miss Goodwin, "to be inside this lovely house, where blazing fires make everything so cozy and comfortable."

As Selena accepted a drink from a footman's tray, she snuck a glance at Dr. Scott, who stood alone with his drink by the hearth. He was as formally dressed as the other gentlemen, in a tailcoat with a white waistcoat and tie. So, Wells had managed to find proper evening attire for the doctor. How wonderful he looked in it! With that scar on his forehead, Dr. Scott reminded her of a handsome pirate—the endearing, redeemable sort of pirate like the one in her favorite adventure novels by Pryor Corbett.

As if aware of her notice of him, the doctor turned, and their gazes collided. Selena felt a strange fluttering in her insides. His brows lifted, and a glimmer lit his eyes. Was he responding to the way she looked?

She *had* taken extra care with her appearance tonight, making sure her hair was attractively dressed. She had chosen her green velvet gown because she'd been told it brought out the green in her eyes. But she hadn't done so with Dr. Scott in mind. She had just wanted to look her best for Christmas Eve ... hadn't she? That was what she told herself, anyway.

Self-conscious to have been caught staring, Selena averted her gaze. She wondered if Dr. Scott had given any thought to their awkward encounter in Mr. Clarke's room. Had he really blundered into the wrong room by mistake? Or was he also on the lookout for the money? Had he noticed how flustered *she* had been, while in his company? She hoped not.

Selena couldn't deny that she was attracted to him. But his medical practice was in Bath. She was the heir to Darkmoor Park and ran a school here. She would never move, and she was *not* looking for a relationship with a man. Even if she had been, he was the kind of person she was always warning herself to be wary of. She had learned that people often used their good looks and charisma to gain one's trust before betraying it.

Her heart still hurt every time she recalled the way Jerome Withers had cruelly deceived her at age twenty, a story so mortifying she'd never shared it with anyone, not even her sisters. Her father had been ruined by a silver-tongued devil who had persuaded him to invest his entire fortune in a risky business scheme, only to disappear when the venture had gone bad. And Selena was still bitter about what had happened two years ago at Thorndale Manor. Although no romantic attraction had been involved, the person who had betrayed her and Athena and had nearly cost them their lives had also been good-looking and had their own kind of charm.

Was Dr. Scott equally untrustworthy? It was too soon to tell. But there was something about him that felt a bit—off. He'd been so reserved and distracted ever since he'd arrived. Once or twice, she'd caught him positively glowering. She suspected he was hiding something. Just in case, she must try to maintain a distance between them. Although, she admitted inwardly, that might be difficult because despite herself, some inexplicable fascination was drawing her to him like a magnet.

Her musings were diverted when Miss Thompson entered the drawing room, looking resplendent in Selena's borrowed gown.

Mrs. Whitlock wrinkled her nose and said, "Dear lord, Miss Thompson, where did you get *that* dress? It makes you look twelve years old."

Miss Thompson froze and blushed to the roots of her dark hair. Selena winced at the remark, which was so typical of Mrs. Whitlock—and so totally unfounded. She was about to rush to Miss Thompson's defense, but Dr. Scott got there first.

"It's a beautiful gown, Miss Thompson," he said, giving the young lady a warm smile. "And you look well in it."

Colonel Blackwood darted Mrs. Whitlock a withering glare

and said in a lowered tone, "Really, ma'am, you *could* be more kind."

Mrs. Whitlock merely shrugged as she sipped her drink. "I only say what I think, Colonel, which is more than most people do. I would wager that everyone in this room is hiding something and working hard to hold their tongue, so as not to give their true thoughts away."

The room went deadly quiet. If there had ever been any validity to the phrase about hearing a pin drop, Selena thought, this moment was the proof of it. Everyone except Mrs. Whitlock seemed to be staring at the floor or anywhere but at each other.

Miss Goodwin broke the silence. "Well, Mrs. Whitlock, you certainly do have a way with words."

Brittle laughter rippled around the room. Conversations began again. Selena took Miss Thompson by the arm and walked her the rest of the way into the chamber. "That woman doesn't have a kind bone in her body," Selena said under her breath as she motioned to Sam to bring over the drinks tray. "I think it brings her pleasure to tear other people down. You look very nice. And I'm not just saying that because you're wearing my dress."

Miss Thompson's features still seemed to be plagued by doubt, and a tear pooled in one of her eyes. "Thank goodness I chose the plainer frock and not the teal velvet."

They shared a laugh at that.

Christmas Eve dinner followed, a delicious repast of roast beef and Yorkshire puddings with side dishes of stewed carrots and turnips. A chocolate cake was served for pudding with a platter of fruits, nuts, and cheeses.

Afterwards, the group made their way to the music room, where Miss Thompson, as promised, took a seat at the grand pianoforte to play Christmas carols. Everyone gathered around the instrument to sing except for Mrs. Whitlock, who sat in a nearby chair, took out her knitting, and began to work.

Miss Thompson played with tremendous skill and grace.

Selena, who was standing close by the instrument, noted that the young lady also a possessed a lovely soprano voice—another talent that, perhaps, had been honed by that early music master but which she had been obliged to hide from her contemptuous employer.

At first, Selena felt ill at ease singing Christmas carols. It seemed disrespectful to indulge in such a cheerful pursuit when a member of their party had died that very morning. Mrs. Hillman, whose eyes teared up and who sniffed several times, appeared to share Selena's discomfort. But the others, most of whom hadn't known Mr. Clarke well or, in the case of Dr. Scott, had never even met him, all sang with enthusiasm, tempered by only an occasional, tentative half-smile. They had all agreed to "go on," Selena reminded herself. Perhaps it was important—and healthy—to find some joy amidst the sadness, and she was determined to comply.

Mrs. Whitlock was the only person not singing. Selena noticed the woman surreptitiously stowing a small vial in her knitting bag and wondered what that was about. The next time Selena glanced that way, Mrs. Whitlock was fast asleep. *Leave it to her*, Selena thought, *to miss Miss Thompson's performance, and the party's enjoyment of it.*

When the first song ended, Dr. Scott crossed to stand beside Selena. "You look lovely tonight," he said softly—the first words he had spoken directly to her all evening. "Your gown matches your eyes."

Selena felt her face grow warm. "Thank you, Doctor. You look very nice yourself. I'm glad they were able to find you a suit that fits."

"Your butler wears the same size I do. This suit is one of his spares. One of your maids kindly let down the cuffs for me."

"That's funny." Selena's senses buzzed at his nearness. "Miss Thompson spilled ink on her dress, so I loaned her one of mine. By some miracle, it also fit—except for the length."

"Ah." He smiled. "Her gown is yours. I wondered."

Miss Thompson began playing "Joy to the World," and as they sang, Selena couldn't help but be conscious of Dr. Scott's proximity. He had a lovely tenor voice. The warm, woodsy fragrance of his cologne, which held notes of sandalwood and bergamot, made it hard for Selena to recall the words to the song.

As they moved on to "Silent Night" and "God Rest Ye Merry, Gentlemen," Selena found herself wishing for a moment alone with Dr. Scott so they could chat in private. She wanted to find out whether or not he thought as she did that there might be hidden treasure at Darkmoor Park. If only the weather were clear tomorrow, perhaps she could arrange to have a path cleared and invite Dr. Scott to take a stroll on the grounds.

Her thoughts drifted, imaging the scenario. She and Dr. Scott would be walking along in the crisp, clean air, surrounded by snowdrifts. He would offer his arm to her. She would take it. Her heart began to pound as she envisioned that contact. He would turn to her with a warm smile, his lips full and his vivid, blue eyes gleaming, and he would say—

"That's the last piece of Christmas music," said Miss Thompson, looking up from the piano bench.

The remark drew Selena abruptly from her thoughts. *What are you doing, daydreaming about the doctor's eyes ... and lips? You just warned yourself to be wary of him,* she silently scolded herself.

"You are quite the proficient, my dear," Mrs. Hillman told Miss Thompson. "Do you know any Christmas carols by heart?"

"I do," Miss Thompson admitted. "Shall I go on?"

"Please!" exclaimed Colonel Blackwood.

Miss Thompson launched into "Hark! The Herald Angels Sing," followed by several more songs of the season. When they had gone through all the Christmas carols that Miss Thompson knew, Colonel Blackwood gently woke Mrs. Whitlock, who sat up in her chair with a start. "I wasn't asleep," she declared, blinking rapidly. "I was just deep in thought."

Selena announced that it was time for a parlor game called "Snapdragon."

"The staff has set up the game in the drawing room," she explained. "Mrs. Hillman has small prizes for all the games."

"I always enjoy Snapdragon." Mr. Davis rubbed his hands together as everyone moved in that direction.

The chandeliers and candelabras had been extinguished in the drawing room, and the only light came from the fire in the hearth. The party assembled around a table that housed a large, shallow bowl containing a pile of raisins. Beside it stood a bottle of brandy, a small bowl of salt, and a lit candle.

Once again, Dr. Scott stood beside Selena. Her heart raced at his nearness, a development she was determined to ignore as she poured brandy into the bowl until it soaked the raisins. "Who would like to set the bowl on fire?"

"I'll do it." Colonel Blackwood dipped a lit taper into the brandy, which came to life in a fiery blast.

Selena stepped back from the table, perspiration breaking out on her brow as another and very different quiver of emotion rippled through her—*fear*. She had enjoyed playing Snapdragon until two years ago, when she and Athena had been trapped inside Darkmoor Park's dower house when it had burned to the ground and they had barely escaped with their lives. Although the house on the far edge of the estate had been rebuilt, Selena had been leery of open flames ever since. She knew the reaction was irrational, but she couldn't help it. Snapdragon, however, was a traditional favorite on Christmas Eve, and Mrs. Hillman had insisted that they play it.

As the flames shot up, Selena's stomach clenched, and she swallowed hard to quell her anxiety. Everyone applauded except Dr. Scott and Miss Thompson.

"I have never played," Miss Thompson said hesitantly. "How does it work?"

"The point is to grab as many raisins as you can and eat them," Mrs. Hillman explained.

"Whoever plucks the most raisins from the bowl wins," added Mr. Davis, "so keep a running count of your total."

Dr. Scott cleared his throat. "I don't wish to spoil the fun, but I would feel remiss if I did not point out that this can be a dangerous game. The raisins are very hot—indeed they are *on fire*—so please be careful not to burn your fingers or your tongue."

Miss Thompson's forehead creased. "I see."

"Don't be such a ninny!" Mrs. Whitlock glared at her. "It's quite safe."

"The instant the raisins reach your mouth, the fire goes out," Mr. Davis assured her.

Miss Thompson didn't look reassured.

"There's an old tradition that goes with this game," Mrs. Hillman professed. "Whoever snatches the most raisins out of the flaming brandy will marry their true love within a year."

A chorus of "*awws*" went around the table.

Mr. Davis glanced at Miss Goodwin. "I warn you—I am determined to win."

Scattered laughter met this declaration. Everyone waited until the yellow flames had died down to blue, reflecting upon the faces of the onlookers in an otherworldly glow.

"Take turns as we go clockwise around the table," Mrs. Hillman announced. "Mr. Davis, since you are so eager, let's begin with you."

In unison, the group began to recite the well-known chant.

"*Dragon! Take care you don't take too much. Be not greedy in your clutch. Snip! Snap! Dragon!*"

Mr. Davis reached into the bowl, grabbed a flaming raisin, and popped it into his mouth. "Ha ha!" he cried, the brief blue flame making him appear to be breathing fire, like a dragon, until he huffed it out.

Mrs. Whitlock, Colonel Blackwood, and Dr. Scott successfully took their turns at the game while the chant continued.

"*With his blue and lapping tongue, many of you will be stung. Snip! Snap! Dragon!*"

"*For he snaps at all that comes, snatching at his feast of plums.*

Snip! Snap! Dragon!"

"But Old Christmas makes him come, though he looks so fee! fa! fum! Snip! Snap! Dragon!"

As Selena watched the players devouring flaming raisins, the dragon-like effect suddenly brought to mind the words that Mr. Clarke had spoken during his final hours. *"I hid it ... under ... the dragon."* It seemed uncanny that he had mentioned a dragon. What had he meant?

Mrs. Hillman tossed in a pinch of salt, which created sparks. Everyone exclaimed with delight. Miss Thompson snagged a raisin and hesitantly ate it, which brought forth applause.

It was Selena's turn. Her heart began to race with trepidation, but she didn't want to spoil the mood. As she struggled anxiously to seize a piece of fruit from the flaming bowl, she must have taken longer than was prudent, for a sudden shriek came from Mrs. Hillman. "Selena! Your sleeve!"

Selena gasped. One of her gown's long sleeves was on fire.

CHAPTER SEVEN

S HOUTS WENT UP from all the players around the Snapdragon table.

Selena leaped back, terror spiking through her as she batted at the flames consuming the lower part of her gown's left sleeve.

"Don't move!" Dr. Scott wrapped Selena in his arms and propelled them both to the floor, where he rolled back and forth, trapping her arm between their bodies. When he stopped moving, Selena lay beneath him, his face just inches from hers, her heart thundering in her ears.

"Are you all right?" Dr. Scott's blue eyes bore into hers. His breath brushed her lips with the sweet scent of fruit and brandy.

Selena was highly aware of the weight and feel of every inch of the masculine body that lay atop hers. A heat raced through her, even though she sensed that the flames on her sleeve had been extinguished. "I … think so," she whispered, wishing the contact would never end. But it did, all too soon.

As Dr. Scott helped Selena to her feet, Colonel Blackwood cried, "Good man. In the army, I learned the practice of rolling over to smother flames when clothing catches fire, but I have rarely seen the method put into practice."

Selena had read about the principle as well and had used it to great effect, two years ago, when Athena had suffered a similar emergency. Dr. Scott held on to Selena's left hand and studied her arm, his eyes worried. The lower section of her left sleeve hung in blackened shreds, revealing red blotches on Selena's pale skin beneath. Strangely, though, she felt no pain.

"You've been burned, Miss Taylor. I'll need to treat that at once." Dr. Scott turned to Mrs. Hillman. "Ma'am, if you would be so good as to ring for a servant? I need several things, and I need them at once."

"Yes, Doctor." Mrs. Hillman pulled the bell cord.

Dr. Scott directed Selena to a sofa and sat down beside her. "I'm afraid I have to tear your sleeve."

"Go ahead. It's ruined, anyway," Selena told him.

As the doctor ripped the fabric to expose Selena's flesh, Mrs. Middleton appeared and crossed to Mrs. Hillman. "You rang, ma'am?"

"We've had an accident," Mrs. Hillman replied. "Dr. Scott requires some supplies."

"Please bring me two buckets, one filled with snow and the other with cold water," Dr. Scott requested of the housekeeper. "I also need clean white cloths, a fork, a bowl, a jar of honey, and two egg whites."

"Honey and egg whites?" Mrs. Middleton repeated uncertainly.

"Yes, and please be quick about it," the doctor replied.

The housekeeper curtsied and hurried from the room.

"I'm so sorry, everyone, but I fear this puts an end to our evening's festivities," Mrs. Hillman announced.

"But who won at Snapdragon?" Mrs. Whitlock demanded.

"Does it matter?" blurted out Miss Thompson, her eyes round with apparent dismay at her employer's unfeeling remark. The moment she'd said the words, she blushed crimson and stared at the carpet, her shoulders hunched.

"We needn't declare a winner," agreed Mr. Davis, "but I'd give the honors to Miss Taylor. She withstood the most perilous quest by fire."

"Hear, hear!" cried Colonel Blackwood. The others voiced their consent.

"I bid you all goodnight," Mrs. Hillman told the group. "I look forward to seeing you tomorrow on Christmas Day, which I dearly hope will be far less stressful than today."

The group said their *goodnights* and departed. A few minutes later, Mrs. Middleton and several servants brought in the items Dr. Scott had requested. Mrs. Hillman hovered, her features etched with anxiety while the doctor tended to the burns on Selena's left forearm.

"Thankfully, you haven't blistered," Dr. Scott remarked, yet he treated the area with care and attention.

First, he immersed Selena's forearm in a bucket of water, to which he added clumps of snow. Selena gasped at the icy coldness, but he assured her that cooling a burn was the best and most vital approach to a cure. After gently drying her skin, he made a poultice by whipping together honey and egg whites, which he applied to the affected skin. "This will help to soothe the region and prevent inflammation," he explained.

During the doctor's ministrations, Selena was too focused on the head of light-brown hair bent over her, the handsome face so close to hers, and the firm hands that gently ministered to her wounds to pay heed to the feeling of the wound itself. But after he'd finished wrapping Selena's forearm with a clean cloth and had tied it in place with strips from the same fabric, she began to feel the sting.

"Thank you, Doctor." Selena gave him a grateful look.

"Are you in pain?" he asked.

"A bit," she admitted.

"I have medication in my bag upstairs. Or a shot of brandy often does the trick."

Selena quirked a half-smile. "I'll take the brandy."

"After all that, I'll have one as well," announced Mrs. Hillman as she sank down in a chair with a sigh.

"So will I, if you don't mind." Dr. Scott chuckled.

While Mrs. Middleton and the servants removed the medical paraphernalia from the room, Dr. Scott poured out three glasses of brandy from the bottle on the sideboard, handed one each to Mrs. Hillman and Selena, and kept one for himself.

"Cheers," the doctor said. After they had downed the brandy, he added, "A good night's rest is in order, Miss Taylor. I'll remove the poultice from your arm tomorrow, and you should feel better in a couple of days."

"Thank you," Selena said again.

Mrs. Hillman picked up her fan from an end table and waved it at her face. "I need to sit here for a few minutes before I move another step. Doctor, Selena, please go on up without me."

After they both bade Mrs. Hillman goodnight, Dr. Scott turned to Selena. "May I escort you to your room?"

Selena realized that her wish for a chance to speak to Dr. Scott privately had just been handed to her. "I would appreciate that." As their eyes met, a tingle swept down from her chest to invade her very core. It rattled her that a simple look from this man could set her senses spinning—it was the exact same response she'd had to that man she'd met the summer she'd turned twenty—the man who had betrayed her so cruelly. Had she really only just met Dr. Scott that very morning? It seemed impossible to believe.

Be wary, she again warned herself as they both picked up candles from the sideboard and ventured from the room.

DR. SCOTT'S AND Selena's footsteps echoed along the floorboards as they headed towards the front of the house, their tapers providing the only illumination in the shadowy corridor.

"Doctor," Selena said, "there's something I've been wanting to ask you."

"Oh?"

"Earlier today, when we were all discussing Mr. Clarke and the question of whether or not he might have had a large sum of money in his possession …"

He glanced at her sharply. "Yes?"

"Everyone else seemed to accept that he had just been boasting due to drink. But I'm not sure I agree."

"Oh?" he said again. His flickering candle flame cast eerie shadows across the angles and planes of his face.

"Alcohol consumption *might* loosen a person's tongue and cause them to lie or boast. But—as a doctor—don't you think it equally possible that it could cause a person to speak in a more unfettered fashion? That is, to cause them, perhaps unwittingly, to spill their secrets?"

He went quiet for a moment. "Speaking as a doctor and purely from a hypothetical point of view … it's possible, yes." His tone held an edge of bitterness.

It suddenly occurred to Selena that he might have had previous involvement with a similar matter. Could that be why he'd seemed so moody earlier? Had the incident reminded him of a past, unpleasant personal experience?

"Well," Selena said as they walked on, "what if that were so in this case? The sum Mr. Clarke named was so specific. Fifty-two hundred pounds. I can't help wondering if it was all true."

She glanced at him. That hard look had returned to his face, as if he had gone somewhere else in his mind again. Did he think her mad for even bringing this up? Then his lips tightened, as though he had made a difficult decision. He said, "I admit, I have been wondering the same thing about Mr. Clarke."

"Have you?" Excitement rose in Selena's chest. "My mother used to say, '*Where there's smoke, there's fire.*' And I smell smoke, Doctor. Earlier this afternoon when I was in Mr. Clarke's room, packing up his things … I found a letter that confirms he was raising funds for The London General Hospital."

He stared at her. "A letter from whom?"

"A woman—I think her name was Mrs. Stout. There was also a cheque made out to bearer for a hundred and fifty pounds. The envelope was addressed to Mr. John Clarke, which I'm guessing was his formal name."

Dr. Scott's scarred brow lifted at that and his eyes darkened. "Interesting."

"We know that Jack Clarke gave two hundred pounds to Mrs. Hillman," Selena rushed on. "But what if he had far more than that with him? What if he had fifty-two hundred pounds, which—as he said—he'd removed from his safe to safeguard it from his scheming business partner?"

Dr. Scott huffed out a scornful breath. "Do you really believe that? That he took the money to protect it?"

"I do." She stared at him. "Why else would he have taken it?"

He paused, then said matter-of-factly, "Perhaps he stole it."

"Stole it? That makes no sense. Why would he steal from his own fundraising venture? Besides, he said the money was in his own safe."

The doctor's lips tightened. "Apparently so."

"I met Mr. Clarke. You did not. I liked him. Everyone said he was a good man with good intentions. But perhaps he worried that he'd said too much that night at the White Hart Inn. Even though he had given two hundred pounds to Mrs. Hillman—money that I presume was his own—the remaining five thousand pounds would be a huge temptation to anyone." Selena took a breath. "After he arrived here, I think he hid that money to keep it safe."

He nodded slowly. "The same things have occurred to me."

Selena's pulse leaped. She'd been right. Dr. Scott felt as she did about all this. She could use an ally in her search—and the idea of spending more time in his company was appealing. But she had known Dr. Scott less than day. She still suspected he was hiding something, and she kept telling herself he was too handsome to be trusted.

But perhaps she was being unduly suspicious. Just because she'd had bad experiences in the past didn't mean that Adrian Scott was duplicitous. He was a *doctor*. He had treated her burned arm so tenderly just now. If you couldn't trust a doctor to be forthright and honest, whom *could* you trust?

She let go of her doubts and plunged in. "Mr. Clarke intended to bring that money back home and tell the police what was going on. Since he's no longer here to do it, let's join forces, find the money, and return it to the hospital building fund for him."

"I beg your pardon?" Dr. Scott's brows shot upwards. "I'm not about to embark on a treasure hunt at Darkmoor Park."

"Aren't you?" As they passed the morning room, she paused and shot him a challenging look. "When you walked into Mr. Clarke's room today, it wasn't by mistake, was it? You went to see if he might have stashed the money there."

Dr. Scott's mouth opened and just as quickly closed. He stopped beside her. "Fine. Yes. I *was* looking for it. Because … perhaps because I know how desperately new hospitals are needed in London. His room seemed like a logical place to start."

"I was there for the same reason," Selena admitted.

"I surmised as much. I take it you didn't find anything?"

"Other than that letter and cheque, no."

He heaved a sigh. "I admit, I'd like to find that money as much as you would. But I'd rather look on my own."

Selena shook her head. "I can't have you investigating this without me. I can snoop anywhere I want, and I know this house like the back of my hand. Besides, two heads are better than one."

One corner of his mouth quirked upwards. "Is that another one of your mother's favorite sayings?"

"Yes, and it's true. A couple of years ago, my sister Athena and I solved a mystery that would have confounded Confucius himself. With your help, I believe we can do this."

Dr. Scott's eyes narrowed, and he seemed to be considering her offer. Just then, a sound broke the stillness—a soft crackle and thud that made Selena jump.

"What was that?" she asked.

"I don't know," Dr. Scott replied in a lowered tone. "It sounded as if it came from the morning room." He put a finger to his lips and quietly entered the open doorway nearby. Selena followed. Raising their candlesticks, they surveyed the darkened chamber. The heavy draperies were shut on the tall windows. Snacks had been set out on the sideboard. A dirty plate lay on the table, suggesting that someone had been here after it had last been cleaned—but no one else was there now.

"I smell smoke, as if from a snuffed candle." Selena, worried, gestured towards the second door on the far side of the room. "Do you think someone overheard our suspicions and fled through the other door?"

"I hope not." Dr. Scott gestured to the hearth, where a red-hot log had tumbled from the stack and lay at the front edge of the grate. "Ah. There's the culprit. That explains the sound we heard, as well as the smoke."

Selena nodded in relief. "Thank goodness. I don't know why I'm so jumpy."

"It's understandable. It's been a long and difficult day."

They left the morning room and headed up the main staircase. As they passed the half-landing, Selena shuddered, remembering the calamity that had occurred there that morning. The doctor was right. It was no wonder that she was jumpy.

When they'd reached the first floor, Dr. Scott stopped and said in a hushed voice, "We should keep our voices down when we talk about this. I'd rather the household at large didn't get the notion to join us on a treasure hunt."

Selena's heart stuttered. "'Join us'?" she whispered. "Does that mean you're in?"

He shrugged his broad shoulders and replied just as quietly, "As you said, two heads are better than one, and I can't very well sneak about on my own *now*."

Selena felt all lit up inside. "True."

"But where would we even begin to look?" he asked softly. "Darkmoor Park is an enormous house. It could be anywhere."

"Perhaps not." Selena glanced up and down the hallway. It was empty. Still, it wouldn't do to discuss this in the hall. She indicated a nearby door. "Follow me." Selena led the doctor into the small parlor at the head of the stairs. "Our students often do their homework in here, but otherwise, it's rarely used," she said as she closed the door behind them.

The cozy chamber was outfitted with several comfortable chairs, a sofa, and a writing desk. A low fire glowed in the hearth and the only other light was provided by their two candles.

The doctor's mouth grew tense. "Miss Taylor. We shouldn't be in here alone together."

Selena waved a dismissive hand. "Let's not worry about propriety, shall we, Doctor? If we're going on a treasure hunt, I suspect we'll be spending a lot of time alone together." The instant the statement had left her mouth, Selena felt a heat rise to her face. She wasn't sure what had given her the audacity to say something so bold—this wasn't how she usually behaved—but it was too late to take it back.

"Won't your beau be upset if he learns about this?" the doctor persisted.

"My 'beau'?" Selena stared at him.

"I can only presume that a woman as smart and beautiful as you would be … if not spoken for, at least involved with a gentleman who was unable to join you for Christmas."

Selena's blush deepened. Had he just called her smart and beautiful? "I am not involved with anyone, Doctor. I am a spinster schoolteacher."

His brows arched. "I see."

Was it her imagination? Or did he seem as pleased to hear that as she had been upon learning that he was unattached? "Anyway," she added swiftly, "if anyone asks, you can say I had a fainting fit and you had to tend to me in here. Who would challenge you? You're a doctor."

His lips twitched. "Very well." He crossed his arms over his chest. "Now, why are we here?"

"Because." Selena clasped her hands with excitement. "With regard to the hidden money … I think I have a clue to its whereabouts."

His eyes widened. "What clue?"

"When you asked me this morning if Mr. Clarke had said anything before he lost consciousness, I wasn't exactly forthcoming. He *did* say something."

Dr. Scott gave her a sharp glance. "What did he say?"

"He grabbed my arm, looked me in the eyes, and—with great intensity—he said, *'I hid it.'*"

"*'I hid it'*?"

"Yes! Don't you see? He was talking about the money!"

"Perhaps," Dr. Scott acknowledged. "Did he say anything else?"

"Yes. He had trouble speaking, but I remember every word. He said, *'Under the dragon.'* And then, *'Four rows! In the ...'* Then he broke off and said no more."

"*'Under the dragon'*? *'Four rows'*?" Dr. Scott repeated slowly, his forehead creasing. "And you think ... what? That Mr. Clarke guessed he might be dying and wanted you to know he'd hidden something, and where it could be found?"

"I'm certain of it."

Dr. Scott paced back and forth before the hearth. "What do you think it means? That business about a dragon? Is there anything or any place at Darkmoor Park that has a dragon motif?"

"I don't know. I've only lived here a couple of years. But there must be. I'll have to ask Mrs. Hillman."

"You're sure he said *'four rows'*?"

"That's what he said." A sudden thought occurred to Selena, and she took a breath. "Wait. I might be wrong. Maybe he didn't say *rows*, as in R-O-W-S, but rather, *rose.* As in the flower."

"I doubt it. If so, he would have said, *'four roses,'* plural."

"Not necessarily. Mrs. Hillman's first name is Rose. Maybe he was saying, *'For Rose.'*"

Dr. Scott took that in. "Hmm. But he had already repaid Mrs. Hillman the money he owed her." He shook his head. "I believe his dying words were about the rest of the money, and where he'd hidden it."

Selena nodded. "Well, then, we have our marching orders. We need to find some kind of dragon motif and presumably, four rows of something nearby." She paused, thinking. "By the way, Miss Goodwin said that Mr. Clarke claimed to have fifty-two hundred pounds in fifty-pound notes in his coat pocket. How big would that wad of cash be?"

The doctor mulled that over. "Not all that big. If in one stack, I'd guess it would be about half an inch tall."

"Too big for his billfold, I suppose. But he could have kept it in a small pouch in his coat pocket."

"Yes."

She hesitated again. "Do you think we ought to tell Mrs. Hillman?"

Dr. Scott frowned. "This is all just a theory at present. Until we find it, let's keep this to ourselves. If she were to inadvertently say something—if someone else were to get there first—we can't guarantee that their intentions would be honorable."

"My lips are sealed."

"And now, we need a plan."

"I'll ask Mrs. Hillman if there are any dragons about the place. And I'll question the servants to find out if anyone saw Mr. Clarke engaged in any suspicious activity yesterday."

"I'll do the same with the guests," he proposed. "Discreetly, of course."

"We must agree to freely share any information we find."

"Of course."

Selena extended her right hand. "Shall we shake on it?"

"Agreed."

His grip was firm and his touch and the look on his face sent a quiver up Selena's arm. Did he feel it, too? Perhaps he did, for his expression seemed to share her own reluctance when he let her hand go.

He cleared his throat. "We've been sequestered in here long enough. Let's hope nobody has noticed."

She accompanied him to the door. He opened it and peeked

into the hallway. Seemingly satisfied, he turned to back face her, his gaze filled with warmth. The grandfather clock on the landing began to chime the hour. *One. Two. Three. Four.*

"Goodnight, Miss Taylor," he said. *Five. Six. Seven. Eight.*

"Goodnight, Dr. Scott." Her voice was so tremulous, it sounded foreign to her ears. *Nine. Ten. Eleven. Twelve.*

When the final bell rang out, he kissed his fingertips and touched them tenderly to Selena's cheek. Sparks coursed through her body as he said softly, "Happy Christmas."

CHAPTER EIGHT

SELENA SHIVERED AS she strode down an unfamiliar corridor, her candle providing the only illumination in the inky darkness.

A scream rang out. Selena lurched to a halt. Before her, Jack Clarke lay on the carpet in a pool of blood, his dead eyes open and staring. "Oh, no!" Selena cried. "What happened to you, Mr. Clarke?"

Diana appeared out of the shadows. Her dark hair was pulled back from her lovely face in a simple chignon. Selena's heart swelled with a fierce ache of recognition. Oh, how good it was to see Diana! It had been far too long. Selena had missed her so. She started to run to her, but Diana's words stopped Selena in her tracks.

"This was no accident," Diana declared.

Selena stared at her sister. "What do you mean?"

Athena stepped into view, the flickering candlelight bringing out the red highlights in her auburn curls. "Open your eyes, Selena."

With a determined nod, Diana added, "The man was clearly murdered."

Selena awakened with a gasp. Her heart raced as she gripped the covers to her throat. What had prompted such a dream? That feeling of inadequacy reared its ugly head again. Even in her dreams, her sisters were admonishing her, insinuating that she was missing something—that a murder had taken place when there was no evidence of one.

She *had* briefly wondered, the morning that Mr. Clarke's injured body had been found, if he might have been pushed down those stairs. Dr. Scott had posed a similar question. At the time, they had both accepted that Clarke's fall had been an accident. But what if their first instinct had been correct?

If so, why would anyone have wished to do away with Mr. Clarke?

A new thought suddenly occurred to Selena. She and the doctor believed that Mr. Clarke had stashed a huge sum of money at Darkmoor Park. Was it possible that someone had murdered him to get their hands on that hidden money? But no—that made no sense. It would have been foolish to kill Mr. Clarke, for his secret had apparently died with him. Hadn't it? As far as Selena knew, she was the only person who had heard his dying words— as cryptic as they had been.

Selena shook off the errant dream. *No.* It was just her mind playing tricks on her. Mr. Clarke's death had been an unfortunate accident, and that was that. She rose, shivering as her feet touched the frigid floor. A low fire burned in the grate, evidence that Gladys had come and gone. Selena gave a silent thanks to the new chambermaid, who performed this early morning duty.

As she parted the bedroom curtains, Selena took in the view of the rear grounds. The wind had eased somewhat, but it was still snowing hard. The ruined abbey rose majestically from a landscape that was blanketed in deep drifts of snow and the trees and hedgerows were frosted like a wedding cake.

Selena wrapped her arms around herself, being gentle with her bandaged left forearm, which now only stung slightly. Her thoughts drifted back to the previous night, and another shiver ran through her—this time from anticipation rather than from the cold. She couldn't forget the heartfelt look in Dr. Scott's eyes before he had said goodnight. The sensation of his fingertips as they had touched her cheek with his parting indirect "kiss" had

kept her awake for hours and still lingered. It seemed impossible to believe that at this time the day before, they had not even met. And now, she couldn't stop thinking about him.

She couldn't remember when she had ever felt such a dramatic attraction to a man. Not even Jerome Withers, the cad she'd fallen for when she'd been twenty years old. She had been living at home at the time in between governess jobs, with no one in the house but her father. Mr. Withers had been an acrobat and equestrian in a traveling circus, and he had singled her out in the crowd after the show.

Selena had been mesmerized and had attended every performance during the four days that the circus had remained on the village green, sharing stolen kisses with Mr. Withers behind the tent. He'd told her he'd loved her, and—she could hardly believe this now—she had been seriously considering his invitation to run away and join the circus. But when she'd brought a freshly baked apple pie to his caravan, to her shock and mortification, he had answered the door *in flagrante delicto*—and in an amorous embrace with another young woman. Selena had fled as fast as her feet could carry her, wishing she'd had the presence of mind to throw the pie in his face.

That, however, had been ten years ago. Selena hoped that she had grown and learned a thing or two since then. She was no longer that naïve girl and Dr. Scott was no circus performer. Yes, he was handsome and charming, but he was also an intelligent, well-educated doctor who wanted as much as she did to find Mr. Clarke's hidden money so that a new hospital could be built in London.

She believed she could trust him. The idea that they would be investigating a mystery together was incredibly exciting. She didn't know what thrilled her more, the notion that she was about to embark on a treasure hunt that was all for a good cause—or the fact that she would be doing so *with him.*

Selena glanced at the clock on the mantel. It was nearly half-past seven. She had an hour and a half before breakfast was served. She could use that time to start phase one of the quest ahead—by discreetly questioning some of the servants, to see if they recalled Mr. Clarke's movements on the afternoon and evening of December 23rd.

As if in response to Selena's thoughts, there came a low knock on the door and Gladys entered, carrying a cloth-covered pitcher. "Happy Christmas, miss," the maid said politely.

Selena had almost forgotten that it was Christmas Day. She returned the greeting, adding, "Gladys, you're just the person I was hoping to see."

"Am I, miss?" Gladys replaced the old pitcher on the dresser with the fresh one, which Selena knew would hold hot water for her morning ablutions.

"Yes. I know you're relatively new here, and I've been meaning to thank you for your exemplary work. It is always a treat to rise to a warm fire in my room."

Gladys curtsied. "Just doing my job, miss."

"There is also something I wanted to ask you. It's about Mr. Clarke."

The maid's face fell. "Oh, miss." She averted her eyes. "Everybody is talking about that downstairs. What happened, it were ever so sad."

"Yes, and I'm sorry you were the one who came upon him like that. It must have been very distressing for you."

"It was, miss."

Selena launched into the speech she had mentally prepared. "It pains me to think that the last day of Mr. Clarke's life was here at Darkmoor Park. I hope it was a good day. I can't help but wonder how he spent it. That afternoon, after our guests arrived, and everyone went up to their rooms to nap or change for dinner—did you see Mr. Clarke anywhere else about the house?"

"No, miss. I were busy helping out in the kitchen at the time." Gladys twisted her hands. "Mrs. Nash needs all hands on deck these days to help prepare the meals."

Their cook, Mrs. Nash, had managed with a trained kitchen

staff while school was in session, but many of those young women had gone home for the holidays. "What about later in the evening?" Selena asked. "Did you notice Mr. Clarke going anywhere other than straight back to his room?"

"No, miss," Gladys said again. "By that time, I were fast asleep myself. I'm one of the first to rise, so Mrs. Middleton gives me leave to retire at nine o'clock."

"I see." Another question came to Selena's mind. "The morning that we're discussing, did you see or hear Mr. Clarke talking to anyone before you found him on the half-landing?"

A flush crept up Gladys's neck and face, and she hesitated before answering. "No. Like I said before, I were just coming up the stairs with the firewood. I'm so sorry, miss. I know I shouldn't have been using the main stairwell, and I'll never do it again, but—but I did that morning and—and I just found him there."

"Understood. Thank you, Gladys."

The maid dipped another curtsey and hastily left the room. Selena watched her go, wondering why she had seemed so nervous. Was she hiding something? In any case, she hadn't furnished a single clue.

Selena splashed warm water on her face, careful not to get the bandage on her forearm wet as she thought about the day ahead. She knew that Mrs. Hillman, even though she had told her guests not to bring gifts, had presents to distribute. Selena, not wishing to attend the Christmas gathering empty-handed, had been working for months making gifts of her own for the guests.

It occurred to her, with a pang, that Mr. Clarke was no longer here to receive his gift. Dr. Scott had arrived unexpectedly, and she was glad that she'd had the presence of mind to make a few extra presents, just in case.

Meanwhile, the clock was ticking. She must get dressed.

Selena had earmarked her new red velvet gown to wear this evening to Christmas dinner. For Christmas day, she selected a tried-and-true favorite: a frock made of dark-green taffeta that featured vertical ruffles in the same fabric on the front-buttoning bodice, which rose to form a high collar. The dress was trimmed with black braiding and its long, bell-shaped sleeves nicely covered the bandage on her forearm without being too tight.

When she had finished dressing and pinning up her hair, Selena made her way down the servants' stairs, the most direct route to the servants' hall. She encountered one of the housemaids, Beryl, on her way up, carrying an armful of clean folded linens.

"Beryl, may I have a word?" Selena gave the same reason for her inquiries that she had given Gladys and repeated the same questions, asking if the chambermaid had noticed Mr. Clarke anywhere about the house on the afternoon in question, before or after dinner.

Beryl paused to readjust her white cap over her dark head. "Let me think. Well, now that you mention it, I did see Mr. Clarke that afternoon wandering about."

Selena's pulse skittered. "Where did you see him?"

"He was coming out of the east schoolroom."

"The east schoolroom?" Selena's mind seized on the fact. Had he hidden the money there?

"After that," Beryl continued, "he headed down the back hall. He was carrying his overcoat. I thought he might be going for a walk outside."

Outside? Selena groaned inwardly. It hadn't occurred to her that Mr. Clarke might have hidden the money outside. "Did you actually see him leave the building?"

"No. I don't know for certain where he went next. I went in the opposite direction."

"Well," Selena said, "if he did take a walk, I hope he enjoyed it. Thank you so much, Beryl."

Selena found Sam, the new footman, exiting the kitchen with a domed silver platter no doubt intended for the breakfast buffet. She posed the same inquiries to him, to which he replied, "Sorry, miss. I don't recall seeing that gentleman about. If you'll excuse me, I must get this upstairs."

George, the head footman, was of no more help. Next, Selena questioned Wells, whom she discovered in the butler's pantry, pouring a bottle of wine into a crystal decanter.

"I did notice Mr. Clarke exiting the library that afternoon, miss," the butler remarked. "I asked if he would like a guided tour of the building, but he declined, saying he preferred to wander about on his own. I gave him leave to do so."

"Did you see where he went next?"

"Yes—the chapel. I thought it very fitting that he had his overcoat with him, for, as you know, it can be chilly in the chapel at this time of year."

The library. The chapel. Selena made another mental note. "Yes, it can. Thank you, Wells."

As Selena hurried back upstairs, she pondered what she had learned. For one thing, it proved that she'd been right. Mr. Clarke *had* been prowling around the manor house after his arrival, perhaps scouting for a place to hide the money. He'd gone into the east schoolroom, where he'd certainly had no business being. He'd been seen exiting the library and entering the chapel. Were there any dragons in any of those rooms? She couldn't think of any, but she'd have to check.

It worried her that he'd had his overcoat with him. Had he left the building? If so—and if he *had* hidden that money outside—it may well prove impossible to find. For the Darkmoor Park grounds were extensive, and it had been snowing steadily since Mr. Clarke had died.

Selena entered the morning room to find Colonel Blackwood, Dr. Scott, Miss Goodwin, and Mr. Davis seated at the table, eating breakfast. The gentlemen were nicely dressed in frock coats and starched cravats or neckties, and the young lady wore her usual black gown.

"Happy Christmas!" Selena greeted them.

The group echoed the sentiment. As Selena's gaze collided with Dr. Scott's, his blue eyes glimmered. "Happy Christmas, Miss Taylor. How is your arm?"

"It doesn't hurt much at all," Selena assured him.

"I need to look at it after breakfast." Although the doctor's statement was matter-of-fact, his brows arched as if to convey some special meaning intended only for her. Perhaps a silent allusion to a need to talk to her in private?

"Very well." Selena was just as anxious for a moment with him, to share what she had learned this morning. She gave him a nod and poured herself a cup of tea.

Mrs. Whitlock and her companion filed in and helped themselves to the bacon, eggs, and toast at the buffet. Selena had just filled her own plate and had taken a seat across the table from the doctor, when Mrs. Hillman entered. Although she wore a gown of rich, burgundy brocade silk that was pleated and flounced to within an inch of its life, she didn't seem to be in a festive mood. Her face was drawn, and her eyes were filled with anguish.

Everyone stood to greet her. "Is something wrong, Mrs. Hillman?" Selena asked.

"Yes. No. Well, it's nothing to worry you about." Mrs. Hillman crossed the room, leaning on her cane. "It's just that my brooch is missing."

Selena's stomach tightened. "Not your iris brooch?"

"I'm afraid so." Mrs. Hillman paused by the table and sighed. "Last night, I put it where I always put in, in my jewel box. But when I went to put it on this morning, it wasn't there."

"Oh, no." Selena knew that brooch was precious to Mrs. Hillman, not just for its significant financial value, but for its sentimental value, for it had been a gift from her husband. "Perhaps you placed it somewhere else and have forgotten?"

"I must have. I am getting more and more forgetful these days. But never mind. It's Christmas." Mrs. Hillman turned to the footmen, who stood like sentinels by the buffet. "Sam, please bring me tea, eggs, and toast." As Sam scurried to fulfill her request, and George pulled out a chair for her, she sat down at the table and addressed the group. "Did you all sleep well, I hope?"

"Like a log," Colonel Blackwood responded. "It's strange, though. Something was missing from my room this morning as well."

A foreboding feeling hit the pit of Selena's stomach. "What was missing, Colonel?"

"My copy of *The London Times*. I brought it with me on the train. Snowed in as we are, it will be a while until we get news of the outside world, so I planned to read that old edition again this morning. But I couldn't find it."

"That *is* strange," agreed Mr. Davis. "Newspapers don't generally walk away on their own."

"Nor do brooches," pointed out Miss Goodwin. "It sounds as if we have a thief in our midst."

Miss Thompson jerked suddenly and her fork clattered to her plate. Her face turned red.

"Clumsy ox!" Mrs. Whitlock glared at her companion, whose flush deepened even further.

"Thieves don't abscond with newspapers," Dr. Scott pointed out.

"I wouldn't think so." Mrs. Hillman scooped up a forkful of eggs. "You said it was an old edition?"

The colonel nodded. "December 23rd."

"Perhaps one of the servants used it as a fire starter," Mrs. Hillman suggested.

"Nothing was taken from *my* room," declared Mrs. Whitlock, "but the wind kept me awake until all hours and my room was absolutely freezing." Her tone was as biting as her teeth, which crunched upon a piece of crisp bacon.

Selena's hackles went up and it was all she could do to keep her ire in check. "I'm so sorry you were cold, Mrs. Whitlock. I shall ask a maid to bring you another blanket tonight and to be sure to build up your fire higher."

"See that you do." Mrs. Whitlock glanced out the window with a frown. "Will this infernal snow *ever* stop falling?"

"I'm *glad* it's snowing," Miss Goodwin said. "It's a perfect

Christmas Day."

"Indeed!" Mr. Davis agreed.

Mrs. Hillman spread marmalade on her slice of toast. "Yes, and as I mentioned yesterday, I'd like to begin with a service in the chapel in Mr. Clarke's honor. Are you still willing to lead it, Colonel Blackwood?"

"It would be my honor, ma'am."

"Good. Afterwards, we will all gather in the drawing room. I have a little something to give you all."

"Mrs. Hillman!" The colonel wagged a finger at her. "You expressly forbade us to bring gifts."

Mrs. Hillman flapped her hand. "You have all come a long way, and at great expense. Your presence here, as the saying goes, is *my* present. But I couldn't very well let Christmas go by without party favors, could I? Later, we'll have an early Christmas dinner at four P.M., followed by parlor games."

"You are our hostess, ma'am, so your word is law," Miss Goodwin said with a smile. "What time shall we meet in the chapel?"

Mrs. Hillman glanced at the timepiece pinned to her frock. "At 10:30—in a little more than half an hour. I have some small matters to attend to. I will see you all there."

Selena had hoped that after breakfast, she could find a moment alone with Mrs. Hillman to ask her if she knew of any dragon statues or motifs at Darkmoor Park. But Mrs. Hillman removed her napkin from her lap and gestured to George, who pulled back her chair. Selena decided she should use this time to speak with the doctor instead. Apparently, he had the same idea, for in short order, all the members of the party had left the room except for her, Dr. Scott, and the footmen, who were clearing the table.

The doctor poured fresh water from a pitcher into a clean, empty bowl, then brought it and his medical bag to the table and sat down beside Selena. "Let me take a look at your arm." He lifted up the bell-shaped portion of Selena's lower left sleeve and removed the bandage.

"I have information to share," Selena told the doctor quietly.

"So do I," Dr. Scott said under his breath. "But not yet." He began gently sponging away the poultice on Selena's forearm.

When the servants had cleared up from breakfast and quit the room, Selena asked in a low tone, "Now?"

He nodded.

"Did you have a chance to speak to any of the other guests?"

"A few. I said I was thinking about poor Jack Clarke and wondering how he had spent his last day on Earth."

"That's the exact same excuse I gave."

"Great minds think alike." His eyes twinkled. "Mrs. Whitlock said that after she and Miss Thompson got here, they took a nap and didn't see Mr. Clarke again until you gathered for drinks. Colonel Blackwood said he arrived with barely enough time to change for dinner. Which isn't very helpful."

"But good to know."

He finished cleaning her forearm, where only mild red patches marred the skin with no blistering. "It's healing nicely," he proclaimed with satisfaction. "That poultice really did the trick."

"You are a medical wizard."

"Hardly." He gently dried her forearm with a clean linen napkin. "You said you have information?"

"Yes." They were seated in such close proximity that Selena was again aware of the heady scents of Dr. Scott's shaving soap and sandalwood cologne. "I spoke to a number of servants."

"And?"

Selena told him what she had learned.

"That's great," he enthused softly. "It confirms our theory."

"Yes, but if Mr. Clarke hid the money outside, we're doomed. It would be buried in snow by now."

"It can't snow forever. And that's what shovels are for."

Selena laughed.

"I can rebandage your arm if you like, but I don't think I need to, as long as you keep it clean and dry."

"I'll do that. No bandage. Thank you."

"My pleasure." He rose and helped her to a stand. "I suggest we start our search in the rooms Mr. Clarke is known to have visited."

Selena nodded. "Beginning with our group's next stop, the chapel."

He glanced at his pocket watch. "Where we are expected in five minutes."

At that moment, Sam reentered the room. "Are you finished, sir?" He gestured to the items still on the table.

"Yes, thank you." Dr. Scott handed the footman his medical bag. "Would you mind returning my bag to my room for me?"

"Of course, sir." Sam took the bag and departed.

When Selena and Dr. Scott entered the chapel a few minutes later, the rest of the party was already inside. Mrs. Hillman was seated in the front row. The others were scattered among the pews. Selena and Dr. Scott slid onto a bench at the back of the room.

Colonel Blackwood addressed the group from the pulpit. "I think I speak for us all when I say what an honor it is to be here, on this blessed Christmas Day, at this extraordinary haven, Darkmoor Park. Christmas is a very special time, a season that reminds us of the importance of shaping a world filled with compassion, kindness, and love. Thank you so much, Mrs. Hillman, for having us here and making us welcome—the motley crew who first met four years ago at the Worthing Seaside Hotel, as well as those who are new to us."

Selena was touched by the colonel's words. At the same time, she couldn't help glancing around the chapel, wondering if Mr. Clarke had hidden the money here.

"But more than that, Mrs. Hillman," the colonel went on. "Thank you for insisting, with your constant letter writing over the years, that I keep in touch with you—for if it were up to me, such a poor correspondent as I am, I fear we would have fallen out of touch. I'm guessing you must have repeated the effort with

Mrs. Whitlock as well as with Mr. Clarke and Mrs. Goodwin, God rest their souls, or this gathering would never be taking place."

"She did," Mrs. Whitlock called out with a nod. "Every three months like clockwork, another letter."

Laughter echoed within the chapel walls.

Selena noticed that Dr. Scott was also sweeping the interior of the sanctuary with his gaze, no doubt looking for a sign of a dragon. She studied the stone walls, the statues in the niches, the tall, ceramic urns. No dragons anywhere.

"I cannot go further," Colonel Blackwood was saying, "without telling you how much I admired the man who ought to be sitting here among us this morning, Mr. Jack Clarke. He was my friend and companion for many a jolly day and evening. Some of you knew him better than I. Some of you only knew him a single evening. And one of you didn't know him at all." At that, he glanced at Dr. Scott, who squirmed in his seat with a strained smile. "But I know we all feel Mr. Clarke's loss and are filled with sorrow about what happened."

Moisture pooled in Selena's eyes. She reached into her handbag for a handkerchief and dried her tears.

"Let us take a few minutes of silence to honor the man." The colonel clasped his hands before him. "Feel free to direct your mind however you like—to memories of Jack Clarke or, perhaps, to thoughts about mortality, and our own good fortune in being here, alive and well, today."

The room fell silent. Selena was about to close her eyes and follow Colonel Blackwood's directive, when the stained-glass window on one side of the chapel caught her notice. She had sat in this chamber many dozens of times but had never paid much attention to the stained-glass windows. In vivid shades of red, green, blue, white, and gold, two panels featuring winged and haloed angels flanked a central panel that was a tribute to St. George.

Selena gasped.

St. George sat astride a white horse and carried a long spear with which he was slaying … *a fierce-looking dragon.*

CHAPTER NINE

FROM HER SEAT in the back pew of the Darkmoor Park chapel, as Selena stared at the stained-glass window of St. George and the dragon, she struggled not to give any clue to the excitement that was building within her.

Was this the 'dragon' to which Mr. Clarke had been referring with his last words? If so, did it mean the money was hidden somewhere beneath the window?

Selena's heartbeat, which pounded in her ears, sounded like the cacophony of insistent drums. She stole a glance at Dr. Scott beside her. His eyes were closed, and he seemed to be in deep reflection. Which was, Selena reminded herself, the proper way to behave at this moment, since Colonel Blackwood had asked everyone to spend a few minutes in silent tribute to the recently deceased Mr. Clarke.

The other members of their party also had their heads bowed in obedient stillness in the pews ahead of them. Selena slid closer to Dr. Scott on the bench. She didn't dare to break the silence— but she had to get his attention somehow. She was about to nudge his arm but paused; that might be noticed. Instead, even though she knew the gesture was too intimate and possibly scandalous, she reached over and, with dancing nerves and a tingling stomach, surreptitiously tapped a fingertip against his thigh.

His eyes flew open, and he turned to her with a raised brow.

Selena shot him a look filled with meaning and gestured with her head towards the stained-glass window. He followed her glance. His mouth dropped open slightly and he turned back to her with a silent, wide-eyed stare that signaled his understanding.

Colonel Blackwood cleared his throat and addressed the group again. "Thank you, everyone. Mrs. Hillman, before we close, was there anything you wished to add?"

"Yes. I wish to thank you, Colonel Blackwood. That was lovely," she said.

"It was my honor, ma'am," the colonel replied.

Mrs. Hillman grabbed her cane, stood, and turned to face the small congregation. "I appreciate you all joining me for this service. I believe it would have meant a great deal to Mr. Clarke that we are thinking of him this morning. I also believe he would have wanted us to celebrate this sacred day, so let us all proceed now to the drawing room for a bit of Christmas cheer."

The guests rose and headed down the center aisle towards the door. Selena swallowed a sigh of frustration. She could hardly wait to search the chapel to see if a bundle of cash had been stashed here. But there was no time for that. She permitted herself to hold back, though, until everyone else had left and noted that Dr. Scott did the same. As they followed the group out of the sanctuary, she said under her breath, "You saw?"

"I saw." His eyes looked bright with anticipation.

"We'll come back immediately after gift-giving," Selena whispered, and he nodded in agreement.

Selena darted up to her room, retrieved her small box of presents, and joined the others in the drawing room, where everyone was taking seats around a low central table.

"It wouldn't be Christmas without presents," Mrs. Hillman announced, "and I wanted to share a token of my appreciation for your friendship." She hesitated, studying the wrapped gifts that were laid out on the table. "I see that several of these are *not* from me."

Colonel Blackwood chuckled. "You cannot blame us, ma'am,

if some of us wished to get in the spirit of the season, despite your directive."

"Well, when you put it *that* way..." Mrs. Hillman gave a graceful shrug. "We'll start with mine, however. The ones wrapped in silver paper are from me to you. Selena, will you please do the honors and distribute them?"

Selena gave out the small boxes to their recipients. She knew what they contained, for she had helped Mrs. Hillman to choose them. Selena was pleased to see that one was addressed to Dr. Scott. She offered him the gift. "Dr. Scott?" His mind seemed to be elsewhere. "Dr. Scott?" she repeated.

The doctor blinked and looked at her. "Sorry, yes?"

"This is for you," Selena said.

The doctor's mouth opened slightly. He turned to Mrs. Hillman. "Ma'am, I cannot accept a gift. I shouldn't even be here."

"Doctor, I must insist," Mrs. Hillman replied. "I have plenty to go around, for I ordered a few extra."

"Even so, ma'am." Dr. Scott stirred in his chair with visible discomfort. "I've come empty-handed."

Selena was impressed by the doctor's humble modesty, which went hand-in-hand with the other positive qualities she had observed him to possess: an upright nature and a sense of decency.

Mrs. Hillman gave the doctor a dismissive wave of her hand. "How could it be otherwise? You had no idea you would be coming to Darkmoor Park. You are far from your family and friends today, Doctor, but I hope you will consider *us* your friends. And I refuse to allow you to be the only one without a gift. Please do me the honor of accepting it."

With a silent, gracious nod, Dr. Scott gave in and accepted the package.

"They're all the same, so please open them at the same time," Mrs. Hillman directed.

The group opened the presents—sterling silver Christmas tree ornaments that had been engraved with a sketch of the manor house and the words *Darkmoor Park, Christmas 1852*, accompanied by a red ribbon for tying to a tree.

"Mrs. Hillman, you shouldn't have," Mrs. Whitlock exclaimed, the appreciative gleam in her eyes seeming to belie the words.

"The picture of the house is based on a drawing my husband and I commissioned years ago," Mrs. Hillman explained. "The original hangs in the great hall."

"It's a lovely memento," proclaimed Colonel Blackwood. "Thank you."

The others professed their thanks with equal fervor. Selena gave out her gifts next, quietly insisting, "It's nothing much, really. Just something I made."

The guests unveiled small notebooks, their cardboard covers wrapped in white brocade fabric and embellished by dried flowers and leaves protected by a clear sealant. Everyone *ooh*ed and *aah*ed and demanded to know how they'd been made.

"I dried and pressed the flowers and leaves last summer," Selena explained. "My students all made something similar so they'd have something to bring home to their parents and siblings for the holidays."

The notebooks were received with obvious appreciation by all. Even Mrs. Whitlock surprised Selena by pronouncing them to be "well-made and thoughtful."

Dr. Scott was the most effusive with his thanks. "Again, I feel undeserving of any gift at all, Miss Taylor, much less something so unique and beautiful, that was created by your own hands."

His gaze was so direct and filled with such admiration it made Selena's cheeks grow warm. "I am pleased if you like it, Doctor, and hope you'll find it useful." While making the notebooks, she had never dreamed that a man like him might be one of the recipients. The notion that Dr. Scott might one day jot down notes in the little book was delightful.

Nearly all of the guests, as it turned out, had ignored Mrs. Hillman's *no gifts* command, where their hostess was concerned.

Colonel Blackwood gave Mrs. Hillman a new style of pen, which had been growing in popularity of late. "It has a reservoir, which you fill by dipping it into an ink bottle and pulling that little lever," the colonel explained. "I thought it just the thing, what with your avid enthusiasm for letter-writing."

Mrs. Hillman was delighted by his gift, and by the others that followed—a crocheted doily from Mrs. Whitlock, a handkerchief embroidered with the initials *RH* from Miss Goodwin, and a box of scented soaps from Mr. Davis.

Selena then gave Mrs. Hillman the gift she had made for her, a black velvet cap embellished by white Belgian lace. The older woman donned the cap immediately and pronounced it to be, "The most beautiful cap I have ever owned, and all the more special because you made it yourself."

Mrs. Hillman had saved her gift to Selena for last. It was a letter opener, shaped like a knife with an ivory handle and a thin, sharp blade. "You get so many letters from your sisters, and sometimes from your brother," Mrs. Hillman said with a smile. "With the advent of the envelope and sealing wax, I hope you'll find this useful."

"I'm sure I will! Thank you so much." Selena studied the letter opener with delight. It was not only a practical gift, but a beautiful one.

With all the presents unwrapped, Mrs. Hillman reminded everyone that in place of luncheon, Christmas dinner would be held early at four P.M. "That gives you time to rest and change for dinner."

The group repeated their thanks and everyone trooped out of the drawing room to go upstairs. Everyone, that was, except Selena and Dr. Scott, who left their gifts on a sideboard and, with a silent nod, headed straight to the chapel.

The sanctuary was deserted. Dr. Scott left the door slightly ajar, for propriety's sake, and they crossed to the stained-glass window of St. George and the dragon.

"I've been bursting with curiosity ever since I noticed it,"

Selena said.

"So have I." The doctor's voice rang with enthusiasm. "But now that we're here … what are we looking for? A hiding place *under a dragon?*"

"Yes. Maybe under one of these paving stones?" Selena suggested.

Dr. Scott knelt down on the floor and tested the stones beneath the window to see if any of them jiggled.

Selena joined in the pursuit, working so closely by the doctor's side that he bumped into her, causing a tingle to skyrocket through her entire being. *I'm just excited because we're searching for treasure*, she told herself. But deep down, she knew that her reaction was due to the man with whom she was searching, and the thrill of his body touching hers.

Dr. Scott sank back on his knees with a sigh. "This floor is as solid as a rock. There couldn't be anything hidden beneath it."

Selena frowned in agreement. She directed her attention to the wall before them. "Maybe there's a cavity behind a loose stone?"

Still on their knees, they pressed here, there, and everywhere on the stone wall beneath the window, but nothing moved. The only other thing of note in the vicinity was a blue-and-white porcelain urn that stood next to the wall.

"Maybe he put the money …" Dr. Scott began.

"… inside that urn?" Selena finished with him.

They got to their feet. Dr. Scott opened the urn's lid and looked inside. "Empty."

"Oh." Selena's spirits deflated.

As Dr. Scott replaced the lid, a sound drew their attention to the back of the room. The door was closing with a soft click.

Selene's pulse quickened. "Was someone else in here?"

Dr. Scott, his eyes flashing, darted to the door, yanked it open, and rushed out. Selena hurried after him down the hall. She caught up to him in the front entryway, at the base of the main staircase. There was no one else in sight.

"Did you see anybody?" she asked softly, catching her breath and looking up the stairs.

"No." He stood still for a moment, his hands on his hips. "If someone *had* been in the chapel, I would have surely caught up to them." He hesitated. "I wonder if the door shut on its own. It *is* a bit drafty in there."

Anxiety pricked at Selena like needlepoints. "If it was due to a draft, wouldn't the door have slammed shut?"

"If the door had been wide open, perhaps. But I only left it ajar a couple of inches."

"Well, I *hope* we weren't seen or overheard, or we'll have an army of treasure hunters competing with us. And as you said, they might not be as willing to return the money to the hospital."

Dr. Scott sighed. "It seems we're back to where we started." He withdrew his pocket watch. "And Christmas dinner is in ninety minutes."

"We had best get dressed." They retrieved their gifts from the drawing room and made their way up the stairs.

"Have you asked Mrs. Hillman if there are any other …" He gestured with one hand, as if breathing fire from his mouth. *"You-know-whats* about the place?"

"I haven't had a chance. But I will."

"Let me know when you do. We'll put our heads together and try again."

The concept of *putting their heads together* sent a sizzle up Selena's spine. She shook her head to clear it. *You really need to get a grip on yourself.*

When they reached the first-floor landing, they nodded in parting. Dr. Scott turned towards the south wing, while Selena moved to her room at the beginning of the north wing. She entered her chamber and was about to unbutton her frock, when she noticed a small piece of white paper lying on the blue coverlet atop her bed. *What is this?*

Selena picked up the note. She read it and felt as though her heart had stopped beating.

A message had been scrawled on the page in pencil.

Stop looking
or you'll be next to die.

CHAPTER TEN

SELENA STARED AT the note in her hands, a chill running through her.

Who had left this on her bed, and when? She glanced around her bedchamber. No one else was there. She yanked open the doors to the room's only possible hiding place, the tall, mahogany wardrobe. To her relief, inside she found only clothes.

Her heart pounded as Selena read the note again.

Stop looking.

It could only mean one thing. Someone knew she was looking for the money. Someone who wanted her to give up the search. Who? And why?

Her hands quivered with rising dread as she reread the second statement.

Or you'll be next to die.

Only one person had died recently at Darkmoor Park: Jack Clarke. Was this note a threat? Did someone intend to kill her if she continued searching for the cash that Mr. Clarke had hidden?

Another horrifying thought swiftly followed. Both she and Dr. Scott had wondered, initially, if Mr. Clarke's death had really been an accident. She'd had an unnerving dream in which her sisters had insisted that it was not. Selena had dismissed that notion as unlikely for a variety of reasons, but what if they were right? What if someone *had* pushed Mr. Clarke down those stairs? Selena's stomach clenched. Had the person who'd sent this threatening note … *murdered* Mr. Clarke?

She needed to speak to Dr. Scott without delay. Gripping the note, Selena dashed out of her room towards the south hall. She had nearly reached Dr. Scott's room when he burst out of his own door and they almost collided.

His eyes were wild, and his voice was low and filled with agitation. "I found this on my bed." Furtively, he showed her a note that looked to be identical to hers in size and shape.

"I got one, too," she said quietly. They exchanged notes. The handwriting style and wording on his note were identical to hers.

"Good lord." Dr. Scott's face drained of color. "We have to talk," he whispered urgently. "But not here."

Selena glanced back towards the north hall. The other guests were presumably in their rooms, getting dressed for dinner, but they could emerge at any moment. To her dismay, there was the sudden sound of approaching footsteps on the main staircase. Alarmed, Selena grabbed Dr. Scott's hand, yanked open the nearest door, drew him inside, and shut the door behind them.

It was pitch black inside. Not a speck of light.

"Where are we?" Dr. Scott's low voice pierced the darkness.

"The linen closet," Selena whispered. The enclosed space was just large enough for two people to stand within.

"What are we doing in the linen closet?"

Selena sensed the warmness of Dr. Scott's body a mere foot away from hers. "It was the closest unoccupied room."

"It's not a *room*. It's a *closet*." Although he kept his voice to a murmur, it rang with annoyance. "Do you have any idea what could happen if we are found together *inside a closet*?"

"Sorry. I didn't think. I just reacted. It's what my sisters and brother and I did as children, when we were up to something of which my father disapproved."

"You hid in a closet?"

"It worked every time."

From the hall beyond, the sound of footsteps grew louder. "Shhh!" he hushed.

Two people were talking just outside the linen closet door. Selena recognized their voices.

"I expressly told you that the doctor was staying in the south hall," Mrs. Middleton was saying, "and that you must clean his room as well."

"I'm sorry. I forgot." Gladys sounded frightened. "I had so many rooms to clean today."

As Selena and the doctor stood in the silent darkness, his cologne enveloped her senses. Sandalwood. A hint of citrus and lavender. It rattled her brain.

"See to it that it doesn't happen again," Mrs. Middleton said.

"Yes, ma'am."

There was a knock, Mrs. Middleton calling out Dr. Scott's name, and then the sound of a door opening and receding footsteps.

"We could have gone into the small parlor at the head of the stairs," he murmured, his voice not quite as even as before.

Selena's heart thudded so loudly in her ears, she feared they might burst. "We wouldn't have made it in time. We would have been seen."

"And if we were? So what?" He took an uneven breath. "We were just talking in the hallway."

His nearness was so overpowering, she had difficulty formulating a reply. "I suppose so." She felt ridiculous now. There had been no need to hide.

"But now that we're in here, we can't very well leave until *they* do."

"True." Selena swallowed hard. "You said we had to talk," she added. "We're talking."

A moment passed. "You realize this changes everything, don't you?" he whispered.

"What does?" Selena responded. Was he referring to the fact that they were standing inches away from each other in a linen closet? Or to the possible ramifications of them being discovered there?

"The *threatening notes*." There was a sharp edge to Dr. Scott's whisper. "Someone *has* been watching us."

Selena chastised herself to keep her mind on track. "Right. Right. Since when, I wonder?"

"I don't know. But they must have been spying on us in the chapel. That door didn't shut by the wind."

Her eyes, Selena realized, must have been adjusting to the darkness because she could see his shadowy outline now, less than a foot away. She sensed frustration in his voice, tinged by some other emotion that she couldn't define. "Someone wants that money as much as we do."

"Apparently enough to kill us for it."

Her insides tightened at the notion. She knew she should have been afraid, but her thoughts were scattering. Although Dr. Scott's figure was ghostly in the darkness, Selena could perceive his eyes boring into hers. The heat from that gaze made her heart bang like a drum. She lowered her glance and found herself looking at the outline of his lips. She wanted to touch them. With her own lips. "What do we do now?"

"Now?" He paused. "Now, we must ..." His voice trailed off. "Hang it all, Miss Taylor. I can't think with you standing here so close to me."

"Neither can I," Selena admitted breathlessly.

"In truth, I haven't been able to think straight since the moment we met." His voice was hoarse and throaty as his hand came up and gently cupped her cheek. "All I want to do right now is take you in my arms and kiss you."

"I wish you would," Selena heard herself reply. She felt a heat take over her face. *Had she really said that aloud?*

He needed no further invitation. His arms wrapped around her and drew her to him until their two figures were pressed so tightly against each other that she could feel every hard line and plane of his body. And then he bent his head and pressed his mouth to hers.

Selena's eyes closed as she melted into his kiss. At first, it was gentle and questing, but it soon became more urgent. His hand pressed against the back of her neck as his tongue danced with hers and then, softly and sweetly, delved into her mouth. Selena gasped at this intimacy but welcomed it. She had only been kissed this intently by one other man, the errant circus performer, but even his caresses had been nothing like this.

Dr. Scott's kiss was so hot, it seemed to set every cell in Selena's body afire and melt away every inhibition. She leaned into his embrace, kissing him back with a fervor and a passion that matched his own. Something deep and powerful seemed to take hold of her, a feeling she'd never known existed, a deep wanting to be with him in every way possible, to mingle her breath and being with his own here, now, and forever.

She heard him groan deep in his throat as his mouth left hers. He drew back a few inches as they both caught their breath.

"Selena." His breath was a sweet exhalation against her face. "For two days, my mind has been full of nothing but you."

It's been the same for me with you, Selena wanted to reply. But she was so spellbound by what they had just experienced, she could barely form a thought, much less a word. To know that he'd been thinking of her, too—it made her feel weak in the knees.

His fingers traced her cheeks to the tip of her nose, finally coming to rest on her parted lips. "You are lovely. And that was a lovely kiss." He was still whispering, and she could see him smiling in the darkness. "I kissed you because I couldn't help myself. But it shouldn't have happened." With a sigh, he let her go and took a step back. "I was out of line. I hope you'll forgive me for overstepping any sense of propriety."

"I played a part in this too," Selena managed softly. "I wanted you to kiss me. And I kissed you back."

"I'm flattered, truly." His voice seemed to be tinged with regret as he added, "But you know as well as I do that we can never be in a situation like this again."

He was right, and Selena *did* know it. If she were caught in such a compromising position, Dr. Scott would have to marry her, or she'd be ruined. Although, after that kiss, the prospect of marrying him didn't seem like such a bad idea at the moment.

Selena instantly chastised herself for the thought. They barely knew each other. That kiss had just been an expression of mutual physical attraction and desire, with no substance behind it. If she ever were to marry, she wanted *substance*. And she wanted *love*. A man she could admire and trust forever, who would love and admire and trust her in return.

"Understood," Selena replied.

From the hall beyond came the sound of a door opening and closing, a few more words being exchanged by Mrs. Middleton and Gladys, and footsteps treading past. At length, the footsteps faded away.

Selena exhaled a long breath. "Now what, Doctor?"

"Now, we have to get out of here and talk about those notes."

They stood still in the darkness and listened.

All Selena could hear was her heartbeat, which still pounded in her ears. "I don't hear anyone in the hall," she whispered.

"Neither do I. Where can we go that is completely above-board, where it's unlikely that anyone will overhear us?"

"My study," Selena replied. "It's on the ground floor near the schoolrooms."

"I remember. Why don't you leave first? I'll wait here a minute just in case."

"Let's change our clothes before we go downstairs. That way, in case we're seen in my study, I can say I was just … showing you some of my students' essays on the way to dinner."

"That works for me."

Selena had the strongest impulse to lean forward and kiss him again. She averted her gaze, afraid that if she kept looking at him, she would follow through on that desire. "I'll see you there in fifteen minutes."

She quietly opened the closet door, blinking as the brighter light of the corridor assaulted her vision. To her relief, the hallway was empty. She returned to her chamber and leaned back against the door, pausing to wrap her arms around herself. The memory of Dr. Scott's scorching kiss was still so fresh in her mind, she didn't want to let it go.

And yet she must. She had to get dressed for dinner before meeting him again downstairs.

Selena quickly put on her new Christmas gown, which she'd had made based on a French fashion plate. The bright-red velvet was the shade of a cardinal's wing, and its short sleeves were gathered at the sides and embellished by gold, diamond-shaped buttons. A narrow trim of gold gimp braid ran vertically at the front of the gathered bodice and decorated the edge of the neckline, which dipped in a slight V, and a gold, satin ribbon cinched in the frock at the waist.

Using the method she had learned in girlhood, Selena dressed herself, reaching behind to fasten the last two buttons and tie the gold ribbon at her back into a bow. She took a quick glance in her cheval glass to make sure she was orderly. Oh, her hair! Her blonde tresses were pinned up as they had been all day, in a simple braided bun at the back—not as fancy as she would have liked for Christmas dinner, and not as tidy, either, after the doctor's kisses—but there was no time to restyle it.

And oh, her cheeks! They were quite pink. In fact, her entire face was flushed. Would anyone be able to tell that she had just been thoroughly and wondrously kissed by Dr. Scott? She hoped not.

She grabbed a gold-toned pashmina shawl from a dresser drawer, which Diana's husband, Captain Fallbrook, had kindly brought back for her from one of his sea voyages. Although this was a formal dinner, she decided not to bring gloves. She wasn't leaving the house, she'd have to take them off while dining in any case, and they wouldn't be needed during the parlor games.

Thinking about her upcoming meeting with Dr. Scott, she fetched her new red velvet handbag and stowed the threatening note inside. Something told her that she might have need of it tonight. After slipping the cord around her wrist, she dashed from the room and down the stairs.

A few minutes later, Selena was at her desk in her study. She lit two lamps. Since the room wasn't expected to be occupied today, there was no fire. Despite the chill in the air, she sank down in her chair and took a minute to breathe in the sense of tranquility that always enveloped her when she entered this cozy space.

She heard approaching footsteps. Her pulse leapt. Any second now, Dr. Scott would appear. She could hardly wait.

CHAPTER ELEVEN

Dr. Scott paused inside the threshold of the study and after some apparent internal debate, he closed the door behind him. "I saw no one in this part of the house," he said quietly, "but I don't want to take any chances of us being overheard."

Selena nodded from her seat behind her desk. It was a treat, as always, just to look at the man. He was dressed for dinner in the gleaming, black frock coat and trousers that had been altered for him so expertly. A white cravat was gracefully tied at his throat above a white shirt and white, embroidered waistcoat. He looked impossibly handsome. To think that she had just spent several minutes kissing him in a dark closet! The memory sent a ripple dancing from her head to her toes that made it impossible not to smile.

Clearing her throat in an attempt to clear her mind, Selena said quietly, "I thought you could sit there." She indicated the chair opposite her desk. "That way, if anyone *should* pop in unexpectedly, they will come upon only the most decorous behavior."

"Agreed." He crossed the room to her. "We have an urgent matter to discuss." He paused to stare at her, though, his eyes lit with appreciation. "You look beautiful."

"You mean my gown? This old thing?" She primped a little and readjusted her shawl about her shoulders. "You are only seeing it from the waist up."

"From what I see, you look like a princess."

She wasn't accustomed to receiving compliments like that from a man. It filled her with delight. "And you look like a prince, Dr. Scott."

"I wouldn't want to stand out as the ruffian in this crowd." He cast his glance about the room. "You said you share this office with your sister?"

"Yes. Years ago, it belonged to Mr. Hillman. When Athena and I moved the Darkmoor Bridge School for Girls here, Mrs. Hillman encouraged us to redecorate this room according to our taste."

The walls were still paneled in dark wood and lined with bookshelves, but they had installed two smaller desks for each of them instead of one large one, along with a bureau for storing school supplies and comfortable chairs for visiting guests and students. They had changed the color scheme and artwork as well. Pale-blue curtains framed the windows. The paintings of hunting scenes had been replaced by pictures of gardens and flowers along with portraits of Selena's mother and father in their prime. In the spirit of the season, festive branches of holly intertwined with evergreens decorated the mantel.

"It's very nice," Dr. Scott said with a nod. "Where is your sister spending the holidays?"

"In Cornwall." She explained the family's plans.

"Ah." He looked at her. "But you chose to remain here at Darkmoor Park? Why?"

"To help Mrs. Hillman host her holiday party," she replied simply.

"That was a kind thing to do."

"Mrs. Hillman has been very good to me." Selena, wishing to learn more about him, asked, "Do you have brothers and sisters, Dr. Scott?"

"I had a younger brother. He passed away when we were very small."

"Oh! I'm so sorry. What about your parents?"

"They also died when I was a child."

Selena's heart went out to him. "How sad that you lost your family at such a young age." It helped explain why he had been traveling up to Scotland to see friends for Christmas—he had no family with whom to share the holidays. "Who raised you?"

"I spent my formative years in an orphanage. But—I see from your expression that you are starting to feel sorry for me now, Miss Taylor. Don't. I've been on my own for so long that I am quite accustomed to it."

Selena's cheeks warmed and she brought a hand to her face, embarrassed that it had given her thoughts away. "Still, I feel bad that—"

He cut her off with a silencing hand. "Enough on that subject."

Selena frowned. She was full of questions. It must not have been easy, growing up in an orphanage. Where had he been educated? And how had he become a doctor? That must have been a difficult road to follow. But he evidently didn't want to talk about it. And she reminded herself they had more important things to discuss.

Dr. Scott was one step ahead of her. "The clock is ticking," he said, his tone turning deadly serious. From his coat pocket, he withdrew the threatening note he'd received and slapped it on Selena's desk. "Someone just threatened to kill us both."

"Yes." A spike of fear jabbed Selena in the stomach at this stark reminder of their predicament.

Dr. Scott sat down in the chair facing Selena's desk. "I'm guessing that whoever wrote these notes is after the five thousand pounds that Jack Clarke hid, and they know we're looking for it."

"Do you think they murdered him?" Selena asked.

"I can't prove it—but yes, I do. I think his killer confronted him, determined to find out where he'd hidden the cash."

"But apparently, he didn't tell them. Wouldn't it be idiotic to kill the only man who knew where the money was?" Selena asked.

"It would. Unless—"

Selena gasped, the answer coming to her before the doctor could provide it. "Oh! I see. Mr. Clarke lied about where he'd put it!"

"That's my thinking. Maybe they came at him with a weapon of some kind, threatening to kill him unless he told them."

"Or they might have appealed to his ego and tried to manipulate him into willingly sharing the information," Selena posited.

The doctor nodded. "Either way, once the killer *believed* they'd gotten the information they needed, they pushed Mr. Clarke down those stairs."

"After he was dead, they discovered that he'd lied, but by then, they were out of luck."

"They knew the money existed but had no clue where he'd stashed it," Dr. Scott said.

"And now, his killer wants that money and wants us out of their way."

"Exactly."

Selena's hand went to her cheek. "Who would do such a thing?"

"That's the question of the hour."

Her mouth went dry. "If this was truly murder, we ought to summon the parish constable."

Dr. Scott met her gaze across the desk. "How do you propose we do that in the middle of a snowstorm? By the way, who is your constable?"

"Our vicar, Mr. Johnson."

"Ah." Dr. Scott frowned. "When I called at the vicarage yesterday morning and ran into your hall boy, the housekeeper informed me that Mr. Johnson was away for the holidays and not expected back until the twenty-ninth of December."

"Oh." That was four days away.

Dr. Scott ran a hand distractedly through his wavy, brown hair. "I don't think it wise to wait that long. Our lives have been threatened. I need to look into this myself."

"Yourself?" Selena stared at him. "I thought we were in this together."

"When we were talking about looking for the money, yes." He glanced grimly at the note on the desktop. "But this could prove to be a treacherous business. We've both been warned. And the perpetrator is not likely to hesitate to kill again."

Selena paused. She had been reading Gothic novels about murder and mayhem for years. But solving a real-life murder was not for the squeamish. Her sisters had both nearly died while investigating such crimes. Selena had come close to losing her own life two years ago while helping to uncover a frightening truth at Thorndale Manor. This was the first time, though, that a murder mystery had fallen directly into Selena's lap.

Did she dare to open that door?

Of course she did. Although a tremor of fear raced through her, Selena couldn't deny that she was excited as well. This wasn't just a treasure hunt any longer. She and Dr. Scott were going to work together to investigate a murder as well.

She had always wanted to investigate a murder.

Selena steeled herself. "I understand. But I am fully invested in this, Dr. Scott. There is too much at stake. Mr. Clarke may have been murdered under this very roof. We can't let his killer make off with that five thousand pounds. We need to learn who killed Mr. Clarke and find that money before they do, return it to the London General Hospital fund, and make them accountable for their crime. And I refuse to sit back while you do all the work."

Dr. Scott blew out a long breath. "Very well, then. But we must proceed with caution. We don't want to disturb Mrs. Hillman or any of the guests. If they suspect a murder has taken place, panic could set in."

Selena gave him a firm nod. "I won't breathe a word of this to anyone. Except to share whatever we learn with Mr. Johnson when he returns."

"Of course."

Selena paused to reflect. "Since the morning that Mr. Clarke's body was found, it hasn't stopped snowing. No one else has come or gone from Darkmoor Park. Which means …"

"Whoever did this is still here," he finished for her.

A shiver raced up Selena's spine. "But who? I find it hard to believe that anyone in our party is capable of murder—even for a sum as tempting as five thousand pounds."

A dark, distant look came into Dr. Scott's eyes. "You'd be surprised by what people—even the nicest, most upright-seeming people in the world—can be capable of," he declared flatly.

Selena sensed that he was speaking from personal experience and wondered at it. But she didn't want to pry. "Where should we start?"

Dr. Scott blinked twice. "Let's start with the threatening notes." He gestured to the one he had received, which lay atop the desk. "Does the paper look familiar?"

Selena picked up the note and studied it. The paper was of good quality. She held it up to the light and took a sharp breath. "I recognize the watermark. It's the same as the one on the notepaper I put in the desk in the library for guests to use."

"Which means that *anyone* in this house would have had access to it." Dr. Scott frowned.

"And literally anyone could have written those notes."

He gave her a half-smile. "Except *you and me* of course."

She half-smiled in return. "And Mrs. Hillman. She adored Jack Clarke, and she has no need of money."

"We'll take Mrs. Hillman off the list." He paused. "Four people whom we know of were aware that Clarke had a vast sum of money with him. He announced it over dinner at that inn before he got here."

"Yes. Mrs. Whitlock, Miss Thompson, Miss Goodwin, and Mr. Davis were all there that night."

"One of them might have decided to kill him at their first opportunity." He glanced at her. "Do you know if any of them are in dire need of cash?"

Selena narrowed her eyes. "Miss Thompson mentioned a desire to open a flower shop. But it sounded more like a distant dream than an obsession. And she's so nice. I can't imagine her killing anyone."

"What about Mrs. Whitlock? She seemed very keen to get her hands on some expensive estate jewelry."

"She did! As for Miss Goodwin and Mr. Davis—I don't know them well enough yet."

"What about the servants?" he mused. "Is it possible that one of them knew about the money?"

Selena drew a sharp breath. "We discussed Mr. Clarke's claim about the money while we were trimming the tree. The footmen were there."

"Yes, but I've just realized—the timing doesn't work. That was after Mr. Clarke was already dead."

"True, true."

"What time was it again that you found Clarke on the staircase landing?"

"Just after six."

"What was Mr. Clarke doing up at that hour?"

"He told everyone the night before that he liked to rise early and have breakfast at six o'clock."

"Which made it convenient for our killer. They knew exactly when and where to confront him." Dr. Scott glanced at her abruptly. "Did you tell anyone else about Mr. Clarke's last words?"

"No."

"Good. Keep it that way."

"How do they know we're looking?" Selena wondered.

"They must have overheard us talking."

Selena reviewed the last two days in her mind. "Oh! Last night, after I burned my arm, when you walked me back to my room ..."

"We paused in the hallway outside the morning room and discussed it."

"Maybe the sound we heard wasn't a log falling in the fireplace. Maybe someone was hiding behind the morning room curtains." Selena inhaled a worried breath. "We didn't say anything about the …" She mouthed the word *dragon*. "Did we?"

"I don't think so."

"What about this morning, in the chapel?"

"I don't think we mentioned *why* we were looking there." He sighed. "Going forward, we'll have to be very careful about what we say and do. We don't want to give away that we have a clue to where the money might be hidden."

Selena nodded in agreement. "Whoever sent those notes will have to search every inch of this house to try to find that money. Whereas you and I can—hopefully—narrow the field." She opened a drawer in her desk, withdrew a piece of paper, and picked up her pen from its stand.

"What are you doing?"

"I'm going to write up a list of what we know so far. It's a thing I do. It lays out all the information in one place and helps me think." Dipping her pen in the inkwell, Selena began to write, narrating as she went and taking input from Dr. Scott along the way.

<u>WHAT WE KNOW SO FAR</u>

<u>Dec. 22</u>:

1. Mrs. Whitlock, Miss Thompson, Miss Goodwin, and Mr. Davis witnessed Jack Clarke announce at the White Hart Inn in Warwick that he had £5200 in cash with him that he had raised to build a hospital.

<u>Dec. 23</u>:

2. Mr. Clarke arrived at Darkmoor Park and paid back Mrs. Hillman £200 that he owed her.

3. Mr. Clarke was seen by Beryl, the housemaid, exiting the east schoolroom and carrying his overcoat.

4. Mr. Clarke may have gone outside.

5. Wells saw Mr. Clarke leave the library and head to the chapel.

6. Mr. Clarke admitted to all that he rose early and wished to have breakfast at 6 A.M.

<u>Dec. 24</u>:

7. Shortly after 6 A.M., Mr. Clarke was found lying on the half-landing of the main stairs, bleeding from a head wound.

8. Mr. Clarke's last words were: *"I hid it. Under the dragon. Four rows! In the ..."*

9. A letter found in Mr. Clarke's room with a cheque for £150 from Mrs. Evelyn Stout confirmed that he had raised money for the London General Hospital Building Fund.

<u>Dec. 25</u>:

10. In the chapel, we searched under the stained-glass window of St. George and the Dragon. We found no hiding place to conceal the cash.

11. We received notes that read, *Stop looking or you'll be next to die.*

Selena set down her pen and slid the page across the desk to Dr. Scott, who read it through.

"That sums it up," he affirmed.

"Now what, Doctor?" she asked, repeating the question she had posed not all that long ago, when they'd been inside the linen closet—a memory that set her nerves atingle all over again. *Focus, Selena, focus.*

"We have three mysteries to solve." Dr. Scott ticked them off on his fingertips. "One: where did Mr. Clarke hide the money? Two: who killed him? Three: who sent the threatening notes? Admittedly, we're working on conjecture for the first two things—but I feel confident that we're on the right track."

"So do I." Selena could feel it in her bones.

"Until you speak with Mrs. Hillman about the location of certain … *mythological creatures*," Dr. Scott said quietly, "I suggest we concentrate on items two and three."

"Yes. Let's make subtle inquiries to find out who, if anyone, needs a large influx of cash."

"And meanwhile, we should figure out who wrote those notes."

An idea occurred to her. "I think I know just how to do that."

"How?"

"A parlor game."

His brows arched. "How would a parlor game help us?"

Selena darted him a veiled glance. "Allow me to surprise you, Doctor."

CHAPTER TWELVE

"CHRISTMAS IS MY favorite holiday," said Miss Goodwin.

The candles in the chandelier and candelabras bathed the dining room in a warm glow, adding further cheer to the holiday greenery on display.

The dining room table had been beautifully set for the Christmas feast. They had begun with white soup, progressed to a boar's head and sweet potato pie, and were now enjoying the main course that included roasted turkey stuffed with chestnuts, beef and kidney pudding, and several vegetable and potato side dishes. The staff had brought each platter around so that guests might serve themselves and then had taken their places at the back of the room to assist as needed.

The partygoers had all dressed up for the occasion, the gentlemen in formal black and white, and the ladies—except for Miss Goodwin, who remained in mourning—in festive holiday gowns that Selena guessed had been purchased for this occasion. Miss Thompson once again looked lovely in the navy-blue satin frock she had borrowed the day before, and a sprig of holly ornamented the braided bun in her dark hair.

Selena had taken care to sit at the opposite end of the table from Dr. Scott to ensure that she didn't make some inadvertent remark to him during the meal. She hugged her secret to her chest, determined that no one should ever guess that they were involved in two clandestine quests. *Or that they had kissed. In a closet.*

"I would enjoy Christmas more if it occurred at a different time of year so that we wouldn't be bothered by all this snow." Mrs. Whitlock's querulous voice drew Selena from her musings. The older woman was attired in a gown of silver satin embellished by thousands of shimmering beads.

"It has been a rather endless onslaught," Selena admitted, taking a forkful of mincemeat pie.

"You ought to move to India, Mrs. Whitlock," quipped Colonel Blackwood. "I promise you'll find the weather there warm enough to suit your taste."

"Or Australia," put in Mr. Davis, sipping his red wine with an appreciative smile. "I hear the seasons are upside down on that continent. Why, it's summer there now, if you can believe it."

"It would be so strange to celebrate Christmas in summer," murmured Miss Thompson.

"It would, indeed." Mrs. Hillman wrinkled her nose. "I, for one, should not like to spend Christmas in a hot, tropical climate, kept in a continual state of inelegance that could only be eased by sea bathing."

Miss Goodwin turned to their hostess with a raised eyebrow. "Have you tried sea bathing, Mrs. Hillman?"

"I have not." Mrs. Hillman swallowed a bite of mashed potatoes. "I have no interest. It is immodest and dangerous."

"Oh! But it is such a thrilling occupation, and it's perfectly safe and modest, if you employ a bathing machine and a dipper to assist you into the water," enthused Miss Goodwin. "I bathe every time I visit the seaside."

Selena paused, her fork halfway to her mouth. "What do you mean, 'visit' the seaside, Miss Goodwin? You *live* by the sea."

Miss Goodwin's lips parted slightly, and her cheeks grew pink. "Of course, I only meant, that whenever I *go down to the beach*, I like to bathe. I don't always have the opportunity, you know," she added hastily, "being so busy running the hotel."

Mr. Davis cleared his throat. "Yes, managing a hotel is an exhausting business. For the proprietor, a visit to the beach is rare, indeed."

Selena narrowed her eyes. It almost seemed as though Miss Goodwin had forgotten that she ran the hotel, and that Mr. Davis was trying to cover for her. But perhaps Selena was reading too much into that?

Changing the subject, Miss Goodwin turned to Mrs. Hillman and said, "What a lovely brooch. Was that a gift from your husband?"

Mrs. Hillman smiled softly as she fingered the small pin. "It was. It's nothing, really. It's made of pewter and the stone is glass."

"It is pretty, and a reflection of his good taste," Miss Thompson said.

"That reminds me." Colonel Blackwood finished off his last bite of turkey and gravy. "Did you ever find that other brooch of yours that went missing, Mrs. Hillman? The one of the iris?"

Mrs. Hillman's smile fled. "I'm afraid not, Colonel. I looked everywhere. I even had the maid pull the furniture away from the walls in my chamber, in case I had dropped it behind something, but it has simply vanished."

"What a shame." The colonel shook his head. "You seemed so fond of it."

"It *was* quite dear to me." Mrs. Hillman sighed. "But we must not dwell on it."

In all the excitement of late, Selena had forgotten about Mrs. Hillman's missing brooch. "I'm sure it will turn up soon," she said, hoping that would be the case.

Mrs. Whitlock nodded. "I cannot tell you how many times I have lost a thing and looked high and low for it, only to find it hiding in plain sight exactly where it was meant to be all along."

"I'll take comfort in that thought, my friend," Mrs. Hillman replied.

Mrs. Middleton soon brought in the plum pudding on a silver

platter. When Selena took a bite of the hot, steaming holiday treat, she closed her eyes with pleasure, savoring the molten combination of fruits, breadcrumbs, flour, eggs, and spices. She and her sisters used to make plum pudding every Christmas when they were growing up.

Her thoughts darted to Christmases gone by. She'd been too young when her mother had died to remember much about her, but Selena was enveloped by a surge of tender feelings as she recalled special times with her sisters; their brother, Damon; and their departed father, talking and laughing and enjoying their holiday feast. With a pang, she wondered if Athena and Diana and their families were enjoying a similar Christmas dinner at Pendowar Hall. Might Damon be leading his congregation in prayer at this very moment? All at once, she missed them with an ache so fierce, it threatened to close her throat.

Did her family miss her as much as she missed them? What would they think if they knew she had become embroiled in her own murder investigation—and a treasure hunt to boot? Selena had become so accustomed to seeing Athena every day, while running the school together. She cherished the moments when they'd been able to steal away and share their thoughts and problems. True, those moments had become fewer since Athena's marriage, but they had still found time for each other.

If only she could write to them—and they to her! But first, the storm had to end. It would be many days beyond that, she reasoned, before the roads were clear enough to post a letter in the village, much less to receive one.

Next year, Selena promised herself, *we will all spend Christmas together. And there will not be a single murder involved.*

AFTER DINNER, THE group returned to the drawing room for parlor games.

Hot brandy, rum punch, wassail, and Christmas coffee spiced

with cloves and cinnamon had been set up on the sideboard, where the guests—despite claiming to be too full to eat another bite—helped themselves to Father Christmas shortbread and gingerbread cookies.

Later in the evening, Selena planned to introduce a parlor game that she hoped would give them information about the person who had written the threatening notes. First, however, they played charades. Mrs. Hillman excused herself from participating since she had prepared everything in advance herself.

A spirited game ensued. Everyone took turns silently acting out the word, phrase, famous person's name, or book or play title that they had drawn from the basket, while the others tried to guess what was being portrayed.

Miss Goodwin mimed "Queen Victoria" by feigning a crown atop her head while holding a scepter. Colonel Blackwood acted out the title for Jane Austen's *Pride and Prejudice* by sticking his nose up in the air, and Selena got it right out of the starting gate. Mr. Davis guessed *A Christmas Carol*, which Miss Thompson expressed by drawing an imaginary Christmas tree in the air and pretending to sing a song.

But Dr. Scott outdid everyone. He cleverly conveyed *pirate ship, penguin, beekeeper,* and *Frankenstein* with his acting antics and was the first to guess a slew of idioms from *fox hunt* and *The Pilgrim's Progress* to *Romeo and Juliet*.

"I declare you the winner, Dr. Scott," Mrs. Hillman announced to universal applause when the basket had been picked clean. "You may claim your prize from the gifts on the sideboard."

His prize was a box of toffee, which Dr. Scott passed around for the assembled group to enjoy. Selena then passed out pencils and pieces of papers and announced the next game, the one she'd been waiting for. "One of my pupils taught me this last term. I call it 'the Memory Game.'"

"'The Memory Game'?" Mrs. Whitlock's forehead creased.

"How is it played?"

Selena set a cloth-draped platter on the low table around which the group was seated. "Beneath this cloth is an assortment of everyday objects." Selena had gathered the items in the few spare minutes she'd had in between her meeting with Dr. Scott and Christmas dinner. "When I uncover the platter, you'll have two minutes to study the contents on the tray before I cover it again. You'll then have three minutes to write down as many of the items as you can remember. Whoever remembers the most things wins."

Selena's aim was to obtain a sample of everyone's handwriting, to compare to the threatening notes she and Dr. Scott had received. She stole a peek at the doctor and detected an appreciative glint in his eyes, a look that sent a pleasant shiver racing through her.

"I don't have the best memory anymore," complained Mrs. Whitlock, placing a hand over her heart. "The very idea of this game gives me palpitations."

Selena wondered if the woman's physical complaint was real—or an excuse not to play. "I'm so sorry. Are you well enough to play, ma'am?"

The woman heaved a heavy sigh. "I *suppose*. If everyone else wants to play."

Mr. Davis gave Selena a thumbs-up. "I think it sounds amusing."

"You would." Miss Goodwin made a face at him. "He has an excellent memory," she added to the others, "so watch out."

Gentle laughter filled the room. Only Mrs. Whitlock looked discomposed.

"All right, here we go. The clock starts now." Selena removed the cloth from the platter.

For the next two minutes, everyone stared hard at the contents of the platter and didn't utter a word. There was a pencil, a coin, a spoon, a comb, a postcard, a feather, a sprig of holly, a key, a tiny vase, a paperweight, a seashell ... twenty objects in all.

The only sound in the room was the *whoosh* of the wind in the trees outside. After Selena re-covered the tray, the players grabbed their pencils and began making their lists. When three minutes were up, Selena called the time.

Mrs. Whitlock threw down her pencil. "That was far too difficult."

Mr. Davis delivered his page to Selena with a shrug. "It was a walk in the park for me."

"Please help yourself to a cup of coffee or one of the other beverages," Selena announced when she had collected lists from everyone. "I'll go tally these."

Selena's heart pounded as she retreated to a table in a corner, where she made a quick overview of the seven entries. She wasn't interested just yet in who had listed the most objects on the tray. She was looking for a handwriting style that matched the threatening notes she and Dr. Scott had received.

To Selena's disappointment, Mr. Davis and Miss Goodwin had written their lists in capital letters, which made it difficult to make a handwriting comparison. But the rest were in cursive, as the notes had been. She disregarded Mrs. Hillman's and Dr. Scott's entries, which left only three.

When Selena turned to the last page of the bunch, she froze. It only listed eight items. But when Selena snuck another glimpse at the note inside her handbag and compared it to the page she was holding, her breath hitched in her throat. The handwriting bore a striking resemblance to that in the threatening notes.

She stared at the signature at the bottom of the page.

It had been written by Mrs. Opal Whitlock.

CHAPTER THIRTEEN

"THANK YOU ALL for your efforts. Colonel Blackwood, you came in third place in the Memory Game with your list of fourteen items out of twenty."

Selena mustered a smile as she addressed the group seated around her on the drawing room sofas and chairs. The Yule log, a bit smaller than its former size, still burned brightly in the hearth, doing its best to reduce the wintry chill in the room.

"I say. Not bad, not bad at all!" Colonel Blackwood beamed as the group applauded his accomplishment.

Miss Thompson had come in second place, and Mr. Davis, who had named eighteen items out of twenty, had won the game. As Selena made the announcements, more clapping ensued from everyone except Mrs. Whitlock.

"I knew you'd win." Miss Goodwin gave Mr. Davis a nudge. "You are so clever, dearest."

Mr. Davis beamed with pride as he claimed his prize: a box of peppermint sticks.

Selena briefly caught Dr. Scott's eye. His scarred brow raised in return. She longed to tell him what she had discovered—that Mrs. Whitlock's handwriting seemed to match that in the threatening notes. But that must wait until after the party had adjourned for the evening. She had to settle for a silent widening of her eyes for now.

"That game has given me a headache," Mrs. Whitlock said as

she rose from her chair.

Selena looked at the woman sharply, wondering if her head ached from the effort of playing the game, writing threatening notes, or a guilty conscience—or all of them at once.

"I bid you a good night," Mrs. Whitlock added, directing an imperious look at her companion. "Miss Thompson?"

The young lady leaped to her feet. "Goodnight, everyone."

The other guests seemed to sense this as a signal that the festivities had ended, for they all got up.

"Wait. Before you go." Mrs. Hillman found her cane and stood. "Tomorrow is Boxing Day. I've given most of the staff the day off after breakfast. But my cook has prepared food in advance, so a cold buffet will be available for lunch and dinner."

"That sounds lovely," Colonel Blackwood said.

"Have someone bring up my hot toddy, please," Mrs. Whitlock told Mrs. Hillman as she and Miss Thompson departed the room.

"I will make sure Mrs. Middleton has that in hand," Mrs. Hillman replied.

Dr. Scott bowed to Mrs. Hillman and Selena. "Thank you both for a delightful Christmas Day."

Everyone exchanged *goodnights* and *thank yous* and made their way to the door. Selena retreated to her study. As agreed, Dr. Scott soon joined her and closed the door. Selena had set up two chairs next to each other and he plunked down beside her.

"Well?" he asked, his tone and expression eager.

"Take a look." Selena handed him the threatening note she had received along with Mrs. Whitlock's entry in the Memory Game.

He studied the list. "Mrs. Whitlock?" His lips pursed. "The writing *is* similar, but not an exact match."

"I have taught handwriting for years. No one's writing is exactly the same every time. Mrs. Whitlock only wrote down eight words, but her style matches the notes in so many respects. Look at the *O*s. They have an identical loop. The letters *G*, *P*, and

E have the same upward tail on the final stroke. And the capital *S* in *Stop* and *Seashell* is distinctive. Rather than being composed at an angle, it is standing at attention."

"'Standing at attention'?" he repeated.

"It is just a term I use to add a bit of fun to my handwriting lessons."

Dr. Scott's eyes sparkled, a look that made Selena's insides vibrate to a strange rhythm. It had probably been a mistake, she realized, to position these chairs so close together. The impulse to brush back the lock of hair that had cascaded down over his forehead and run her fingers over that intriguing scar of his was so overpowering, she had to clasp her hands in her lap to keep them still.

"You might be right." He handed back the pages. "That game was a clever tactic. And Mrs. Whitlock may well be our culprit. Unfortunately, though, this doesn't prove anything."

His words put a damper on Selena's excitement. "What do you mean?"

"We have a possible motive—Mrs. Whitlock may have threatened or cajoled Mr. Clarke into disclosing where he'd stashed the money, perhaps to buy that jewelry collection she craves. She may have killed him, thinking he had revealed the hiding place. She may have gotten wind that we are searching for it and left those messages. But we can't *prove* any of that. All we know for sure is that a man died halfway down the stairs, and someone wrote two threatening notes. It's not enough to arrest anyone."

Selena let out a long sigh. "I guess not. But I still think she's behind all this." She pressed her lips together. "I know it's horrible of me to say this—but if it *is* Mrs. Whitlock, I'm glad. She is so rude and critical, and she treats her companion in such a condescending manner. I would feel no compunction about reporting her to the constable when he returns."

"Nor will I. But that's four days away, presuming the storm ends and the trains are even running again by then." He seemed to be lost in thought for a moment.

"What should we do in the meantime?"

He rubbed his face. "Let's keep searching, quietly and discreetly. I doubt anyone is in danger, except potentially *us*."

Selena nodded. "We can start tomorrow with the other rooms we know Mr. Clarke visited: the schoolroom and the library. I'll think up an excuse to ask Mrs. Hillman about dragon motifs."

"Good plan." Dr. Scott rose and helped Selena to her feet. He brought one of her hands to his mouth and kissed it. The imprint of his lips against her flesh sent a flurry of sparks up Selena's arm.

He stepped back and gave her a bow. "Until tomorrow," he said softly.

"Until tomorrow," she repeated. As the man turned to leave the room, Selena called out, "Dr. Scott?"

He turned back to face her.

"Do you think Mrs. Whitlock is truly mad enough to kill us?"

"I hope not," was all he said before leaving the room.

A SOFT KNOCK on the door awakened Selena from a deep slumber.

She sat up in bed, startled and fuzzy-headed. A hint of early morning light was visible beneath the window curtains. It was the second time in as many days that she'd been roused from sleep at an early hour.

"Miss Taylor?" someone called out quietly but urgently from beyond the door. It sounded like Miss Thompson.

"Coming!" Selena rose, threw on her dressing gown and slippers, lit her candle, and crossed to the door, where she halted in her tracks. A folded note lay on the inner threshold, a note that looked similar to the threatening notes she and the doctor had received.

Selena grabbed the note and read it.

I don't like games.

Horror blazed through her. The handwriting was the same as on the other notes.

Whoever had written this must have seen through her intentions with the parlor game the night before. Which meant her study of the writing styles had been a waste of time. The culprit had no doubt disguised their handwriting, either on these notes, or when they had played the game.

But there was no time to think about that now. Selena shoved the note in her dressing gown pocket and yanked open her door.

Miss Thompson stood before her, carrying a candle and dressed in a plain, brown frock—no doubt her 'spare dress' since her ink-stained one had been taken away by a servant for cleaning. The young woman's face was struck with terror. "Oh, Miss Taylor, come quickly! It's Mrs. Whitlock."

Selena's body filled with dread. "Where is she?"

"In her room," Miss Thompson explained as they rushed down the north hall corridor. "Last night, Mrs. Whitlock was angry with me and refused to let me help her undress for bed. That's not unusual. I'm always to rouse her, though, at 7:30 A.M. so she can be bright and chipper by eight. But she's just lying there, and I can't get her to waken!"

Mrs. Whitlock's chamber door was open and so were the drapes. The whitish-grey light of a wintry dawn, combined with the radiance from the fireplace and their two candles, illuminated the disturbing scene before Selena's eyes. Mrs. Whitlock, still wearing the clothes she'd worn the previous evening, lay atop the tufted counterpane on the four-poster bed. Her eyes were closed, her face was ghostly white, and her lips were blue. "Oh, no."

Selena's stomach twisted as she approached the bed. She gave Mrs. Whitlock a gentle shake. "Mrs. Whitlock?" The woman didn't stir. Selena touched Mrs. Whitlock's face. It was as cold as ice.

"Is she ...?" asked Miss Thompson shakily.

"I don't know. Wait here, I'll get help." Selena hurried down to Dr. Scott's room and knocked on his door.

A moment later, he answered. He was dressed in his shirt sleeves and trousers, his face was covered in shaving cream, and he held a razor in his hand. "Miss Taylor?" Apparently taking in her alarmed expression, he added quickly, "What's wrong?"

"I need your help. It's Mrs. Whitlock. I fear she might be dead."

His eyes widened. "Wait here. I'll be two seconds." He reappeared a few moments later with a clean face, his frock coat on, and his black bag in hand. "Where is she?"

They hurried off together. "In her chamber. It was Miss Thompson who woke me. She said Mrs. Whitlock refused her offer to help her undress for bed last night."

When they reached Mrs. Whitlock's chamber, Dr. Scott took Mrs. Whitlock's pulse and his features tightened in a deep frown.

"I'm sorry. She's gone," he said quietly.

Miss Thompson gasped. "Dear heavens."

Selena bit her lip in shock and dismay. This felt like an eerie reprise of the morning when Jack Clarke had been found on the half-landing. Could that really have only been two days ago? Last night, Selena had been so certain that Mrs. Whitlock had written those threatening notes and had killed Jack Clarke. But now that seemed most unlikely, for she was dead. "How did this happen? And when?" Selena asked.

"I'll have to examine her more closely to make that determination." The doctor turned to Miss Thompson. "Did you find Mrs. Whitlock like this?"

"Yes." A sob escaped Miss Thompson's throat. "It's my job to help her undress for bed, but when she's in one of her moods, as she was last night, she doesn't allow it."

It was the second time that Miss Thompson had brought up her excuse as to why Mrs. Whitlock was still fully dressed. Selena's suspicions were aroused. Did the young woman feel guilty about the circumstance? Or was she trying to cover up something?

"At 7:30 A.M.," Miss Thompson continued, "I brought in Mrs. Whitlock's cup of tea as usual and opened the drapes. But I couldn't get her to stir."

Selena noticed a tray atop the dresser, holding a teapot and cup. Dr. Scott, however, was eyeing the bedside table, where a glass medicine bottle and spoon stood next to an empty crystal glass.

From where she stood, Selena could read the label on the bottle. In bold letters it read, *LAUDANUM. POISON.* It was half full. Selena's pulse skittered. She knew that laudanum could be a dangerous drug. One of the women she had worked for as a governess had suffered from a laudanum addiction.

Dr. Scott studied the bottle and gestured to the tumbler beside it. "What's this?"

"It was her hot toddy, I'd imagine." Miss Thompson wiped a tear from her eye. "She had one every night before she went to bed."

Dr. Scott picked up the glass, swiped his index finger against the slight residue of dark-brown liquid at the bottom, and touched it to his tongue. Darkly, he said, "This drink was laced with laudanum. Alcohol and laudanum can be a deadly combination." He set down the glass and turned back to Miss Thompson. "Was Mrs. Whitlock in the habit of putting laudanum in her nightcap?"

"No." Miss Thompson's voice caught. "That is, I don't think so. She does—she *did* take laudanum quite regularly, for headaches and whenever her stomach was bothering her. She sometimes took a few drops on a spoon, and sometimes from a vial she carried in her handbag."

Selena remembered that Mrs. Whitlock had stealthily returned a small vial to her knitting bag on Christmas Eve, when they'd been singing carols, and soon after had fallen asleep in her chair. Had that been laudanum? "Mrs. Whitlock complained of a headache last night," she pointed out.

"I remember." Dr. Scott leaned over the bed and gently opened Mrs. Whitlock's eyes with his fingertips.

Selena noticed that Mrs. Whitlock's pupils were as tiny as pinpoints.

"That confirms it." The doctor stood back with a heavy sigh. "I wish I'd known she'd had laudanum with her. I would have warned her not to take it with her hot toddy. But even if Mrs. Whitlock hadn't had that nightcap, two or three teaspoons of laudanum in an otherwise-healthy adult can depress the respiratory system so severely that they stop breathing entirely. The blue lips, and the constriction of the pupils—they're both signs of a laudanum overdose."

"You mean she accidentally killed herself?" Miss Thompson sounded dismayed.

"It would seem so," Dr. Scott replied.

"Unless," Selena blurted out, "someone else added laudanum to her beverage."

"'Someone else'?" Mrs. Thompson's brow furrowed. "But how could that be? Are you suggesting that Mrs. Whitlock might have been deliberately poisoned?"

Selena wanted to bite her tongue. She shouldn't have said that in front of Miss Thompson. Selena didn't want anyone to know that she and the doctor suspected that murder had been afoot at Darkmoor Park. And it still seemed suspicious that Miss Thompson hadn't helped Mrs. Whitlock get ready for bed. "I'm … just thinking out loud," she said quickly.

"Anything is possible at this point," Dr. Scott interjected, arching his scarred eyebrow at Selena as if to say, *Let's keep mum on that subject.* "Miss Thompson," he added, "did your mistress come straight up to her chamber last night after we all left the drawing room?"

Miss Thompson shook her head. "No. She wanted a foot massage—she sometimes liked one before retiring, and she preferred the chair in my room. So, she demanded to go there first. And while I was giving her a foot massage, she …" Miss

Thompson hesitated, her cheeks coloring. "She started berating me. She said I had made a spectacle of myself during charades and should not have been so gregarious. She insisted that I should have made a shorter list during the Memory Game so that her own list wouldn't have looked so bad. She was so angry, I started to cry. I was still crying when we returned to her room, where I was supposed to help her get ready for bed. But she said, 'If you're going to cry at every little thing, I have no use for you. I'll undress myself. Get out!'"

"And did you go back to your room?" Selena asked.

Miss Thompson nodded. "I did. I was so miserable, I sank down on my bed and cried."

Despite herself, Selena's heart went out to the young woman, whose story seemed entirely credible.

"Getting back to the moment or two when you entered *this* room, did you notice if the hot toddy was on the bedside table?" Dr. Scott asked.

"Yes, it was," Miss Thompson replied.

Dr. Scott's mouth set. "Which means it had been brought up in the meantime."

"Oh, this is all my fault!" Miss Thompson's face crumpled.

"Your fault?" Selena looked at her. "How so?"

"I should have ignored Mrs. Whitlock's order to leave her room. I should have stayed and helped her to undress. If I had, I could have warned her not to take laudanum." Miss Thompson's lips trembled. "Her doctor was always telling her to be careful how much she took. I kept warning her to keep the dose to a minimum, but she didn't always listen. I have found her too many times to count so deeply under the influence of that drug that it was difficult to rouse her. This was the first time, though, that she wouldn't wake up at all." Her voice broke.

"Please don't blame yourself, Miss Thompson." Dr. Scott hesitated, then added, "If anyone is at fault, it is I. I knew she had a headache and had ordered a hot toddy. I had also noted that she'd consumed rum punch earlier in the evening. I should have warned her not to take any pain medication."

"She wasn't your responsibility, Doctor." The tragic circumstances filled Selena with sorrow, but at the same time, her mind was buzzing with an alternate theory—a theory that involved a deliberate poisoning. Which she didn't want to discuss in front of Miss Thompson. "How could you have known that she had laudanum with her?"

"Even so, I blame myself." He heaved a sigh. "In any case, it appears that sometime after you left this room, Miss Thompson, your employer ingested a dose of laudanum as well as her hot toddy. The combination proved lethal. My guess is that she fell asleep fully dressed, and sometime during the next hour or two, she stopped breathing and died."

"Oh! It's too, too awful." Miss Thompson retrieved a handkerchief from her skirt pocket and wiped her eyes.

"Please accept my condolences, Miss Thompson." Dr. Scott's tone was gentle and kind. "We can talk later to discuss whom we might notify about Mrs. Whitlock's passing. For now, you may return to your room. Miss Taylor and I can take over from here."

"Thank you." Miss Thompson left the room, still sniffling.

The moment the door had closed, Dr. Scott turned to Selena with a hard look. "There was an interval, when Mrs. Whitlock was getting a foot massage, when this room, and that drink, were left unattended."

"Which means anyone could have slipped in and added a lethal dose of laudanum to Mrs. Whitlock's hot toddy."

"Possibly."

"But wait," Selena said, with sudden doubt. "I was prescribed laudanum once for a headache and I never took it again. It has a distinctive color and a bitter taste. Wouldn't Mrs. Whitlock have noticed?"

"A hot toddy contains whiskey, honey, lemon juice, and spices, potent flavors that would have masked the taste of the laudanum," Dr. Scott explained. "I detected a trace of it, but I am trained in the matter and was looking for it. As for color, both whiskey and laudanum are reddish brown. A dose of laudanum wouldn't have changed the color of her drink."

"I see," Selena replied. They turned to the bed, where Mrs. Whitlock lay, grey-faced and still. "What do you think happened, Doctor? Did she accidentally poison herself? Or did someone do her in?"

"An excellent question. Although for the second theory to hold water, we'd need to find a motive."

Selena took a breath, an idea spinning in her brain. "We know Mrs. Whitlock coveted that expensive estate sale jewelry. We thought she may have risen early and tried to threaten or persuade Mr. Clarke into revealing the hiding place of his five thousand pounds and then killed him. But what if someone else got there first, and Mrs. Whitlock was merely a *witness* to the man's death?"

Dr. Scott went quiet. "And, later, Mrs. Whitlock threatened to turn in Mr. Clarke's killer if they didn't pay her a particular sum?"

"Exactly."

"That could be." Dr. Scott nodded. "Even if she wasn't a killer, I believe her unscrupulous enough to have tried to blackmail the actual villain. But the perpetrator didn't want to pay up, so they silenced her forever."

"It's possible, isn't it?"

"Yes. But if this *was* murder, it's a theory we must keep to ourselves."

"Agreed."

Dr. Scott's features tightened. "That isn't all. About the threatening notes. We thought Mrs. Whitlock might have written them. But another note was slipped under my door late last night or early this morning. It couldn't have been earlier because I was up until the wee hours reading. It said, '*I don't like games.*'"

Selena gasped. "I got one, too!" She retrieved hers from her pocket and showed it to him.

"Whoever wrote these this wasn't fooled by the parlor game

last night. They must have disguised their handwriting."

"And Mrs. Whitlock couldn't have written them because by then, she was already drugged or dead."

"Precisely."

"This was supposed to be a jolly holiday gathering, Doctor. Things are getting far too messy and complicated." Selena's mouth tightened. "But I refuse to be intimidated by this villain."

"So do I."

"What now? Do we remove Mrs. Whitlock's body to the icehouse to … to join Mr. Clarke?"

"That's what I'd suggest. Perhaps you might summon the footmen to help?"

Selena didn't look forward to the dismal task ahead. "I will."

Later, after Sam, George, and Dr. Scott had departed with Mrs. Whitlock's body on a stretcher, Selena was still standing in Mrs. Whitlock's room, steeped in distress.

She hadn't liked Mrs. Whitlock, but she hadn't wished her to die. The thought of the dead woman, dressed in a thin evening gown, being transferred to the icehouse to literally … *freeze* … made Selena's stomach churn. Mrs. Whitlock, as annoying as she had been, had deserved a better fate than this.

Selena's mind flashed back to the day Mrs. Whitlock had arrived at Darkmoor Park, and to the stunning, black velvet coat she had been wearing, the one trimmed in white fur. *Mrs. Whitlock should be wearing her coat*, Selena told herself. She recalled that, upon arrival, Mrs. Whitlock had insisted on storing her coat in her bedchamber, rather than in the cloakroom.

Selena knew it was mad, but she didn't care. She threw open the doors to the wardrobe, seized the velvet coat, and darted from the room.

She stopped briefly in her own room to get dressed in a warm gown, hat, and gloves. She rushed downstairs to the cloakroom, where she donned her boots and her warmest, burgundy woolen coat. With Mrs. Whitlock's velvet coat over her arm, she hurried down the servants' stairs.

Although it was Boxing Day, the servants didn't get off until ten A.M. As Selena made her way through the lower hall, the staff was too busy preparing breakfast and attending to their other duties to pay her any heed.

"That's two deaths in two days," remarked someone from the kitchen—Selena recognized the voice as belonging to a scullery maid.

"What a cursed Christmas!" muttered Mrs. Nash.

Selena winced as she hurried out through the back door.

Although the wind had abated, it was, incredibly, still snowing for the third day in a row. The kitchen yard was buried in a white blanket that looked to be at least a foot deep. Selena was grateful to see that, as per her recent instructions to the staff, a pathway had just been carved out across the yard leading to the back gate in the brick wall.

Selena crunched along the path and through the gate to find a group of men from the groundskeeping staff, in coats and scarves and carrying shovels, on their way back to the house. They had roped in the thirteen-year-old hall boy, Billy, to help with the task.

Selena nodded to the team and addressed the head groundskeeper, whose nose was red from the cold. "Mr. Brown, I presume that Dr. Scott and George and Sam have come by this way?"

"Yes, miss." He tipped his cap. "We just finished clearing the way. They're in the icehouse now."

"Thank you all," Selena said before she hurried to the icehouse. The domed, partially subterranean structure was built solidly of red brick and fronted by a small, red brick building whose heavy wooden door was standing open. Selena had never been inside.

The frigid air within the structure seemed to permeate straight through her coat and gloves and made her shiver. The entryway was a few feet wide and about six feet long and paved in stone. Farther on, a steep, stone staircase led downwards.

Selena hadn't thought to bring a lantern—but thankfully, daylight from the open door behind her illuminated part of the stairwell and a glow beyond promised that there was a source of light below.

As Selena followed the steps down, the air, already impossibly frigid, became noticeably colder. At the bottom of the stairs, she nearly collided with Sam and George, who were on their way up, carrying an empty stretcher between them.

"Miss Taylor!" said George as the two men ground to a halt. "Don't go in there."

"It's cold as the devil," agreed Sam, visibly quaking. "If you'll excuse us."

The footmen made a hasty retreat up the steps. Selena ignored their warning and continued into the icehouse itself. The high-domed chamber was lined with brick, and its walls were insulated with straw. Large blocks of ice that had been cut from a nearby frozen river were stacked in massive piles, surrounded by barrels holding smaller chunks of ice.

A lantern stood on the floor inside. Nearby, Dr. Scott was arranging Mrs. Whitlock's body atop a pile of ice that looked to Selena like a frozen bed. In the distant shadows, Selena spied a dark, frosty form, which she guessed to be Mr. Clarke's frozen body, similarly laid out on a bed of ice. The realization that she was in an enclosed, underground space that was temporarily being used as a crypt to house two bodies made her cringe inwardly, and she shivered again, both from the pervasive cold and the creepiness of it.

The doctor saw her and frowned. "Miss Taylor, you shouldn't be here."

"I know I'm on a fool's errand," Selena admitted, "but I couldn't bear the thought of Mrs. Whitlock being down here in all this ice without her coat." She gestured with the fur-trimmed velvet coat in her arms.

Dr. Scott's jaw opened at that, but to his credit, he didn't reprimand her or make her feel foolish. Instead, he gave her a nod. "All right, but let's move fast. It's not safe for us to be down here very long."

He speedily repositioned Mrs. Whitlock's body so that Selena could dress her in the velvet coat. It took some doing, but when the garment was on, Dr. Scott lay Mrs. Whitlock back down on the ice slab. As Selena buttoned up the coat, she felt an odd lump beneath it in the upper chest area. Curious, she felt again. Sure enough, there was something there that didn't belong.

"Let's go," the doctor warned.

"One second." Selena opened Mrs. Whitlock's coat and inhaled in sharp surprise. Pinned to the inner lining of the coat … was a gold and bejeweled brooch.

A brooch in the shape of a blue iris and fitted with diamonds, sapphires, emeralds, and pearls.

"What's that?" Dr. Scott asked.

"It's Mrs. Hillman's heirloom brooch."

The doctor's eyes widened. "She didn't misplace it, after all."

"*Mrs. Whitlock stole it.*" Selena was stunned.

"Detestable woman. It doesn't surprise me. Take it—and let's get out of here." He picked up the lantern.

Selena's fingers were growing numb, despite the protection of her gloves. She finally managed to unpin the brooch and stow it in her own coat pocket. Shivering harder now, she followed Dr. Scott up the steps. When they'd reached the upper landing, to her surprise, it was dark—because the icehouse door was closed.

"Did you shut the door when you entered?" Dr. Scott asked in a worried tone.

"No."

He frowned. "I told Sam and George to be sure and leave it open when they left. Wells informed me that the door has a tricky lock and sometimes jams in winter." Dr. Scott turned the handle. The door didn't budge. He cursed aloud.

Selena's stomach clenched as the doctor rattled the door handle again and yanked hard. It didn't open.

"Dear lord," he said. "I think we've been locked in."

CHAPTER FOURTEEN

T HEY WERE TRAPPED inside the icehouse.

"Do you have a hairpin?" Dr. Scott asked.

"No." Selena hadn't taken the time to put her hair up before she'd rushed out to the icehouse. "But I have Mrs. Hillman's brooch." She retrieved it from her pocket and inserted the point into the lock. But no matter how hard she wiggled and twisted it, the door lock appeared to be jammed.

Dr. Scott pounded on the icehouse door. "Help! We're trapped in here!"

Selena's heart thudded with apprehension as she joined in the pounding. "Help! Help us!"

Although they were standing aboveground in the icehouse's entryway, it was so cold, their breath formed clouds in the air. Selena's face felt as if it were made of the same ice that was piled up in blocks in the storage area below.

The doctor paused and slowly shook his head. "I doubt anyone will hear us. We're quite a way from the house, and these walls are thick."

Selena swallowed hard. "You said the lock sometimes sticks?"

"That's what your butler told me before we headed out here. But ..." Dr. Scott broke off, his jaw tense.

"What are you thinking?" Selena's mind went to a dark place. "That someone might have deliberately locked us in here?"

He opened his mouth as if to reply, then shut it gain. "No.

No. Of course not." Bracing one foot against the doorjamb, he turned the knob again and pulled with what seemed to be all his might, but still, the door wouldn't open.

"Is there another way out?" Selena wondered.

"Icehouses generally only have one entrance and exit. But I'll go check. I'm afraid I'll have to take the lantern."

Selena didn't relish the idea of being left alone in the dark. "I'll come with you."

She followed him down the stairs back to the icehouse floor, where the intense cold enveloped her like a frozen shroud. While Dr. Scott perused the perimeter of the chamber, Selena took in the two bodies on the ice slabs and wrapped her arms around herself, trembling, struck once again by the eeriness of the place. It felt like a frosty tomb.

"There's no other exit," Dr. Scott said, returning with the lantern.

A cough broke the stillness nearby. Selena started in astonishment. "Is someone there?"

A fair-haired, lanky lad straightened up from behind the slab of ice upon which Mrs. Whitlock lay. It was Billy, the hall boy. He was shivering in a thin coat, his eyes were sheepish, and his lips were blue.

"Billy!" Selena recalled that he'd been a member of the group who had shoveled the path to the icehouse. "What are you doing in here?"

The lad's cheeks, which were already pink from the cold, turned a deep shade of red. "I wanted to see the dead body."

"Did you shut the icehouse door?" Dr. Scott demanded, his features hard.

Billy twisted his hands. "I ... I don't know, sir. I don't think so. But I may have done."

"That was foolish, boy." Dr. Scott scowled. "Now all three of us are trapped in here."

"Wells knows we're here," Selena said. "Surely, when we don't return, he'll send a party to look for us."

"He'll have to be quick about it," the doctor pointed out. "Hypothermia can happen in minutes. We'll all be dead within the hour."

Selena gasped. "Oh, no." She hadn't realized how cold and terrified she was until the doctor had put that reality into words.

"I'm scared," Billy whined.

"So am I, Billy." Selena felt bad for the boy, who looked like he was about to cry. She crossed to him and embraced his thin frame. In her most reassuring tone, the one she used when her students were anxious about something, she said, "Don't worry. We'll get out of here." If only Selena could believe that.

Billy was trembling even harder now.

"Dr. Scott," Selena said softly, "Billy needs a coat. Mrs. Whitlock's will do. Would you help me?"

"Of course," the doctor replied. They removed the coat from Mrs. Whitlock's body and offered it to the boy.

"I'm not wearin' no dead woman's coat!" Billy cried, his eyes wide.

"Take it and be grateful." Dr. Scott shoved it at him. The lad reluctantly put it on.

A shiver now took over Selena's entire body and her teeth started chattering.

Dr. Scott unbuttoned his overcoat and offered it to her. "Wear this."

"What? No! I couldn't," Selena objected. "You'll freeze."

"Take it," he insisted.

"I already have a coat." Although in this frozen chamber, even her woolen coat felt as thin as Billy's had been.

Ignoring her protestations, Dr. Scott wrapped his overcoat around her like a cape. "Let's go back upstairs. It's a bit less cold there, and we can call again for help."

They traipsed up the stairs to the entryway, where Selena and Dr. Scott pounded on the door and all three began yelling at the top of their lungs, "Help! Help! We're trapped in the icehouse!" They continued the chant over and over until Selena's mouth went dry, and her voice became hoarse.

All at once, there came an answering call.

"Miss Taylor? Dr. Scott? Is that you?" It was Colonel Black-wood's voice.

"Yes! Yes!" Selena cried, her pulse leaping. "We're stuck in here."

"The door won't open," Dr. Scott explained urgently. "I fear the lock is jammed."

"Got it," the colonel replied. The doorknob rattled. "Give me a moment. I've got a penknife."

Selena waited with bated breath as the sound of metallic scraping ensued. An eternity seemed to pass while the threesome stood there, shivering uncontrollably. Selena had never been so cold in her life. She couldn't feel her hands anymore and she was beginning to feel drowsy. Then suddenly and miraculously, the door burst open. Colonel Blackwood stood there with a penknife in his hands.

"Thank you, Colonel." Dr. Scott's features sagged with relief. Putting an arm around Selena's shoulders, he drew her out the door and urged Billy to come with them.

Without a word, Billy darted out, threw Mrs. Whitlock's coat on the ground, and dashed off in the direction of the house.

"Who was that?" Colonel Blackwood asked.

"The hall boy, Billy," Selena said. "He followed us in."

"How did you find us?" Dr. Scott asked as they stood outside beneath the gently falling snow.

"I just learned of Mrs. Whitlock's death from Gladys when she laid my new fire," Colonel Blackwood said. "I still don't understand what happened, but I heard that you were bringing her body to the icehouse. I rushed out here, hoping to have one last moment with Mrs. Whitlock before she ..." He took a breath, as if struggling to calm himself. "Anyway, that's when I heard you pounding on the door and shouting."

"Thank you." Dr. Scott gave him an appreciative look. "I hate to think of what might have happened if you had not come,

Colonel."

"We're so grateful." Selena couldn't believe how close they had come to losing their lives just now.

"I'm glad I could be of help. I've had more than one man in my regiment freeze to death. Not a pretty sight—and a grim way to die." Colonel Blackwood hesitated. "May I ask—how did Mrs. Whitlock die?"

"A lethal combination of laudanum and alcohol, in her bedtime drink," Dr. Scott replied.

"Good heavens." Colonel Blackwood shook his head. "Would you mind if I go in and take a moment to pay my last respects to her?"

"Be my guest, Colonel." Selena picked up the velvet coat from the ground where Billy had tossed it. "Would you do me a favor, though?" She explained how and why the coat had come to be there. "Would you mind bringing this back to Mrs. Whitlock?"

"It would be my honor," the colonel replied.

"Take the lantern." Dr. Scott handed it to him. "And please be quick. I need to get Miss Taylor back to the house, but I don't want to leave until I see you safely out of the icehouse, Colonel— not with that tricky door lock."

"I'll fly as fast as a bird," Colonel Blackwood assured them. He disappeared into the icehouse with Mrs. Whitlock's coat.

"Doctor, please take back *your* overcoat." Selena began to unwrap it from around her shoulders, but he stopped her.

"Keep it for now. You can return it later."

Snow was drifting down at a steady pace. When he refused her second plea, Selena gave up, her heart turning over at his display of gallantry. "I still can't help wondering if someone knew about that tricky door lock and deliberately shut us in."

"Who? You mean the author of the threatening notes?"

She nodded. "They warned us to '*stop looking or die.*' And said, '*You're next.*'"

He let out an uneasy laugh. "It would have taken great audacity and tricky timing for someone to have pulled that off." He shook his head. "I'm sure Billy shut the door, with no idea that it would lock. I understand why you're suspicious, though. Who knows what the person who wrote those notes is thinking or intending."

Colonel Blackwood rejoined them, and they hurried back to the great house. Selena was so cold that she kept the doctor's coat when she returned to her room to change, promising to meet the gentlemen downstairs again later.

Once inside her chamber, Selena stowed Mrs. Hillman's brooch in a dresser drawer, wondering when the right moment would be to apprise Mrs. Hillman about her friend's misdeed.

She paused gratefully before the hearth, warming her frozen hands and feet by the fire. Her mind spun with a mix of churning emotions: shock over all that had happened that morning and anxiety about what lay ahead. For with Mrs. Whitlock dead, they had no idea who had sent the threatening notes or who had killed Jack Clarke—if indeed he *had* been killed. Or if Mrs. Whitlock's poisoning had been deliberate or accidental.

And what about that terrifying experience just now in the icehouse? Had Billy truly shut the door? Or had someone else closed it, knowing that the lock might jam and trap her and the doctor inside? All of these things were a conundrum, and not one she'd be able to solve today.

While she waited for the numbness to recede and her body to return to a normal temperature, she became aware of the familiar scents of sandalwood, citrus, and lavender emanating from the overcoat still wrapped around her shoulders. Impulsively, she hugged the coat to herself, reveling in the feel of the fine wool and the pleasing fragrance. The knowledge that this coat had been wrapped around the doctor's body filled Selena with an almost overpowering sense of delight ... and want.

She wished, suddenly, that the man himself were wrapped around her, rather than just his overcoat. That she were in his arms again, and he were kissing her the way he had in the linen closet. The memory of that interlude came back to her full force and caused a thrilling sizzle to reverberate in Selena's very core.

Her face grew warm. She really *must* stop thinking about that. Dr. Scott had insisted that their kiss had been outside the bounds of propriety, and it should never happen again. She might not like that assessment, but she had to respect it. He was only here by chance, after all. They may have been working together to try to solve a mystery or two, but as he'd said, their theories were all built on conjectures and fueled by a couple of anonymous notes. Whether or not they were on the right track remained to be seen.

If the pair was lucky enough to find that hidden money, Dr. Scott could well be out the door as soon as the weather cleared. And she wouldn't blame him. He was a doctor with a medical practice to return to. Someday, she would look back on this time with him as a brief, exciting, merely stolen romantic moment.

With a sigh, Selena gave the overcoat one last, full-body caress. In doing so, she felt something inside one of the inner pockets. She pulled out a calling card. It read:

DR. ANDREW DALTON

Licensed Physician

26 Brompton Road, Hampstead, London

Selena stared at the card. What was Dr. Scott doing with another man's card in his pocket?

Unless … A sudden thought occurred to her that made her stomach tighten and her head spin. *Was Dr. Scott the man he claimed to be?*

SELENA, DRESSED NOW in a gown of deep lavender silk, marched down the south hall corridor with Dr. Scott's overcoat over her arm. She got to Dr. Scott's chamber just as he was exiting the room.

"Doctor," she said, offering him the coat.

He stopped before her, a sparkle in his blue eyes as he accepted the garment. "You are very prompt in returning it."

Selena saw no reason to beat around the bush. "I found this in the pocket." She handed him the calling card.

He studied it and went still. The color seemed to drain from his face—or had she, wondering if he was hiding something, just imagined that? He cleared his throat. "I didn't realize I still had his card in my pocket."

"*Whose* card?" Selena persisted.

"Dr. Dalton's—a colleague of mine." He shrugged his shoulders. "He called on me the day before I left London for the holidays."

"London?" Selena shot back. "You said you're from Bath."

He blinked. "I am. But … I was in London for a few days before I traveled north. Dr. Dalton and I met for a drink at my hotel."

"Oh." Selena's face warmed with sudden embarrassment. His explanation was perfectly reasonable.

He shot her a quizzical look. "Why are you so concerned about his calling card?"

"I'm not," she replied quickly. "I just wondered, that's all."

Dr. Scott's eyebrows drew together. "All right. I'll just put my coat—and my friend's card—in my room. And I'll meet you downstairs?"

"Yes, yes." Selena hurried off. *Why do you see deceit everywhere?* she silently chastised herself as she fled down the stairs. *You must stop that.*

Her stomach growled. Selena recalled that she hadn't had anything to eat or drink that day. She wanted desperately to get a quick bite in the morning room, but a more important concern suddenly struck her.

Selena spotted the housekeeper below and stopped her at the base of the stairs. "Mrs. Middleton! I presume, by now everyone has heard what happened to Mrs. Whitlock?"

"Yes, Miss Taylor." The housekeeper's expression was grim.

"Such a sad business."

"How has Mrs. Hillman taken the awful news?" Selena was worried, for Mrs. Hillman had just lost another friend.

"As well as can be expected, miss. Mrs. Hillman said she is grieved and confused about what happened, but she has not taken to her bed. And she had the presence of mind to distribute Boxing Day gifts to the staff not half an hour ago."

Selena had forgotten, in the madness of the morning, that it was Boxing Day. Mrs. Hillman's reaction was both a relief and illuminating, since she had practically fallen apart when Mr. Clarke had died. "And our guests? How are they faring?"

"I'll leave you to draw your own conclusions, miss. Mrs. Hillman and the others are all waiting for you in the drawing room."

Selena nodded. *No quick bite in the morning room, then.* "Thank you, Mrs. Middleton." She paused. "But wait—why are you still here? You and the rest of the staff were off duty at ten o'clock."

"Yes, miss. But the weather's so bad, none of us can go any-where. I thought I may as well help out as long as I'm here."

"I appreciate that, but it's Boxing Day. Please, take this time for yourself. You have earned it."

Mrs. Middleton thanked her, curtsied, and took her leave.

As she headed for the drawing room, Mrs. Hillman's pro-nouncement that she was *grieved and confused* repeated in Selena's mind. She was grieved and confused herself.

Had Mrs. Whitlock's death, she wondered once again, been an accident? Or had someone poisoned her nightcap? Either way, how were she and the doctor to ever learn the truth? There would be a great many questions, she feared, from the group who were awaiting her. What should she tell them?

In the drawing room, Selena found Mrs. Hillman and all the guests except Dr. Scott fully dressed and in hushed conversation. Selena couldn't help but notice, with a sharp twinge, how their group had dwindled since the day the house party had begun.

"Is it true?" Miss Goodwin rose from her chair, her voice

ringing with incredulity as she addressed Selena. "Mrs. Whitlock is *dead*?"

"I'm afraid so." Selena did her best to appear composed, even though her mind was still buzzing with a thousand questions.

"How on Earth did it happen?" asked Mrs. Hillman, from her seat on the wingback chair beside the fire. She was, as promised, much calmer than she had been two mornings ago, when Mr. Clarke had died. "Miss Thompson and Colonel Blackwood said that Mrs. Whitlock died during the night from some kind of overdose?"

"Yes, ma'am," Selena answered.

"But how?" Mrs. Hillman asked.

"I can answer that." Dr. Scott strode into the room and stopped by the hearth, where he addressed the group. "I regret to say that at 7:30 this morning, Miss Thompson found Mrs. Whitlock unresponsive in her bed. We found a half-empty laudanum bottle on Mrs. Whitlock's bedside table. In the residue from her bedtime drink, I detected the taste of laudanum. I believe she must have added some of the tincture to her hot toddy and the combination of the drug and alcohol proved to be lethal."

"Dear lord." Mrs. Hillman's face went ghostly pale.

Colonel Blackwood's mouth turned downwards. "In effect, she accidentally killed herself."

"It certainly looks that way." Dr. Scott clasped his hands and stared at the carpet.

"'*Looks* that way'?" Mr. Davis sat up straighter on the sofa. "What do you mean, Doctor? Could there be some other explanation?"

"I didn't say that," Dr. Scott replied.

"And yet you implied it." Mr. Davis spread his hands wide in inquiry. "Do we know for certain that Mrs. Whitlock knowingly took that much laudanum? Or did someone douse her hot toddy on purpose?"

Selena caught Dr. Scott's eye. His forehead turned down in a frown, echoing Selena's inner turmoil. They had agreed not to mention this alternative theory—but it seemed the idea was not to be silenced. How would they explain this without raising a general panic and drawing attention to the missing money?

Another thought crossed Selena's mind, adding to her anxiety. If Mrs. Whitlock had indeed been murdered, was the perpetrator in this very room?

CHAPTER FIFTEEN

A HUSH DESCENDED on the drawing room. Everyone turned to stare at Mr. Davis, who had raised the alarming question about Mrs. Whitlock's death, asking if her poisoning had been accidental or deliberate.

"Bite your tongue, sir!" cried Mrs. Hillman, her tone aghast. "It's bad enough that the poor woman died. To say she was murdered? Don't make such absurd insinuations."

Mr. Davis raised both hands now as if in apology. "Forgive me. I know that Mrs. Whitlock was your friend, Mrs. Hillman. And that she was your employer, Miss Thompson. But I have to say, she was not a kind woman. I didn't like her. Did any of you?"

An awkward moment followed. At length, with a shrug of his shoulders, Colonel Blackwood admitted quietly, "She *could* be rather ... prickly."

"'Prickly'?" Miss Goodwin made a scoffing sound. "She was hateful and always complaining about everything."

"You didn't know her as I did." Mrs. Hillman held her head high. "Mrs. Whitlock has always been a good friend to me."

Selena knew this wasn't true. Mrs. Whitlock had shamelessly stolen her 'friend's' brooch—a valuable pin that had been a treasured gift from Mrs. Hillman's departed husband—and then lied about it. But this wasn't the time to bring that up.

"Mrs. Whitlock may have had a negative view of things at times, but there was a reason for it," Mrs. Hillman continued.

"Her husband, whom she adored, passed away six years ago and since then, she has had to live in much-reduced circumstances, which has been very hard on her."

"That's no reason to plague the life out of her companion." Miss Goodwin gave Miss Thompson a compassionate look. "We all saw the way she treated you, my dear."

"If you ask me, it would have served her right if *you* had done her in, Miss Thompson," Mr. Davis added with a chuckle.

Everyone seemed to freeze at this remark. Mr. Davis colored slightly as if aware that he had once again spoken out of turn. Selena noticed that everybody else, except for Mrs. Hillman, stole a hooded glance at Miss Thompson. Selena couldn't deny that Mrs. Whitlock *had* treated her companion very shabbily. But for the young woman to resort to murder? Selena didn't believe it. Or maybe she just didn't want to believe it.

Miss Thompson's face went pale. "Don't look at me," she said quickly. "I admit, I didn't like Mrs. Whitlock. But I didn't kill her. Why would I?" Her lips trembled. "I needed that job. Now, I am unemployed, and I have no idea how I shall make ends meet."

Miss Goodwin's brows lifted, as if she hadn't considered that. The rest of the group universally lowered their gazes as if processing this idea.

Dr. Scott pierced the ensuing silence. "I'm sorry, Miss Thompson. I can see that this has proven very distressing for you."

Miss Thompson nodded, tears pooling in her eyes. She gave Mrs. Hillman an appealing glance. "I hope you will allow me to stay on, ma'am, after the weather clears? Even though my employer is … is no longer with us? Just for a few days at least?"

"Of course I will, young lady." Mrs. Hillman gave her a warm smile. "You are one of us now. And pray, don't be upset. No one in this room believes that you had anything to do with Mrs. Whitlock's demise, believe me."

Selena also rushed to the young lady's defense. "Miss Thompson explained to us that Mrs. Whitlock was … how shall I put it … prone to taking laudanum quite regularly and did not always follow the advice of her doctor."

"You mean she was an addict," Mr. Davis blurted out.

Mrs. Hillman shot him a glare.

"I didn't mean to suggest that," Selena responded quickly.

"The evidence I found points to an accidental overdose." Dr. Scott's voice rang with authority. "Unfortunately, this is not an uncommon occurrence. It is my belief that laudanum is too widely prescribed for even the most minor of complaints. I have observed nurses spoon-feeding laudanum to quiet crying infants. The drug ought to be regulated, and yet it is available without limit at every chemist's and apothecary shop in the nation." He shook his head. "If I had known that Mrs. Whitlock had had a bottle of laudanum with her, I would have warned her about the dangers of mixing it with alcohol. But I didn't know. She took too much, and to my great regret, she is gone. And now let that be an end to it."

Another silence fell. Colonel Blackwood crossed one leg over the other and nodded, as if in agreement with this pronouncement. Miss Goodwin and Mr. Davis exchanged a look and a shrug. Miss Thompson wiped her eyes.

Mrs. Hillman was the first to speak. "I'm sorry this happened, everyone. I don't know what to say. It's been a long while since we've had a death at Darkmoor Park. And now to think we've had two in two days."

Selena was also wrestling with the strangeness of that. A new thought occurred to her. "It's also a bit of a coincidence," she couldn't help but observe, "that the two people who have just died were both at the Worthing Seaside Hotel with you four summers ago, Mrs. Hillman." As she spoke the words, a jolt of doubt ran through Selena's body as she recalled another one of her mother's favorite sayings, which she and her sisters had adopted. *I don't believe in coincidences.*

A faraway look came into Mrs. Hillman's eyes. "You're right. It does seem extraordinary, now that you mention it," she noted.

Colonel Blackwood pursed his lips. "What are you saying? Do you think there might be a connection?"

Mrs. Hillman shook her head. "Of course not. How could there be? But it *is* peculiar. Especially when you consider the awful incident that transpired that summer."

Selena's entire body went on alert. "What incident?" She remembered Mrs. Hillman mentioning that something untoward had happened that summer, but she had never shared the details.

"Oh, that poor porter." Mrs. Hillman glanced at Colonel Blackwood. "You remember, don't you, Colonel? The boy who worked at the hotel and was accused of stealing?"

"Yes. A young chap." Colonel Blackwood nodded. "He stole jewelry from several guest rooms. Took Jack Clarke's prized gold watch, as I recall, my diamond stickpin, and some necklace belonging to Mrs. Whitlock."

Mrs. Hillman's eyes looked troubled. "What was the young man's name again?"

Colonel Blackwood's eyes narrowed. "Webster, I think it was?"

"That's right! Clive Webster. He was accused of those thefts, convicted at trial, and sentenced to prison." Mrs. Hillman frowned. "Mrs. Goodwin wrote to me last year to say that after serving two years, Clive Webster became ill and died in prison."

"Oh! I had no idea." Colonel Blackwood's voice went quiet. "A sad end to the story. But then, he *was* a thief."

"Perhaps." Mrs. Hillman worried her lower lip. "I have always wondered if that was true. Mr. Webster seemed like such a nice young man to me. He carried my bags in and out with a smile, he ran errands for me on a moment's notice, and once, I'll never forget it, he left a bunch of wildflowers in a vase in my room with a note wishing me a lovely day. But apparently, Mr. Clarke told the police that the porter had eyed his gold watch covetously. Mrs. Whitlock maintained that Mr. Webster had asked if her pearl necklace was real, which it was—and then both items, along with the colonel's diamond stickpin, mysteriously vanished. You spoke to the police as well, didn't you, Colonel?"

"Yes," Colonel Blackwood affirmed. "They asked me to describe my stickpin."

"Mr. Webster had access to all the guest room keys—his little sister was one of the maids, you see. So, he was blamed." Mrs. Hillman glanced at Miss Goodwin. "It was your mother, Miss Goodwin, who initially called the constable."

Miss Goodwin nodded slowly. "I remember Mr. Webster." Her cheeks deepened in color as she spoke. "I was away on holiday with friends when you all stayed at the hotel that summer, and I didn't attend the trial. But Mother was frightfully distressed about it at the time. So was I."

"I told the constable that I didn't believe the young man was responsible." Mrs. Hillman shook her head. "But at the trial—none of us were there except Mrs. Goodwin, who wrote me all about it—she insisted that Mr. Webster should pay for his crimes."

"Mother took great pride in our hotel." Miss Goodwin's eyes grew distant and appeared troubled. "If there was even a *hint* of any wrongdoing from the staff, she would let them go. She had to make an example of Mr. Webster, she said."

Selena had been listening to all this in silent wonder. Mrs. Hillman had never spoken a word to her about this before.

"How terribly sad," Miss Thompson said softly, "if Mr. Webster was actually innocent of those crimes."

"Yes, very sad." Miss Goodwin let out a long sigh.

The hairs on the back of Selena's neck stood on end as an idea began to formulate in her brain.

She knew that Mrs. Whitlock had brazenly stolen Mrs. Hillman's bejeweled brooch and hidden it inside her coat. Given this illicit proclivity, was it possible that Mrs. Whitlock had also stolen those pieces of jewelry from the hotel that summer? The woman's claim about her own stolen necklace might have been a ruse to divert suspicion from herself. Had Mrs. Whitlock allowed an innocent young man to go to prison for thefts that she had committed?

If so, how awful! And furthermore, if so ... could that crime all those years ago have become a motive for her murder today? If so, Mr. Webster couldn't have done the deed, since he had died. But perhaps someone else had sought revenge on the lad's behalf?

"Mrs. Hillman, did you say the porter had a younger sister?" Selena asked.

"Yes. I don't remember her at all, I'm afraid. She was the under chambermaid and kept out of sight." Mrs. Hillman tilted her head to one side. "There was an older brother too, as I recall, who worked as a footman in a great house somewhere. I never met him, but Mr. Webster used to talk about both of his siblings, Maisie and Joe, with such fondness."

"I never heard that old story about a theft at the hotel," Mr. Davis remarked to Miss Goodwin.

"I saw no reason to tell you, dearest," Miss Goodwin responded.

"Miss Goodwin." Selena turned to her abruptly. "How did your mother die?"

The young woman's eyes widened. "What? Why do you ask?"

"I was just wondering." Selena cleared her throat. "When Mrs. Hillman wrote to you, and you mentioned that your mother had passed away, I don't believe you ever said what had happened."

"That's true." Mrs. Hillman turned to Miss Goodwin. "I didn't want to pry. But I should dearly like to know. Was your mother ill?"

Miss Goodwin's face grew pink again. She darted a glance at Mr. Davis. He averted his gaze. "No, she wasn't ill." She seemed to be searching for words. "She ... She ..." Her voice trailed off.

Was she unwilling, Selena wondered, or unable to complete the thought? Selena leaned forward in her chair. "Miss Goodwin. Your mother and Mrs. Hillman had written to each other for years. They were dear friends. And we are all *your* friends now.

I'm sure that whatever happened, your mother wouldn't have minded you sharing it."

Miss Goodwin nodded almost imperceptibly and took a little breath. "Well. If you must know, Mother had been suffering from insomnia. All the stress of running the hotel, you see, and people coming and going at all hours. She'd been taking laudanum to help her sleep. And … she died from an accidental overdose in her cup of tea."

A gasp went around the room. Selena's heart seemed to skip a beat.

Mrs. Hillman clutched at the collar of her satin gown. "But that's … exactly what happened to Mrs. Whitlock. Except the laudanum was in her hot toddy."

For the third time, an awkward hush enveloped the room. Colonel Blackwood's bushy brows drew together. Mrs. Hillman wrung her hands. Miss Goodwin bit her nails. Miss Thompson and Mr. Davis fidgeted in their chairs. Dr. Scott's features tightened, even as Selena felt her own jaw clench. What did this mean?

Colonel Blackwood suddenly slapped his thigh. "I say. Why does everyone look so fretful all of a sudden? So, we happen to know two women who weren't very smart about their laudanum intake. My deepest condolences, Miss Goodwin. Your mother was a dear woman and deserved better. But you heard what Dr. Scott said. This kind of thing happens all the time. Why, I know at least six ladies who are addicted to the stuff. I just hope and pray it doesn't happen to them. Again, I'm very sorry for your loss."

Miss Goodwin exhaled a long sigh. "Thank you, Colonel."

"Colonel Blackwood is right," Dr. Scott remarked with a self-effacing nod. "Meanwhile, this is a reminder to us all to be careful when taking a drug of any kind. And if a doctor prescribes something, be sure to ask him how to take it."

Mrs. Hillman gave a long, sad sigh and looked around the room. "What a time we have had, my friends. After this, I wouldn't blame you if you all chose to leave Darkmoor Park this very day."

"I wouldn't think of leaving," Miss Goodwin insisted with a flap of her hand.

"And how could we, in any case?" Mr. Davis nodded towards the drawing room's tall casement windows. "We are still snowed in."

Selena followed his gaze. Snow was still falling from a moody, grey sky. The rear grounds were covered in a thick, white blanket, and the trees and hedges were generously frosted in white. Selena knew, from her earlier glance out front, that the long drive leading up to the house was also deeply buried. "We are indeed, Mr. Davis. And even if it stops snowing tomorrow, it will no doubt be many days before the roads are cleared."

"No matter. We all came to stay through New Year's, didn't we?" Colonel Blackwood said. "I say, let's take all this in stride and make the best of it."

The rest of the group nodded and voiced their agreement.

"I propose a quiet day," Mrs. Hillman announced. "Let us begin with a short service in the chapel in honor of Mrs. Whit-lock, as we did for Mr. Clarke. After that, you may feel free to do whatever suits your fancy. There is a library full of books to read. There's a chess board in that cupboard there, and as you know, a very good pianoforte in the music room. Since it's Boxing Day, our meals will all be cold, so you can dine at your leisure. Let us hope for a better day tomorrow." With that, Mrs. Hillman stood. "And now, I beg you to accompany me to the chapel."

As Selena rose along with the group and filed out of the draw-ing room, her thoughts returned to the story of the unfortunate porter, Clive Webster. Three people who had been at the Worthing Seaside Hotel that summer, and who had reported Clive Webster as a thief, had died: Mr. Clarke, Mrs. Whitlock, and a few months ago, the proprietor of the hotel, Mrs. Doris Goodwin—who had called the authorities and had seen to it that Mr. Webster had been charged for the crimes. Two of the victims had died from the same apparent cause: an accidental overdose of laudanum. Was it just a coincidence?

Selena didn't believe in coincidences.

The party reached the chapel, where once again, Colonel Blackwood moved to the pulpit and began speaking about Mrs. Whitlock. Selena, seated on her own at the back of the room, was unable to focus on his words. An idea began to brew in her mind … a dastardly and frightening idea that might explain a way in which the seemingly disparate deaths were connected.

Mr. Clive Webster had apparently had a sister and a brother, Maisie and Joe Webster, with whom he'd been very close. *What if*, Selena wondered, *one—or both—of Clive Webster's siblings had murdered Doris Goodwin to avenge their brother's death?*

And what if one—or both—had come to Darkmoor Park seeking revenge on the other participants in the awful proceedings?

Selena dared a glance at Dr. Scott, who was seated a few rows ahead of her, at the far side of the sanctuary. He was staring at the floor, as if his mind, too, were elsewhere. Was he thinking what she was thinking?

Was it possible that she and Dr. Scott had been wrong, all this time, about the motive behind Mr. Clarke's death? If the man had indeed been murdered, had it had nothing at all to do with the hidden money? Might it have been, instead, an act of revenge for what had happened to Clive Webster?

A cold tremor dashed up Selena's spine. If she was right, the three deaths that had occurred would not be the last. The danger was still ongoing.

She needed to talk to Dr. Scott—and fast.

CHAPTER SIXTEEN

A S EVERYONE ELSE dispersed to go about their day, Selena followed Dr. Scott to the morning room, where he began making up a plate for the breakfast that they had missed.

Selena grabbed her own plate, made a quick sandwich with two pieces of bread and a slice of ham, and whispered to him, "Meet me in the east schoolroom in ten minutes." At his nod, she slipped from the room.

She was waiting when he arrived and closed the door behind him. "I've been anxious to talk to you."

"So have I." His eyes were bright and alive with speculation. "This new information about what happened at the hotel that summer may put a new light on things."

"It may have." She beckoned him to the cushioned window seat and sat down beside him. "*If* Mrs. Whitlock was poisoned ... and *if* Jack Clarke was pushed down the stairs ... it might be just as we've theorized—that it's about Mr. Clarke's hidden money. On the other hand, it may have nothing at all to do with the money."

"My thoughts exactly." He leaned forward. "The porter who was convicted of theft and died in prison—he had a sister and a brother."

"Maisie and Joe Webster."

"Mrs. Hillman said that Clive Webster was very close to his siblings."

Excitement rose in Selena's chest. "If they thought their brother was innocent, they may have been distraught by his death."

"Yes! Something tells me that Mrs. Whitlock stole those jewels that summer and let that poor boy pay for it."

"That wouldn't surprise me." Selena stood up and paced back and forth before the window seat. "What if the brother and sister decided to get revenge? They plotted to kill every person who had been instrumental in their brother's arrest and conviction?"

"They started with Mrs. Goodwin and moved on to Mr. Clarke and Mrs. Whitlock," he shot back.

"If we're right, it has to be a member of the house party—or one of the servants. Someone who has been at Darkmoor Park at least since December 23rd and is here under an assumed name."

"How old do you think Maisie and Joe Webster would be now?"

Selena paused to think. "The thefts took place four years ago. Mrs. Hillman said the sister was an under chambermaid who kept out of sight."

"Let's presume that the sister-chambermaid was between fifteen and twenty years old at the time. That would make her anywhere from nineteen to twenty-four today."

"We have several maids about that age, but all of them have worked at Darkmoor Park more than four years ... except Gladys. She's only been here a few months."

Dr. Scott's brows arched. "If she's Maisie Webster, she could have taken this position with a specific goal in mind. What about the brother?"

"Mrs. Hillman didn't say much about him. Just that he was a footman." Selena took a breath. "Wait, we have a temporary footman—Sam. Wells hired him just for the holidays. He's the only new male employee whom I know of."

He rubbed his jaw. "Sounds like it's time to have a chat with Gladys and Sam. But we can't stop there. We have the guests to consider. Miss Thompson is the right age to be Maisie Webster."

Selena shook her head. "No, it can't be her."

"Can't be? Or you don't want it to be?"

She hesitated. "The latter, I suppose. I really like Miss Thompson."

His eyes dimmed. "Sometimes, the people we trust the most are the ones who are most likely to stab us in the back."

Selena recalled him saying something similar a few days ago. "I take it you had a bad experience with someone you'd trusted?"

"You could say that." His tone was bitter.

"I'm so sorry." Her heart went out to him. "May I ask what happened?"

"I'd rather not discuss it. It's in the past. Let's get back on topic. Didn't Mrs. Whitlock say that Miss Thompson was a new hire?"

"She did." Selena's spirits fell as she considered that. She *really* wanted the young lady to be innocent. "I suppose Miss Thompson *could* be Maisie Webster. Apparently, she had only been serving as Mrs. Whitlock's companion for a few months."

"She may have deliberately sought a position in that lady's household with the intent to kill her."

She sat back down beside him. "If so, why did she wait three months to kill her, until *after* she'd arrived at Darkmoor Park?"

He considered that. "Perhaps she changed her plans when the invitation to this holiday house party came in the post. Maisie—now going as Miss Thompson—may have decided that the party would be the ideal opportunity to dispatch some of the other people who had doomed her brother to prison and death."

"So, she waited and came along." Selena tilted her head. "If that's true, did she kill Mrs. Goodwin at the hotel as well?"

"She may have. The woman apparently died from an overdose of laudanum in her tea, similar to the way Mrs. Whitlock died. Remember, Maisie was an under chambermaid at the Worthing Seaside Hotel. All these years, she may have despised Mrs. Goodwin for turning in her brother Clive."

Selena inhaled sharply. "I just remembered. Miss Thompson

said she'd started out as a chambermaid. And she mentioned a brother."

"Well, there you have it."

"For all we know, Miss Thompson—if she's Maisie—may have still been working at the hotel three months ago when Mrs. Goodwin died."

Dr. Scott ran a hand through his hair. "Or, she may have known the hotel so well that she was able to sneak in unseen, poison Mrs. Goodwin's tea, and then dash off to take a position as Mrs. Whitlock's companion."

"The timing fits." Selena hated to admit it, but the whole thing was possible. "Miss Thompson freely admitted that she disliked Mrs. Whitlock. The reason for that dislike could go far deeper than her dissatisfaction with the way that woman treated her."

"It could, indeed." It was Dr. Scott's turn to stand up and pace. "If so, she's an excellent actress. I truly believed that Miss Thompson was shocked and horrified when she found Mrs. Whitlock dead in her bed this morning."

"So did I. And I felt sorry for her, when she shed tears about being newly unemployed."

"Well. She is innocent until proven guilty," Dr. Scott reminded Selena as he paced.

"What about our other guest, Miss Goodwin? She's the right age, too. When the subject of Clive Webster's arrest and conviction came up, Miss Goodwin seemed oddly upset about an incident that had occurred four years ago to an employee at the hotel."

The doctor hesitated. "How could *she* be Maisie Webster? She's Mrs. Goodwin's daughter."

"Is she?" Selena asked skeptically.

"What do you mean?"

"Mrs. Hillman had never met Mrs. Goodwin's daughter. No one in the group had. The young lady was away on holiday with friends the summer they all met at the hotel. In fact, the night

Miss Goodwin arrived, Mrs. Hillman mentioned that she looks nothing like her mother and must take after her father."

"So, you're saying anyone could show up here and pretend to be Miss Goodwin, and no one would be the wiser?" Dr. Scott mused.

"Yes. Think about it. If a few months ago, Maisie was still working at the hotel, perhaps in a more elevated position now, as parlor maid, she would have had access to Mrs. Goodwin's post."

"Her post?" Dr. Scott whirled to face her. "Ah. I see where you're going with this. Maisie might have intercepted the invitation that Mrs. Goodwin received from Mrs. Hillman."

"And then, she could have written to Mrs. Hillman, *pretending* to be Mrs. Goodwin's daughter, to explain that poor Mrs. Goodwin had died."

"Maybe," he theorized, "the woman already *was* dead. Or maybe the invitation prompted Maisie to get rid of Mrs. Goodwin by putting laudanum in her tea."

Selena raised a finger. "The real Miss Goodwin may have known nothing about Mrs. Hillman's invitation to Darkmoor Park."

"Maisie could have continued to intercept the mail and correspond with Mrs. Hillman, seeing this holiday party as the ideal opportunity to exact her revenge."

Dr. Scott ground to a halt a just a foot away from her. "This all presumes that Maisie Webster knows how to read and can write well enough to sound like the daughter of a hotel proprietor."

Selena paused to reflect. "We don't know what kind of education the real Miss Goodwin had. But Maisie had years to plot her revenge. She might have gotten help writing the letters. Or she could have spent that time bettering herself and learning to write and speak well."

"It's possible."

Another thought occurred to Selena and her heart jumped. "There were a couple of instances over the past few days when

Miss Goodwin seemed to have forgotten that she was a hotel manager."

"If she really *is* Miss Goodwin," Dr. Scott pointed out, "that could simply be because she is new in the role and still grieving the loss of her mother."

"True. But if she's Maisie Webster, it could have been her mask slipping. After all, she refused to play the pianoforte on Christmas Eve."

His brow wrinkled. "How does that signify?"

"All well-bred young ladies in the upper and middle classes are expected to learn to play the pianoforte. That's why we include music in our school curriculum. Piano playing is seen as a key accomplishment, even for the daughters of tradespeople, to demonstrate their refinement to help secure a good marriage. Whereas a chambermaid would rarely have the means or the opportunity to learn to play."

"I see." He crossed his arms over his chest. "A fair point, but not conclusive. If she *is* the real Miss Goodwin, even if she did learn to play, she might not consider herself an accomplished musician."

"True. But—oh! If only we could write to the Worthing Seaside Hotel and see if Miss Goodwin is there right now. But with this storm, that's impossible. And even after the weather clears, who knows how long it would take to hear back?"

Dr. Scott squinted at her. "If the woman really is Maisie Webster, how does Mr. Davis play into this?"

Selena considered that. "Mr. Davis is the right age to have been a footman four years ago. And now that I think of it, he and Miss Goodwin have the same dark hair, and they do resemble each other."

He gave a little gasp. "They could be brother and sister, posing as an engaged couple."

"And doing a fine job of it, for I never suspected a thing." Selena steepled her fingertips as the notion sunk in. "I wonder what Mr. Davis does for a living? I never thought to ask." She crossed to the teacher's desk and retrieved paper and a pen.

Dr. Scott chuckled. "Are you going to write this down?"

"I am." Selena sat and jotted a few words.

ARE THEY MAISIE OR JOE WEBSTER? HERE TO SEEK
   REVENGE?

- Gladys
- Sam
- Miss Thompson
- Miss Goodwin
- Mr. Davis

She handed the list to Dr. Scott, who reviewed it in silence. At last, he said, "You must realize, we may be completely wrong about this."

"We may be," she acknowledged.

"This entire Webster siblings plot might be a figment of our imaginations. The deaths of Mrs. Goodwin, Jack Clarke, and Mrs. Whitlock may very well have all been accidents. Or, with regard to the last two at least, related only to the stolen money."

"I realize that. But the *Webster siblings plot*, as you put it—it's possible, isn't it?"

"It is. I admit, I'm intrigued. And I want to know if those three people were murdered or not."

"If so, the villain might not be finished." Worried, Selena darted her eyes towards the doctor. "Colonel Blackwood also told the police that Clive Webster had stolen from him."

Dr. Scott's mouth opened slightly. "I'd forgotten that. And Mrs. Hillman was there as well."

"But Mrs. Hillman said that she spoke in the boy's defense."

"Right, right. So, if Maisie and Joe Webster are aware of that and are truly here seeking revenge …"

"The colonel might be next on their list."

"Good lord." The doctor clasped his hands and stared at the floor. "This could be even more dire than I'd thought."

"I know."

He glanced out the window, beyond which snow still sifted down in a vast expanse of white. "Under normal circumstances, we'd call in your parish constable. But he's not here, and it'll be days before we can go anywhere. It looks like, once again, it's our responsibility to investigate this. Not only to find out the truth, but to protect Colonel Blackwood from becoming the potential next victim."

"How shall we go about this?"

He flapped the list in his hand. "Let's start asking questions, learn everything we can about the people on this list."

"It's the perfect day to do that. Everyone is pursuing their own interests in different parts of the house. If one of them is Maisie or Joe Webster, maybe they'll admit something that gives them away."

"One can only hope."

Selena paused. "Wait, what about the threatening notes? Could one of the Webster siblings be responsible?"

"Of course. Even if they're here for revenge, they might want that cash as well—and they wouldn't want us to find it first."

"The footmen were present on Christmas Eve when we discussed Mr. Clarke's missing money!" Selena recalled suddenly. "And gossip spreads like wildfire downstairs."

He nodded, and his expression turned even more serious. "To recap the situation to date: did someone kill one or all of those people? Did they write the threatening notes? And what happened to Mr. Clarke's money? Recovering that money was our first mission and I don't want to lose sight of that—it's the only one I know in my gut to be real."

"Of course! We *have* to keep looking for the money. Whoever wrote those notes may be out there as we speak, checking every nook and cranny for that five thousand pounds."

"For all we know, they may have already found it."

"Let's hope not." Selena's mouth pulled downward. "Because I'm sure *they*, whoever they are, mean to keep it for themselves."

"I say, we search quietly and inconspicuously."

"Agreed." Selena stood. "By the way, we're in the east schoolroom—one of the places Mr. Clarke was known to have visited on his last afternoon. Shall we take a look around for a dragon?"

They spent the next fifteen minutes searching the chamber, glancing inside all the students' desks, every drawer in the teacher's desk, and every storage cupboard. They found nothing out of the ordinary.

"Mr. Clarke didn't hide that money here," Dr. Scott proclaimed when their examinations had come to an end.

"It may be difficult to explore any further today," Selena noted. "The other guests could be anywhere in the house."

Dr. Scott nodded and shoved his hands in his coat pockets. "Let's put the treasure hunt on hold for the present and go do some discreet questioning."

Selena raised a hand. "First—although we agreed not to say anything to anyone about the hidden money, I think we should tell Mrs. Hillman and Colonel Blackwood about the Websters. If there's even the tiniest chance that the colonel could be in danger ..."

Dr. Scott's expression turned grave. "We need to warn them."

"And as much as I hate to do it," Selena added as they left the room, "I ought to tell her who stole her brooch."

CHAPTER SEVENTEEN

SELENA AND DR. Scott entered the drawing room to find Colonel Blackwood and Mrs. Hillman seated by the fire, playing a game of chess. Thankfully, they were alone.

"Clever move, ma'am," the colonel was saying. "But then, I knew what I was getting into when I invited you to play." He and Mrs. Hillman looked up as Selena and the doctor approached. "Miss Taylor! Dr. Scott. You have arrived just in time to see me on the brink of defeat by my worthy opponent."

Mrs. Hillman grinned. "How many times did I beat you at the hotel that summer?"

"I stopped keeping count." Colonel Blackwood chuckled.

Selena briefly returned their smiles. "I'm sorry to interrupt your game, but Dr. Scott and I would like to have a word with you both if we may."

"By all means." Mrs. Hillman gestured to a pair of velvet-tufted chairs opposite.

Once the pair was seated, the colonel sat back in his own chair and said, "What's on your mind?"

Dr. Scott cleared his throat. "Ma'am. Colonel," he said, his voice low and solemn, "What we're about to impart, we share in the strictest confidence. It must not be repeated to anyone else in this house."

"Oh, dear. You sound so serious." Mrs. Hillman placed a hand over her heart. "What is it?"

"It relates to the unfortunate deaths of Mr. Clarke and Mrs. Whitlock," Selena murmured in the same quiet tone, "as well as that of your mutual friend, Mrs. Goodwin."

"Mrs. Goodwin?" Colonel Blackwood narrowed his eyes at them. "What has she got to do with anything?"

"As Mrs. Hillman mentioned," Dr. Scott explained, "it *is* quite odd that three people you met at the Worthing Seaside Hotel that summer have died in such short succession."

Mrs. Hillman's eyebrows pulled together. "I wouldn't say it's odd, but rather a terrible coincidence. One which I would rather not think about just now."

"I'm afraid we must think about it, Mrs. Hillman, and without delay," Selena replied. "What we're going to say is important."

"When you brought up the Clive Webster case, it got us to thinking." The doctor folded his hands in his lap. "And we have formed a theory."

The colonel's brows drew together. "What kind of theory?"

Selena checked again to make sure there was no one else in the room. "Mrs. Hillman, you said you believed that Clive Webster might have been innocent of the thefts of which he was convicted?"

The older woman gave a long sigh, but her expression seemed to signal her reluctant acquiescence to discuss the matter. "He was such a nice young man. To steal valuables from the guest rooms—to me, it didn't fit with his character. I felt certain that someone else must have done it. I tried to voice my opinion, but no one listened."

"You may have been right." Selena leaned forward in her chair. "You know your iris brooch that went missing?"

"Yes?"

Selena knew this wasn't going to be easy for Mrs. Hillman to hear. But for her to truly accept Clive Webster's probable innocence, she felt it necessary to tell her. "It pains me to report this but, after we found Mrs. Whitlock this morning ... I discovered your brooch hidden inside her coat."

Mrs. Hillman's eyes widened. "What?" She sounded aghast. "What are you saying? That Mrs. Whitlock stole my iris brooch?"

"I'm afraid so." The doctor gave her a grim nod.

"And you're certain it was *my* brooch you found?"

"Yes, ma'am." Selena had retrieved the brooch from her room and withdrew it now from her skirt pocket.

Mrs. Hillman took the brooch and held it to her chest. "Oh, thank goodness! I'm so glad to have it back." Then her face crumpled. "But this is too awful. How could Opal have done such a thing? She kept insisting that I had misplaced it."

Colonel Blackwood shook his head. "The woman had her eye on that brooch from the minute she first saw it. And she was forever commenting about jewels and such that summer at the hotel."

"Given that Mrs. Whitlock was so fond of jewelry," Dr. Scott stated calmly, "and that she apparently wasn't shy about stealing something she wanted, we can't help wondering if she has done it before. In short, we believe it may have been Mrs. Whitlock, and not Clive Webster, who stole the guests' jewelry at the hotel."

Mrs. Hillman's hand went to her mouth. "Do you really think so? Oh! If it's true, my heart breaks for that poor, innocent boy."

"So does mine." Selena had never met the young man in question, but the unfairness of it all deeply rankled.

"Which brings us to the real point of this discussion—and the most delicate part." Dr. Scott raised his hands, palms upward. "You mentioned, Mrs. Hillman, that Clive Webster was very close to his brother and sister. If they believed Mr. Webster was unfairly convicted, we think it possible that after he died in prison, either Joe or Maisie Webster, or both of them, decided to seek revenge for their brother's death."

"'Revenge'?" repeated the colonel, scratching his head.

"They may have decided to come after the people responsible for Mr. Webster's conviction," Selena explained, "and make them pay with their lives."

Mrs. Hillman tilted her head to one side. "What people responsible?"

"The ones who had reported him to the police," Dr. Scott answered. "It would explain why three of you have died in such quick succession—first Mrs. Goodwin, and now Mr. Clarke and Mrs. Whitlock."

"Don't be absurd. Those were accidents," Mrs. Hillman insisted.

"Perhaps," Dr. Scott replied. "Or perhaps they were made to *look* like accidents."

The colonel's eyes widened. "Dear lord. I spoke to the police about Clive Webster. They asked about my missing diamond stickpin."

"We know," Selena put in. "What did you tell the police, Colonel? Did you believe the boy was culpable?"

"Yes, and I told them so," the colonel admitted.

"What about you, Mrs. Hillman?" Dr. Scott asked. "You said you spoke in Clive Webster's defense?"

"I did." Mrs. Hillman's eyes narrowed. "But what are you all on about? I don't understand."

"I think I do." Colonel Blackwood nodded slowly. "You think Clarke didn't fall down those stairs. You think he might have been pushed—by Joe or Maisie Webster, as an act of revenge. And you think one of them might have poisoned Mrs. Goodwin and Mrs. Whitlock with lethal doses of laudanum."

"What? That's ridiculous!" cried Mrs. Hillman. "And impossible. Maisie and Joe Webster aren't even here."

"How can we be sure of that, ma'am?" Dr. Scott gave her an earnest glance. "Do you know what either of them looks like?"

Mrs. Hillman went quiet for a moment. "Well, no, I suppose not," she replied falteringly. "But they *can't* be here," she said again. "I know every single person at Darkmoor Park."

"Do you?" Selena countered quietly. "You never met Miss Goodwin, Mr. Davis, nor Miss Thompson until they arrived here. And we have two new servants, Sam and Gladys."

Mrs. Hillman listened in stunned silence as Selena went on to explain their suspicions about the five people in question. Dr. Scott threw in a few comments of his own. When they had finished speaking, the colonel appeared to be deep in thought, but Mrs. Hillman's face was tarnished by a deep frown.

"I don't believe a word of that." The older woman gave a great sniff. "I understand that a woman I thought was my dear friend has stolen from me, and perhaps, *perhaps*, she was the thief at the Worthing Seaside Hotel—but you have no proof of that whatsoever. And as for this business about Mr. Webster's brother and sister coming for revenge, I think you two are quite mad."

Colonel Blackwood was staring at the carpet with a worried frown. "I, on the other hand, can see the point that Dr. Scott and Miss Taylor have made. There *are* three people at this house party whom none of us has ever met. And how much do you know about those two new servants, ma'am?"

"I have no doubts that the Misses Goodwin and Thompson, and the enchanting Mr. Davis, are exactly who they say they are," Mrs. Hillman declared. "And Mrs. Middleton and Wells assured me, before hiring them, that Gladys and Sam are the salt of the earth. They couldn't possibly be here posing as someone else." She wagged a finger at Selena. "I know where this is coming from, my dear. It's that mother of yours! She put ideas into your head, and the heads of your sisters. It's put you on the lookout for danger, deceit, and duplicity. I know what Diana went through at Pendowar Hall, and what you and Athena had to deal with two years ago at Thorndale Manor—and with that horrible fire! But I assure you, nothing of the kind is going on here today at Darkmoor Park."

"I don't know," the colonel persisted. "It does seem fishy that three of us who were at the hotel that summer have died in circumstances that can be explained away as accidents. Not to mention that two of them died in the *exact same way*. Killers often repeat their actions." He raised his gaze, worry haunting his eyes. "If this is all true, do you think the villain—or villains—are finished?"

"They may not be, Colonel," the doctor said quietly.

"That's why we wanted to warn you," Selena added. "You might be next on their list."

"Oh, piffle!" Mrs. Hillman flapped a hand with disdain. "Please desist with all these morbid suspicions about revenge and murder. I repeat—you are all three out of your minds."

"Even if you don't agree with us, Mrs. Hillman," Dr. Scott cautioned, "it would be prudent for Colonel Blackwood to lock his bedroom door at night."

Selena turned to the doctor. "That isn't possible, I'm afraid. None of the bedchambers at Darkmoor Park have locks on their doors."

Dr. Scott's jaw visibly tightened. "Don't they? I didn't notice. That's too bad."

"I suppose no one worried about madmen entering their chambers when those knobs were installed in the seventeenth century." Mrs. Hillman rolled her eyes heavenward.

"What do you plan to do about this?" Colonel Blackwood asked Selena and Dr. Scott. "We're snowed in. And even if we weren't, it's not as though we could go to the constable. We have no real case. At present, this is all speculation."

"True." Dr. Scott glanced at Selena, who nodded in silent encouragement. "We intend to discreetly question the people we mentioned, to find out about their backgrounds and such. If one of them is here under an alias, perhaps they will let something slip."

"An excellent plan," the colonel replied. "I'd offer to help, but if I'm on their list, that doesn't seem prudent."

Dr. Scott nodded. "Leave this to Miss Taylor and me. And," he advised, "I urge you to be alert and vigilant at all times."

"Duly noted." Colonel Blackwood sat up straighter and puffed out his broad chest. "But don't worry. I spent thirty years in the Royal Army. I can take care of myself. No one is going to sneak up on me unannounced."

"I pray you're right," Selena said as worry coursed through her veins. "But do be careful. And please keep this between ourselves. We don't want anyone to get wind that we suspect them."

Mrs. Hillman shook her head. "Believe me, I will say nothing to anyone. This Christmas party has been marred enough by two tragic and quite *accidental* deaths." She stood with a scowl. "We will have to finish our game at another time, Colonel. All of this has given me a nasty headache."

As Dr. Scott opened his mouth to speak, she cut him off by adding, "Don't offer me something for the pain, Doctor. After what you've just insinuated, I may never take another drop of medicine again."

"I FEEL BAD that we gave Mrs. Hillman a headache," Selena said moments later, when she and Dr. Scott had been left alone in the drawing room. "That's why I'm always afraid to tell her any-thing."

"I'm sorry about that, too." Dr. Scott leaned forward in his chair. "But I'm glad to see that Colonel Blackwood, at least, took our advice to heart."

A thought occurred to Selena, and she sighed. "This was the first time I've had a quiet moment with Mrs. Hillman in days. I meant to ask her if there are any dragon motifs at Darkmoor Park."

"She probably wouldn't have been in the mood for such a weird question, anyway," Dr. Scott said. "Considering that she thinks us both mad."

"Good point."

"Next time."

"Next time," she agreed.

Now that it was just the two of them, Selena was suddenly

aware of how close she and the doctor were sitting to each other. His eyes sought hers, and his direct look sent sparks cascading through her. She took a deep breath, commanding herself to focus. There were dire matters at hand. She and Dr. Scott were partners in two investigations—a treasure hunt and a murder inquiry. There was no time nor was this the place for romance, and in any case … there was no future in it for either of them.

"I have a thought as to how we might proceed," she offered quickly. "I hate to bother the servants on their day off. But the library is next door."

He bobbed his head. "Let's see if any members of our party are in there."

Moments later, they entered the library to find Miss Thompson within. Selena's pulse rattled. How fortuitous—here was one of the very people they were seeking. Seemingly unaware of their presence, Miss Thompson was pulling out books a few at a time and barely glancing at them before replacing them.

Dr. Scott cleared his throat. "Good afternoon."

Miss Thompson jumped with a sharp gasp. She shoved the books in her hands back onto the shelf and whirled around. "Dr. Scott. Miss Taylor! How are you?"

"We are well, and here seeking a book to read," Dr. Scott remarked.

"So am I." Miss Thompson gave them a brief smile. "After the events of the past few days, I'm in the mood for something light to read. Perhaps a novel? Can you recommend something?"

Selena's mind buzzed. Had Miss Thompson really been seeking a book? Or had they caught her snooping? Whether or not the young woman was Maisie Webster, might she be interested in the hidden money—and checking to see if it had been stashed behind the books on the shelves? "You can never go wrong with Miss Austen," Selena told her brightly. "Have you read any of her works?"

"Only *Pride and Prejudice*, which I greatly enjoyed." Miss Thompson clasped her hands. "I have longed to read another."

"I recommend *Persuasion*," Selena offered. "It's about a second chance at love. And being shorter than many of Miss Austen's novels, you will hopefully have time to finish it during your stay at Darkmoor Park."

"That sounds lovely," Miss Thompson replied. "Where would I find it?"

"I'll show you." Selena headed towards a bookcase across the room, with Dr. Scott and Miss Thompson following. She considered her next words, seeking a way to direct the conversation to Miss Thompson's background. "Have you always been a great reader, Miss Thompson?"

"Not as much as I would have liked." Miss Thompson gave a sigh. "My father frowned on novel-reading."

"Where did you grow up?" Dr. Scott asked.

"In Hampshire," Miss Thompson responded.

Selena took that in, intrigued. Hampshire was next door to West Sussex, where the Worthing Seaside Hotel was situated. "I recall you mentioning the other day that you were writing a letter to your brother. What does he do?"

"He ..." Miss Thompson seemed to be choosing her next words carefully. "He runs a dry goods shop."

Is that true? Selena wondered. Why had Miss Thompson hesitated, unless she was hiding something? *But then, I always sense deceit everywhere.* They had reached the fiction section.

"What about that book?" Miss Thompson said quickly. "*Persuasion*, I think you said?"

"Yes. Miss Austen's books are on the top shelf with the As. We'll need the ladder."

"Allow me." Dr. Scott began rolling the library ladder into position.

Selena contemplated her next line of questioning. If Miss Thompson was Maisie Webster, she must have carefully plotted her revenge. "You said you were a chambermaid and then a governess before you took a position with Mrs. Whitlock," Selena remarked in her most casual tone. "How did that transition come about?"

Miss Thompson glanced aside and picked at her fingers. "I ... required a change. About four months ago, I was at the post office when I happened to overhear Mrs. Whitlock saying that she needed a new lady's companion. I'd never met the woman, but I ... I drew up my courage and said I would like to apply. She interviewed me twice at her house before she offered me the job."

A scenario, Selena thought, *that fits perfectly if this young woman is Maisie Webster.* "I'm so sorry about what happened to that unfortunate lady," she remarked softly.

"She was not an easy woman to work for, but I'm sorry, too, that she is gone, and in such an awful way." Miss Thompson seemed to be avoiding Selena's gaze.

Selena wondered what the young woman was nervous about. "Will you seek a new, similar position, or go back to being a governess?"

"To be honest, I don't know what's next for me."

Dr. Scott descended the ladder, carrying two gilded, brown-leather volumes. "When you learned about this Christmas party at Darkmoor Park, it must have seemed like a nice thing to look forward to."

"It did," Miss Thompson said ruefully. "Although Mrs. Whitlock wasn't sure she wanted to attend."

"Oh?" Selena was surprised by that.

"Mrs. Whitlock hated traveling. It was too far to go, she said, and the weather was sure to be horrid. But it sounded like such fun to me. Had I known what was in store, of course, I should never have encouraged her to come."

With a grim look, Dr. Scott handed Miss Thompson the two-volume set. "Indeed."

Miss Thompson accepted the books with a sigh. "I look forward to reading this. Thank you both. Good afternoon."

"What do you think?" Selena quietly asked Dr. Scott, after Miss Thompson had quit the library.

"She hesitated when you asked about her brother," he said

under his breath. "And it was interesting to hear how she came to work for Mrs. Whitlock."

"Many women find such positions by placing advertisements in the newspaper. But Maisie Webster, no doubt, would have sought a position directly with Mrs. Whitlock—exactly as she said."

"If she's Maisie, she put up with Mrs. Whitlock's abysmal treatment for months, waiting for this house party—the ideal time and place to exact her revenge."

"She seemed strangely nervous. What was she up to when we entered the room?"

"We may have just startled her," he pointed out.

"She was searching for something."

"A book."

"Or the money?" Selena wondered. "Even if she's here for revenge, finding that money would be an unexpected bonus."

They exchanged a glance. In unison, they dashed to the shelves that Miss Thompson had been perusing when they entered and surveyed the titles. They were all books related to science, nature, and landscaping.

"Hardly light reading," the doctor pointed out.

"It might be, though, for her," Selena noted. "She did say she dreamt of opening a flower shop someday."

"Perhaps, after seeing these, she changed her mind and asked for a novel." He paused. "On the other hand, if she *is* Maisie, everything she said could have been a lie."

Selena gasped. "Could Miss Thompson have written the threatening notes? And deliberately disguised her handwriting?"

He nodded slowly. "It's possible. She would have been familiar with her employer's handwriting. She may have deliberately made it look like the notes were from Mrs. Whitlock."

"If so, it's a good thing that she doesn't know about Mr. Clarke's last words." Selena pursed her lips, thinking. "When Mr. Clarke said, '*Under the dragon,*' might he have been referring to a book about a dragon?"

Dr. Scott tilted his head. "There are a number of books from antiquity and the Middle Ages that feature a dragon, but offhand, I can't think of a single book with *dragon* in the title. And somehow, I can't see Clarke giving you such a sophisticated clue."

Selena's brow furrowed. Oddly, he had dropped the inclusion of 'Mister' when referring to Mr. Clarke—almost as if they'd been previously acquainted. "How do you know what kind of clue he would have given? You'd never met Mr. Clarke until after he'd died."

The doctor paused. "True. I could be wrong. But after hearing so many descriptions of Mr. Clarke, I almost feel as if I've grown to know the man."

That made sense. "We *have* been thinking and talking non-stop about Mr. Clarke for the past few days," she acknowledged.

"I think it more likely that his clue was about an object," Dr. Scott added, "something that is blatantly recognizable as a dragon."

"No doubt you're right. So, we're probably looking for a picture or a statue of a dragon."

They searched the library but didn't notice anything remotely dragon-like.

As they prepared to leave, Dr. Scott sighed. "We've checked all the rooms that Mr. Clarke was seen entering on his last afternoon. But in truth, he could have gone anywhere, inside or out."

Selena shared his frustration. "Let's wait until I get a chance to speak to Mrs. Hillman before we search further."

"Good, because I'm starving. Didn't she say there'd be cold food available all day?"

"She did. And after dinner, let's see if we can find Miss Goodwin and Mr. Davis."

Who may, Selena thought as they left the room, *not be a betrothed couple at all, but rather, a sister and brother: Maisie and Joe Webster.*

CHAPTER EIGHTEEN

AFTER AN EARLY dinner with the colonel in the dining room, Selena and Dr. Scott excused themselves and found Miss Goodwin and Mr. Davis in the billiard room.

They watched from the sidelines as the pair finished off a lively game, challenging and critiquing each other's every shot. Miss Goodwin was equally as skilled a player as her companion, and when she sunk her last ball and gave a victory shout, Mr. Davis bowed in smiling defeat.

"You get better every time we play," the young man admitted.

"But you put up a good fight," Miss Goodwin teased.

Selena and the doctor applauded.

"The table is all yours." Mr. Davis gave Selena and Dr. Scott a nod.

"We aren't here to play." Dr. Scott crossed to where the couple stood by the table.

"We were hoping to have a chat with you," Selena put in, joining them. "We haven't had a moment with just the two of you since the day this house party started. I should so like a chance to get to know you better."

Miss Goodwin darted a glance at Mr. Davis. "Actually, I'm rather tired. I was thinking of retiring."

"So was I," Mr. Davis admitted.

"It's far too early to go to bed." Dr. Scott gave them a warm smile.

"And we wouldn't want to waste that good fire." Selena gestured towards the four comfortable-looking chairs arranged before the marble fireplace, where a good-sized log gave off a splendid glow.

Miss Goodwin averted her eyes as if uncertain and then said, "Well, I suppose we could stay for a minute."

Mr. Davis frowned, but Miss Goodwin was already moving to seating area, where Dr. Scott and Selena sat down across from the pair.

"It has been *such* a strange day," Miss Goodwin remarked with a sigh.

Selena nodded. "It has."

"Such an awful event this morning." Mr. Davis's posture looked tense and rigid.

"And then being told that we were all on our own." Miss Goodwin idly straightened the skirts of her black gown. "We hardly knew what to do with ourselves."

"I hope you found some pleasant occupation?" Selena asked.

"We napped after breakfast," Mr. Davis responded.

"And this afternoon we found some books in the library," Miss Goodwin added.

Selena wondered if that was true. The pair hadn't been in the library when she and the doctor had been there. "It was a pleasure watching you both play billiards."

"Where did you two learn to play such a good game?" Dr. Scott asked.

"We have a billiards table at the hotel," Miss Goodwin replied smoothly. "I've been playing since I was a child."

"What about you, Mr. Davis?" the doctor persisted. "Not, I suppose, at the great house where you served as a footman?"

Mr. Davis froze. His face turned red. "I beg your pardon?"

Selena thought it was an ingenious question on the doctor's part—for if Mr. Davis *was* Joe Webster, he would have worked in just such a position.

"I have *never* been a footman, nor a servant in any capacity." Mr. Davis's voice rang with indignation.

Doth the gentleman protest too much? Selena wondered.

Dr. Scott raised a hand. "Forgive me. I thought someone mentioned that you had."

Mr. Davis straightened his tie, although it wasn't the least bit askew. "I work *in a bank*," he said emphatically. "And I learned to play billiards at home and at the pub."

"Graham is just a bank clerk now, but he is on his way up," Miss Goodwin put in. "I'm sure it will be no time before he is the manager of the place, just like his father was. Isn't that right, *dear?*"

Mr. Davis stirred uneasily in his seat. "Yes, *dear.*"

Was it Selena's imagination, or had they both placed unnecessary emphasis on the word *dear?* And why, Selena wondered, did the man look so uncomfortable? "Your father is also in the banking profession?" she asked.

"Yes, but he's no longer in England," Mr. Davis said quickly.

"His family had a lovely house in Haverstock Hill," Miss Goodwin explained. "But Graham's father sold it several years ago when his parents moved to India."

Selena had the strangest sense that the pair was speaking from a script they had memorized. Or was she just thinking too hard? "India? How exciting. Do they like living there?"

"I've heard that the climate in India can be difficult for a woman raised in England," Dr. Scott remarked, his gaze focused on Mr. Davis.

The young man cleared his throat. "My mother is a hardy woman. I miss my parents, but they are apparently content and have no plans to return to England." Mr. Davis offered nothing more. A silence fell.

Dr. Scott turned to Miss Goodwin. "I'm fascinated to hear that you grew up at the Worthing Seaside Hotel, Miss Goodwin. Did you enjoy living there as a child?"

"Yes. It is a lovely house."

"It must have been nice living by the sea," Selena remarked.

Miss Goodwin gave a small sigh. "I didn't get to enjoy it as much as I would have liked. I was so busy with my duties, making the beds and ..." She stopped herself.

"'Making the beds'?" Selena looked at her. "Isn't that a job reserved for the chambermaid?"

Miss Goodwin's face became suffused with color. "It's embarrassing to think of it now, but for many years, after my father passed away, my mother couldn't afford to keep more than one chambermaid. There was so much work to do, Mother made me help out whenever I could, before and after school."

"I'm sure Nancy hasn't made a bed in many a year," Mr. Davis maintained with a tight smile.

"Indeed, you are a young lady now." Selena fluttered a hand. "And the proprietor of the hotel."

"Precisely," Mr. Davis affirmed. "Running a hotel is a demanding and all-consuming position."

"I imagine it must be expensive, too," Dr. Scott remarked.

"It certainly is!" Mr. Davis shot back. "In addition to all the daily expenses, there's always something in an old house that needs to be fixed or replaced."

Miss Goodwin nodded. "They're saying we need all new windows now and have to replace the roof as well! How we're going to afford that, I have no idea."

Selena filed that information away in her brain. "How did you two meet?"

The pair went quiet. After exchanging a glance, Miss Goodwin said brightly, "Graham was a guest at the hotel last summer. I didn't even notice him the first week he was there. But *he* noticed *me*."

Mr. Davis nodded. "I couldn't take my eyes off her."

Beaming, Miss Goodwin added, "He introduced himself one morning and told me his life story, about his house in Haverstock Hill and graduating from Oxford and his parents moving to India.

He was so sweet and attentive, and he brought me flowers. After that … I suppose you could say *I* was smitten."

Mr. Davis stared down at his hands. Once again, Selena had the sense that something was *off* here, but she couldn't put her finger on it. "I don't wonder that Mr. Davis claimed your heart," she said. "He is a very charming man."

Dr. Scott crossed one leg over the other and said off-handedly, "All this talk about the hotel—it has made me think of that sad business about Clive Webster, poor fellow. I believe you said you knew him, Miss Goodwin?"

Once again, Miss Goodwin's cheeks turned rosy. "I—" she began.

"All that happened when Nancy was away from home," Mr. Davis interjected.

"It's all right, Graham, I can answer." Miss Goodwin took a breath. "To be honest, I *did* know Clive. He and … and his sister started working at the hotel when I was twelve years old."

Selena leaned forward in her chair. "What was the sister's name again?"

Miss Goodwin pulled her lip between her teeth. "Maisie."

"What was Maisie like?" the doctor asked.

Miss Goodwin's eyes grew distant, as if she were wrapped in a memory—or was she carefully choosing her words? "A good girl," she finally said.

A good girl. What a strange choice of words. Selena adopted an encouraging tone. "What do you remember about Mr. Webster?"

"Clive?" Sudden tears pooled in Miss Goodwin's eyes.

"See here, why are you asking her all these questions?" Mr. Davis's face contorted in a frown. "Nancy, you don't have to answer."

"I don't mind." Miss Goodwin retrieved a handkerchief from her handbag and used it to dab the moisture in her eyes. "Clive was so sweet. He always had a grin on his face. When he entered a room, it was like he brought sunshine with him. If someone required assistance, he was always the first person to offer to help.

When he was convicted of theft and imprisoned … it nearly broke my heart. It's impossible that he could have done such a thing." A tear rolled down her cheek.

The young woman's reaction was so strong, it must have meant something. Selena decided to get straight to the point— and force a confession. "You were very fond of Clive Webster," she declared with compassion. "Which is understandable, since he was your brother."

A silence fell. The young lady stared at her. "I beg your pardon? What did you just say?"

"Only that I sympathize with you, Miss Webster. You must miss your brother terribly," Selena said softly.

Miss Goodwin's brows arched skyward. "You're confused. My name is not Webster. I am Miss Nancy Goodwin."

"That may be the name you're going under," Selena persisted, "but admit it. Your name is really Maisie Webster."

Miss Goodwin—Selena supposed she must think of her as such, until she was certain—let out a disbelieving huff, then shook her head, blinking rapidly. "What are you talking about?"

"Why else were you so distraught when you spoke of Clive Webster, unless he was your brother?" Selena charged.

Mr. Davis stood up abruptly. "This conversation has gone on long enough."

"It has, indeed." Miss Goodwin also rose. "If you'll excuse us. Graham, will you see me to my room?"

"Of course." Mr. Davis gave Selena and Dr. Scott a dark glare.

The pair started out of the room, when Miss Goodwin stopped and turned back to face Selena and the doctor. "If you must know, the reason I get distraught about Clive is because he was the first boy for whom I had an infatuation. I was very young, but I fancied myself terribly in love with him. And when he died, it pained me deeply." She turned and hurried from the room, with Mr. Davis at her side.

Selena and Dr. Scott sat in silence for a long moment as Selena contemplated all that they had just heard. Selena didn't know what to think. Had Miss Goodwin been sincere? Or was that merely a clever lie?

"Did we just interview Miss Goodwin and Mr. Davis?" she asked under her breath. "Or Maisie and Joe Webster?"

"I wish I knew," Dr. Scott responded, with a contemplative frown.

THE GRANDFATHER CLOCK in the hall rang out the hour of two A.M. Selena tossed and turned in her bed, going over all that had transpired the previous day.

It had been such an exhausting cavalcade of events, from Mrs. Whitlock's untimely death to the many tense conversations that she and Dr. Scott had had amongst themselves and with others.

Were they right in their assumptions? Had Mrs. Whitlock indeed been the thief at the Worthing Seaside Hotel that summer four years ago? Even if Mrs. Whitlock hadn't been to blame for those thefts, they had heard such good reports about Clive Webster—that he had been a kind, sweet young man who would never have stolen anything. Had Maisie and Joe Webster indeed come to Darkmoor Park seeking revenge for their brother's unjust imprisonment and death? *If so, who are they?*

Selena and Dr. Scott had gone over the matter in detail before retiring for the night. There were reasons to believe that any of the suspects they had so far interviewed—Miss Thompson, Miss Goodwin, and Mr. Davis—could be Maisie or Joe Webster in disguise. Miss Thompson had admittedly once served as a chambermaid. She had gone out of her way to seek a position with Mrs. Whitlock. She had persuaded the older woman to come to Darkmoor Park. And she had seemed nervous about something.

Miss Goodwin had claimed that, while growing up at the hotel, she had been obliged to make beds and undertake other chambermaids' duties to help. Was that true? Or had she in fact *worked there* as Maisie Wester? On the other hand, she'd said she had learned to play billiards at the hotel—which seemed unlikely if she had worked there as a servant. Most interesting was Miss Goodwin's longsuffering reaction when she had spoken about Clive Webster. She had shed tears for him—and had called him, familiarly, by his Christian name. Had he been her first young love? *Or her brother?*

As for Mr. Davis, he had seemed fidgety and uncomfortable throughout the entire conversation. Selena felt certain that he'd been hiding something. Had he really grown up in an affluent neighborhood in London, the son of a banker who had moved to India? Why had Mr. Davis blushed as red as a beet when Dr. Scott had asked him if he had once been a footman? Could he be Joe Webster? If so, was Miss Goodwin his sister, Maisie, and a part of his plot? Or was she merely an unwitting companion?

All these scenarios seemed plausible. But if one of them were true, how were Selena and Dr. Scott to prove it?

Thinking about Dr. Scott brought all these other contemplations to a standstill. She recalled a moment, during their conversation in the schoolroom, when he had glanced her way with a spark in his blue eyes, as if to share his excitement about the missions they had embarked upon. Solving these mysteries together was certainly one of the most thrilling things that had ever happened to Selena.

One of the most being the operative phrase. For the most thrilling thing of all had been the kiss they had shared. Selena still could not believe how brazen she had been, to shut herself in a linen closet with Dr. Scott! What had she been thinking?

She *hadn't been* thinking, that was the problem. Selena knew they lived and worked in different parts of the country and could never be together, but she couldn't get that kiss out of her mind. She went back to that delectable interval, allowing herself to revel in the memory, as she drifted off to sleep in a happy haze.

She was in the linen closet again, in Dr. Scott's arms. His

breath was sweet and warm against her cheek. And then his lips followed where his breath had been. A soft, delicious series of pecks that ran up and down her face and then captured her mouth in a wondrous, heart-stopping kiss. Oh, if only the kiss could go on forever …

A gentle clicking sound came from somewhere in the distance. Selena tried to ignore it and to concentrate on the joy of kissing Dr. Scott, but it sounded like a doorknob turning. Was someone opening the door to the linen closet? A hint of unease rippled through her. She couldn't be found in here kissing Dr. Scott! But when she opened her eyes, Selena wasn't in the linen closet anymore. She was in her own room, alone in bed.

Selena knew she was still asleep, and this was just a dream. Or was it? The dark chamber was pierced by only a single point of distant light—the glow of embers in the fireplace. A new sound caught her attention. Footsteps creeping across her floor.

Was someone in her room?

The footfalls grew closer. Selena's heart began to pound in fear. A dark shadow of a figure loomed over her now, holding something directly above her face. *A pillow.*

Selena screamed.

CHAPTER NINETEEN

SELENA SWIFTLY ROLLED away from the shadowy invader and, looking up from her bed, screamed again at the top of her lungs. The dark figure above her seemed to freeze—and then it darted away.

She heard pounding footsteps. Her door opening and shutting. Then silence.

Selena closed her eyes and lay trembling in the dark, her mind a fog of confusion. *What just happened?* Was she dreaming or awake?

There came an urgent knock. "Miss Taylor?" It was Miss Thompson's voice.

Selena blinked, now fully conscious. Throwing back the covers, she rose, lit a candle, and opened the door. Moonlight from a hall window cast a muted glow on Miss Thompson's tense form. She stood in her bare feet and nightgown, anxiety written all over her face. "Are you all right?"

Before Selena could reply, Dr. Scott rushed up, also in his nightclothes, his jaw clenched. "Who screamed? Was that you, Miss Taylor?"

"Yes." Selena's legs began to tremble beneath her.

"What happened?" Dr. Scott's voice was marked by puzzlement and concern.

"I heard footsteps and then I thought I saw someone standing over my bed in the dark, holding a pillow over my face. I screamed and they ran off." As she said the words, Selena knew how ridiculous they sounded.

"Dear lord." Dr. Scott's eyes flashed with apprehension.

"Did you see anyone running down the hall?" Miss Thompson asked the doctor.

"Not a soul," he replied.

Selena glanced back at the bed. Her cheeks grew hot. "Never mind. My second pillow hasn't moved. It's still untouched on the opposite side of the bed. I'm sure I dreamed the whole thing."

Dr. Scott opened his mouth as if to speak, but at that moment, three doors opened in the north hall, and Miss Goodwin, Mr. Davis, and Colonel Blackwood emerged, carrying candles.

"I heard a scream." Colonel Blackwood was wide-eyed beneath his nightcap.

"What is happening?" asked Miss Goodwin, her face pale.

"I'm so sorry to have disturbed you all," Selena told the assembled group. "I just had a bad dream. Please go back to bed."

As everyone returned to their rooms, Dr. Scott asked, "Are you sure you're well?"

"Yes. Yes. I'm fine. Again, I'm so sorry."

Selena went back to bed, where she lay awake in the darkness for what seemed like hours, scolding herself for having an overactive imagination. And yet the dream had felt so real, as if someone had actually come into her room.

And had tried to kill her.

SELENA AWAKENED TO a glorious view outside her bedroom windows. At last, after three long days, the storm was over!

Her spirits lifted. The sky was a cloudless, cerulean blue. Sunlight sparkled like diamonds on the endless white expanse beyond. The windowpane felt less cold than it had of late—a sign that a milder day was ahead. But even if that were so, the grounds and roads might remain buried in snow for quite some time, and it could be days before a path was cleared to permit anyone to take a walk.

Selena was thankful though for the sunshine. It would be a cheerful change for everyone, after the gloomy weather of the past few days. *Not to mention the deaths of two of our guests.* Her mind veered to the nightmare she'd had the night before. A wave of doubt swept over her. It *had* been a dream, hadn't it?

Or had someone really broken into her room with the intent to smother her while she slept? The notion filled her with sudden dread.

If so, who might it have been? Had one of the three people Selena and the doctor had questioned the day before been Maisie or Joe Webster, and had they guessed the purpose of those interviews? She had brazenly accused Miss Goodwin of being Maisie. Perhaps she shouldn't have done that. Someone else might be here under an assumed name, though, someone who had overheard those interviews. Although the servants had had the day off yesterday, they hadn't been able to leave the house due to the weather. Could Sam or Gladys be one of Clive Webster's siblings?

A shudder ran through her. Had the intruder intended to silence Selena before she could expose them?

No, no, no. Selena swept these ideas away with a firm swipe of her hand. She was just overthinking the matter. *It was a dream, and nothing more.* So many dreadful things had been happening of late, it was no wonder that she'd had a nightmare. She would think of it no more.

After freshening up and pinning up her hair, Selena opened her wardrobe and studied its contents. Not in a party mood, she chose her cobalt-blue woolen gown, one of her simpler dresses that she often wore while teaching school. She added a dark-blue woolen jacket with a braid trim in the same lighter blue.

She had just left her room when another door opened at the end of the north hall. Mrs. Hillman emerged from her chamber, clad in her silk dressing gown and her ruffled nightcap.

"Selena." Mrs. Hillman beckoned to her.

Selena crossed to her. "What is it, Mrs. Hillman?"

"I thought I heard a scream in the middle of the night. Did I dream it?"

"No. I did scream," Selena admitted ruefully. "But *I'm* the one who was dreaming. I had a frightful nightmare."

"What did you dream about?"

Selena fluttered a hand. "It was silly and not even worth talking about."

Mrs. Hillman made a face. "I had a nightmare, too. I was in the icehouse and Mrs. Whitlock's frozen body rose from the dead. She pointed a finger at me and cried, 'Give me your brooch!'"

"Oh, no! I'm so sorry." Selena shuddered. "How ghastly."

Mrs. Hillman heaved a deep sigh. "This has been a most trying and ghastly week. You were right, you know."

"Right about what?"

"You worried that something unexpected would occur. When you said that, I thought, perhaps the plum pudding might fall off the platter or a candle might set a branch of the Christmas tree on fire—that happened one year, and we put it out in half a second. I never imagined that two of my friends would perish in this very house." Mrs. Hillman scowled. "Fate has a very dark sense of humor."

Selena was tempted to bring up the theory about the Webster siblings' revenge plot again but decided there would be no point. "At least the weather has cleared," she said, hoping to brighten Mrs. Hillman's mood.

"Yes, I'm so relieved. I hope that will bring a bit of cheer to the proceedings and that nothing else will go wrong." Mrs. Hillman turned to go back into her room.

Selena remembered that she'd been hoping for a moment alone with her for days. "Wait—Mrs. Hillman. May I have a word?"

"Certainly. I was just going to drink my morning tea."

Selena followed Mrs. Hillman into her chamber, a comfortable room with beautiful carved mahogany furniture and a blue-and-gold coverlet on the four-poster bed. The older woman took a seat at her dressing table, where a tray held a bone china tea service. "I'm sorry there's only one cup," Mrs. Hillman said as she poured herself a cup of tea.

"It's no problem. I'll have mine downstairs as usual." Selena settled in a chair nearby.

"Now what's on your mind?" Mrs. Hillman remarked as she blew on her tea to cool it.

Selena hesitated. She still didn't think it prudent to tell Mrs. Hillman about Mr. Clarke's last words for fear of overagitating her or raising her hopes and expectations, lest they were wrong about the hidden money or were never able to find it. She had thought of an unobtrusive way to ask about dragons, though.

"It might seem as though this is coming out of the blue, but it's been on my mind for days." *At least that part is true*, Selena told herself. "I'm contemplating a lesson for my pupils for next semester about the mythology of dragons."

"Dragons?" Mrs. Hillman's brows rose. "What an interesting subject."

"Yes, and I thought it'd be fun to take the girls on a hunting expedition. You know, to visit any place in the house or on the grounds that might feature a dragon motif. Do you know of any?" Selena waited, trying not to look too eager.

Mrs. Hillman pursed her lips. After a moment, she said, "I can think of one place. The folly."

Selena's heart seemed to skip a beat. "'The folly'?" The Darkmoor Park folly was a little Greek temple on the far side of the grounds.

"I believe it was built in the eighteenth century by one of Roger's more whimsical ancestors. A completely useless structure but quaint nonetheless. In former years, I used it occasionally as a summerhouse—for picnics and such. There are statues in the niches and if I recall correctly, one of them might be a dragon."

Excitement rose in Selena's breast. She had only visited the folly a couple of times, for it was situated at least a third of a mile away from the house, in a direction she rarely ventured. She had forgotten that the interior was outfitted with niches and statues. "That sounds perfect. I'd love to visit the folly and check it out."

"That will be impossible for a while, I'm afraid." Mrs. Hillman nodded towards the scene outside her window, where although the skies were clear, the snow looked to be a good fifteen inches deep.

Selena frowned. Somehow, she needed to visit the folly—and she didn't want to wait for the snow to melt away. She considered asking Mrs. Hillman to have the groom rig up a sleigh but thought better of it. It would be dangerous for a horse to walk out in such deep snow. To hike such a long distance on foot by post-holing was too difficult to even contemplate.

A thought suddenly struck her. "Mrs. Hillman, did I once spy a couple of pairs of snowshoes in a closet in the mudroom?"

"Is that where those old things are?" A smile curved Mrs. Hillman's lips and her eyes grew misty. "When Roger and I first married, we spent a winter holiday in Scotland, and our guide took us on an adventuresome hike. Roger enjoyed it so much, he insisted on keeping the snowshoes, promising that we would return there someday. We never did, but oh, what a lovely time we had."

Selena smiled in return. "Mrs. Hillman. Would you mind if I borrowed them?"

"HOW WONDERFUL IT is to be outside." Selena inhaled the crisp, fresh air, an invigorating tonic that seemed to make every cell in her body feel more alive. "It seems like weeks since we've been out of doors instead of days."

"Yes, and these are stunning grounds." Dr. Scott's face lit up as he took in the vista before them.

The Darkmoor Park grounds were covered in a deep, white blanket as far as the eye could see. The sun beamed in a cloudless, azure sky, glistening on the snow-frosted branches of the trees and hedgerows on either side of them. It was so much milder today than it had been yesterday, the icicles on the trees were already dripping. Beyond the long, open expanse of clean, white snow, the folly, a fanciful white building that resembled a small Grecian temple, stood on a distant rise.

When Selena had quietly informed the doctor that there was apparently a dragon statue inside the folly, they had both been anxious to explore it without delay. Mr. Clarke might have hidden the money there. He'd been seen carrying his overcoat in the vicinity of the rear door to the house—and there had been no snow on the grounds at the time.

Snowshoes were not commonly used in England and although neither had ever tried them, Dr. Scott had been willing to give it a go. After a hasty breakfast, they had informed the others that they were going to attempt a snowshoe trek across the grounds to the folly—a professional quest, regarding a lesson plan for Selena's upcoming school term.

They had put on coats, hats, scarves, and gloves, had found and donned the snowshoes, and had begun the journey in high spirits, each carrying a handmade wooden pole with a wicker-basket-shaped device on the end, that Mrs. Hillman had explained would help them keep their balance.

When they'd first set out, Dr. Scott had brought up Selena's nightmare and, with a concerned look, had asked, "Are you certain it was just dream?"

"Absolutely certain," Selena had replied, ignoring the wave of doubt that still rippled through her. "It was just my imagination running away with me—while I lay fast asleep. Mrs. Hillman had a nightmare, too." She had told the doctor about the older woman's dream, and they had shared an uneasy laugh.

After that, both had agreed to leave all worrisome topics behind them—no more talk about recent deaths, poisoned tea, bad dreams, the Webster siblings, or threatening notes. Their aim was twofold: to enjoy the day and to search for the money Jack Clarke had hidden. Everything else could wait.

"I love every season at Darkmoor Park," Selena enthused. "But sometimes I think winter is my favorite because everything looks so magical when it's draped in snow."

Dr. Scott grinned. His cheeks, burnished a bright pink from the wintry air, made a lively contrast to the dark blue of his eyes. Since the day they'd met, he had generally been serious or had seemed preoccupied. This was one of the few times that she had seen him truly smile. The obvious delight he was taking in their surroundings made him seem younger, almost boyish—and *oh-so-handsome.*

"I take it that was an abbey?" Dr. Scott gestured to the standing walls of the ancient stone ruin nearby.

"Yes, it dates back to the twelfth century. During Henry VIII's reign, the nobleman who'd acquired the property used stone from the abbey to build the mansion, and later generations continued to mine the building to make improvements to the house until there was nothing left but these poor ruins."

"What a shame. I'm sure it was a stunning building." He glanced around. "I don't see a cemetery."

"There isn't one. The graves of the people who've lived here for centuries are all buried in catacombs beneath the ruined abbey."

"Fascinating." He took a deep breath as they marched along. "To be here and see all this is such a treat. I haven't had much of an opportunity to enjoy the country in winter. I've lived almost my entire life in London."

"Oh? When did you move to Bath?"

An odd look came into his eyes, and he said quickly, "A few months ago. There is a great need for doctors in Bath."

He said nothing more, but Selena inexplicably had the strangest sense that he didn't live in Bath at all—that for some reason, he only wanted her to think he did. But that was absurd. Why should she care where he was from?

"Snowshoeing is harder work than I'd expected," he declared, interrupting her thoughts.

Selena nodded in agreement. The hardwood frames, shaped like a teardrop and much wider than a normal shoe, were filled in with latticework and attached to their boots with leather straps. Even though the snowshoe's displacement of their body's weight made it possible to walk atop the deep drifts of snow without sinking in, every step still took great effort. Even with the assistance of the pole, Selena had to walk carefully and deliberately to avoid tripping herself. After only fifteen minutes of trekking, they were both huffing and puffing.

"When I was a boy, I was thrilled by William Parry's account of his attempt to reach the North Pole," Dr. Scott went on. "I never imagined that I would be attempting something equally challenging on the grounds of an English estate."

She laughed. "How did you have access to such interesting reading material while growing up in an orphanage?"

"I was fortunate. From a young age, I caught the eye of one of the patrons of the foundling home—a gentleman who saw promise in me. He singled me out and brought me interesting books to read. I have no idea why. Perhaps it was because, when I happened to meet Mr. Brown one day—I think I might have been seven or eight years old—he asked me what future I saw for myself, and I told him that I wanted to become a doctor."

"You knew at such an early age?"

"I did."

Selena was impressed. "How?"

He glanced at her. "It is not a happy story. And we agreed to speak of nothing troublesome today."

She chewed on her lip. "We did. But we were referring only to recent events. Stories from our past do not count. I am interested in learning more about you, Dr. Scott," she admitted, hoping she wasn't being too nosy or forward. "That is, if you're willing to share it?"

"I am," he said. "If you don't mind hearing it."

CHAPTER TWENTY

T HE LATE-MORNING SUNSHINE was even brighter now as Selena and Dr. Scott continued their snowshoe trek across the snowy grounds of the estate towards the folly.

"I suppose you have already heard the saddest part," Dr. Scott said as they marched along. "I told you that my parents and brother all died when I was young?"

"Yes. I was so sorry to hear that." Selena had wanted to ask more about it at the time and was glad he was willing to share the story now.

"I had a brother, Cameron, who was a year younger than I." Dr. Scott's voice grew quieter, and his eyes grew distant. "My father—he was a blacksmith—died when I was two years old, leaving our mother with two small boys to raise. She worked as a laundress to provide for us. We lived in a London slum." He stopped to catch his breath, and Selena paused with him. "When I was five years old, Mother and Cameron both died from consumption."

"Oh, no! When you were five?" Selena's heart twisted.

"I tried so hard to care for them, but I was just a child. They wasted away before my eyes."

"How horrible. For them to lose their lives so young, and for you to be a witness to it."

"It *was* horrible." He gestured with his pole. "The worst part was that I felt so helpless. I decided, later, that I must have been spared for a reason. That I had been put on this Earth to learn about health and medicine to prevent people from dying from such awful diseases."

"A noble goal, Dr. Scott. Especially at such a tender age."

"I don't know how noble it was. But it felt like a calling."

"I find it admirable. How many people know what they want to do with their lives when they're a child? I certainly didn't. And how fortunate you were to find a benefactor at the orphanage."

"I was." They moved on again. "Not every boy received much schooling. Most were set up as apprentices to learn trades. One morning, I overheard the director of the orphanage telling Mr. Brown that he intended for me to either train to become a blacksmith like my father or a coffin-maker at a funeral home. Mr. Brown insisted that I would be wasted in such occupations. He offered to pay for my education at a good local school, as well as at Oxford, and provided financial assistance during the years in which I trained and apprenticed at a London teaching hospital."

"What a kind and generous man."

"Indeed. Mr. Brown has since passed away, but he changed my life. I shall be forever grateful to him."

As they forged on across the snow, Selena contemplated all that he had told her. It meant so much to her that Dr. Scott had been willing to share these details about himself. It made her feel closer to him. "Do you enjoy your profession, I hope?"

"Yes. I cannot imagine doing anything else."

"I suppose you must work long hours?"

"I do."

"Are you on call in the middle of the night?"

"I am. But I don't mind the hours. Having the opportunity to alleviate my patients' suffering and to help improve their lives, it is immensely fulfilling." Excitement infused his words and was evident in the brightness of his eyes. "I enjoy the problem-solving aspect of it as well. There is always something new to learn and explore, even in a small private practice."

"It is the same for me," Selena admitted. "As a governess, I was never really off-duty. And as a teacher and now the headmistress of a school, my hours are equally long. And yet it is thrilling to know that I am helping young girls to discover their strengths and potential. And as you say, I learn something new every day."

He nodded his head. "Working so hard, though, I have found, doesn't allow much time for socializing outside of work." He darted her a glance. "Which I suppose is why I've never met … why I have never married." His eyes locked with hers, and his expression seemed to be filled with some deep, unspoken meaning.

Selena's pulse began to drum in her ears. Why did he feel it necessary to explain his unmarried state to her? She hadn't asked him to. Although she had wondered. It did seem to her that a man so caring, accomplished, and good-looking ought to have been married by now.

"The same for me," she said again. "Over the past thirteen years, I have not had many opportunities to meet … unattached gentlemen." She felt her cheeks grow warm at this declaration. "I am fortunate, though," she went on quickly. "Mrs. Hillman and my students are like a second family to me."

"I am fortunate as well. I treasure the friends I do have."

Selena dug her pole into the snow as they trudged on. "Like the ones in Edinburgh."

"Edinburgh?"

"The friends you were going to see for Christmas."

He blinked. "Yes! Yes, indeed. They are my family now that—" He broke off. A shadow seemed to cross his features.

Selena wondered what had driven away his enthusiasm. But before she could process that further, he spoke again.

"We have talked far too much about me." His voice was grim and he appeared to be directing all his attention to the movement of the snowshoes beneath his feet. "I have told you about my childhood. Now I should like to hear about yours."

"My childhood?" Selena considered. "It started off like a dream. My father was a gentleman, and I grew up in a comfortable household, with two wonderful sisters and a brother and parents I cherished. However, like you, I lost my mother when I was young—I was also only five."

"Oh! And how young *she* must have been." His brows drew together as he gave her a sad glance. "What did your mother die from?"

"She had a stroke."

"I'm sorry."

"So am I." Selena was perspiring from exertion, and it was hard work to walk and talk and breathe at the same time. "I wish I had more memories of my mother. I recall sitting on her lap as she read to me. She was a wonderful storyteller. I remember the fragrance of her cologne—gardenia. She once said she felt it her duty to share her life experience with us. I know her favorite sayings because my sister Diana repeated them over and over to us as children." Selena smiled at these remembrances but then let go a long sigh as sadness enveloped her. "I remember the nursery maid telling us to stay quiet and out of the way because Mama was sick in bed, and the apothecary coming and going, and the awful silence in the house when my mother was gone."

"I'm sorry," he said again. "My memories are quite different. We couldn't afford an apothecary or a nursery maid. And my mother never read to me. Not because she didn't know how to read, but because we couldn't afford books, and she didn't have time. But the end result is the same. You and I, unfortunately, grew up without a mother's love. And that is hard for any child to bear."

"It was a tragedy for my entire family. Diana is only two years older than I am, but she took it upon herself to serve as 'mother' in every way she could to my sister Athena and me and our brother, Damon."

"And she was how old? Seven?" His voice rang with incredulity.

Selena nodded as they tramped along. "It was far too much responsibility for such a little girl, but Papa seemed to be lost with

Mama. He was fond of hunting and riding—and accustomed to a woman running the household. Diana, even as a little girl, was willing and efficient, so he allowed it. As for me, I was the baby of the family. I was pampered and indulged. Until age sixteen, that is."

"What happened when you were sixteen?"

"My father lost his fortune in a bad investment." Selena sighed. "He had followed the advice of a charming friend, one who hadn't invested a penny of his own and who vanished when all of my father's money was gone. We were thrown into very difficult financial straits. There was a question as to whether or not we could even keep our house, a modest cottage in the Derbyshire countryside. My brother secured a position as a curate at a poor parish in London. My sisters had to finds posts as governesses. A year later, I entered the same trade."

"You became a governess at age seventeen?" They were getting closer to the folly now and paused again to catch their breath. "Isn't that rather young?"

"A bit, but Athena did it at the same age a year before me and proved to be such a success that her employers' friends took me on to care for their young daughters. Thankfully, I had received a good education at school and Diana had served as a tutor to me and Athena since childhood, so I was ably prepared to teach children the basics."

"Did you enjoy your profession, I hope?" he asked, echoing her own words from earlier.

The sadness of that time returned to Selena in a flash, but she gave her head a shake to dispel it. "A governess is neither a member of the family she serves nor a servant, but somewhere in between, and in many cases, respected by no one. But none of my siblings were at home anymore and I was lonesome without them. I needed a job. I survived in the occupation for nearly ten years and so did my sisters. In fact, I think those years were good for all of us. They made us stronger and more independent. And they instilled in us a love of teaching, which led to Athena and me opening our school for girls."

"An enterprise I applaud. We haven't had a chance to talk much about your school. With all the pupils away on holiday, it's easy to forget that Darkmoor Park is actually the home of such a valuable institution."

Selena was pleased to hear his positive assessment of her life's work. "It is a long-held dream come true. As you said—I cannot imagine my life without it."

They forged on again and after a small silence, he said, "How, may I ask, did you come to meet Mrs. Hillman and to open the school?"

"That is a two-part question." Selena glanced at him. "You and I have both been extraordinarily fortunate to have had a benefactor who changed our lives. In your case, it was Mr. Brown. For me, it started with Diana's husband, Captain William Fallbrook. He acquired Thorndale Manor, a lovely estate less than a mile from here, and put it in Athena's name, expressly to house our school. The estate now belongs to Athena and her husband, Ian Vernon—the property had once been in his family for centuries, so when they married, it felt as though the universe had righted itself. Athena and I ran the school at Thorndale Manor for the first two years. Mrs. Hillman welcomed us to the neighborhood, became a close friend, and then volunteered to be a patron of the school. In time, she requested that we move the school here and we decided it was an excellent idea. Darkmoor Park is equipped to host more students, and the manor house and grounds are such a delightful place for teaching."

"I imagine so." He gave her a smile. "You and Mrs. Hillman seem to be very close. If I were to guess, I would say that she considers you the daughter she never had."

Selena felt her cheeks grow warm, despite the frosty air. "You aren't wrong. In fact ..." She broke off.

"In fact, what?"

Selena hesitated—but they had been so honest and open with each other, it felt natural to tell him the rest. "Mrs. Hillman has no children or natural heirs. To my great honor, she named me as the successor to Darkmoor Park."

Dr. Scott halted mid-step and turned to her, his eyes widening. "The successor? But that's wonderful!"

"I know. It's not something I could have ever anticipated happening to me, and I don't like to speak of it."

"Why not?"

"Because I'm not her blood relative. I worry that it will change people's perception of me. They might see me as underserving."

Dr. Scott shook his head. "No one who knows you would ever think that. We only met a few days ago and yet I understand why Mrs. Hillman chose you as her heir. It's obvious how much you love this place. You're putting it to excellent use and I'm sure she knows it will be in good hands after she's gone."

The fondness and admiration in his gaze were so warm, it made Selena's heart turn over. "Thank you for saying that."

"It's true. Mrs. Hillman is as lucky to have found you as you are to have found her."

"I hope so," she said softly. They had reached the folly now and stopped. "Here we are."

They took in the small building before them. Several wide, snow-covered steps led up to a raised platform that housed the structure, which was fashioned of white stone in the Grecian style. Four fluted Doric columns at the front held up a roof topped by a triangular pediment decorated with scrollwork. Pairs of arched casement windows and decorative pilasters designed to resemble columns flanked a double front door.

"An elegant structure," Dr. Scott pronounced.

"It is." Selena tilted her head. "But at the same time, it's a bit useless, isn't it?"

He studied it. "I don't know. People built these things to catch the eye and enhance the landscape, didn't they? And as a display of wealth?"

"I believe so."

"If that was the intent, it has succeeded. If I owned an estate like Darkmoor Park and had nothing but money, I might build something equally as whimsical."

"Would you? I don't know what the family's ancestors did with the folly. It may have been purely decorative. Mrs. Hillman says she has used it every now and then as a summer house, a place to read and picnic."

"Looks like a good place for it." He rested his gloved hands atop his pole. "She said it has a dragon statue?"

"Yes." Selena chuckled. "This was such a difficult trek, I almost forgot why we came! I don't remember a dragon, but I've only been inside a couple of times. This could be it. The money could be hidden here!"

His eyes glinted. "What are we waiting for?"

They scooped away the soft new snow that covered the steps, clearing a path just wide enough for them to gain access. After helping each other to unstrap their snowshoes, they climbed up to the platform, where Dr. Scott wielded one of the snowshoes like a shovel to laboriously clear a path to the temple's front doors.

The doors wouldn't open.

"Oh, no," Selena cried, struck by the eerie similarity to the events of the morning before at the icehouse.

He noticed her reaction and paused. "I know what you're thinking. Here we are with another stuck doorknob, trying to break in instead of out."

"But we're not breaking in," Selena pointed out. "Mrs. Hillman gave us permission to come. She assured me the folly would be unlocked."

"Maybe it's just frozen shut." Dr. Scott jostled the doorhandle again and then threw his full weight against the door. To their mutual relief, it finally burst open.

They entered the temple, which was about the size of a standard bedroom in the manor house. It was colder inside than out, well-lit by four arched casement windows, and completely empty. Leaves and dirt were scattered across the stone floor. The interior walls, made of the same white stone as the exterior, were outfitted with six niches at about waist height, each of which held a carved stone statue.

As they began to make their way around the room, Selena inhaled with surprise. "Look, the statues are all—"

"—from Greek mythology," Dr. Scott finished with her, his grin reflecting her own delight.

They named the creatures as they moved along. "Cerberus, who guarded the gates of Hades," he proclaimed, pointing to the statue of a three-headed, giant hound.

"The Sphinx, known for its riddles," Selena pointed out as they passed a winged lion with a woman's head.

"A pair of sirens?" he asked, gesturing to a statue of two women with the lower bodies of a bird, who reclined seductively on a rock.

"I think so. They lured sailors to their deaths on rocky shores with their enticing songs."

They discussed the next statues, the winged horse Pegasus and a Centaur. Selena was enchanted to discover yet another connection that she and Dr. Scott shared: a love of mythology.

Selena became aware of something else: the circumstances in which she had placed herself. They were alone inside a remote building, separated from the manor house by such a vast expanse of snow that there was no possibility of anyone coming upon them.

Dr. Scott was standing oh-so-close. The personal details they had discussed during their walk seemed to have built a bridge of intimacy between them. And his proximity was doing strange things to her equilibrium. She wanted, suddenly, more than anything in the world, to reach out and touch him. *To kiss him.* But before she could act on that impulse, he called out in triumph.

"There it is! The dragon!"

Selena followed his gaze to the statue in the last niche, and her breath caught in her throat. "It's Jason, drugging the dragon who's guarding the golden fleece!" A laugh escaped her chest and once again, their gazes collided. She read her own excitement mirrored in his eyes. "We found it!"

"Well. We found *a* dragon." He rubbed a hand across his face. "We don't know if it's *the* dragon."

"What safer place could Mr. Clarke have found to hide that cash than all the way out here in the folly?"

"He said, '*Under the dragon.*' How could anything be hidden under this statue?"

"I guess we'll find out." She ran her hands over the smooth stone base of the statue and the niche beneath it, searching for a gap of some kind. There was none.

Together, they replicated what they had done in the chapel, pressing on the wall and, on their hands and knees, testing the floor for loose stones. "There's nothing here," he said, sighing.

He was right. Dr. Scott rose, took Selena's hand, and helped her to her feet. The touch of his strong hands through the layers of their gloves sent a tingle racing up her arms. "This," she said, "was a long way to come for nothing."

"It wasn't all for nothing." There was a rough edge to his voice.

Selena looked up at him. He stood barely a foot away. His gaze glimmered as it caught hers. Despite the cold air, a wave of heat coursed through her.

"Selena." It was the first time he had called her by her Christian name, and the single word was infused with affection. He hesitated and then added softly, "I was in a dark place when I arrived at Darkmoor Park. I feared I would never have a happy moment again. And then I met you."

Her heart began to thunder in her chest. She wondered what he meant about being in a dark place—but the thought was overridden by the need to touch him. She raised a hand and gently traced the jagged scar on his forehead. "How did you get this?" she whispered.

"I was two years old. I fell in my father's blacksmith shop. It's ugly, I know."

"It's beautiful," she insisted. Every molecule in Selena's body seemed to be aware of his nearness and a deep and burgeoning *want* for him to kiss her again. Could he sense her desire?

Perhaps. His lips parted, but there was hesitancy in his eyes.

She didn't wait for him to make the first move. She stood on her tiptoes and pressed her lips against the scar.

He inhaled sharply. All at once, he tossed off his hat, dropped his gloves to the floor, and took her in his arms as his mouth claimed hers.

This time, the kiss didn't begin slowly or searchingly. He embraced her with a fevered passion, as if it had been pent up inside him for days. Selena had felt the same longing and wanting and matched him kiss for kiss. Their mouths possessed each other with an almost hungry desperation, unleashing a surge of heat throughout her body that threatened to consume her.

Despite the layers of their clothing, his hands roved up and down her back as she pressed herself against him, one hand tangling in his hair. Selena reveled in the scent of him, the familiar blend of his shaving soap and sandalwood cologne, and the taste of him, a pleasing essence that could only be described as *him*. She had never been kissed like this before, by a man who was so obviously thrillingly engaged by the touch of her, who was breathing her in as if she were some intoxicating being, in the exact same way that she was breathing him in.

A hoarse sound filled her ears, and she realized it was a moan of pleasure coming from his throat, mingling with a similar moan of her own. The feel of his tongue as it wrapped around hers blotted out all other thoughts and memories. There was only the here and now and the feeling of being in his arms, alone together in this temple filled with tributes to the gods, far away from the eyes and ears of the world.

All too soon, he was ending the kiss. "Selena." He was breathing fast and raw against her ear, and his voice was gruff. "Selena."

She wanted to say his given name in return, but her mind was spinning, and she could barely remember it. Then it came to her. "Adrian," she murmured breathlessly. "Adrian."

He froze in her arms. Then he took a step back. The color had drained from his face, the fiery expression in his eyes had vanished, and he stared at the floor.

Selena's insides clenched with bewilderment. "What's wrong?"

It was a moment before he answered. He was still avoiding her gaze. "If I could have conjured the perfect woman for me," he said quietly, "it would be you. Just knowing that you exist in the world, it has given me hope."

Her mind reeled with confusion. Had he just called her the perfect woman? "Hope for what?"

"Hope that things might be better in the future. That you and I …" His expression grew deeply troubled. "Even though I know it's impossible."

After that incredible kiss, why did he look so forlorn? "Nothing's impossible," she said breathlessly. "We get to choose our own paths in life."

"Do we?" He heaved a breath that seemed to be filled with bitterness.

Why was he suddenly so dejected? "What did you mean before, about being in a dark place?"

"I was … *It* was …" He swallowed hard. "It's hard to explain. I need some time to …" He gripped her hands in his and stood gazing at her, his features contorted by what looked like affection mingled with burning frustration. "Selena. Everything we're hunting for together—Mr. Clarke's hidden money, the truth about what happened to him and to Mrs. Whitlock—they're vitally important. I want to return that money to the hospital. I want to know who sent those threatening notes and why. And if one or both of the Websters is here, I want to prove it and turn them in. The weather has changed and I'm guessing that in a few days, if there is a villain in our midst, they'll be able to leave. We need to solve these riddles as quickly as possible." He raised one hand and cupped her cheek tenderly. "Can you trust me while we figure all this out? Together?"

The expression in his blue eyes was so appealing that Selena's stomach did a little flip. "Yes. Of course I can. I do."

"Thank you." He heaved a sigh of relief. "And now I think we'd better get back, before the others start worrying about us."

They exited the folly. During the long hike back to the manor house, they were both quiet, concentrating on the effort it took to walk in the snowshoes. No sooner had they reached the house and propped up the snowshoes in the mudroom to dry than the announcement came that luncheon was being served.

Selena and Dr. Scott hurried up to their respective rooms to change. She was hungry, thirsty, bathed in perspiration, and completely drained. She took a long drink of water followed by a quick sponge bath at her pitcher and basin. As she donned fresh clothes, Selena thought back to that delectable kiss, and what Dr. Scott had said before and after.

"If I could have conjured the perfect woman for me, it would be you." Her mind reeled with pleasure at the thought. Was Dr. Scott the perfect man for her? She was beginning to think so. Even though it might be difficult for them to be together.

What had he meant, though, about being in a dark place?

There was clearly something he wasn't telling her. But, Selena reassured herself, whatever it was, there must have been a good reason behind it. Because he was a good man, and she did trust him.

CHAPTER TWENTY-ONE

D URING LUNCH, EVERYONE was interested in hearing about Selena and Dr. Scott's adventure.

"We lost sight of you through the window after you passed the ruined abbey." Colonel Blackwood took a spoonful of split pea and ham soup. "Did you make it to the folly?"

"Yes." Selena stifled a yawn. "I am bone-tired and every muscle in my body aches."

Mrs. Hillman motioned to Sam to refill her wine glass, then turned to Selena. "Was I right? Did you find a statue of a dragon to show your students?"

"Yes, a lovely one." Selena buttered a piece of bread. "It's of Jason poisoning the dragon guarding the golden fleece."

At the word *poisoning*, the room went quiet. Everyone stared down at their soup bowls. Selena's cheeks grew hot as she realized her *faux pas*.

Mrs. Hillman, apparently noticing the change of mood, took command of the conversation "If you're thinking of Mrs. Whitlock, I promise you, my friends, she accidentally poisoned *herself*. And don't worry. All of the soup came from the same pot, and you saw it served before you."

"Ditto for the bottle of wine." Mr. Davis raised his glass and took a sip.

A ripple of laughter went around the table. As everyone resumed eating and drinking, Selena studied their expressions. Had

Mrs. Whitlock, she wondered, indeed inadvertently poisoned herself? Was one of these people Maisie or Joe Webster? Had one of them killed Mr. Clarke and Mrs. Whitlock? If so, which one of them had written the threatening notes? To her frustration, it was impossible to tell.

When lunch concluded, Mrs. Hillman proposed that they play cards in the drawing room. Everyone agreed except for Dr. Scott, who said he would prefer to read, and Selena, who wanted to take a nap.

As the pair left the dining room, the doctor nodded cordially to her in parting. No one could have a clue that they had just exchanged passionate kisses a couple of hours before. Selena hugged her secret to herself.

Back in her room, Selena undressed and crawled into bed, sighing with relief when her head hit the pillow. In minutes, she was fast asleep.

SHE KNEW IT was a dream because she and Dr. Scott were inside the Grecian folly again. Except that the temple was immense, with a dozen doorways that opened to beckoning corridors.

Dr. Scott took Selena's hand and led her down a long, dark hallway. Flames leaped from torches mounted on the stone walls, where there was a seemingly endless row of niches filled with statues of dragons.

"There are so many dragons!" Selena cried. "How are we ever going to find the right one?"

"Maybe we never will." Dr. Scott stopped and ran a gentle finger across Selena's lips, an intimate touch that sent sparks careening through her body. "Maybe we aren't meant to." With that, he brought his mouth to hers.

Selena wrapped her arms around his neck, rejoicing in his kiss and the feel of his strong body against hers.

"I love you," he whispered against her lips.

"I love you, too," she said back.

Selena awakened with a gasp, her heart racing. The last glimmer of fading daylight filtered in beneath the curtains. She lay curled on her side, cradling her extra pillow to her chest, and wishing it were Dr. Scott.

The last moment of the dream played again in her mind. *"I love you."* Heat bloomed in her face and chest, then radiated down to the deepest part of her being. With it came a realization.

I do love him. And not just in a dream.

Selena knew it seemed absurd. Five days ago, she hadn't known that Dr. Adrian Scott existed. How could a person fall in love in just four days? And yet she had. Every day since had been a discovery, a series of windows opening to provide insights into the man. And she loved what she had seen.

He had risen from a difficult childhood with few prospects and had made something of himself. He'd had the financial backing of a patron who had seen his worth, but Dr. Scott wouldn't have achieved what he had without determination and many years of hard work. He had dedicated his life to healing the sick. She had observed his meticulous techniques from the moment of his arrival, from his assessment of Mr. Clarke to his considerate treatment of Mrs. Hillman to his tender ministrations when Selena had burned herself.

She admired him for more than his professional skills, though. She loved that they had so many things in common. He was intelligent and shared her love of reading. They had bonded over their mutual loss, at a young age, of a mother's love. She had only caught glimpses of his sense of humor, but she knew it existed. He was just as tantalized by the unsolved mysteries that lay before them as she was—which thrilled her no end. He had become such an invaluable ally in her quest to uncover whatever misdeeds might have been happening at Darkmoor Park.

And when it came to kissing, he was the very definition of tenderness and passion. Just thinking about the embraces that they had shared made her cheeks grow even hotter. He had made her feel like the most desirable and cherished woman in the world.

She loved him. Did he love her? Or was the scene in her dream merely a fantasy?

"I kissed you because I couldn't help myself," he had said the first time they'd kissed. *"If I could have conjured the perfect woman for me, it would be you,"* he had told her at the folly.

Yes! *Yes.* It might not yet be love on his part, but he *did* care for her. The idea brought a smile to her face, and Selena hugged her pillow again. Unable to help herself, Selena closed her eyes and tried to imagine what the future might hold.

She had hoped to find the perfect man who would understand her desire to work and would encourage it. Now, it seemed that she had met the perfect man. They both had work they enjoyed and valued. Dr. Scott had said her school was a cause he championed.

Her brows drew together as uncertainty rose within her breast. That was an easy thing for him to say, she realized, if, after the holidays, he intended to leave and never see her again.

Surely, Dr. Scott would never give up his medical practice in Bath, a city teeming with thousands of ill people seeking treatments, to remove to Darkmoor Bridge, a village so tiny that one apothecary was able to attend the needs of its population.

Dr. Scott was aware of these problems, she realized. He had implied that he thought it would be impossible for them to be together. Some other matter was troubling him as well. He had mentioned being in a *dark place* when he'd arrived at Darkmoor Park. She had no idea what that meant, but the two things must be tied together.

Was he experiencing difficulties at work? Perhaps a patient was suing him for some reason? The idea made her heart catch. In any case, it must have been a private issue that he couldn't talk about, and that he must solve upon his return to Bath. And Selena couldn't follow him there. She had told him, plainly and clearly, that her school was her life's work and a long-held dream come true. *"I cannot imagine my life without it,"* she had said.

Perhaps he would take her at her word and never bring up the possibility of a future between them. That would be the gentlemanly thing to do.

Disappointment surged through her, and a lone tear ran down her cheek. Selena wiped it away and let out a sad sigh. Perhaps her whirlwind relationship with Dr. Scott could never be more than that, just a brief affair, with no prospects, after all. She loved him—but she would never tell him. When the holidays ended, he would go home and she would remain here, where she belonged. She would never see him again, but she would look back on this interval as a thrilling moment in time, spent with a thrilling man.

In the meantime, there was no use moping in bed about it. She must be sensible. Selena donned her dress again, reminding herself that the clock was ticking. The temperature outside had begun to rise. Soon, the snow would melt and make it possible to travel again. Before their guests left Darkmoor Park, she and Dr. Scott still had mysteries to solve.

She picked up her pen, sat down at her writing desk, and made a list.

QUESTIONS TO BE ANSWERED

1. Where did Mr. Clarke hide the money?
2. Were Mr. Clarke's and Mrs. Whitlock's deaths accidental? Or were they murdered?
3. Was Mrs. Goodwin's demise at the Worthing Seaside Hotel three months ago related?
4. Were Mr. Clarke's and Mrs. Whitlock's deaths connected to the hidden money?
5. Or were all three the marked victims of the vengeful siblings of Clive Webster?
6. If *that* is so—who is in this house, posing as Maisie and/or Joe Webster?

DINNER WAS A tedious affair. Dr. Scott appeared to be wrapped in his own thoughts throughout the meal. Selena was so distracted herself that she found it difficult to concentrate on the conversations around her.

Mrs. Hillman was wearing the precious brooch that her husband had given her, and Miss Goodwin remarked upon it. "So, you found it, ma'am? Had you just misplaced it after all?"

Mrs. Hillman responded with a tight smile. "Yes, dear. I'm getting older. These things happen."

Selena understood why Mrs. Hillman had chosen to conceal the truth. To know that her friend Mrs. Whitlock had been a brazen thief must have been heartbreaking. Everyone kept secrets, and that was to be hers.

After dinner, the group removed to the drawing room to play the card game Speculation. Dr. Scott once again excused himself, explaining that he wasn't a card player. Selena, resuming her role as hostess, dutifully brought out the deck of cards and counters. But as the rounds of the game progressed, she found her mind wandering.

What other secrets, Selena speculated, might all these people have been keeping? When Miss Goodwin and Mr. Davis exchanged a few whispered words, Selena wondered how to characterize the affection that they displayed. Were they truly a young, betrothed couple? Or were they Maisie and Joe Webster, a sister and brother?

When Miss Thompson won a round and gleefully collected her counters, Selena thought about the hidden money. Did Miss Thompson crave that fortune so she could open a flower shop? Had she written the threatening notes? Could she be Maisie? Had she had anything to do with her employer's death? Selena hoped not. Of all the potential subjects, she would be so disappointed if it turned out that Miss Thompson were culpable for such heinous deeds.

What about the servants? She still hadn't had a chance to speak to Sam or Gladys. Selena's mind buzzed with so many questions, she couldn't recall which cards had been played or which suit was trump and found it difficult to make any intelligent bids. She was relieved when the game ended, and she was at last able to retire for the night.

When Selena reached her chamber, the door was standing open. Her pulse skittered. From within, there was a thumping sound. Someone was in her room.

Her stomach clenched as she cautiously glanced around the doorjamb. Gladys was inside, building up the fire. Selena's heart skittered. Who *was* Gladys, really? All Selena knew was that the young woman had been hired a few months ago. Could Gladys be Maisie Webster, a former chambermaid at the Worthing Seaside Hotel?

Here was the perfect opportunity to question her. Selena entered her room. "Gladys."

The maid started and dropped the piece of firewood in her hands. "Miss Taylor."

"I'm sorry if I startled you." Selena began unbuttoning her velvet jacket.

"Oh, don't mind me, miss. I startle easily." Gladys's expression was reserved as she returned to her duties.

"I know we've put you to a lot of extra trouble this past week, and I wanted to thank you for doing such excellent work."

"It's my job, miss."

Selena hung her jacket in the closet. "I hope we haven't tired you out too much."

"No, miss." Gladys stacked new wood in the hearth. "I just feel bad about all that's happened. First that gentleman dying, and then that old woman who passed away after stealing Mrs. Hillman's brooch."

Selena froze inwardly. She hadn't discussed that theft with anyone other than Dr. Scott and Mrs. Hillman, who had vowed to keep it quiet. "Where did you hear that? About the brooch?"

Gladys shrugged. "I think someone mentioned it downstairs."

It was a reminder that at a manor house like Darkmoor Park, the servants often knew more about what was going on than the other residents. Selena saw it as an opportunity to place her first test. "Mrs. Hillman wants to honor her friend's memory, and she'd prefer that you didn't discuss that matter with anyone else."

"Yes, miss."

"You don't mind, do you?"

"Mind what, miss?"

Selena focused on the maid's face. "Keeping a secret."

Gladys blinked at that. "I think everyone has secrets, don't you? At least, that's what my mother always used to say."

"My mother had favorite sayings, too. She used to quote the Buddha who said, 'Three things cannot long stay hidden: the sun, the moon, and the truth.'"

Gladys's forehead creased, and she turned her gaze to the hearth. "If you say so, miss."

Selena wondered if the maid had ever even heard of the Buddha. She sat down at her dressing table and removed the pins from her hair. "Gladys, how long have you been at Darkmoor Park?"

"Three months, miss." Gladys grabbed a brush and dustpan from her bucket and began sweeping up ash by the hearth.

Mrs. Goodwin died three months ago. "Where did you learn your exemplary skills? Mrs. Middleton said you worked at a hotel?"

"A hotel?" Gladys paused, her brows quirking. "She must have me muddled with someone else. I never worked in a hotel."

"No?" Selena tried to hide her disappointment. "Where *did* you work before coming to Darkmoor Park?"

"For a family in Nottinghamshire. I was there eight years, from under chambermaid to parlor maid, but they moved to Boston, and I didn't wish to go with them."

Boston? A convenient explanation, Selena thought, *if she is hiding her true identity.* A reference letter could be forged, and it would be difficult to check up on Gladys's history if her former employer had left for America. "Did you come from a big family?"

"No, miss. I just have one brother."

She has a brother. "Where were you and your brother raised, may I ask?"

"Nottinghamshire."

Selena ran her hairbrush through her long, blonde locks. "I've heard that Nottinghamshire is a beautiful county. But if you had to choose, which would you say has the finest beaches, Nottinghamshire or West Sussex?"

A laugh escaped Gladys's throat. "Nottinghamshire is landlocked, miss. There are no beaches."

Selena brought a hand to her face, as if in chastisement for her mistake. "Oh! Silly me. Of course you're right."

"In any case, I wouldn't know about beaches. I've never even seen the sea."

Was that just a clever remark, Selena wondered, *to divert any connection to Maisie Webster?* Selena tried another tactic. "I don't know why I was thinking about West Sussex. I supposed it's because of the story I heard."

"What story?" Gladys asked.

Selena continued brushing her hair. "It was about a girl in West Sussex whose brother was imprisoned for a crime he hadn't committed. The poor lad died in prison."

Gladys paused, her cleaning tools in midair. "What a sad story, miss."

"I felt bad for the boy who died, but also for the sister who must surely mourn him." Selena dared a glance at Gladys, who was staring down at her hands. "I've often thought," Selena went on, "I would not blame the young woman if she were to be furious with the people who had contributed to her brother's unfair conviction."

Gladys's features tightened. "I wouldn't blame her, either, miss." She stood abruptly and emptied the ash from her dustpan into the bucket, her motions so rapid and disjointed that they caused a cloud of dust to billow in the air. "If you'll excuse me, I must get on with my work." She curtsied, gathered her buckets and tools, and hurried from the room.

Later, as Selena climbed into bed and blew out the candle, she wondered if anything that Gladys had told her was true. The Clive Webster story had seemed to perturb her.

Was Gladys really a maid from Nottinghamshire who had never seen the sea and whose employer had moved to America? Or was she Maisie Webster, here to exact revenge?

CHAPTER TWENTY-TWO

SELENA HAD JUST finished pinning up her hair the next morning, and was about to get dressed, when she noticed another note lying on the threshold just inside her chamber door.

She raced to it and unfolded the small piece of white paper. Her heart seemed to gallop in her chest as she read the words inscribed therein.

Stay out of this or die.

Perspiration broke out on Selena's brow. Who was writing these? What was she being warned to stay out of? The hunt for the hidden money? Or the search for the Websters? Or both?

As fast as her shaking fingers would allow, she threw on a day dress and a matching jacket of rose-colored wool and hurried from her chamber, intending to find Dr. Scott. As she emerged into the corridor, she found him striding quickly and purposefully towards her, his features drawn.

"I got another note," Selena whispered when he stopped at her side.

"I got one as well," he replied under his breath. They compared them. Again, they were identical.

Before she could ask the doctor what he thought, Colonel Blackwood exited his own chamber. "Doctor! Miss Taylor." The colonel's face was pale.

Selena shoved her note into her skirt pocket, all thoughts about the notes fleeing from her mind as she took in the colonel's beleaguered state. "Colonel! What's wrong?"

He met them in the middle of the hall and spoke in a low voice. "It's … the sandwich."

Dr. Scott stared at him. "What sandwich?"

"The one I ordered before I retired." Colonel Blackwood's lips trembled. "I was feeling a bit peckish last night, so I told Mrs. Middleton that I fancied a toasted cheese sandwich. She said she would have the cook make one up and have it brought to my room."

"Did someone bring you the sandwich?" Selena asked.

"Yes, that good-looking footman, what's his name, Sam?"

Dr. Scott's brows drew together. "Then what seems to be the problem, Colonel?"

"Well, it's the mouse, you see," the colonel answered.

A dark foreboding took hold of Selena. "What mouse?"

"By the time the lad had brought up the sandwich, I was too tired to take more than a single bite," Colonel Blackwood said, "so I left the rest and went to sleep. I soon awoke with terrible cramps and then I became very ill. I presumed it was something I had consumed at dinner. But this morning, I saw that the sandwich had been nibbled at, and I found a dead mouse next to the plate."

The hair stood up on the back of Selena's neck. "Oh, no."

"Let me see it." Dr. Scott's voice was as stern as his expression.

Selena and the doctor followed the colonel into his chamber, where a partially eaten toasted cheese sandwich lay on a plate atop the dresser, with the body of a small, grey mouse beside it.

Selena's pulse jangled in alarm. She turned to the doctor. "Might it have been poisoned?"

"I'll have to check." Dr. Scott lifted the plate to his nostrils and inhaled. He then gently peeled away the top slice of bread from the sandwich and studied the layer of melted orange cheese beneath. His facial muscles tensed. "Colonel—you said you were unwell in the night?"

"Yes." Colonel Blackwood's face colored. "I lost my supper into my chamber pot."

"It may be a good thing you did," Dr. Scott declared. "And it may be a blessing that you didn't take more than a bite of this sandwich. There's a textural difference here in this layer of cheese. Do you see it?" He held out the plate for them to study.

The cheese looked like melted cheddar and did have a slightly bumpy appearance. "What does it mean?" Selena asked.

"I suspect it was sprinkled with granules of some sort, which melted into the cheese," the doctor answered. "Possibly arsenic, which is odorless and tasteless—but when ingested, even a small amount can be fatal."

Selena's throat constricted and she was overcome once more by a sense of déjà vu—reminded of the morning that they had discovered Mrs. Whitlock and the remains of her poisoned hot toddy. Except that this time, although Colonel Blackwood was shaky and pasty-faced, he was thankfully alive.

"Arsenic?" the colonel repeated. "I don't understand. Why would ...?" He gasped and his eyes grew huge. "You don't mean ...? Good heavens!"

"Where would someone get arsenic?" Selena asked.

"Arsenic is the key ingredient in rat poison," the doctor explained. "Its natural color is white. The Arsenic Act of 1851 aimed to help prevent poisonings by requiring it to be colored indigo or soot, but that's been difficult to regulate and isn't common yet. Mind you, I can't prove the sandwich was poisoned. If we could send it to Scotland Yard, there's a new test that might be able to detect the presence of arsenic. But cut off here as we are, I can only go on the evidence before us. The dead mouse, the textural difference in the cheese, and the fact that you became ill, Colonel. You said Sam brought up the sandwich?"

"Yes," the colonel replied.

Sam, Selena thought, suspicion rising. "Did anyone else enter your room last night after it was delivered?"

The colonel shook his head. "No one. I was already undressed for bed. I took one bite and then went to sleep."

"If it was poisoned, then, it happened before it was delivered." The doctor frowned. "Who knew you had ordered a sandwich?"

Colonel Blackwood narrowed his eyes. "Everyone in our group was there. I asked for it after our card game last night—just after Miss Taylor had quit the room."

Dr. Scott turned to Selena. "Who would have had access to rat poison?"

She thought about it. "Anyone who went looking for it, I suppose. I think it's stored in a cupboard in the servants' hall."

"Could it have been the cook?" asked Dr. Scott.

Selena shook her head. "Mrs. Nash has worked at Darkmoor Park for more than a dozen years. She came as a widow with her infant son, Billy, and is a woman of high principles. It cannot have been her."

The colonel's face was still pale. "I hoped you two were mistaken when you said someone had done in Jack Clarke and Mrs. Whitlock and that I might be next. But now … I don't know what to think."

"I think it must have been Joe or Maisie Webster," Selena said, her lips tightening. "A determined guest could have found that poison. Or perhaps it was Sam, who brought up the sandwich. We'll have to find out if the sandwich had ever been left unattended, and who else was in the servants' hall at the time."

"Yes. And we ought to tell Mrs. Hillman what just occurred," Dr. Scott said flatly.

Selena nodded in agreement. "We've already shared our theory about the Websters. This is the first concrete evidence that seems to verify there's a killer amongst us—whether she believes it or not is up to her."

"I suggest we say nothing of this to anyone else, though," Dr.

Scott insisted. "You're the only other person here, Colonel, who had anything to do with Clive Webster's conviction. If our theory about the Websters is correct, then everyone else is perfectly safe."

"And *if* Maisie or Joe Webster is here and poisoned that sandwich," Selena added, "they'll be surprised—and no doubt upset—to find you still alive, Colonel. Their reaction might give them away."

The colonel sank down onto a chair, blinking rapidly. "This is a shock. But it will take a lot more than a poisoned sandwich to kill me. I dare the villain to try again. I'm on my guard now."

"Please, Colonel," the doctor warned, "be careful. I advise you to stay with the group during the day and move a chair up under your door handle before you retire for the night."

"And don't eat or drink anything unless it's with us in the dining room," Selena insisted.

"Very well." Colonel Blackwood rubbed his belly with a grimace. "I'm going to return to bed for the rest of the day. I still feel unwell."

"Would you like me to give you something for a bad stom-ach?" offered Dr. Scott.

The colonel made a face. "As long as it's not laudanum."

"Understood." Dr. Scott gave him a half-smile. "I'll dispose of the dead animal and sandwich and get my bag."

"Thank you, Doctor. In the meantime," Selena declared, "I'll have a chat with Sam ... and find out everything I can about that sandwich."

SELENA DESCENDED THE servants' stairwell to find a beehive of activity. Gladys was scrubbing the floor. Beryl hurried by with piles of folded linen. A kitchen maid was making pastries in the still-room. In the scullery, Billy and another maid were up to their elbows in sudsy water, scrubbing dishes and pots and pans from the morning's breakfast—a meal Selena had yet to enjoy.

But the matters on her mind took precedence over food. She stopped in the housekeeper's office, where Mrs. Middleton was working at her tiny desk. "Mrs. Middleton? May I have a word?"

The housekeeper stood. "Yes, Miss Taylor?"

"Last night, after the parlor game ended, did any members of the house party come downstairs?"

"Not that I'm aware of," Mrs. Middleton responded. "Colonel Blackwood did order a toasted cheese sandwich, but he made that request upstairs."

Selena had agreed to say nothing of the sandwich being poisoned. "Do you recall who was in the servants' hall at the time?"

Mrs. Middleton tilted her head. "I think we were all here, miss. Normally, I let some of the staff go to bed by nine, but there was too much to do last night with all the dishes and clean-up required, to make up for our day off on Boxing Day."

"As I understand it, Sam brought up the sandwich to the colonel. Would he have picked it up in the kitchen?"

"As a general rule, yes. But last night, there was too much going on. I saw the sandwich sitting on a table in the hall and reminded Sam to bring it up. Why?"

"I was just curious." *So, the sandwich had been set out where anyone could have tampered with it.* "By the way, the colonel found a dead mouse in his room this morning. Dr. Scott disposed of it, but I wondered if anyone had recently laid out any bait?"

"I routinely set out bait in the kitchen area," Mrs. Middleton replied, "and the other day, I put some in the storage closets on the first and second floors."

"But not in the guests' bedrooms?" Selena asked.

"No." Mrs. Middleton shook her head.

"Where do we keep the rat poison? Would you show me?" Selena asked.

"Certainly." Mrs. Middleton led Selena briskly down the hall to a storage closet. She opened the door and Selena followed her inside. "It's here on this shelf." The housekeeper indicated a small box marked DANGER! RAT POISON!

Selena's shoulders fell with disappointment. Somehow, she had hoped the box would be missing—to prove that it had been stolen. "Is the closet ever locked?"

"No, never."

"How do you use the poison?" Selena asked.

"I coat a few pieces of cheese with the granules or mix it into a pat of butter."

Mrs. Middleton opened the box and showed it to Selena. It was half-full of tiny, white pellets. *Granules. Just as Dr. Scott predicted.*

"I tell the maids to be careful not to touch it directly and to immediately wash their hands and clean any tools they use." The housekeeper closed the box. "I'm sorry the colonel found a dead mouse in his room, but as you know, in a house this old, mice live in the walls. Do you wish me to have bait set out anywhere?"

"Not now. As I said, I was just curious." Selena turned to go, then paused. "Where might I find Wells?"

"He's in the butler's pantry, I believe."

"Thank you." As Selena headed down the hall, she thought about the box of rat poison. Although no one had stolen it, that closet was never locked. Perhaps someone had made a paper sachet and stolen just enough granules to poison that sandwich when it had been left out on a table in the hall.

The only people she could imagine who would want to harm Colonel Blackwood were Maisie or Joe Webster. Had one of them, or the pair working as a team, murdered Mrs. Goodwin at her home, then killed Jack Clarke and Mrs. Whitlock, and finally tried to silence the colonel? What about the hidden money? Were they after that as well? Selena was still pondering this when she reached the butler's pantry.

The utility chamber, ringed by glass-fronted cabinets, held the manor house's fine china, glassware, serving dishes, and silver. The grey-haired butler stood at the central wooden table, his black tailcoat covered by a clean, white apron. On the table before him lay the gleaming silver tea service and he was vigorously polishing its large, silver tray.

Selena mustered a smile and entered. "Good morning, Wells. I wondered if I might have a word?"

"Of course. Do you mind if I keep working, Miss Taylor? I polished the tea service last week for Christmas, but I noticed spots of tarnish this morning."

"Please, continue." Selena stopped beside him. The silver teapot, coffee pot, sugar bowl, creamer, pitcher, and tray already gleamed as if they were brand new—which showed how particular the butler was. "I wanted to speak to you about Sam."

"Oh?" Wells poured more polish onto his rag.

"As I recall, you hired him just to help over the holidays?"

"That's right. He leaves after the first of the year."

"What can you tell me about him?"

"Sam?" The butler paused "Why? Has he done something wrong?"

"Not at all," Selena replied congenially. "You did a fine job in choosing him. So fine that I was thinking of recommending him to Mrs. Hillman as a permanent hire." Selena felt bad lying to this man, but it was the only excuse she could think of to gain the information she needed.

"Indeed?" Wells stood straighter, his chin raising. "What do you wish to know?"

"What is his training and experience? Where did he work before he came to Darkmoor Park?"

"He was—rather he *is*—second footman at Thurley House in South Yorkshire. Started there as hall boy when he was a lad, apparently. He's only here on loan to us. The family went abroad for holidays."

Selena's heart skipped a beat. She recalled Mrs. Hillman mentioning that Clive Webster's older brother had worked at a great house, but she had been vague about the details. It was certainly possible that Joe Webster had worked in South Yorkshire, even if his siblings had been employed at the hotel in West Sussex. "How did you find him?"

"I placed an advertisement in *The London Times* and several Yorkshire newspapers."

Yes, Selena thought. Joe Webster could have learned about Mrs. Hillman's upcoming holiday house party from his sister, Maisie, at the Worthing Seaside Hotel. If he had spied the advertisement for a temporary holiday post at Darkmoor Park, it might have seemed like the perfect opportunity to exact his revenge. "He came with good references, I imagine?"

"He did."

"What do you know about his family?"

"His family? I didn't ask about that." Wells energetically polished the platter in his hands. "He was only to be here such a short time, you see." He held up the platter in front of his face, as if testing its mirror-like qualities. Frowning, he poured more polish on his rag.

"Is there anything else you can tell me about him?"

The butler pursed his lips. "Sam is pleasing to look at—an essential quality for a footman. He follows orders, knows how to polish a boot and carry a tray, and he sets a good table." He hesitated. "However—may I be frank, miss?"

"Please."

"I wouldn't say he has the temperament to stay on at Darkmoor Park."

"No? Why is that?" Selena's brows lifted.

"He isn't particularly well-liked by the staff. I suppose because he is a man of few words. Keeps himself to himself. In any case, I wouldn't feel right poaching him from Thurley House. And in truth, I can't say that we'd need additional help after Mrs. Hillman's guests leave."

"Good to know." Selena was intrigued. If Sam was Joe Webster, with a vendetta to carry out and a secret identity to maintain, he would surely lie low and be careful not to say too much. "Thank you, Wells. I appreciate your input. Have a good morning." Selena turned for the door, when the butler spoke again.

"Wait. I remember now. Sam did say something about family."

Selena glanced back at him. "Oh?"

"I mentioned, out of kindness, that I hope he didn't mind spending the holidays away from home. He said it made no difference to him because his parents and brother were all dead. He had nothing left but a sister, he said."

Goosebumps prickled on Selena's arms. "Did he say where his sister lives?"

"In the south of England, I believe?"

"I see." It was all Selena could do to keep her expression even. "Oh, one last thing, where might I find Sam? I want to speak to him."

Wells glanced up at the clock. It was a quarter to eleven. "Breakfast ends soon. He should be clearing away the dishes. Which reminds me that I ought to head upstairs." He began untying his apron.

Selena thanked him again and hurried from the room. Everything the butler had told her about Sam added up. The footman had been working at a great house at the time of Clive Webster's trial. His brother was dead. And he had a sister still living—who resided in the south.

Selena had almost reached the servants' stairs when footsteps pounded down from above and Sam himself darted into view, balancing a tray of dirty dishes and glassware. Selena ground to a halt.

Sam stopped abruptly before her, tray in hand. "Pardon me." He looked dapper in his livery uniform.

"No, pardon me. I am in your way." Selena retreated two steps and nearly ran into Wells.

"Has everyone left the morning room?" Wells demanded of the footman.

"All except Mrs. Hillman and Dr. Scott," Sam replied.

"When you have cleared the room completely," the butler instructed, "Mrs. Hillman wants coffee, tea, hot chocolate, and biscuits brought up to the library for all the guests."

"Yes, sir." Sam nodded.

As Wells plodded up the stairs, Selena asked, "Sam, may I have a word?"

The footman paused with his carefully balanced tray of dishes. "Miss?"

Selena chose her words just as carefully. "I have been negligent, Sam."

"Pardon?"

"You have been with us—what is it, two weeks now? And I have not had the opportunity to give you a proper welcome."

He shrugged. "I didn't expect one."

"But you deserve one. Mrs. Hillman and I are grateful that you were able to help at Darkmoor Park for the holidays. Indeed, I don't know what we should have done without you."

"Thank you, miss."

"I understand that you are employed at a great house in South Yorkshire?"

"I am."

Selena went fishing. "And you grew up in West Sussex?"

A line formed between his brows. "No, miss."

"I must be remembering wrong. Perhaps I heard that you went to West Sussex on holiday?"

He seemed to be at a loss for words. "I did, a few months ago. How did you know?"

Selena fought hard to keep her face impassive. *Mrs. Goodwin died at the Worthing Seaside Hotel a few months ago.* "I think your employer mentioned it to Wells? It's no matter. I don't know why it even occurred to me." Selena lowered her voice. "Sam, the other reason I wanted to speak to you is to offer my condolences. Wells told me that your brother died. I am so sorry."

The wrinkle in his forehead grew deeper. "That was a long time ago."

"Even so, I can only imagine how difficult it must be to lose a sibling. I have two sisters and a brother. I don't know what I would do if anything happened to them."

He stared at the floor. "It was hardest on my mother, I think. She said there's nothing so hard to bear as the loss of a child."

Selena took that in, seeing the truth in it. It would indeed, she thought, be devastating to lose one's child. She was searching for an appropriate response when George sprinted down the stairs with his own tray of dirty dishes and called out, "Sam! Why are you lolling about? Get a move on!"

"Pardon me, miss." Sam rapidly followed George down the hall.

Here was Selena's chance to catch him. "I say, Joe!" she called out.

Sam stopped in his tracks and turned back.

Got you! Selena thought in silent triumph.

He stared at her. "My name is Sam."

"Of course, sorry. Keep up the good work, Sam," Selena told him.

Without a nod or a *thank you*, he whirled and disappeared into the kitchen. Selena's pulse pounded as she hurried upstairs. Had he turned around because she'd called out his real name? So many of the other pieces of the puzzle fit to perfection.

She could hardly wait to tell Dr. Scott. And she ought to inform Mrs. Hillman as well.

CHAPTER TWENTY-THREE

S ELENA FOUND MRS. Hillman and Dr. Scott in the morning room, finishing their breakfast, with Wells standing at attention at the back. The sun shone in through the casement windows, bathing the room in its brilliant light.

The aromas of bacon and eggs from the warmers on the buffet table were too tempting to resist. Selena quickly filled a plate. "Good morning," she said, taking a seat at the table. Mrs. Hillman and Dr. Scott returned her greeting. *This would be the ideal opportunity to bring them both up to date about what I learned,* Selena thought, *if only the butler weren't in the room.* She didn't want him thinking she suspected Sam and Gladys of anything, lest word might somehow get back to the pair.

"Mrs. Hillman," Selena said in a congenial tone, after taking a bite of toast, "How are you?"

Mrs. Hillman looked up from her cup of tea. "Well enough. I wish I could say the same for the colonel. And please don't get started about that toasted cheese sandwich. Dr. Scott has already filled me in and once again, I say the two of you are barking up the wrong tree."

Selena caught Dr. Scott's eye, surprised that the doctor had mentioned the sandwich in front of Wells. His brow furrowed and he shrugged slightly. It occurred to Selena that the doctor might have broached the subject before Wells had entered the room, and that Mrs. Hillman might have continued to talk about it unfettered.

But then, maybe it didn't matter? Wells must have been in his late fifties or sixties. He had worked at Darkmoor Park for ages and could hardly have been Joe Webster. And the butler was so honest and steadfast, Selena couldn't imagine that he would have been behind the poisoning. Dr. Scott gave her a slight nod, as if to say, *It's all right. Go on.*

"But, ma'am," Selena replied, "Dr. Scott detected the presence of arsenic in the sandwich."

"That is just a theory," Mrs. Hillman pointed out. "He has no proof."

"A mouse *died*," Selena pointed out. "And the colonel became ill."

Mrs. Hillman waved an unconcerned hand. "Mice have very short lives. That one may have died a natural death. If it was indeed poisoned, it probably ingested it in the servants' hall, which is regularly baited, and died in Colonel Blackwood's room. As for the colonel, I believe he suffered from indigestion last night. We have been eating so many rich foods all week, one of us was bound to fall ill."

Selena released an exasperated breath. She wanted to bring up the threatening notes, but perhaps this was not the time. That subject, however, was apparently out of the bag as well.

"And if you're about to bring up that business about the notes you've received, don't bother," Mrs. Hillman said. "Those notes were nothing but a prank."

"'A prank'?" Selena repeated, her mouth agape. "How so?"

"It was just Billy. He's at that age, you know—thirteen years old, and boys will be boys. He got up to all sorts of mischief when he was a young lad. One day, he put pepper in my tea. Another time, he put a mouse inside a cook pot, scared his poor mother out of her wits. He got a sound whipping for that. But he's Mrs. Nash's son," she added by way of explanation to Dr. Scott, "and he's a good boy at heart. He'll grow out of it soon, I have no doubt."

Selena ate her eggs, struggling to think of a convincing argument. "Billy has played tricks on me, too—I can't count how many times he's jumped out at me in the corridor to make me scream. But I doubt that he could write threatening notes like those."

"Billy's been to school, and I assure you he's quite capable," Mrs. Hillman insisted. "Dr. Scott showed me the notes. The handwriting is nothing but a scrawl and the wording is so simplistic."

"Pardon me, ma'am," Wells said, stepping forward. "Would you like me to have a word with Billy about this?"

Mrs. Hillman shook her head. "Thank you, Wells, but no. I'll take care of it." To Selena and the doctor, she added, "Please, don't let the machinations of a hall boy bother you."

"Mrs. Hillman," Selena said calmly, hoping to appeal to her sense of reason. "I understand your reticence in these matters and why you don't wish to believe that anything untoward is going on at Darkmoor Park. But two people have *died*. And too many strange things have been happening the past few days."

"We cannot simply pretend that all is well," Dr. Scott affirmed gently.

The light in Mrs. Hillman's pale-blue eyes dimmed and the corners of her mouth turned downward. She sighed. "Fine. I am not an idiot. This has indeed been a trying and heartbreaking time. But everything you've brought up is mere conjecture! You haven't any proof!"

"Not yet," Selena admitted. "But we're working on it."

"And what is it that you wish of *me*?" Mrs. Hillman demanded. "To summon the parish constable? Impossible. We're still trapped here, and, in any case, Mr. Johnson has gone away." She picked up her napkin and toyed with it distractedly. "I said I'll talk to Billy, and I will. I'm sure the notes were just a prank. In the meantime, this is a *holiday house party*. Isn't it bad enough that I have lost two friends? Must I truly spend the rest of the week worrying that some villain in disguise is here to kill the colonel and wishes the both of you harm? It sounds like something out of a Gothic novel! I want to go on as we planned and I don't want to alarm anyone!"

"But—" Selena began.

"Not another word on that subject!" Mrs. Hillman slapped her hand on the table emphatically and then glanced out the window with a sigh. "Oh! How annoying it is to go so long without any news! I can't properly enjoy breakfast without a newspaper to read. To think that we've been cut off from the world for nearly a week. Perhaps by tomorrow, the snow will have melted enough that the trains are running, and I can send someone to the village for a newspaper."

Dr. Scott's teacup slipped from his hand into its saucer with a clatter, sloshing tea onto the tablecloth. A flush crept up his neck. "Pardon me. Just call me butterfingers."

"Happens to me all the time, Doctor," Mrs. Hillman said with a dismissive wave of her hand.

Selena was so annoyed by Mrs. Hillman's refusal to take their warnings seriously, she required a moment to switch gears to this new topic. She'd been too preoccupied this morning to give any notice to the weather. But she saw now that most of the snow was already gone from the trees, and the snow on the ground had melted away considerably since her trek with the doctor the day before.

"Now, Selena, let us talk about today's activity." Mrs. Hillman set her napkin on the table. "I want to have dramatic readings tonight after dinner. I sent everyone to the library to find a passage in a novel to read aloud. Perhaps you can go in and see if anyone needs help selecting a book?"

Selena was too frustrated to care. "Yes, ma'am," she managed, finishing off a last bite of eggs and toast and pushing back her chair.

"Wait, before you go!" Mrs. Hillman added. "There's something I wanted to tell you."

Selena struggled for patience. "Yes?"

"It's for that school activity you asked about. I thought of another place where we might have a dragon," Mrs. Hillman said.

That grabbed Selena's attention. "Where?"

"In the catacombs."

"The catacombs?" Selena had never been there.

"I haven't been down there in ages," Mrs. Hillman admitted, "but I have a vague recollection of a dragon motif on one of the tombs. It is not a pleasant place, but it might be an interesting history lesson for the girls."

A glint appeared in Dr. Scott's blue eyes. "How does one gain access to the catacombs?"

"The entrance from the old abbey church was bricked over centuries ago when the structure was torn down," Mrs. Hillman explained, "but there's a door in the chapel, just behind the altar, to an underground tunnel that leads to the catacombs. As I heard it, during the reign of Queen Elizabeth, monks and priests used the secret passageway to escape and hide in the catacombs."

Selena tried not to show her rising excitement. She recalled that Mr. Clarke, on the afternoon of his arrival, had been seen heading in the direction of the chapel. Was it possible that he'd found the door leading to the underground burial site and had hidden his cash there? "Are there a great many tombs in the catacombs?"

Mrs. Hillman nodded. "Oh, yes, they are quite numerous. The coffins of the hoi polloi are stacked here and there on shelves and in open chambers, but the burial crypts were for the more important people in the family." As Sam and George entered the room and joined Wells by the back wall, Mrs. Hillman turned to the butler. "Wells, you may clear now. And please send the coffee, tea, hot chocolate, and biscuits to the library, will you?"

"Right away, madam." Wells motioned to the footmen to begin clearing up.

Selena and Dr. Scott rose and excused themselves. As they headed down the corridor, Dr. Scott said under his breath, "I had brought all that up in confidence with Mrs. Hillman, but then

Wells walked in."

"I figured," Selena whispered back. "I wouldn't worry about it. Wells is very discreet." With a sigh, she added, "Mrs. Hillman can be the most frustrating woman on Earth, though. For her to think those notes were a *prank*."

"She has very determined views," he agreed.

A shiver of apprehension raced through her. "Are the notes a warning to stop searching for the hidden money? Or to stay out of Joe or Maisie Webster's way?"

"Perhaps both."

"I spoke to Gladys and Sam. She claims that her previous employers moved to America, so it would be difficult to check up on her—*and* she has a brother. He seems even more suspicious. Sam had a brother who died. And when I called him 'Joe,' he turned around as if by instinct."

"Or," the doctor pointed out, "he may have turned to correct you for misremembering his name."

"Either way, I'm not backing down now," Selena insisted fiercely.

"Neither am I. Mrs. Hillman has given us a new lead. Have you ever been to the catacombs?"

"No. Are you game for a visit?"

"Yes!" His blue eyes flashed with anticipation. "The sooner, the better."

"Let's do it. But I need to check in with our guests first."

They entered the library to find Miss Thompson, Miss Goodwin, and Mr. Davis searching the shelves. Miss Thompson's brow creased as she approached Selena and Dr. Scott. "The chambermaid told me that Colonel Blackwood fell ill during the night. Is he all right?"

Dr. Scott nodded. "Yes. We believe it was indigestion. I gave him a tonic to soothe his symptoms and help him sleep. Hopefully, he will feel better this evening."

"Thank goodness he's all right," Miss Thompson said.

Selena wondered if the young woman's concern was genuine

or manufactured. Selena glanced aside at Miss Goodwin and Mr. Davis to gauge their reaction to this news. If one or both of *them* had poisoned the colonel, surely, they would have hoped to hear of his death—and Selena ought to be able to glimpse guilt or disappointment on their faces. But the pair seemed to be intent on their search for a book and neither batted an eye.

"Give me two minutes. I'm going to choose a book," Dr. Scott said, slipping off.

Miss Thompson turned to Selena with a sigh. "I'm reading Miss Austen's *Persuasion* and think it delightful. But I'm at my wit's end about tonight's dramatic reading. What do you recommend?"

Selena suggested a scene from *Persuasion*, for which Miss Thompson was grateful. Miss Goodwin and Mr. Davis came up to her next. Judging by their tight-lipped expressions, Selena sensed that the pair were still upset about the accusation she had made the evening before. But perhaps they had forgiven her, for they also requested help locating appropriate novels from the library's vast collection.

"How about something from Mr. Dickens's *A Christmas Carol*?" Selena suggested.

"I've never read it," Mr. Davis said.

"Neither have I, but I've heard of it," Miss Goodwin put in.

"It's about a curmudgeon who is visited by the Ghosts of Christmas Past, Present, and Future and discovers the true meaning of Christmas. It's the perfect tale, given the time of year. You could read aloud from the same scene or chapter together, taking turns and voicing the different characters."

"It sounds like an excellent suggestion," said Miss Goodwin. "Thank you."

As Selena located Mr. Dickens's novel and indicated a passage that might be appropriate, an army of servants, including Sam, George, Wells, Mrs. Middleton, Beryl, and Gladys, entered with the silver coffee and tea service, the chocolate pot, cups and saucers, dishes, and trays of biscuits. Selena took advantage of the diversion to give Dr. Scott a meaningful glance and they started for the door.

Just as they were about to slip from the room, Wells headed them off, declaring, "I beg your pardon, Miss Taylor? If you and the doctor plan to visit the catacombs to research that school activity of yours, I wanted to mention—the door is hidden behind a bookcase by the chapel altar. It's not readily apparent unless you know what to look for. The spring hinge works both ways. Press hard and it will open."

"Thank you, Wells," Selena replied. A rush of uneasiness washed over her. The message in the notes that she and Dr. Scott had just received echoed in her mind.

"Stay out of this or die."

Who had sent them? It was impossible to know, but the threat was deadly.

She glanced back at the other occupants of the room. Everyone seemed to be staring in their direction. Had they all overheard the butler's remarks? If so, they would know where she and Dr. Scott were headed and how to follow. She blinked, and now all the heads were turned away. Had she just imagined those stares? Was she just letting her paranoia get the best of her?

Selena's stomach clenched with anxiety as she and Dr. Scott hurried from the room. *I refuse to be intimidated,* she reminded herself. Besides, hadn't the butler made it clear that she wanted to visit the catacombs as research for a school activity? Whoever had written those notes couldn't have a clue as to why she and Dr. Scott were *really* interested in the catacombs. Could they?

IT WAS AN ordinary-looking bookcase, painted white, with candlesticks and various religious paraphernalia on the shelves.

"Wells said to press hard," Selena remarked as she and Dr. Scott studied the set of shelves behind the chapel's altar.

He pushed on the bookcase's frame in several places until

with a soft creak, the bookcase swung outward. A musty smell emanated from the dark space beyond where a narrow stone staircase descended. Dr. Scott lit the lantern they'd brought and carried it as he and Selena slowly made their way down the steps. The farther they went, the colder it got, and the more the musty aroma increased.

As she and the doctor moved down the stairs, Selena was suddenly reminded of another time and place, when she and Athena had been obliged to flee by a secret staircase—and she shivered at the thought. But, she reminded herself, that had been a very different circumstance. She and her sister had been running for their lives. This time, Selena and Dr. Scott were running *to* something exciting. They were scouting for hidden treasure.

The stairs ended at a dirt floor. In the lantern's beam, Selena could make out the beginning of a long, subterranean passage, also lined in ancient stone and just wide enough for two people to walk side by side.

"This must lead to the catacombs," Selena said, her heart thumping with excitement. "Come on."

They had been walking in silence for a couple of minutes when a faint, distant creak broke the stillness. Selena started in surprise. "What was that?" The noise seemed to come from behind and above them.

"It sounded like the door at the top of the stairs."

Dr. Scott held the lantern aloft as they both stared down the corridor in the direction from which they had come. An eerie silence reigned.

Selena let go a nervous laugh. "I thought someone might be following us."

"As did I." He chuckled quietly in return. "Let's go."

The dark passage seemed to go on endlessly, but at last, they passed through an age-old, arched, stone-and-brick entryway into a wider space about eight or nine feet across. Dim light filtered in from a small, round opening in the ceiling, which Selena judged to be a tunnel to the surface above. The lantern provided further illumination. They were standing in a room with a dirt floor. It was partially enclosed by lofty walls of brick and stone. On both sides, vertical shelves held ancient, dusty, cobweb-laden wooden coffins that had been slid in end to end.

It was both fascinating and nerve-wracking to be so far beneath the ground, in an area accessible by only one long tunnel. "It's strange to think that people have been buried down here for many hundreds of years."

"These are, according to Mrs. Hillman, the less important people. Servants and lesser family members and going back further, no doubt members of the monastic order," Dr. Scott remarked, studying the coffins.

"We're looking for a tomb," Selena pointed out.

They moved on through the archways of brick and stone that opened from one room into the next. Selena heard water dripping. Was it melting snow from above? The tiny apertures in the ceiling that let in fragments of natural light were few and far between, leaving large sections of the catacombs shrouded in darkness. The stale air was a mix of aromas including dusty earth, stone, decaying wood, damp, and mold.

The aspect of the chambers changed slightly from room to room. In some, the coffins on the shelves were open to view, while in others, they were partially concealed behind rusted metal grates or stacked up on the floor. In one room, the walls were made up entirely of engraved stone plaques in tribute to the deceased, behind which coffins no doubt rested. Some of the rooms also included an ancient, wooden door. A few doors were closed, while others stood open and led into small, private crypts where a stone sarcophagus stood in state. None of tombs, however, had a dragon motif over the doorway or on the coffin itself.

As they marched on, surrounded by so much evidence of death, Selena was keenly aware of the passage of time. She contemplated all the people who had once lived at Darkmoor Park from the time it had been an abbey. One day, *she* might be buried here. Would she be in a coffin slid onto an open shelf? Or would she be worthy enough to merit a private tomb? The idea made her shudder.

A slight shuffling sound made her heart skip a beat. "Are those footsteps?"

Once again, they halted in place and stared behind them. The long pathway was shrouded in blackness. Suddenly, two rats dashed into view, freezing with blazing eyes when they came in contact with the lantern's beam. A second later, they scampered off and disappeared into a crevice in a wall.

"*Rats.*" Dr. Scott shook his head. "This is a creepy place, but we mustn't allow ourselves to get spooked."

They continued into the next chamber, where the only light was provided by their lantern. Coffins were stacked up willy-nilly in piles across the floor. Selena spied an open doorway that led to a tomb. On pedestals on either side of the door, stood stone statues about three feet high that depicted women in Renaissance-era dress.

The stone pediment above the door was adorned with a mythical creature with the body of a lion and the head, wings, and talons of an eagle. "Look!" Selena cried.

"A griffin," Dr. Scott noted.

"An unschooled person might mistake it for a dragon."

His eyes widened. "Let's take a look."

They entered the tomb. A stone sarcophagus within was topped by the figure of a gentlewoman lying on her back, her arms folded in prayer. Selena ran her fingers along the finely carved stone lid. "I wonder who she was?"

Dr. Scott squatted and studied the plaque on the side of the sarcophagus. "Lady Georgina Mason, Born May 9, 1532, Died March 18, 1584. A good and honest woman."

"A nice tribute," Selena remarked, "to focus on the woman's honesty."

A frown took over Dr. Scott's face. His cheeks reddened, and his mouth opened and closed, as if he were deliberating how to reply. Suddenly, his head snapped up, he stood abruptly, and whirled away, taking the lantern with him. Selena, surprised by his sudden departure, wondered what was wrong. Had he heard a suspicious sound?

Selena felt her way out of the tomb by the dim remaining light. "Dr. Scott?" She didn't see him. She heard a rapid scuffling sound from behind a stack of nearby coffins. Was it rats again? She shrank away with a terrible sense of foreboding.

All at once, something hard and heavy struck Selena's back and shoulders. A bolt of pain shot through her as she cried out and tumbled to the ground.

And everything went black.

CHAPTER TWENTY-FOUR

SELENA'S HEAD WAS pounding. Her eyes were so heavy, she couldn't open them. Her body was free floating and jostling. Was she being carried?

The sound of deep, rapid breathing reached her ears. Her head was cradled against something hard. The scratchy texture of wool was against her cheek. The scent of woodsy cologne infused her nostrils. Dr. Scott wore that scent. Was it his labored respiration that she heard? Was she in his arms? *How wonderful to be in Dr. Scott's arms.*

But something was wrong. Selena managed to open her eyes a slit. It was dark, but they were surrounded by a halo of flickering light.

"Stay with me, Selena." It was Dr. Scott's voice, and it was deep and filled with anxiety. "Stay with me."

I'm here, she wanted to tell him. *I'm here.* But the throbbing in her head intensified, and blackness claimed her once more.

"SELENA! SELENA!"

Selena opened her eyes, squinting at light so dazzling, it made her head pound. Dr. Scott, in his shirtsleeves and waistcoat, was bent over her, his dark-blue eyes filled with concern. He let out a deep inhalation. "Oh, thank heavens."

Still struggling to adjust to the brightness around her, Selena stared up at a high ceiling of grey stone. Sunlight bathed the white walls in a rainbow of colors. She spotted the stained-glass window of St. George and the Dragon. *Ah.* They were in the chapel. She was lying on a pew. Her head was cushioned by something. She reached up behind her to touch it. Woolen fabric. Was it Dr. Scott's folded frock coat? Selena tried to go back in her mind to the last thing she remembered, but her brain pulsated with pain and confusion. *Think, think. Oh, yes. We were in the catacombs. Looking for a dragon.*

"How do you feel?" Dr. Scott asked.

"Like my head was hit by an anvil."

"That's understandable. You've suffered a mild concussion." Dr. Scott looked intently into her eyes. "Can you tell me your name?"

Why was he asking that? she thought irritably. Did he think she was a fool? "Selena Taylor." She recalled stepping out of a burial chamber. And then—nothing.

"Can you lift your right hand?"

Selena suddenly understood. He was being doctorly and giving her a medical overview. She raised the requested hand and saw relief cross his face. "How long have I been out?"

"About ten minutes or so, but you briefly awoke once or twice." He took one of her hands in both of his and clasped it warmly.

Her mind felt clearer now. "I remember being in the catacombs." She rubbed her shoulder, wincing as a spasm of pain shot through her. "We didn't find the dragon tomb."

"We'll go back when you feel up to it."

She remembered something else. "Why did you run off like that, with our only light?"

A faint blush stained his cheeks. "I thought I heard something and hurried out to check. I shouldn't have left you in the dark. I'm sorry."

"What happened after that?"

His lips compressed. "Do you remember the stone statues on the pedestals beside the tomb's entrance?"

"Yes."

"One of them fell. When I turned around, I found you and the statue on the ground. If you'd been standing a few inches farther back, it might have killed you."

Thoughts tossed through Selena's brain like stones in a tumbler. "Wait. Did you say a statue *fell* on me?"

"Yes. It must have been precariously balanced, and we disturbed it when we walked by."

Selena dredged up the memory of the last thing she had heard before she'd blacked out. "That statue didn't fall," she exclaimed. "It was pushed."

"'Pushed'? What do you mean?"

"Someone else was in the catacombs and they shoved it onto me."

A line formed between his brows. "I thought I heard someone, too. But if anyone else had been there when I left the tomb, I would have seen them."

"Did you check behind the stacks of coffins, or the closest archway?"

"No."

Selena blinked rapidly. "When we entered the tunnel, we heard a door creak. We thought somebody might have followed us in, but we discounted it. Later, we heard another strange sound. We thought it was rats."

"It *was* rats."

"Yes, but why did they scamper away like that? Unless they were running *from* something ... *or somebody?*"

He frowned. "If so, I repeat, we would have seen them."

"Would we? Remember, there were only pockets of light."

"Still, I don't think—" he began, but she continued.

"Just before I was hit, I heard a scuffling sound. Someone must have been hiding while we were in the tomb. When I came out, they pushed the statue off the pedestal and hid again. Did you look inside the tomb?"

"No. It never would have occurred to me. You were unconscious. My only thought was to get you out of the catacombs as quickly as possible."

Selena realized she hadn't yet thanked him for that. "I'm so grateful that you did. I can't thank you enough." She took a breath. "But, Dr. Scott, don't you see? I might not have been the only target. That fallen statue may have been meant for both of us. Have you forgotten the threatening notes?"

"Of course not, but—"

"For days, we've been on the trail of a purported killer whom we believe is after the hidden money. They warned us to *stay out of this or die*. They may have just tried to do away with me—and had you been standing closer, you as well."

Dr. Scott rubbed his chin pensively. "I understand what you're saying. But to think that someone might have followed us all that way, intending to do us harm ... it seems incredible."

"It's not." Selena shook her head, which caused a splitting pain to spear her forehead. "If you only knew what happened to Athena and me two years ago, the lengths to which a determined killer went to try to murder us ... you wouldn't doubt what occurred here today. And it's not the first attempt. I think when we were trapped in the icehouse that someone shut the door on us deliberately."

"Possibly," he conceded, although his voice rang with doubt.

"We're lucky we got out or poor Billy would have died in there with us," Selena insisted. "Plus, I don't think I had a nightmare the other night. I think someone really did plan to smother me in my sleep."

Dr. Scott's frown deepened. "But you said yourself, the second pillow hadn't moved."

"The perpetrator must have brought their own pillow with them."

He raised his hands in acquiescence. "All right. I've heard

enough." He ran an agitated hand through his hair. "Let's say, for the sake of argument, that you're right. That someone did try to kill you, and possibly *us* today. The question is: what shall we do about it?"

A wave of relief washed over her. At last, he was listening. "Whatever we do, we have to hurry." From her prone position on the bench, Selena squinted towards the chapel windows. The sun beat down on the landscape beyond. Although snow was scattered in drifts across the lawns, in most areas, it was nearly gone, leaving wide, muddy patches in its wake. "Even if the roads are clear of snow by tomorrow, they'll be sunk in mud and untraversable. But the trains might start running again. Our guests may decide to leave."

"I thought they were staying through the new year?"

"That was the intention, but with all that's happened, I wouldn't blame them if they want to depart early." Selena pondered. "When you arrived in Darkmoor Bridge, you learned that our vicar, Mr. Johnson—the parish constable—was away for the holidays. When did you say he is supposed to return?"

Dr. Scott seemed to flinch at her question—an odd reaction, Selena thought. Perhaps he was just thinking hard, as she was. "December 29th."

"That's tomorrow." Selena clasped her hands. "If the trains do start running, and Mr. Johnson returns, we can tell him everything that's happened."

"I suppose we *could*." Dr. Scott's forehead creased. "But we still don't have a shred of evidence to support any of our theories. No way to prove that anyone's actually been murdered, or that *attempted* murder has occurred, or even that any cash is hidden here."

Selena blew out a sigh. "I know. But Mr. Johnson is a thoughtful and intelligent man. He'll listen, at least. In the meantime, we have to *find* that proof and the truth of what's been happening."

"The truth." Dr. Scott fell silent and glanced away, a haunted expression in his eyes.

Selena wondered what he was thinking. "Are you all right?"

"Yes." He shook his head as if to clear it. "And *in the meantime*," he said, echoing her words, "I must get you to bed. You need to rest and recover."

"I'm all right," Selena assured him. But when she tried to sit up, her head hammered with such violent pain that she fell back, groaning.

"What hurts?" he demanded.

"My head."

"I'm not surprised. Let me help you up." With the gentlest of care, he assisted her to a sitting position on the pew. "For the next forty-eight hours, you must lie in a darkened room. Doctor's orders. No exertion of any kind that will tax body or your brain. Just peace and quiet."

Selena made a face. "That doesn't sound like fun."

"You're not supposed to have fun. You've suffered a concussion. Being overly active right now can be dangerous."

"Oh, Doctor, don't be so dramatic. I'll be fine," Selena insisted.

"We can't be certain of that." He was emphatic and his eyes were worried. "I've done some research on the condition. Pushing yourself too soon might worsen your symptoms, delay the healing process, and increase the risk of a second concussion or even brain damage."

Selena started to shake her head, which once again caused it to ache more. "Fine, whatever you say."

Dr. Scott put his frock coat back on. "Do you feel well enough to stand?"

"I think so." As he helped her to her feet, a wave of dizziness took hold of her, and she wavered and fell against him. "Sorry."

"When we get upstairs, I'll give you something to help with the pain," he said, supporting her firmly with both arms.

"Not laudanum," she quipped, remembering that Colonel Blackwood had said the same thing.

Dr. Scott's lips twitched. Whatever had been troubling him seemed to have left his mind. "I won't give you a drop more than is required for a restful sleep."

As they made their way across the chapel, Selena said, "As soon as we can, we need to visit the catacombs again and work on a plan to entrap the villain before they can strike again."

"We'll see. Only when you feel better," he cautioned. "To-night, I'm going to ask Mrs. Hillman to post a servant at your bedside to watch over you."

"Why? That's unnecessary."

"If someone really did just try to kill you, it's completely necessary," he insisted. "Plus, you've had a head injury. You may need help during the night. Someone needs to be on guard to alert me if anything changes."

Selena couldn't think of an argument against that. "Very well, but please make sure it's not Gladys."

"Duly noted."

"What about you?" she asked, aware that the villain might have it in for both of them. "Who's going to keep you safe?"

"I can take care of myself." They were nearly to the chapel's exit. Dr. Scott paused and, to Selena's surprise, he bent his head to hers and kissed her full on the mouth.

It was an absolutely lovely kiss that sent sparks shooting through Selena's entire body and literally curled her toes.

"What was that for?" she asked, her pulse racing.

"For believing in me," he said simply. With that, he opened the chapel door and escorted her out.

SELENA AWAKENED THE next morning to find Beryl asleep in the chair beside her bed.

Her memory of the night before was hazy. When she and Dr. Scott had returned from the catacombs, he'd given Selena medicine to help her sleep. She had been lost to the world for the rest of the day and night, waking intermittently only long enough to accept a glass of water from the maid who had been watching over her, and to drink the cup of beef tea the doctor had ordered.

As Selena slowly sat up in bed, her head began to pound, and pain shot up the back of her neck. She couldn't prevent a groan.

Beryl opened her eyes. "Miss!" She yawned and stretched her arms. "I must have dozed off. I wasn't supposed to. How do you feel?"

"My head hurts," Selena admitted.

"I'm sorry. Dr. Scott said you might be in pain. I was to watch out for confusion and seizures, he said, and call him if you seemed worse."

"Thank you for staying. I'm sorry you had to sleep in that chair. I seem to be all in one piece and not any worse for wear."

"Thank goodness for that." Beryl stood and opened the drapes.

Sunlight beamed into the room. The light seemed overly bright. Selena held up a hand to shield her eyes as she squinted out the window, where moisture sparkled on the sodden back lawns and the remaining drifts of snow. When Beryl helped Selena rise and perform her morning ablutions, she felt dizzy and was grateful to crawl back into bed afterwards.

"The doctor said you're to stay in bed until he has a chance to see you. Before I call him, I'll have your breakfast brought up," the maid explained before exiting the room.

Selena closed her eyes to rest them. It seemed that Beryl had only been gone a few seconds when Gladys entered the chamber.

"Good morning. Mrs. Hillman told me to bring you breakfast in bed," Gladys announced as she crossed Selena's room with a tray.

Selena's entire body tensed. *Is she Gladys or Maisie? Could it have been Gladys who pushed over that statue in the catacombs?*

"I hope you're feeling better?" Gladys set down the breakfast tray over Selena's lap and removed the silver domes from two plates, revealing scrambled eggs and bacon, toast, a dish of butter, and a cup of coffee.

The tantalizing aromas distracted Selena from her musings. Her head still throbbed, but she realized she was famished. "Yes, thank you." To her surprise, a folded newspaper lay on the tray—an edition of *The London Times*. "How did we come by a newspaper, Gladys?"

"The snow being mostly gone, Mrs. Hillman sent Billy into the village this morning to fetch a paper," Gladys replied. "The trains aren't running yet, but he said they might be back in operation this afternoon. He managed to get copies of this old newspaper, though—it arrived just before the storm."

"I see." Selena unfolded the linen napkin on her lap and picked up the fork and knife. "Thank you, Gladys."

The maid curtsied and left the room. Selena was glad to see her go. She tasted a slice of bacon, relishing the smoky flavor. As she ate, her headache dissipated. It occurred to her that she had slept through everything last night. Selena wondered if the dramatic readings had taken place without her, and if so, she hoped they'd gone well. She was so hungry, she ate nearly everything on the plate before she took time to open the newspaper.

It was dated December 23rd, 1852. The day that their guests had arrived at Darkmoor Park. As always, the news was featured in multiple columns of short, blocklike snippets of identically sized text, each item separated by a horizontal line. Selena took a sip of coffee as she glanced over the news. There was an article about a concert at the London Harmonic Society, a notice that a steamship sailing from London to Dunkirk and Lille had been postponed due to poor weather, an article about a public meeting to consider the policies of *The Times*, and a shopkeeper's list of food items for sale for Christmas dinner.

Another item caught Selena's attention, and it made her freeze.

A LETTER HAS JUST BEEN RECEIVED BY THE TIMES

from a MR. JOHN CLARKE, a businessman. Mr. Clarke writes:

"I am writing to The Times *to ensure that there is a written record of the dire situation in which I find myself. I am the co-founder of the LONDON GENERAL HOSPITAL FOUNDATION. I have raised £5000 in cash for this worthy project. My business partner, DR. ANDREW DALTON, who resides in Hampstead, is thirty-one years of age, a tall man of gentlemanly appearance with a jagged scar on his forehead. I have reason to suspect that he intends to murder me, steal all the funds, and flee the country. I am afraid to leave my house or go to the police. Should anything happen to me, should this villain carry out his threat, I pray that he may be apprehended, and justice may be served."*

Please note: The Times *does not endorse this message nor purport any part of it to be true. Should you have information about the above proceedings, please contact Scotland Yard or* The London Times *office.*

Selena read the article once, twice, and then a third time. She couldn't believe her eyes.

She was shocked for two reasons. Firstly: that *The Times* had printed such a libelous letter, even while admitting that they did not endorse a word of it. And yet they *had* printed it, which implied that they must have thought it had merit and needed to be seen.

Secondly: the names contained therein were all too familiar, starting with the author of the piece, *John Clarke.*

The letter she had discovered in Mr. Clarke's bedroom had been addressed to John Clarke, apparently the man's formal name. When he'd spoken out of turn at the White Hart Inn, he had confided that he'd brought money with him to protect it from a potential thief who had threatened his life. But Selena now realized, he had never identified the man who had vowed to rob and kill him. Until now.

Dr. Andrew Dalton.

A tall, thirty-one-year-old man of gentlemanly appearance with a jagged scar on his forehead.

It was a perfect description of Dr. Scott.

The name on the calling card Selena had found in Dr. Scott's coat pocket had been Dr. Andrew Dalton. As she recalled, it had included an address in Hampstead. Dr. Scott had explained that card away, claiming that it belonged to a colleague who had called on him the day before he'd left London. Had that been a lie?

Were Dr. Scott and Dr. Dalton one and the same person? *They must be.*

Dr. Scott was Mr. Clarke's business partner. The thought was so astonishing it made Selena's body go cold. She'd had a feeling all along that something wasn't right about Dr. Scott, but she had always talked herself out of it—*and she had never considered this.*

Anger, embarrassment, and disappointment flooded her every pore. The doctor, she realized, had been perpetrating a fraud the entire time he had been at Darkmoor Park. He was a liar, a scoundrel, and a thief—and she had fallen for it. The signs had been there from the very beginning. How could she have missed them?

When he had arrived that first snowy morning, he had seemed stunned to discover that the dead man on the stairwell landing was Mr. Clarke—but she had discounted that. On more than one occasion, he had not responded when Selena had called him Dr. Scott—and no wonder, since he'd apparently made up the name. And no wonder, when she had called him *Adrian* after they'd kissed in the folly, he had reacted with such guilt and confusion.

To think that she had kissed him! Heatedly! More than once! And had told herself she had fallen in love with him!

On one occasion, he had referred to the deceased man as "Clarke" without the "Mr." title—an informality that she had wondered about. She'd suspected that he wasn't from Bath—and now she knew she had been right. She should have listened to her gut.

Selena seethed inwardly. The doctor must have been furious to discover that Mr. Clarke had left London with all the money meant for the hospital—money he had planned to steal himself. Somehow, he must have learned where Mr. Clarke had gone and followed him. His excuse for being on the train that had brought him here—to visit friends in Edinburgh—had been a total lie. How convenient for him that there had been a patient at Darkmoor Park in need of medical attention. How relieved he must have been to find that the patient in question had been Mr. Clarke himself—and that the man was already dead! It had paved the way for the doctor to search for the money himself.

Selena's hand went to her face with dismay as she realized that their entire hunt for the money had not been an effort on his part to return the funds to the hospital foundation, but for his own personal gain. How could she have allowed herself to be taken in by this confidence man? Had she learned nothing from her liaison with Jerome Withers? Once again, she had allowed herself to be swept off her feet by a handsome, charming man in a whirlwind romance that had ended in deceit and heartbreak.

Selena's throat constricted and she choked back tears. She felt like an utter fool. She had told the doctor about Mr. Clarke's dying words, believing she could trust him. What else, she wondered, had he lied about?

Selena removed the breakfast tray from her lap and stood. The room began spinning around her and she sank back down onto the bed again. *Wait, wait,* she thought. *What about the Webster siblings? How did they figure into all this?*

The doctor had alleged that the Websters' plot for revenge was a valid theory, and perhaps a separate crime that had nothing to do with the hidden money. But what if he'd just said that to distract her from his true purpose in coming to Darkmoor Park? What if Maisie and Joe Webster weren't here at all—and never had been? What if, as Mrs. Hillman had so often insisted, the entire Websters conspiracy had been a figment of Selena's imagination?

Selena thought back to Mr. Clarke's death. Had he indeed been murdered? Or had he simply taken a misstep on the stairs in the dark?

And what about Mrs. Whitlock? Selena and the doctor had both believed, in those first days on the case, that Mrs. Whitlock had wanted that five thousand pounds so badly, she'd written the threatening notes, warning them to *stop looking*. To what lengths, Selena wondered with rising dread, would Dr. Scott—or rather Dr. Dalton—have gone, to ensure that no one else found that money before he did?

Another equally horrifying thought followed.

Yesterday, in the catacombs, just before that statue had come down upon her, Dr. Scott had moved away, taking the lantern with him. Later, he had apologized, saying that he'd thought he'd heard something—a shoddy excuse for leaving her alone in the dark. When she had exited the tomb, she'd lost sight of him. Was it possible that Dr. Scott himself had pushed over that statue onto her? Had he wanted Selena dead, so that once he found the money, he could keep every penny for himself? Having failed at that attempt to kill her, would he try again?

Selena went stiff with terror. What now? Their search yesterday had been aborted. The doctor would surely go back to the catacombs on his own and keep looking. Selena glanced out her bedroom window, blinking at the intense glare. Billy had been able to reach the village on foot today. Which meant that the doctor could do so as well. If he found the hidden cash, he would flee.

Somehow, she had to stop him. Before he made another move. If only she could go to the parish constable! Selena's breath caught in her throat. Today was the twenty-ninth of December—the day that the constable had planned to return. If Mr. Johnson were coming home by carriage, he would be delayed, for the roads would be impassable. But if the trains started running again, he might be back this very afternoon.

She could send word to the vicarage and ask Mr. Johnson's housekeeper to let Selena know the minute he was back, explaining that she had important information to share with him.

Meanwhile, Selena decided, she needed to talk to Mrs. Hillman. The older woman had dismissed everything Selena had told her so far, but Selena had new information now. It was time to tell her not only about the doctor's deception, but about Mr. Clarke's dying words. She glanced at the clock. It was a few minutes past nine. Mrs. Hillman might still be in her room.

Selena quickly got dressed and pulled on her shoes. Pain erupted in her skull. She ignored it. The doctor had told her she must lie quietly in bed for another full day, or it could have unwelcome repercussions. But there was no time to think about that now.

Moments later, she was knocking on Mrs. Hillman's bedroom door. There was no answer. *Perhaps*, Selena thought, *Mrs. Hillman has already risen?*

Selena made her way downstairs, ignoring the throbbing in her head and neck. She peeked into the morning room. All the guests, with the exception of the doctor, were at breakfast. Mrs. Hillman wasn't there. Selena knew that her friend sometimes started the day with a visit to the chapel. She hurried there, but to her disappointment, the sanctuary was empty.

It suddenly occurred to Selena that she was only steps away from the entrance to the tunnel to the catacombs. If she could take another look—if she could find the hidden cash—she would have proof to help back up her claims against the doctor. And she needed to get that money before he did. Dread pooled in her stomach at the thought of entering that underground chamber again. But it had to be done.

Selena hurried to the shelving unit behind the altar. She was about to grab a candle when the bookcase door suddenly swung open.

And the doctor strode out through it.

CHAPTER TWENTY-FIVE

S ELENA GASPED AND froze, an action mirrored by the doctor, who had just burst into the chapel through the bookcase door that led to the underground tunnel.

"Selena!" His eyes were wide with shock. "Why are you out of bed?"

Selena's heart thundered in her ears as, too stunned to speak, she recoiled backwards.

The doctor set the lantern he was carrying atop the altar. "I told you it's vital that you rest for the next day or two. Any physical or mental activity could delay your recovery." He paused, his forehead furrowing. "What's wrong?"

She considered fleeing the chapel, but her legs were suddenly wobbly, and that simple backwards motion had caused another spasm of pain to ricochet through her head. She doubted she could outrun this man in her current state. Instead, she grabbed a large, brass candlestick from the altar and clutched it in a tight fist before her. "You went back to the catacombs while I was sleeping," she blurted out.

He shifted uncomfortably from one foot to the other. "I did."

"Did you find the money?" she snapped.

He shook his head. "But that doesn't mean it isn't there."

Selena blew out a disgusted breath. To know that he had continued searching while she had lain in bed drugged by whatever medication he had given her … It made her blood boil.

"If we could get a clearer picture from Mrs. Hillman about the dragon image she saw, we might have better luck, and ..." He broke off, eyes narrowing. "Why are you holding that candlestick as if it were a weapon?"

"Shouldn't I be, Dr. Scott?" Selena demanded coldly. "Or should I say, Dr. Andrew Dalton?"

At that, his jaw dropped, and his body stiffened. For a long moment, he said nothing. At last, he said quietly, "So, you know. Yes. I am Andrew Dalton."

Anger rose in Selena's breast. "How could you do it?"

"Do what?" he replied, his tone flat.

"Mr. Clarke wrote to *The London Times*. All about your plan to murder him and steal the money he'd raised for the London General Hospital Foundation."

"Ah." He nodded slowly. "You've read the December 23rd edition?"

"The hall boy fetched it from the train station this morning." A thought occurred to Selena, and she inhaled abruptly. "The colonel brought a newspaper with him, but it was stolen. It was *that* edition, wasn't it? It was *you* who stole it!"

"I did take that newspaper. I'm sure you can understand why." A dark glare took over his face. "It was highly irresponsible of *The Times* to print that letter. I'm guessing Clarke knew or paid off an editor there. I intend to speak to my solicitor in Town at the earliest opportunity and file a libel suit. All it takes is one accusation like that to ruin a man's reputation, or his life. And there isn't a word of truth in what he wrote."

"Forgive me if I don't believe you." Selena took another step back. "Mr. Clarke told his dining companions at the White Hart Inn that he had taken the money to protect it from his business partner, to whom he had been coerced into giving the combination to his safe. He never said *who* his partner was, but now I know. It was *you*."

He blew out a sigh. "I did work with Clarke—but the issue of the money didn't happen the way you think."

Selena ignored his look of protest. "I trusted you! I thought we were searching for the money together, to return it to the foundation. But all this time, you intended to keep it for yourself!"

"No—" he began, but she cut him off.

"You followed Mr. Clarke here, determined to get that money. How shocked you must have been to find him dead—and yet how convenient that was. Now he could never come after you! All you had to do was find the cash and flee." Selena's stomach churned with fury. "What a fool I was to play your willing dupe in this sham of a treasure hunt, and a 'murder investigation' to boot! Just how badly did you want that money? Did you kill Mrs. Whitlock to remove her from the equation?"

"*What?*" He stared at her, his eyes wide. "Don't be absurd."

"You're a doctor. You would have known exactly how much laudanum it would take to kill a person."

He shook his head emphatically. "No! You've got it all wrong."

"Have I? Please enlighten me."

"I will. But first, put down that candlestick. I swear, I mean you no harm."

Selena hesitated, but to her surprise, she didn't see any threat in the doctor's eyes. He just looked tired and frustrated. Still, she didn't trust him for an instant. She set down the candlestick on the altar but kept it close just in case. "I'm listening."

He crossed his arms and stared at the stone floor beneath their feet. "A year ago, I was just a struggling doctor with a small medical practice in London, working hard to make ends meet. Out of the blue, John Clarke came to me with a proposal—to be the co-founder of a new hospital. That's the name I knew him by—John, not Jack. He said he'd heard great things about me from my patients. He needed a doctor on board to make the foundation more legitimate. And he wanted it to be me. He was a man of immense charm and presented himself as a legitimate and respected businessman. I was flattered. I saw it as an unexpected opportunity. To help found a new hospital—I couldn't have dreamed of taking such a step so early in my career."

He paced back and forth beside the altar with rising agitation as he continued. "I willingly joined him. He put me in charge of the building phase of the project and its financial management so he could concentrate on fundraising. He appealed primarily to private investors—successful businessmen and wealthy widows and matrons who sought to do good in the world. Clarke said he didn't trust banks. He'd lost a bundle once when a bank had failed, he claimed. Fool that I am, I believed him. Although I opened a bank account in the name of the foundation, he had me turn every investment into fifty-pound notes, which he kept in a safe at his house. While continuing my private practice, I also sought out investors and put in nearly every penny I had, over three hundred pounds. Two months ago, on Clarke's orders, I signed a lease on a building for the future hospital, hired contractors to begin renovating it, and purchased the equipment we would need—all on credit with the promise to pay."

Selena listened to all this with a frown. He had lied about so many things. How could she trust a word he was saying? Even if what he'd said was true, it didn't make him blameless if he had ultimately decided to go after the money for himself. "This is a nice little story, doctor, but—"

"It's not a *story*. It's the truth! Hear me out, will you?" His blue eyes flashed. "On the morning of December 23rd, I saw that article in *The Times*. I was dumbfounded. Clarke had made absurd, totally false statements, accusing me of being a potential murderer and thief. I realized that I'd been duped—Clarke must have intended all along to flee with that money. I felt like an idiot for having fallen for his scheme. I raced to his house in a panic, but he wasn't there. His housekeeper had just arrived—she knew me and let me in. The furniture in his study was in disarray. His wall safe was standing open and empty. There were bloodstains on the carpet. Where the blood came from, I don't know—an animal, I imagine—but it looked like someone had been murdered there."

This was too much. Selena shook her head. "Doctor, this is beginning to sound like a serial installment from one of Mr. Dickens's more sensational tales."

He heaved a sigh of frustration. "I am only telling you what actually occurred. I guessed at once what his letter to *The Times* had been for. Clarke had intended to fake his death, frame me for his murder, and disappear with the funds. His housekeeper walked in, screamed, and ran off, I presume to summon the police. I knew I had to get out there and fast, or I might be arrested on suspicion of Clarke's murder as well as theft. So, I fled and hopped on the first train north."

Selena wished she could believe him. But looking at him as he stood before her, his eyes frantic, his hand raking through his hair, she saw only a desperate man who would say anything to try to convince her of his innocence. "You just hopped on a train?" Selena charged, shaking her head. "And it just magically brought you here, where Mr. Clarke happened to be?"

"No! *No.* I guessed that Clarke had gone to Darkmoor Park."

"How?"

"My first thought was that he meant to flee the country—and had he lived, he undoubtedly would have. But I recalled him mentioning, a few months ago, that he'd received an invitation to spend the holidays at Darkmoor Park in Yorkshire, from a wonderful woman to whom he owed some money. He said he had always wanted to pay her back. At the time, he probably hadn't made his escape plan yet. I'm sure it never occurred to him that I'd remember what he'd said, but I did. I figured he might have stopped there on his way to Scotland. At least it was worth a try."

It was a simple and clever answer—but had he just made it up? "What did you imagine you would do when you got here? Confront Mr. Clarke and demand that he hand over the money?"

His face colored. "Something like that. It wasn't much of a plan, I know, but there wasn't time to think of a better one. I was determined to prove that he *had* the money so I could return it to the hospital fund."

"'Return it to the hospital fund'?" Selena repeated with heavy skepticism. "I'll bet."

"Yes! That was my primary goal—and still is. And at the time, my life was on the line. If Clarke's accusations in that letter were believed, I knew I could be tried and imprisoned for embezzlement and worse yet, possibly convicted of murder—and hanged."

"That's all just words, words from a man who is so very good at lying. Your story is impossible to swallow, Doctor. You wouldn't have been convicted of murder. This house is full of witnesses who could attest that they saw Jack Clarke alive and well the day he arrived."

"The London police would never have thought to look for Clarke hundreds of miles away here in Yorkshire," the doctor exclaimed. "Why would they? They wouldn't have had any idea where he'd gone. I'm telling you, the case against me would have been closed in ten seconds flat."

Selena shook her head. "If Mrs. Hillman or anyone who knew Mr. Clarke had read that letter in *The Times*, they would have known he hadn't died in London."

"Clarke is a common name," the doctor countered. "They wouldn't have connected a story about John Clarke to a man they knew as Jack. At least, that's what *he* was hoping, I'm sure. And I didn't know the people here when I set out. For all I knew, Clarke had friends who would have lied for him. I *had* to come. If nothing else, I had to prove that Clarke was still alive so that I wouldn't be blamed for his 'death.'" He heaved another sigh. "The rest of it, you know. My train was stopped by the snow. I walked the last few miles and encountered your hall boy. Upon learning that you needed a doctor ..." His voice trailed off.

"You saw it as the perfect way to gain entry to Darkmoor Park."

"Yes."

"And you introduced yourself as Dr. Adrian Scott—which

was a lie."

"How could I do otherwise?" He braced both hands on the altar and said impatiently, "For all I knew, you were already in possession of that edition of *The Times* that incriminates Dr. Andrew Dalton as a potential thief and murderer. And if not— when I saw that Clarke was here, and dead, I worried that he might have told you or someone else the same lies he had spewed in his letter to the newspaper—which indeed turned out to be the case. I feared that if you knew who I was, you would turn me in to the law."

"So, you pretended to be Dr. Scott, a man who was *so grateful* to remain at Darkmoor Park for the holidays." Selena looked at him, heartsick to her very core. "When I—naively—shared Mr. Clarke's dying words with you, and my suspicion that he may have been murdered for his money, you were only too happy to foster those ideas and join me in a treasure hunt. And why not? Two heads *are* better than one. And working with me meant you didn't have to sneak around, and it gave you easy access to every room in the house."

His face turned a darker shade of pink. "I'm sorry. It did start that way, but ..."

"You're *sorry?*" Selena spat the words. She felt used, ridiculous. How effortlessly he had taken advantage of her and exploited her good nature. He must have been laughing at her all this time.

"Don't you see? I *had* to find that money." His voice rang with desperation. "Every penny of it had been spoken for. Creditors were clamoring to be paid. I knew *I* would be liable for the entire sum. There was no way I could come up with fifty-two hundred pounds. When I couldn't pay back that money, I would have been put in debtors' prison. I've visited patients who are incarcerated, although I wasn't allowed to do much to treat them. I know how horrible the conditions are—cruel wardens, severe overcrowding, lack of sanitation, and starvation all lead to the spread of diseases like typhus and typhoid. Who knows how long

I would have survived in such a dark and dismal place? My freedom and possibly my very life were at stake."

He was breathing rapidly, and his eyes reflected such deep pain and anxiety that an unexpected wave of doubt washed over Selena. She was aware of the awful conditions in the nation's prisons. It made sense that he would be terrified of facing such a fate. But although his fear seemed genuine, was there any truth to the rest of it? Or was it just a clever tactic to pull the wool over her eyes? "Why would Mr. Clarke have told his dinner companions at the White Hart Inn about the money if he'd stolen it from a hospital fund?"

"*That*, as Mrs. Whitlock said so eloquently the other day, must have been the drink talking. Clarke did tend to run off at the mouth when he'd been in his cups. I'm guessing he was furious with himself the next day for revealing that—if he remembered it at all. And it may have proved to be his undoing. It may have led to his murder and all the threatening notes."

There might be truth in that, Selena realized. Her thoughts veered to that bit about the blood on the carpet in Mr. Clarke's study. She was fairly certain Dr. Dalton had made up that sensational detail, as easily as he'd made up a new name. But if, perchance, it were true, what did it mean? Might Mr. Clarke really have sprinkled blood around and sent that letter to *The Times* to frame Dr. Dalton? But no. That seemed impossible to believe.

"Even if Mr. Clarke did pay someone at *The Times* to publish that letter," she reflected slowly, "or it slipped in without proper editorial oversight, it doesn't prove that Mr. Clarke's *concerns* were invalid. He may have been truly afraid. He wasn't a thief or a cad. He paid Mrs. Hillman back, after all! She adored him."

"You put a lot of stock in Mrs. Hillman's opinions of the man," the doctor shot back.

"Why shouldn't I? I like to think that she's a good judge of character. I only wish I could say the same for me." Selena fixed him with her gaze and let out a huff of self-derision. "All this time,

I've been on a wild goose chase, haven't I? When the Webster siblings came up, you must have seen *that* as quite an amusing diversion."

"No! *No.* You're wrong there." He raised his hands as if in self-defense. "I legitimately thought, and still think, that theory may be possible, even if it means there are two crimes going on here. Otherwise, who tried to poison Colonel Blackwood?"

Selena hesitated. Could he be right about that? Could Joe or Maisie Webster be at Darkmoor Park, after all, determined to complete their revenge plan—by getting rid of Colonel Blackwood and anyone who stood in their way? Or was the doctor merely spewing clever words again to throw her off track?

Selena's head began to pound. The whole story was getting muddled in her mind.

"You sound so earnest," she asked quietly. "But you have been lying to me through your teeth since the day we met."

"I know. It was wrong. And I can't tell you how sorry I am." The doctor took a step forward, then stopped himself, his features tense with apparent self-recrimination. "Selena, from the moment I arrived at Darkmoor Park, I have been drawn to you. I told myself to keep my distance, knowing that I wasn't being honest with you. But I wanted to get to the bottom of these mysteries as much as you did. It made sense to work together. I was already in too deep before I realized I had feelings for you. And—"

"'Feelings for me'?" Selena repeated in disbelief. "What a joke. Is that something you feel compelled to say to try to win me over to your side?"

"What? No!"

Selena let out a bitter laugh. "When you shared that story about growing up in an orphanage, and your love of helping the sick, had every word been calculated? A ploy to arouse my sympathy and admiration? To distract me from the scheme you were perpetrating?"

The color drained from his face. "How can you even think that?" He hunched over, clutching his hands to his chest. "Selena.

I wish, from the bottom of my heart, that we could turn back the clock and start over. I wish that we had met under different circumstances. But ... after that first kiss, I told you I couldn't help myself. I wanted to be with you any way I could. There were so many times I wanted to tell you ..."

The plaintive look in his blue eyes looked so genuine that it ripped at her heart and made her stagger back a step. She wanted so desperately to believe him. But how could she?

Vivid images of moments that she and the doctor had shared began to play in her mind—hunting in this chapel for hidden treasure, their midnight talks in her study, the snowshoe trek to the folly, the caring manner in which he had tended her burned arm, the kisses they had shared.

He'd had plenty of opportunities to tell her the truth about himself, but he hadn't even tried.

She felt so stupid for falling for his lies—for actually imagining that she had fallen in love with him.

At the same time, a voice nagged at the back of her mind. Could that man, the man with whom she *thought* she had grown so close, be guilty of the charges that Mr. Clarke had laid at his feet? Was he a thief? Could he truly have threatened to murder Mr. Clarke? Had he poisoned Mrs. Whitlock?

Her gut, at war with her mind, told her otherwise. *No. No! He couldn't be.*

And yet ...

"One may smile, and smile, and be a villain." That line had been spoken by Shakespeare's Hamlet after he'd learned about the deceptive nature of Claudius, the new King of Denmark, who had hidden his villainy behind a façade of smiles and pleasantries after murdering his brother.

Selena had only known the doctor less than a week. People, she had learned, were not always what they seemed. The side they presented to the world might not represent their true character at all. How was she to know what he was capable of? He could just be a very good actor.

The throbbing in her temple made it difficult to think. Selena pressed her fingers to her forehead as another saying sprang to mind, the one she and her sisters had been taught in childhood. *"Where there's smoke, there's fire. If something doesn't feel right, it probably isn't."*

Dr. Scott—*no, no, Dr. Dalton*—it would take some time to get used to *that*—had romanced her and used her and lied to her face for days on end, and yet she had trusted him. She would be an even greater fool to trust him now.

"I'll tell you what I believe, Doctor," she said wearily. "I think the first part of your story is true. I think Mr. Clarke *did* invite you, an up-and-coming doctor, to be his partner to establish a new hospital—to give it legitimacy, as you said. Your claim about Mr. Clarke intending to flee the country—that was *your* intent, not his. You followed Mr. Clarke here, not to clear your name, or to rescue the money for the hospital—but so you could keep it for yourself and disappear. And you used me as a pawn in your scheme. Does that about sum it up?"

"No." Dr. Dalton shook his head vehemently. "It does not. I'm telling you—"

"Did you push that statue onto me in the catacombs?" she heard herself exclaim. "Were you trying to get me out of the way so you could keep the entire fortune for yourself?" She didn't believe that anymore, not deep down, and didn't know why she was saying it—perhaps to hurt him, as much as he had hurt her.

Her accusation made him hunch over and visibly wince. "Is that what you really think of me?" His voice broke. "Dear lord, how low I have sunk in your estimation."

His despairing response once again gave Selena momentary pause, but she swallowed hard, determined not to be taken in. "It's the twenty-ninth of December. Our parish constable might be returning today. I'm going to show him that newspaper article, tell him all that has happened here, and your part in it."

The doctor blinked. "I see." He drew in a long breath and looked away. When he spoke again, his voice was deadly quiet.

"Before you do that, allow me to set you straight about two things. Earlier, you accused me of killing Mrs. Whitlock. May I remind you that there was only a brief interval, the night she died, where someone might have had the opportunity to poison her nightcap—the few minutes when she had gone to Miss Thompson's room before retiring. If you recall, you and I were in your study at the time, discussing the results of the Memory Game."

Selena processed that. "Very well," she conceded, "but—"

"As to whether I tried to dispatch you yesterday in the catacombs … I did lie about why I walked away and left you in the dark for a moment. It was because the plaque on the sarcophagus in that tomb had praised its occupant for her honesty, and I was steeped in guilt that I hadn't been honest with you. But that was my only fault. Had I wanted to kill you, after that statue fell, I would have finished the job then and there. It would have been easy enough to do. And I could have hidden your body in any one of a hundred ancient coffins. But I did no such thing. Instead, I carried you out of there as fast as my legs could carry me and tended to you to make sure you were all right."

Selena saw the truth in that and wondered why she hadn't thought of it herself. She struggled for a reply.

"In fact, I lay awake most of the night," the doctor continued. "I was worried sick that your injuries might be more extensive than they had appeared, for the true nature of a concussion can take hours or even days to manifest. I would have sat by your bedside all night myself if I hadn't worried about propriety. I couldn't bear the thought of losing you. But it's clear to me now that such feelings were out of line and pointless—for you were never mine to lose." His eyes looked sad, and he sighed again. "With regard to your other allegations: everything I've told you is true. What you do with that information is up to you. And now, I will not infect you with my unwanted presence a moment longer." His jaw clenched as he strode past her and down the center aisle of the chapel.

Selena's mind reeled with sudden confusion as she watched him go. "Wait!" she exclaimed, but it was too late; he was already out the door. She started for the exit but felt unsteady on her feet again and only made it as far as the first pew, where she sank down on the hard bench, waiting for the dizziness to pass.

Uncertainty enveloped her like a dark cloud. Her concerns were valid, weren't they? Even if, as far as she knew, the doctor hadn't killed anyone, he *had* come here under a false name and had lied about so many things—much of what he'd just told her might be untrue. Although it did seem odd that Mr. Clarke had written that letter to *The London Times*, instead of going to the police, and unusual that the newspaper had risked a libel suit to publish it ... Mr. Clarke's worries might have all been genuine. The doctor had followed him here, after all, determined to find the hidden money, and used Selena as his unwitting accomplice. She *had* to turn him in to the constable. Didn't she?

The chapel door opened, interrupting Selena's thoughts. Her heart lurched. Had the doctor returned? To her disappointment, it was Mrs. Hillman who entered the sanctuary, her face marred by a frown.

"Selena! Why are you up? I thought you were supposed to stay in bed for another day."

Selena shrugged her shoulders. "I've been looking for you. I wanted to talk to you."

Mrs. Hillman made her way down the aisle and sat down beside Selena. "I just passed Dr. Scott in the hall. He had the most thunderous look on his face. Do you know what that's about?"

"I do." Tears welled up in Selena's eyes. "Oh, Mrs. Hillman, there's so much that I haven't told you—things that have been going on here this past week. Secrets I've kept, hoping to protect you. And now it's all gone horribly wrong."

"'Secrets'?" Mrs. Hillman looked at her. "You have already shared many wild theories with me of late, my dear. But go on, tell me what's on your mind."

Selena wiped her eyes, took a deep breath, and plunged in,

admitting to Mr. Clarke's dying words and her theory that he'd not only hidden the five thousand pounds he'd raised for the hospital but may have been murdered for it. She explained that she had teamed up with the doctor to find the money and revealed her suspicions about the death of Mrs. Whitlock. She decided to lead up slowly to the part where Dr. Dalton had been here under an assumed name—the reasons behind it were still too confusing and heartbreaking.

Mrs. Hillman listened in silence and then turned to Selena with raised eyebrows. "What an interesting time you've been having, Selena. I thought the past week was already full of shocking events and turmoil, but I see now that what you *did* tell me wasn't even the half of it." With hooded eyes, she added, "As for Mr. Clarke's message, you said your search for a dragon was for a school lesson."

Selena's cheeks warmed. "Forgive me. You had been so resistant to every idea I had presented and so adamant that Mr. Clarke was innocent, I couldn't bring myself to tell you about that. The five thousand pounds has so far eluded our grasp. There was nothing hidden at the folly and we didn't find a dragon on a tomb in the catacombs."

"It wasn't a dragon *on* a tomb," Mrs. Hillman corrected, her lips pursing. "It was more a dragon *in* a tomb."

"What do you mean?"

"It was on the side of a sarcophagus resting on pedestals in a tomb near the end of the passage, I believe."

"Oh!" Selena committed that information to memory. If the stone coffin was on pedestals, it might be possible to have hidden something beneath it. She heaved a sigh. "But I haven't told you all. The doctor and I have been questioning the guests, trying to determine if the Webster siblings are here at Darkmoor Park. And when we were in the catacombs yesterday, someone followed us in and tried to murder me."

"*Murder* you?" Mrs. Hillman's jaw dropped.

"That's why I was laid up last night. I suffered a concussion."

"You said you had tripped and fallen."

Selena shook her head grimly. "Someone pushed a stone statue onto me."

"Who?"

"I don't know. They came at me from behind." Heat bloomed in Selena's cheeks and her chest tightened. Even if she wasn't entirely sure of all that the doctor had done, she felt bad that she'd thought him culpable of *that*.

Mrs. Hillman's brows drew closer together. "Are you sure the statue didn't fall on its own?"

"I'm sure. Other things have happened this week that could be explained away as accidents, but not this."

"Oh, my dear. I'm so sorry. I don't know what to say about that. Or do."

"Neither do I, to be honest. Apparently, the constable is due back soon. However, I have no idea who's behind all this yet and no way to prove any of it." Selena sighed. "And there's more."

"More?" Mrs. Hillman put her hand to her heart.

Selena took a deep breath. "As it turns out, Dr. Scott isn't who we thought he was. He's been lying since the day he arrived. *He* was Mr. Clarke's business partner. And his name isn't Scott. It's Dalton."

Mrs. Hillman grew still at this revelation. At length, she said, "I know, my dear. I know."

Selena stared at her. "How do you know?"

"Billy brought back two copies of that December 23rd edition of *The London Times*. I just finished reading it in my front parlor. It was plain as day that Dr. Scott is really Dr. Andrew Dalton." Mrs. Hillman's tone was matter-of-fact.

"But ... aren't you shocked? Aren't you angry?"

"Not really. I thought it proved what I'd always known about Jack Clarke. Or should I say, *John* Clarke, which I suppose must be his real name."

"What do you mean? What had you always known about him?"

Mrs. Hillman shrugged. "That Mr. Clarke was a complete and utter rascal."

Selena was so shocked by this admission that it took her a moment to reply.

CHAPTER TWENTY-SIX

THE CHAPEL WAS so quiet, Selena felt as though time were standing still. She stared at Mrs. Hillman, who sat on the pew beside her.

"But I thought you *adored* Mr. Clarke. You said you had *a little romance* with him. He was going to ask you to marry him! I thought you worshipped the ground he walked on."

"He was a fascinating man, but I wouldn't go *that* far." Mrs. Hillman narrowed her eyes. "I think I always knew what he really was, from the moment we first met. We were strolling along the boardwalk in front of the Worthing Seaside Hotel, and he bragged about a hospital he had helped to build in Liverpool for wounded soldiers. The details were so vague, the whole thing seemed unlikely to me. But he was ever-so-charming. So, I let him charm me. He described himself as a successful businessman. I didn't think he was really harming anyone. I got the impression that the investments he took were from wealthy people he believed wouldn't miss the money, people who were grateful to him for giving them a sense of purpose."

As Selena processed that, a pressure rose in her chest. "Are you saying that Mr. Clarke was a fraud?"

Mrs. Hillman sighed. "I suppose he was. But I wanted to believe the best of him, and I looked the other way."

Selena swallowed hard. It sounded as if Dr. Dalton's description of Mr. Clarke's financial proclivities might have been true, after all. "Didn't you invest two hundred pounds in a project of Mr. Clarke's, a school, I think it was?"

"I did." Mrs. Hillman shrugged. "I never expected to see a penny of that money again. I hoped he would prove me wrong, even though I knew, deep down, that I was lying to myself."

"And yet he did pay you back," Selena pointed out, struggling to find some worthy action on that man's part. "Which means he must have thought very highly of you."

"I doubt it." Mrs. Hillman lowered her gaze. "The night he handed me that envelope … he mentioned another project he was developing. In Brazil. Which would require even more money."

"Oh, Mrs. Hillman." Sadness welled up behind Selena's eyes.

Mrs. Hillman turned to her with a frown. "I made no promises. Not that it would have mattered, anyway. And don't judge me or feel sorry for me, Selena. In spite of everything, I found Mr. Clarke amusing. He made me feel special and adored, which isn't something that often happens to a woman of my age."

Selena's stomach twisted. "Dr. Dalton claimed that Mr. Clarke's letter to *The Times* was a complete lie—an attempt to frame him for murder and theft so Mr. Clarke could steal that money for himself and vanish. Do you think that's true?"

"I do. And now that I think about it, I would bet my life that the two hundred pounds Mr. Clarke repaid me came straight from the hospital fund."

"Oh, no." As Selena thought of all the accusations she had just hurled at the doctor, she sank back in her seat, a hollow ache invading her chest.

"I have liked Dr. Sco—Dr. *Dalton* from the first moment I met him, when he came to my aid after Mr. Clarke passed away. Consider how much he had on his mind that morning and yet he treated me with such empathy. Dr. Dalton has all the qualities I adored in my own dear Roger—he's smart, thoughtful, and kind. And he listens. From what I see, the only thing Dr. Dalton is guilty of is giving us a false name and pretending that he hadn't met Jack Clarke."

Selena realized now that Mrs. Hillman was right. Dr. Dalton *was* all of those things. It was why she had fallen in love with him.

And still was in love with him.

Yes, he had lied to her about his name and connection to Mr. Clarke, but perhaps everything else that had transpired between them—including the sharing of his personal history, and his professed affection for her—had been true. Their entire murder investigation, especially their hunt for the Webster siblings, had only been tangential at best to his desire to find the hidden money, and yet Dr. Dalton had been there at her side, every step of the way.

Mr. Clarke, in contrast, had perpetrated a truly egregious fraud—one that he had apparently pulled off many times before. He had sent that letter to *The Times*, incriminating Dr. Dalton, before any crime had even been committed. He'd written that he'd been afraid to leave his house—but when Selena had met Mr. Clarke, he hadn't behaved like a man in terror of losing his life. On the contrary, he had been jovial and charming.

Charming. There was that word again. Both the doctor and Mrs. Hillman had called Mr. Clarke *charming*. The descriptor that Selena had learned to equate with a trickster or charlatan. It seemed she had been wrong about Mr. Clarke all along.

A wave of remorse rushed through Selena like a tide. "If only Dr. Dalton had told us the truth about himself and his situation from the outset."

"But he could have had no idea how you—or I—would have reacted," Mrs. Hillman insisted. "For all he knew, I might have kept him under lock and key until the parish constable returned— and I would have been within my rights to do so. And he needed to remain free to find the hidden money, to prove his innocence—to avoid debtor's prison. I understand his reticence."

Selena heaved a sigh. "I suppose you're right."

"Of course I'm right. Just look at the way you reacted today when you read that article."

Selena grimaced. "I should have given him the benefit of the doubt, instead of jumping to the conclusion that he was guilty."

Mrs. Hillman cast Selena a glance. "Why, I wonder, were you so quick to believe the worst of the doctor, rather than of Mr. Clarke?"

"Because you've known Mr. Clarke for years, whereas we have only known Dr. Dalton for a matter of days. And you had insisted over and over that Mr. Clarke was such a good man."

"Perhaps I should have been more transparent about my thinking where Mr. Clarke was concerned," Mrs. Hillman admitted sheepishly. "But I couldn't bring myself to admit the truth before the entire company after he had died. I didn't want to disrespect his memory. I was a bit embarrassed that I'd given him so much money. And although I had doubts that he had 'rescued' any money from a hospital fund, there was no way to prove him guilty of wrongdoing—or that he had taken any more than the two hundred pounds he had repaid me. I told myself the whole story had just been puffed-up bravado."

Selena bit her lip. "And yet Mr. Clarke had actually *stolen* all that money."

"Dr. Dalton, on the other hand, is a man of sense and good character. I saw how tenderly he took care of you, Selena, after you burned your arm, and after what happened in the catacombs." Mrs. Hillman paused. "You know, I accept everything you've told me about Mr. Clarke and the hidden money. But it still seems fantastic to think that anyone's been murdered at Darkmoor Park, or that someone tried to kill you."

"They did. I'm certain of it. And Dr. Dalton brought me to safety." Gutted by remorse, Selena covered her face with her hands. "I feel so bad that I didn't believe his explanations for everything that happened."

"I think," Mrs. Hillman asserted, "you were so hurt that Dr. Scott—Dr. *Dalton*—had lied to us—and to *you*—that you let it cloud your judgement. You forgot what he has shown us on a daily basis about his basic nature, that he's a decent man whom I would doubt would ever hurt anyone. Can you really imagine him planning to steal from a hospital fund?"

"No," Selena admitted, wondering now how she could have ever imagined him capable of such a thing. Tears pricked her eyes. "I've been so foolish. If you only knew what I just said to him."

"What did you say?"

"I accused him of being the worst sort of villain and thief. I told him I was going to report him to the parish constable."

"Oh. That explains the look on his face just now. And it's a shame. I've been observing the two of you together." Her gaze wandered into the distance. "You and Dr. Dalton remind me of me and my Roger when we first met. I think you've fallen in love with him."

Selena felt her face grow hot. "I don't know about that," she lied.

Mrs. Hillman cast Selena a sidelong glance. "And what's more, I think he's in love with you."

The moisture in Selena's eyes spilled over and ran down her cheeks. "If he did have any feelings for me, they're surely gone now. He thinks I'm going to turn him in. He must hate me. Oh! What do I do now, Mrs. Hillman?"

The older woman turned to her with a kindly smile. "I suppose you go to him. And you tell him how you really feel."

SELENA HURRIED FROM the chapel to find Dr. Dalton.

When she'd read that letter in *The Times*, she had felt like an idiot for trusting him and for falling for his charms. Now, she felt equally idiotic for having believed the allegations in the newspaper, instead of opening her mind to the truth that he'd tried so hard to share. She understood now why he'd kept his secrets. As he had tried so desperately to tell her, he'd been facing debtors' prison, a fate so appalling that he might not have survived. His freedom, and possibly his very life, had been at stake.

She needed to find him and tell him she'd had a change of heart. Jack Clarke had been the rascal. She would never report Dr. Dalton to the constable. Moreover, she wanted to reprise their mission and help him find that money.

As she passed the morning room, Selena heard the murmur of conversation and the tinkle of cutlery from the guests who must have been dining within. Sam exited with a tray. *Sam. Who might be Joe Webster.* Selena had no time to think about that, however.

"Sam," she called out, "have you seen Dr. Dalton—I mean, Dr. Scott?" She flushed at her blunder. She doubted anyone else knew that the doctor was using an alias. If the footman really was Sam, and not Joe Webster, he must have thought she was truly terrible with names.

Sam hesitated, his eyes narrowing. "I saw him head upstairs a little while ago."

"Thank you." As Selena rushed up the main staircase, her head began to thud again. She was about to knock on the doctor's chamber door when it opened and Beryl stepped out, carrying an armful of used linens.

"I beg your pardon, miss." Beryl halted in her tracks.

"No, forgive me. I'm in your way." Selena stood aside, allowing the maid to join her in the corridor. "Is Dr. Scott within?"

"No, miss. When I came in to make up his room, he was packing up his things. In a big hurry he was, and he left without a word."

Oh, no. A heavy feeling descended in the pit of Selena's stomach. *He packed and left.* No doubt, he had gone to the village to catch the first train out. She didn't blame him. She'd made it clear that she was going to turn him into the constable at the earliest opportunity.

Selena thanked the maid, who walked off.

As Selena headed down the corridor, her mind spun. There

was only one possible course of action now. She had to go to the village, find the doctor, and beg him not to leave. Hopefully, the trains weren't running yet, or she'd at least get there before he left.

Selena hurried to her room, where she donned a hat and gloves. She considered asking one of the grooms to saddle up a horse, but it had been years since she'd gone riding. In any case, she wouldn't feel comfortable taking out one of Mrs. Hillman's horses under current conditions. The roads, she knew, would be mired in deep mud, which would put a great deal of strain on the animal. No, she would walk. Billy had done it. So could she.

A few minutes later, after grabbing her coat in the cloak room and changing into her oldest pair of boots, she was out the front door, struggling to ignore the pain that pulsed in her temple. When she came to the end of the gravel drive, Selena ground to a halt as she took in the scene before her.

The unpaved lane leading from the estate to the main road was a long stretch of filthy slush and mud imbued with scattered drifts of snow and pockets of filthy water. Selena's heart sank. How on Earth had Billy made it to the village this morning? How had the doctor made his escape? The drive was so enmired, it would have been impassable by foot or carriage. And the road beyond would be just as bad—or worse.

She saw no footprints in the mud. They couldn't have gone this way, Selena realized. They must have found another route. The front lawns, she noticed, were partially covered by snow-drifts and a veil of wet snow, but pockets of grass and mud showed through. Perhaps they had gone that way and then had found a shortcut through the woods, sticking to the still-frozen spots. Yes, that was it. She would look for footsteps and follow them.

Selena struck out with this in mind, picking her way across the lawn. But her boots instantly sank into the water-logged grass and became immersed. The freezing dampness soaked through her shoes and stockings, and in minutes, her feet were chilled to the bone. She pressed on, her shoes squishing and splashing with every step. Before long, her feet felt so cold and heavy, it became a struggle to lift them.

From a distance, she heard voices. "Miss Taylor!" "Stop!" She glanced back towards the house, wondering what the commotion was. People were gathering on the front drive. Miss Thompson and Miss Goodwin were staring at her. The colonel and Mr. Davis were waving their arms. Mrs. Hillman had a hand to her mouth. Selena trekked on. But now, her head and body began to feel strangely light. It was as if she were floating and unconnected to the ground.

All at once, to her dismay, the ground literally fell out from beneath her feet. With a cry, she pitched forward, landing face-first in the cold, deep mud. She lay there for a moment, stunned, trying to make sense of what had happened, and deduced that she had stepped into a hole. With effort, she pulled herself out of the muck and sat up on the freezing, flooded ground.

Had she broken anything? She hoped not. She wiggled one foot and then the other. They seemed to be undamaged. Her boots and stockinged shins, though, were sopping wet and caked in mud. So were her gloves. Her coat was covered in mire, her skirts were equally as filthy, and her woolly hat lay nearby in a muddy pool. What must her face have looked like?

The voices grew louder. Mrs. Hillman was beckoning to Selena to return. Mr. Davis and Colonel Blackwood had left the safety of the gravel drive and were tramping towards her across the expanse of mucky grass.

"Come back!" cried Colonel Blackwood.

No, Selena thought. *I must go on.* Time was of the essence. She had to reach Dr. Dalton before it was too late. With effort, she rolled to her knees.

"Where are you going?" Mr. Davis called out as the gentlemen caught up to her.

"To the village." Selena shakily rose to a stand. Another wave of lightheadedness took over and she began to sink down again.

The men darted up and each slid an arm under Selena's shoulders.

"You're not going anywhere," Colonel Blackwood commanded, "except back to the house."

"I *must* get to the village," Selena insisted. But when she took a step, her legs bowed out from under her.

"You're clearly in no condition to walk, Miss Taylor," the colonel pointed out kindly as he and Mr. Davis propped her up. "Come back with us now. I won't take *no* for an answer."

Tears pooled in Selena's eyes. She felt powerless to disobey. Heaving a frustrated sigh, she allowed the men to support and guide her back to the house, where she received bewildered looks and questions from the ladies.

"What on Earth were you doing?" asked Mrs. Hillman.

"I went in search of the doctor," Selena answered. "I thought he might have gone to the village."

"Ah." The older woman nodded. "Well, this is no day to be out walking."

"We heard he'd left." Miss Goodwin frowned. "Does anyone know why?"

"It's strange," Miss Thompson said softly. "He didn't even say goodbye."

So, Selena thought. *No one else had read that article in the newspaper yet.* Or if they had, they hadn't put two and two together.

"I believe he had to get back to his medical practice," Mrs. Hillman said smoothly. "Apparently, the trains are expected to start running again today."

"Yes." Selena darted her friend a look, grateful for her discretion.

A bevy of servants appeared in the foyer where Mrs. Middleton, clicking her tongue with disapproval, took over. Within minutes, Selena's filthy shoes and coat had been removed and taken away.

"Sam! George!" the housekeeper barked. "Fetch the tin tub upstairs to Miss Taylor's bedchamber. Gladys! Beryl! Heat water for a bath and bring it up to her."

A rush of dread hurtled through Selena's form. The last thing she wanted was to sit in a bathtub in her room, naked and vulnerable. Someone had tried to kill her the day before. They might walk in and try to drown her now.

"I don't want a bath," Selena insisted. "I'll use the cold water in my basin to clean up."

Mrs. Middleton frowned. "Very well." The servants bowed or curtsied and vanished. "I'm worried about you," the housekeeper said as she helped Selena upstairs to her room. "You're so pale, you look like you might faint dead away at any minute."

"I'll be fine," Selena lied. "I'm just tired. I want to sleep."

"Ring if you need anything else," Mrs. Middleton told her as she withdrew.

Selena peeled off her mud-streaked frock and stockings and sank down on her bed, devastated that her plan had failed. She had missed her one and only opportunity to talk to Dr. Dalton. He would flee and she would never see him again.

She had not only lost the man she loved, but a killer was still at large, a villain whom she believed had murdered at least twice and had attempted to murder at least three more people—her, Dr. Dalton, Colonel Blackwood, and also Billy, if only by accident, when they'd been locked in the icehouse. The killer would no doubt make another attempt if no one stopped them.

Selena swallowed back tears. She suddenly, desperately, wished she could talk to her sisters. They had been out of touch for so long due to the bad weather interrupting the delivery of the post. Oh, how she missed them! The ache inside her was so deep, it felt like an empty chasm.

Selena's cheeks grew hot, however, as she imagined what their reactions might be if she told them what she'd been going through. She had always felt *lesser* when compared to her older sisters, but she had never felt that sting as sharply as she did right now. Diana and Athena had both solved mysteries and uncovered secrets, and they had proven their intelligence and worth in so many other ways. But although two mysteries had been laid at Selena's door, she hadn't solved either one of them.

Despite all her efforts, she hadn't found the hidden money or identified the culprit who had murdered Mr. Clarke and Mrs. Whitlock—or even proven that they *had* been murdered. Even though she knew in her bones that they had. All she had were unproven theories and, as the doctor had so astutely pointed out, not a shred of proof to bring to the authorities.

The doctor.

He had said, *"I was already in too deep before I realized I had feelings for you."* His remembered words were like a stab to Selena's heart. She had fallen in love with him, and he'd cared for her as well. But now, she'd lost his love—and *him*—forever.

The tears she had been holding back burst forth and rolled down her cheeks.

Although Dr. Dalton could not be held accountable for murder, since Mr. Clarke had died at Darkmoor Park in full view of many witnesses, still, after that letter in *The Times,* the London police might look into Dr. Dalton's affairs. Or—given his honest nature, which she had now come to understand and admire—the doctor may well turn himself in. He would be held liable for the fifty-two-hundred pounds that was owed to creditors from the London General Hospital foundation. With no way to pay it back, or to prove that Mr. Clarke had stolen it, Dr. Dalton would surely be sentenced to debtors' prison.

Selena wept even harder at this probability. If Dr. Dalton were unjustly imprisoned, unable to practice the profession he loved and locked away in filthy, overcrowded conditions that might kill him—it would be a calamity. And it would be partly her fault. He had struggled so hard to explain himself, but she hadn't listened.

If only she had believed him, he wouldn't have dashed off and disappeared. If only they had found the money Mr. Clarke had hidden, the doctor would have been able to pay off the creditors, and walk away free and clear.

If only … If only. Filled with regret and shame, Selena sobbed, great floods of tears that made her shake. She had failed miserably at everything she had tried to do the past week.

As she wept, though, a new thought took hold of her. She hadn't *completely* failed. She had, after all, gathered a great deal of information. So much information, perhaps, that she was having difficulty seeing the forest for the trees.

This didn't have to be the end. Defeat, she decided, was an unacceptable outcome. She wouldn't—*couldn't* give up.

She may not be able to search for the money *with* Dr. Dalton, but she could continue the search *for* him. And while she was at it, she would find out, once and for all, who was behind the murders at Darkmoor Park and stop the killer before they got to the money or harmed Colonel Blackwood or anyone else.

Selena found a handkerchief, dried her eyes, and blew her nose. She wasn't certain she could do this, but she had to try. She started going over, in her mind, all that had transpired over the past week and the things she had learned. So much had happened, however, it was impossible to keep it all straight in her head. She had to write it down.

She sat down at her desk, grabbed a piece of paper and a pen, and jotted a list of random thoughts.

OVERVIEW OF THE CASE TO DATE

- Mr. Clarke died. Accident? Or murder?
- Mr. Clarke had hidden £5000 *under the dragon. Four rows.*
- Mr. Clarke had visited the chapel on his last afternoon.
- Tunnel to catacombs begins in the chapel.
- Dragon on a sarcophagus?
- Mrs. Whitlock's hot toddy: overdose. Accident? Or murder?
- Mrs. Goodwin died three months ago. Related?
- Threatening notes!
- Maisie Webster? Joe Webster?

- Trapped in the icehouse with Billy.
- Poisoned sandwich. Dead mouse.
- Gladys could have been a chambermaid at the Worthing Seaside Hotel.
- Sam is a footman, like Joe Webster. His brother died.
- Miss Thompson was a maid and governess. Needs money to open a flower shop. She hated Mrs. Whitlock.
- What is Mr. Davis hiding?
- Miss Goodwin resented her mother's penny-pinching ways. Needs money to repair her hotel.

There were reasons to believe why any one of these suspects could have committed murder. She needed to narrow the list down. Selena went over a raft of things in her mind. Who might have had the easiest access to poison Colonel Blackwood's sandwich? Who was most likely to have written the threatening notes? Who was most likely to seek revenge for Clive Webster's death? The letter Mr. Clarke had received from an investor. The letter that had been published in the newspaper. The people who seemed to be in want of cash. Five thousand pounds was an enormous fortune. Who might have killed to get their hands on it?

Selena read the list through again and when she'd reached the last item, she paused. Miss Goodwin's poor opinion of her mother sent Selena's mind spiraling down another path. Over the past week everyone, it seemed, had mentioned their mother at some point.

"I think everyone has secrets, don't you? At least, that's what my mother always used to say." Who had said that? Selena couldn't remember. Her head felt heavy again, as if someone had filled it with sand. She ordered herself to *think. Think.*

She vaguely recalled someone saying something about their mother that now seemed to be of great importance. What? The memory preyed on Selena's mind, frustratingly just out of reach.

What did someone's *mother* have to do with any of this?

Suddenly, Selena let out a gasp as all the pieces of the puzzle fell into place. She guessed who might have been behind everything—and why. It was so simple. Why hadn't she seen it before? But how to prove it? That was the rub.

She stood up, determination racing through her veins. She had to work fast. She needed to stop the villain from killing again. And she had to find that money before they did, to exonerate Dr. Dalton.

She would go down to the catacombs here and now. Her last foray had been unsuccessful, but she had clearer information now about where the dragon image might be. It was inside a tomb, on the side of a sarcophagus near the end of the passage. Although Selena couldn't be certain the money was there, it seemed like her best bet at present.

She might be able to kill two birds with one stone, so to speak, with this mission. The villain had followed her once into the catacombs, to try to kill her. If she set this up right, they might do so again. It could be a way to entrap them into revealing themselves.

A quick glance in her mirror gave her pause. Her hair was in disarray and streaked with mud. Her face and legs were dirty, too. But there was no time to clean up. She dashed to her wardrobe and put on a simple frock of sprigged, grey muslin. As she pulled up clean stockings over her dirty legs, another thought struck her.

If only she could get word to Dr. Dalton, to let him know that she would not alert the authorities, and that she was determined to find that hidden cash. Selena decided to write him a note and ask Billy to deliver it to the train station.

Selena grabbed another piece of paper and scribbled a message, addressing it to the doctor by the name he'd been going by, so as not to arouse suspicion.

Dear Dr. Scott,

Please come back. I was wrong. I shouldn't have doubted you.

I vow to find the money so you can be debt-free.
Forgive me,
Selena

No sooner had she finished writing, however, than she changed her mind. She couldn't send the hall boy to the village again in all that mud. It was too much to ask. Selena crumpled the note and tossed it in her rubbish bin.

As Selena rose to her feet, a wave of dizziness engulfed her. She blinked hard and shook it off. She didn't relish the idea of going back to the catacombs—she shuddered at the thought of being underground again, surrounded by coffins—with a possible killer on her tail. Especially when she wasn't feeling her best.

She recalled what the doctor had told her—that it was dangerous for her to be up and about so soon after her concussion. It might delay her recovery or have even more severe consequences. But she couldn't let that stop her. She had to do this. She would finish what she and the doctor had started, unmask the killer, and find the proof to clear his name.

But this time, before she entered that crypt, she would bring protection. She grabbed several items from her desk drawer and shoved them in her skirt pockets, then found a long, satin ribbon and tied it around her waist.

She was ready. She knew she was taking a risk—in terms of her health, and perhaps even her life. But it was a risk she had to take.

EN ROUTE TO the chapel, Selena stopped in the cloak room to don her spare pair of boots and slip into a coat. She then made her way to the drawing room, where she was pleased to see all the guests playing a card game and several members of the staff standing at attention or arranging refreshments nearby.

"I hope you are all amusing yourselves without me," Selena announced to the group at large.

Miss Thompson's eyes widened. "Miss Taylor! I thought you were taking a nap?"

"I'm not tired, after all. I'll be in the chapel if anyone needs me." Selena darted away. She had baited the trap. Would the villain follow?

Minutes later, she was in the chapel. As she had hoped, the lantern that Dr. Dalton had used that morning still stood upon the altar. Selena lit the candle and, just in case, stowed a box of matches in her pocket with the other items she'd brought.

The bookcase door opened easily and no longer creaked. Had Wells or one of the other servants oiled it? As she made her way down the stone steps and along the underground passageway, Selena glanced over her shoulder several times, but all was still and silent.

She reached the catacombs, where the moldy, earthy smells enveloped her as she passed through all the familiar rooms. When she reached the chamber with the tomb of the gentlewoman, the fallen statue still lay on the dirt floor, intact except for a broken nose. Selena shuddered at the thought of how close she had come to death.

A sense of trepidation rushed through her. She was deep underground, with only one way out. If the villain did come this way again, did she really have the means with which to defend herself?

Yes, you do, she reassured herself. *You will find Mr. Clarke's hiding place, and the money to pay off Dr. Dalton's debts—and if the culprit shows up, all the better. You will force a confession and nab them, too.*

Selena steeled herself and moved on. Just then, a soft sound caught her attention—as if of footsteps trodding against the packed dirt floor. Sweat broke out on her chest and brow. Had the villain pursued her? Selena raised her lantern and peered behind her, all her senses on alert. But no one was there. The only sound she perceived was the drum of her own heart in her ears. Perhaps she had imagined the footfalls?

She moved on. Farther along the passage, she came upon a bronze door that had turned green with age and was decorated with a coat of arms. Could there be a dragon motif on a coffin within? Selena entered the crypt. It held two stone sarcophaguses, topped by the carved figures of a nobleman and his wife. The sides of the sarcophaguses held memorial plaques in tribute to the deceased, but no sign of a dragon.

Before leaving the tomb, Selena paused cautiously in the doorway. She saw no sign of anyone in the room beyond, and there were no coffins to hide behind. It seemed that nobody had followed her down here, after all. *So be it.* Perhaps it was for the best.

After passing through the next arched division, she found herself in a passageway rather than a room. Her head spun suddenly, and she pressed a hand against the wall for support. For some reason, this wall was lumpier than the others. Selena raised the lantern and recoiled in horror. Dozens and dozens of ancient skulls had been impressed into the walls on both sides—four long rows of them, all dark with age, their empty eye sockets and creepy rows of teeth seeming to taunt and sneer at her.

A tremor traveled down Selena's spine. She fought to restore her sense of balance and started forward—but then paused as Mr. Clarke's last words dashed into her mind. When he'd said, *"Four rows,"* she'd had no idea what he'd meant. Later, she had wondered if he'd actually said, *"For Rose."*

But what if Mr. Clarke had been referring to the *four rows of skulls* impressed into this very wall? Did it mean she was close to the spot where he'd hidden that money?

Selena's breath came faster now. The dizziness dissipated as she proceeded down the passage of skulls and entered the adjoining chamber. Another ancient bronze door that had faded to a greenish-brown patina was embossed with an intricate bas-relief design of another coat of arms.

Selena turned the blackened brass doorknob. It opened with only the slightest creak. Inside the cozy burial chamber, surrounded by moldy stone walls, a single stone sarcophagus stood about four inches off the floor, resting on stone pedestals.

Her heart began to pound. Mrs. Hillman had said the sarcophagus she remembered had been raised off the ground. Selena glanced at the carved lid. It featured a knight in armor in the usual position, lying on his back as if asleep, his hands pressed together in prayer. The sides of the sarcophagus had been decorated with a similar sculptural technique to that employed on the door. Selena crouched down and studied the engraving on one side of the stone casket.

Pins and needles raced through her, and she drew a sharp breath.

There it was, as plain as day. *A battle scene of St. George fighting the dragon.*

Selena's heart hammered even faster now. What lay under it?

She got down on her hands and knees and placed her lantern on the floor. Tilting her head sideways, Selena rested her cheek upon the cold paving stones and peered beneath the ancient coffin. The angle was difficult, but she thought she glimpsed an object lying beneath it. She slid one hand under the sarcophagus as far as it would go ... and her fingers touched something. She picked and tugged at the article until she was able to grab hold of it and slide it out from under the sarcophagus.

Selena could hardly breathe. In her hands was a wallet-sized pouch made of thin, brown leather. She got to her feet, opened the purse, and gasped in excitement.

Inside the purse was a thick bundle of fifty-pound notes. There could well be five thousand pounds here. She had done it. She had found the money!

Just then a distinctive, metallic *click* broke the silence.

Selena looked up to see a man standing just inside the open doorway of the tomb. He held a revolver in his hand. And it was pointing directly at Selena's heart.

CHAPTER TWENTY-SEVEN

"**P**UT THE PURSE on top of the sarcophagus and step away."

Colonel Blackwood's eyes blazed and his voice was as cold as the stone floor beneath Selena's feet. He took two more steps into the crypt, his pistol trained on her.

Selena felt as though her heart had stopped. She had wondered if he was following her, and yet she had been so thrilled to find the hidden money that she had let her guard down. *Where did he get a gun?* she wondered. Then she remembered: he was a retired colonel from the Royal army; he must have brought it with him.

She thought about the weapon she had brought, which lay hidden in her skirt pocket. It was the letter opener that she'd received for Christmas, which was as deadly as any knife. She had hoped it would be her protector. But what good was a knife in a gunfight?

"Do it!" the colonel demanded sharply. "Put the purse down and step away with your hands where I can see them."

Selena did as he commanded. He strode forward, grabbed the purse, stuffed it in his coat pocket, and stopped a yard away from her, his gun still aimed straight at her chest. Panic shot through her. She had faced death before—she'd been trapped in a burning building and an icehouse, and she had survived an attempt to smother her and to kill her in these very catacombs—but she had never been held at gunpoint. Colonel Blackwood stood between her and the door—her only means of escape—but she had no hope of darting past him.

Buy yourself some time, she silently commanded. "Colonel. I know why you're doing this. It's perfectly understandable. You need that cash to save your house." She remembered him talking about it on his first night at Darkmoor Park—the ancestral home that had been in his family for centuries and was in desperate need of repair. And she recalled what he had said about his mother, who spent money like water and was driving him to the poorhouse.

"Figured that out, did you? It took you long enough."

"Take the money," she said, struggling to keep the fear from her voice. "You're welcome to it. Just allow me to leave."

His lips curled. "Do you take me for a fool? I can't let you go. I've seen the way you operate. You and that doctor friend of yours, who's been passing himself off by the name of Scott. You've been on the prowl for that money since the day Clarke died. I know you want to return it to the hospital foundation. You'd never let me walk away with it. I'd always be looking over my shoulder, waiting for the authorities to pounce."

"I won't tell anyone, I swear." But Selena could see from his expression that he wasn't accepting that.

"I've had a devil of time dispatching the two of you." His eyes glinted like steel. "Now that the doctor has left with his tail between his legs, I just have to get rid of you. Thank you for announcing your intentions just now. I had followed you down here once without a lantern and knew I could do it again. You've made my job easy. You've not only led me to the money, but to the ideal location for your death."

Every muscle in Selena's body seemed to be strained to the breaking point. How long before he pulled the trigger? There must be some way she could save herself. "It's been you all along, hasn't it?" she demanded. "You killed Mr. Clarke."

Colonel Blackwood scowled. "*That* was an accident. I only meant to frighten him into telling me where he'd hidden the money."

"You knew about the money because you'd read that letter in *The London Times* on the train on your way up here, didn't you?" It was the colonel's newspaper, after all, that the doctor had stolen.

He nodded. "I knew at once that it was a scheme to steal from philanthropists and frame someone else for the crime. I've always known Clarke was a scoundrel, but I told myself it wasn't my business to interfere. Until it hit too close to home."

Selena had worked that out. The colonel had said his mother's name was Evelyn. And the letter Selena had found in Mr. Clarke's dresser had been from an Evelyn Stout. "Your mother remarried and was widowed a second time, wasn't she, thus why she has a different surname? And when you discovered that she had invested a hundred and fifty pounds in Mr. Clarke's hospital fund, you were furious."

His lips tensed and his face flushed. "When Mother told me about the charming Mr. Clarke, and the money she had sent him, I wanted to murder him. But she hadn't kept a record of his London address. When I got to Darkmoor Park, I was astonished to find Clarke here. I figured he would have left the country, never to be seen again. Which I presume he would have done, after he repaid Mrs. Hillman—if he hadn't met such an early demise. And you, my dear, are going to follow in his footsteps."

Selena swallowed hard. She couldn't die, not here, like this. There must be a way out. *Keep him talking.* "So, before dawn on the morning after you arrived, you confronted Mr. Clarke and threatened to turn him in to the police if he didn't reveal where he'd hidden the money?"

The colonel uttered a sound of disgust. "I told Clarke if they found the money at Darkmoor Park, they'd know he had stolen it, not his business partner. Clarke refused to comply. He said he'd hidden it where no one would ever find it. He shoved me. I shoved him back. Before I knew it, he was tumbling backwards down the stairs. I thought he was dead."

"You panicked and ran." Selena eyed her lantern, wishing she could use it as a weapon, but it was out of reach.

The colonel frowned fiercely. "The secret to the money's hiding place died with him. But I was determined to find it. Then I overheard you and the doctor talking and saw you searching inside the chapel. I knew you were looking for the money, too. Ever since, I've been watching you two like a hawk." He nodded towards the sarcophagus. "How did you know to look here?"

Selena held that information smugly to her chest. "I'll tell you if you let me go."

He smirked. "I'm afraid it's too late for that. I did warn you and the doctor several times to back off, you know."

She understood his reference. "We thought at first that it was Mrs. Whitlock who wrote the threatening notes. How did you imitate her handwriting?"

"I found a draft of a letter she'd been writing in the rubbish basket in her room."

Clever, Selena thought with annoyance. She hadn't considered that possibility.

"That woman was a nasty piece of goods," he went on. "Bullied and abused her companion. And you said yourself she stole Mrs. Hillman's brooch and was probably the thief all those years ago at the Worthing Seaside Hotel." His mouth twisted. "I'd kill her again in a heartbeat. Just like I'm going to kill you."

Selena swallowed her fear. "You admit it—you poisoned Mrs. Whitlock? Why? Did she have the same idea, to get up at the crack of dawn to persuade or threaten Mr. Clarke into giving her the cash? Did she see you push Mr. Clarke and try to blackmail you?"

He blew out another annoyed breath. "Blasted woman, she came at me the next day and claimed she'd seen everything from the shadows. Said if I didn't give her five thousand pounds, she'd tell everyone I had killed Clarke. I had to get rid of her. She won't be missed."

"And having learned that Mrs. Goodwin had died from an accidental overdose of laudanum, you copied that method?"

"Like I said, killers often repeat their actions. It was an excellent red herring. And it was quick and easy to disguise as an accident."

The man was a fiend. Selena felt lightheaded again. *Do not faint*, she warned herself. *You must not faint.* "Joe and Maisie Webster never had anything to do with this, did they?" That entire plot had been a figment of her imagination.

He shrugged his shoulders. "That theory of yours was a convenient way to divert your attention from the money and me. I may have … helped once or twice to further the illusion that the Websters were here."

"The toasted cheese sandwich?" An idea occurred to Selena—it might not work, but it was worth a try. She slowly reached one hand into her skirt pocket. "You poisoned it yourself to throw us off the scent and just pretended to be sick?"

"After taking a bite, I sprinkled enough rat poison on it to kill a man. Or a mouse, as it turns out." He grinned, clearly pleased with himself. "Yesterday, that statue would have killed you if you hadn't moved. Enough questions now—"

"Wait! Did you try to smother me in my bed?" Selena demanded as, with hidden fingers, she unscrewed the cap from the bottle she'd stashed in her pocket. "And lock us in the icehouse?"

Colonel Blackwood gave another shrug. "A shame you woke up. As for the icehouse, that would have worked, if that fool Billy hadn't snuck in after you. I overheard the footmen talking about it and I had to let you all out. I couldn't have it on my conscience to kill a thirteen-year-old boy. I'm not a monster."

"That's debatable," Selena said coldly. Which was a mistake.

The colonel's eyes lit like twin flames. He moved closer, his gun still leveled at her heart. "After I kill you, you may lie here for days before you're found. And your precious doctor? Andrew Dalton? That sad fellow will be on the hook for fifty-two-hundred pounds. He'll end up in debtors' prison for the rest of his natural life." He bared his teeth in a smile. "While I'll be safe at home, with my house paid off and enough money to live comfortably for the rest of time."

Selena withdrew the uncapped ink bottle from her skirt pocket and flung its contents at the colonel's smug face. He gasped, startled, as black ink splashed him in the eyes. Selena took advantage of this reprieve to grab her letter opener from her pocket and, springing forward, she stabbed the thin, sharp blade into the colonel's hand.

He gasped in agony and outrage. The revolver fell from his grasp, spun across the floor, and vanished beneath the sarcophagus. Dropping to her knees, Selena reached under the stone coffin, desperately feeling for the gun with her fingers. If she fled without the gun, he would find it and come after her, firing. But the colonel grabbed her from behind, wrestled her to face him, and pressed his hands forcefully against her throat.

"Goodbye, Miss Taylor." His face flushed and his jaw clenched as he pronounced the fatal words.

Selena clawed at him, struggling to break free, but he was far stronger, and she couldn't breathe. The pressure of his fingers on her throat was the most intense pain Selena had ever felt. Spots appeared before her eyes and her ears began to ring. *Is this how it ends?* she wondered. *Is this how and where I die?*

All at once, the colonel's hands took leave of her throat and—somehow—he was tumbling sideways. Choking and gasping, Selena drank in precious oxygen. It took a few moments before her head and vision cleared and she perceived that someone else was in the chamber.

Dr. Dalton.

The two men were grappling on the floor, fighting for their lives. A second lantern stood nearby. Selena's mind whirled. *What was Dr. Dalton doing here?* But there was no time to process the notion.

Selena reached under the sarcophagus, but to her frustration, the gun was just out of reach. She needed a weapon—a way to knock out the colonel. Her glance fell on her lantern. It was framed in brass and fitted with glass. *That will do.* She nabbed it, waiting for the right moment as the men struggled.

Before she could act, however, the grappling duo rolled up against the sarcophagus. The colonel reached under it and half a second later, he had the gun in his hand and was leveling it at Dr. Dalton. *It's now or never.* Selena bashed the lantern with all her might onto Colonel Blackwood's skull. Glass shattered and flew. The colonel slid to the floor and lay still.

Dr. Dalton, breathing hard, rose to his knees. "Are you all right?"

"Yes." Selena's pulse pounded and her entire body began to quake as she stared down at the colonel's insensible form. "Is *he?*" Although he had just tried to murder them both, she hoped she hadn't killed him.

Dr. Dalton used his fingertips to check the colonel's pulse. "He'll live." His frock coat was streaked with dirt and his boots were caked in mire. "I can't believe it was him."

Selena struggled to clear her head. "The Webster siblings' theory was a bust. Colonel Blackwood has been behind everything—he wanted the money."

The doctor caught sight of the bloodied, fallen letter opener and stared down at the man on the floor. "Is that ink on his face? And did you stab his hand?"

"I did. And I brought this to tie him up with, just in case." She untied the ribbon she had wrapped around her waist and offered it to him.

"Good thinking." The doctor took the ribbon and began binding the unconscious man's hands behind his back.

The room started turning again and Selena blinked hard to make it go away. "You'll be happy to know—I found the money."

He finished tying the colonel's wrists and stared up at her, his eyes huge. "What? *You found it?* Where?"

"Under the dragon." She gestured to the sarcophagus.

Dr. Dalton turned to study the carvings on the side of the stone coffin. A grin lit up his face. "Well, what do you know? St. George was a popular man."

"He was." Selena rested against the sarcophagus to keep from falling over. "The pouch is in his coat."

The doctor fished out the purse from the colonel's pocket and glanced inside. Relief and joy lit his face. "Thank you for finding this."

"Thank you for saving my life."

"Thank *you* for saving *mine*. In more ways than one." He stood up, holding the money pouch to his chest as if it were manna from heaven. "I can go back to my life now with my name and debts cleared." Sliding the purse into his own pocket, he crossed to Selena and briefly touched the side of her throat, cringing at whatever he saw there. "I'm sorry he hurt you. I wish I'd been here sooner."

The touch of his fingertips sent a jolt through Selena's being. "I wish you'd never left at all." She reached up, yearning to touch him as well, but stopped short at the sight of bright-red blood dripping down from his forehead. "Your head is bleeding."

"That can wait. We should leave this place." He blinked as blood dripped into his eye.

"Let me take care of this first." Selena cradled his neck with her hand and urged him to bend his head down towards her. She parted his hair to reveal a wound that was leaking blood. "Stay still. There's a piece of glass stuck in here."

He complied. As Selena carefully maneuvered the small piece of glass out of the wound—unable to bear the suspense any longer—she asked, "Why are you here?" She didn't dare to guess the answer. "When I heard you'd left, I thought you would take the first train out."

"That was my plan," he admitted. "But on my miserable hike to the village, trudging through muck and mire, I had a lot of time to think. How was it, I wondered, that I had come to this? The only wrong I had done was to lie about my identity and motives for a few days—which, although inexcusable, are not criminal offenses."

"True." She inspected his scalp wound for any remaining

shards, then withdrew a handkerchief from her pocket and quickly mopped his brow. "I think I got all the glass."

"Thank you." A frown took over his face. "Still, my responsibility seemed clear. I had to go back to London, turn myself in, and face debtors' prison. I learned that a train was expected within the hour. But as I waited for that train … I thought of you."

Selena pressed the handkerchief tightly against his head to staunch the flow of blood, her pulse thumping like a runaway locomotive. "Of me?"

"Yes, you. I knew a villain was still out there, someone who had warned us off repeatedly and had attempted to kill you—or us—several times. Even though I knew you thought the worst of me—that I was a scoundrel and a thief—"

"I shouldn't have been so quick to judge," she interjected, remorse gnawing at her insides. "I'm so sorry. I—"

"Let me finish." He took over the job of pressing on his scalp wound himself. "I couldn't leave you here, unprotected, when you might be in peril at any moment. So regardless of your low opinion of me, I came back to protect you if I could."

Tears burned behind Selena's eyes. "Thank you. But how did you know where I'd gone?"

"I checked your room and found the note you'd written, in your rubbish bin. I was relieved by your change of heart but panicked. I figured that you might have come back here to look for the dragon tomb. A maid told me she had seen Colonel Blackwood heading for the chapel. That's when I suspected the awful truth about him, although I still don't understand *why*."

"I'll explain it all later."

"I ran through that passage as if the Devil were after me." He shook his head at her. "You do know that it was absolutely crazy—and very dangerous—for you to come back here again on your own?"

Sheepishly, she nodded. "I'm not sure I was thinking straight. I did, after all, hit my head yesterday. But you're right, it was risky." With a rush of gratitude, she added, "If not for you, I'd be dead."

The handkerchief dropped from his hand, and he closed the space between them. His eyes sparkled with affection as he said softly, "That's a thought I cannot bear." And suddenly, Selena was enveloped in his arms, her cheek pressed against his chest. "I didn't want to leave you."

"I didn't want you to leave," she murmured breathlessly.

He dipped his head to face her, until their mouths and noses were but a hair's breadth apart. "Selena," he said softly.

"Andrew," she echoed back at him.

His eyes lit up at her usage of his real name. And then he kissed her, hard and fast.

Just then, a groan erupted from the man on the floor beside them. Selena and the doctor broke apart as the colonel began to stir.

"I think," Dr. Dalton said, "it's time to get out of here and bring this man to justice."

CHAPTER TWENTY-EIGHT

T HE VILLAIN WHO had committed two murders and had attempted two more was incarcerated under lock and key in a room on the basement level of Darkmoor Park.

"It's more comfortable than he deserves," Mrs. Hillman proclaimed in a huff after she and the entire house party had been apprised of the colonel's malicious dealings. "He will remain there until the parish constable comes back."

Selena spent the next two days in bed, where quiet and rest helped to alleviate most of the symptoms that she'd been experiencing from her concussion. She would still need to be careful. Dr. Dalton had told her not to overdo it for the next two months, and she had agreed to follow his orders.

While bedridden, Selena tried several times to write to her sisters and her brother. But so much had happened since Christmas Eve, it was difficult to find the words to explain it all. And since penning a note without admitting to all the tragedies, mysteries, and terrifying circumstances—not to mention the complicated story of Dr. Dalton's appearance in her life—felt like cheating, she crumpled up every attempt and threw it away.

She was glad she had taken the time, a couple of days before Mrs. Hillman's guests had arrived, to send letters with Christmas greetings to her siblings. Those would have to tide them over for a while. In the meantime, now that the trains were running again, Selena hoped to hear from Diana and Athena. Damon wrote so rarely, she knew better than to expect a letter from him.

In between naps, Selena welcomed visits from Mrs. Hillman, Dr. Dalton, and the other house guests, who filled her in on what was going on downstairs. Every time she saw Dr. Dalton, her heart raced, and she wished for time alone with him ... but there was always someone else in the room.

She learned that soon after the colonel was apprehended, Dr. Dalton had admitted his true identity to Miss Goodwin, Mr. Davis, and Miss Thompson, who were at first shocked and disturbed. But by the end of the day, all three had accepted the news and found it in their hearts to forgive him for his ruse.

Learning that a murderer had been among their company all this time, however, was another matter. Miss Goodwin was so upset that she considered leaving, but Mr. Davis insisted, "We always intended to stay through New Year's Day. That scoundrel is gone from our midst and we're perfectly safe. Why should we bolt now?"

Mr. Johnson returned to Darkmoor Bridge the following morning. Dr. Dalton and Mrs. Hillman gave the parish constable a full accounting of all that had occurred. Mr. Johnson reassured Dr. Dalton that he would press no charges and, after the new year, would accompany the doctor back to London to ensure that the money was safely invested in the London General Hospital bank account.

Everyone in the house gave a sigh of relief when Colonel Blackwood was carted away to the lock-up in the village square, where he would be held until he could be transferred to York Prison to await trial, and no doubt the noose. The bodies of the two unfortunate people who had met their end at Darkmoor Park that week were packed in ice and summarily dispatched to coroners in their own hometowns.

On the evening of December 31st, after spending her prescribed two days in bed, Selena was relieved to rise at last and to discover that her headache and the bouts of dizziness were gone. She had just finished dressing for that night's New Year's Eve festivities, when a knock sounded on her door. It was Wells, with two envelopes on a silver salver.

"Good evening, miss," he said with a solemn nod. "I hope you are feeling better?"

"I am, thank you!" Selena spirits lifted as she glanced at the letters. "Are those for me?"

"They are. They arrived a few hours ago, but I didn't wish to disturb you. The postman said that mail bags have been sitting for days on trains stopped due to snow, and it took a while to get it all sorted."

"I'm so glad to have some post at last. Thank you, Wells."

The butler bowed and departed. Selena exclaimed with delight when she saw the return addresses on the missives. One was from Damon in London, and the other was from Pendowar Hall.

She eagerly sat down at her desk and retrieved her letter opener—shuddering despite herself when she recalled the last time she had used it, during her struggle with Colonel Blackwood in the catacombs. She was thankful to employ the device for its intended and more benevolent purpose.

Damon had a sent a Christmas card. It was a concept so new in England that Selena had only received a handful of such cards before, most of them from him over the past few years. The simple image on the card's front featured a black-and-white sketch of an evergreen wreath framing a view of a distant church set in a snowy landscape. Inside the card he had merely written:

Dear Selena,

I hope you are well. I'm sorry I won't see you in Cornwall and hope to make it up to Darkmoor Park again one of these days.

Wishing you a very Happy Christmas and a prosperous new year!

With love, your brother,
Damon

Selena was grateful for the message, despite its brevity. Damon had always been a man of few words, and she knew how busy he was. She propped up the card on her desk, where it would serve as a lovely reminder of her brother every time she saw it.

Filled with joyful expectation, she opened the second envelope. It contained two letters. The first one was from Athena.

Pendowar Hall
Portwithys, Cornwall
December 22nd, 1852

My dearest Selena,

By the time this letter reaches you, I hope you will have enjoyed the most wonderful Christmas on record! We all miss you, but you made the right choice in staying with Mrs. Hillman. I know how much she was looking forward to her guests' visit for the holidays and how much she appreciates your help in entertaining them. I trust Mrs. Nash is outdoing herself with one delicious meal after another and I pray that the activities and parlor games you planned have been a great success!

Our journey down to Cornwall was smooth and uneventful. Ian and I took turns holding the baby on our laps, pointing out the window at the passing scenery and telling him stories. During the longest portions of the train rides, Henry napped most conveniently on the seat between us. We arrived at Pendowar Hall tired but excited and received a warm welcome from Diana and her family. She has a splendid Christmas Day feast planned, and I look forward to Damon joining us a few days later.

How has your weather been? Mild, I hope, with no threat of snow. As for me, I am once again positively mesmerized by Cornwall's temperate climate. The last few days have been as sunny and warm as late summer in Yorkshire. I know I said this last year, but it astonishes me to see palm trees and tropical ferns in the gardens here at Pendowar Hall—it's hard to believe I'm still in England!

It is a treat as well to awaken to the sounds of waves crash-

ing on the rocks and beaches below these towering cliffs. We all took a stroll on the beach yesterday, collected seashells to add to Emma's collection, and visited Smuggler's Cave. Henry enjoyed digging his fingers into the sand and laughed when the foamy water rushed up to tickle his tiny, bare feet.

We had a little mystery this morning. (Not a murder mystery, thank heavens!) Henry's favorite cuddly toy, Mr. Bear, went missing. My mind immediately created various calamitous explanations for its disappearance. Perhaps one of the new servants, who had been hired for the holidays, had taken it? (It is a very nice bear, after all, and I believe cost his aunt and uncle a pretty penny.) Might it have accidentally fallen out of Henry's perambulator during our walk in the village, never to be seen again? Or (this scenario from little Charlotte) maybe Mr. Bear had gotten fed up from being hugged too tightly and had run away?

I told Henry, "I'm so sorry, darling, but we can't find Mr. Bear. Do you know where Mr. Bear might be?" You will never guess what happened. Fast as lightning, Henry crawled off to a low cupboard in the parlor and opened the door to reveal Mr. Bear sitting within atop a stack of linens. Henry, grinning from ear to ear, grabbed the toy and dragged him over to me. Can you believe it? At age nine months, our little boy understood exactly what I'd said—and knew exactly where to find his toy. (Which I presume he had hidden himself.) Ian and I believe we have a little genius on our hands. Perhaps Henry will grow up to create his own mystery society with his future siblings or friends—a group I trust will be worthy of a title as apt as the Audacious Sisterhood of Smoke and Fire.

I must say, it is strange to be so far away from you, Selena, especially at this time of year. I miss our daily conversations. And, strange as it may seem, although I am enjoying our holiday, I find myself missing the routine of our days at school. I'm proud of what we've built, Selena. It is gratifying to think that we are helping to shape the minds—and lives—of the bright young ladies in our care. Thank you for stepping forward and taking over as headmistress so that I may spend more time at *present with my young son. You have proven yourself to be most estimable in the role—an undertaking which I know, all too well, can be daunting. If you find it to be too much, if you wish, I would be happy to share the duties of headmistress with you at some point. It is just a thought.*

Meanwhile, I look forward to receiving a letter with all your news. I send you hugs and kisses. Ian asks me to send his love as well.

With greatest love,
Athena

Selena held the letter to her chest with a happy sigh. Reading these lines were the next best thing to a conversation with Athena. It helped to close the distance between them, making it *almost* feel as though her sister were sitting there beside her.

After a quiet moment, Selena turned to the second letter, which was from Diana.

Pendowar Hall
Portwithys, Cornwall
December 22nd, 1852

My dearest Selena,

I hope you are celebrating the season in grand style at Dark-moor Park, that all of your holiday festivities are going off exactly as planned, and that a good time is being had by all!

I am thrilled to have Athena, Ian, and their darling Henry here. I wish you could have come as well, and I miss you more than words can say. I understand, however, why you chose to remain at home. Although I've only met Mrs. Hillman once, that summer we came to visit, she is a dear soul, and it was both thoughtful of you and I think important to put her needs and wishes first. You owe her a great deal—you are, after all, her heir and Darkmoor Park is your forever home!

It is so wonderful to have William home for the holidays. I missed him so much this year when he was at sea, and he has missed so much of Charlotte's daily development. But he is on leave from the Royal Navy for four months, which is a great blessing. Charlotte has grown and changed so much since you saw her last Christmas! To think that, a year ago, she wasn't even walking yet, and now she runs like a cheetah! She is talking now, too—not just babbling but real words and short phrases, and she is so happy and curious about everything. I have decided that nothing inspires pure joy as much as a child's smile and laugh.

Emma is quite the young lady now. She wears her hair up and insists on having her frocks made to mirror the newest fashion plates. Her reading and writing have improved a hundredfold since I began tutoring her three years ago. Last month, I finally persuaded her to read Jane Eyre. She adored it. (If she hadn't, I believe I would have had to disown her as our cousin.)

Emma turned eighteen this year and dreams of having a coming out ball. William and I have been discussing the matter. Since we have so little society here, a season in London might be a better way for her to meet a suitable gentleman—but that will require us to move to Town as soon as possible for a few months' stay before William returns to sea. Charlotte would come with us, of course. It would be quite an undertaking—but I am more and more inclined to make it happen.

Which leads me to another thought. Yesterday evening, when we were all gathered around the fire, I took in all the love in the room—the heartfelt affection that Athena and her husband and son so visibly share, and the loving bond that I have formed with my own dear husband and family—and I thought of you. It is my dearest wish, Selena, that you will find your own perfect soulmate one day and experience the same deep joy from that relationship that Athena and I have found in ours. I believe, in the depths of my soul, that it will happen for you— that you will encounter the man of your dreams—and when it happens, I cannot wait to meet him!

I think of you often, sister dearest, and look forward to the day when we can be in each other's arms again. Until then,

Happy Christmas and Happy New Year!
With all my love, your sister,
Diana

Tears pricked Selena's eyes as she read—and re-read—the last paragraphs of Diana's letter, and the phrase, *your own perfect soulmate.* Selena felt that she already *had* met such a man. She loved Dr. Dalton. She sensed that he had feelings for her. In spite of all that had happened between them, he had come back for her. Saved her life. And kissed her with such passion.

And yet, after all the suspicions she had leveled at him, was there any way that he could forgive her? Even if he did, was it even possible for them to build a future together? She didn't see how.

She moved to her mirror, where she smoothed the skirts of her new evening gown, a confection of iridescent ice-green silk that featured silk roses and leaves along the edges of the bodice and cap sleeves, as well as a cascade of flowers and embroidered butterflies trailing down the front. Mrs. Hillman had been so generous with Selena's clothing allowance, and this stunning gown fit her to a "T." Selena had ordered it to wear on New Year's Eve—having no idea, of course, that a gentleman would be in attendance, for whom she would want to look her very best.

The idea that the doctor would have to leave Darkmoor Park, and soon, filled her with such anguish, it caused those threatening tears to spill over and roll down her cheeks.

With firm hands, Selena wiped her face dry. She and Mrs. Hillman had, weeks before the guests had arrived, put a lot of effort into planning a grand New Year's Eve party—and Selena was determined to enjoy it. Even though, she thought sadly, there were three fewer guests present tonight than they had counted on.

She put on a smile and descended to the dining room, where the Christmas boughs and holly that decorated the mantelpiece and the centerpiece of the beautifully-set table had been joined by twice as many candles and sparkling ornaments made of blown glass and gilded and silver paper.

Everyone had dressed up in their finest clothes for the evening festivities and were in fine spirits to match. Selena was the last person to arrive, and to her regret, she found herself sitting at the far end of the table from Dr. Dalton, making it impossible to talk to him. His brows lifted when she walked in and the bright-eyed stare he gave her, combined with a gentle shrug of his shoulders, seemed to indicate both his appreciation of the way she looked, as well as his own frustration with the seating arrangements.

Mrs. Nash and the kitchen staff had prepared a delicious feast, which was enjoyed by one and all. The group lingered at the table laughing and chatting so long that before they knew it, it was almost time to ring in the new year.

The night was clear and the weather, after all those days of storms, was so comparatively mild, that after leaving the table, Selena and all the members of the party donned their coats and hats and mingled on the back terrace, where everyone gazed with undisguised pleasure at the vast array of stars sparkling in the heavens against the inky sky.

Selena spotted Dr. Dalton across the veranda. She had just started towards him when Mrs. Hillman appeared, took Selena by the arm, and turned her in the opposite direction.

"How are you feeling, my dear?" Mrs. Hillman asked.

"Better, thank you. I understand that I may not be fully recovered for a while yet. When school starts, I thought I might ask Athena to take over one or two of my classes."

"A good idea. Or you might want to hire another teacher?" Mrs. Hillman's gaze darted to Miss Thompson, who was pacing back and forth by the veranda railing, staring at the ground rather than the night sky. "I've been thinking how sad it is that Miss Thompson is out of a job."

Selena understood the older woman's implication and smiled. "I've been thinking the same thing. Miss Thompson was once a governess and said she has always wished to teach at a school. She *is* quite proficient at the pianoforte and has a beautiful singing voice. We need a music teacher and I'm sure she could teach other subjects as well."

Mrs. Hillman's lips curved upwards. "I suppose you would have to get Athena's approval before you could formally hire her?"

Selena shrugged. "I am headmistress now. Athena wrote and offered to share the duties of headmistress at some point if I find the duties too taxing. I might take her up on that in future. But for now, I can hire whomever I like. That is," Selena amended, "*if* Miss Thompson is interested in the position."

"Oh, I know for a fact that she is," Mrs. Hillman replied with a knowing look, "for I *may* have proposed the idea to her in passing."

"Mrs. Hillman!" Selena cried, both amused and admonishing.

Mrs. Hillman beckoned to Miss Thompson and then drifted away to chat with other guests.

The young woman darted up to Selena, her eyes wide and a slight blush staining her cheeks. "It's a lovely evening, isn't it?" she said.

"It is, indeed." Selena saw no reason to waste any time. "Miss Thompson, I know that you have dreamed of owning a flower shop. But while you save to make that dream a reality, would you like to join the staff at the Darkmoor Bridge School for Girls to teach music and perhaps some other subjects?"

"Oh!" Miss Thompson cried. "Thank you so much. I'd be thrilled to work at your school."

Satisfaction bubbled up inside Selena's chest. "I'm so glad."

Miss Thompson returned her smile and then, hesitating, she lowered her gaze. "By the way, Miss Taylor, there's something I've been wanting to tell you."

"What is that?"

"A few days ago, when you questioned me about my background, and about my work with Mrs. Whitlock? I was so nervous, I worried that you might suspect me of something unseemly. I wanted to explain why I was anxious. It's because I had known that Mrs. Whitlock was a thief. When we would call on other ladies or visit them for tea, Mrs. Whitlock always came home with some new bauble that I knew she had stolen from our hostess. For the past three months, I have lived in fear that I would be blamed for the things that Mrs. Whitlock stole."

"Ah. I see. Thank you for sharing that with me." Selena gave her a warm nod. "Perhaps, when you go back to Mrs. Whitlock's home to gather your things, you can get in touch with her solicitor and see to it that the purloined items are all returned to their rightful owners."

"I'll do that, miss. Thank you again for your offer of employment. You can't imagine how much it means to me."

"Something tells me that we'll be lucky to have you." Selena opened her arms, and the two women embraced. Miss Thompson dashed off to join Mrs. Hillman, to whom she began excitedly imparting the good news. Selena looked again for Dr. Dalton, but at that moment, Mr. Davis strode up.

"Miss Taylor. May I have a word?"

Selena turned to him. "Yes, Mr. Davis?"

"I wanted to ask you a favor." Mr. Davis's face colored. "It's about … some things that were said that evening when you and the doctor questioned Nancy and me in the billiards room."

"Oh?" Selena waited, all ears. She thought Mr. Davis had been hiding something. Would he reveal it now?

He darted a brief glance at Miss Goodwin, who was standing out of earshot some distance away. "I was upset when you accused Nancy of being Maisie Webster. It was so ridiculous! Nancy is the best girl on Earth. She would never lie to anyone. It's not in her nature. I can't say that *I* have been as forthcoming, though." He twisted his hands and gave Selena an appealing look. "What I'm about to say, will you promise not to breathe a word of it to anyone? Especially to Nancy?"

"That depends, Mr. Davis, on what you tell me. If you've committed a crime, I can hardly keep it to myself."

"It's not a crime. It's just … an avoidance of the truth." He lowered his voice to just above a whisper. "I'm ashamed to admit it, but I lied to Nancy and her mother. My father wasn't a manager at a bank, and I didn't grow up in Haverstock Hill. We lived in a squalid flat in the East End, and my parents ran a dry goods shop. The shop went bankrupt a few years ago. That's why they moved to India, to start over. From what I understand, they are barely getting by. I worked myself up from nothing to get my job at the bank. I worried that Nancy wouldn't give me the time of day if she knew—that she'd think I want her for her money— so I made all that up about myself and my family. I love her to distraction. But so much time has gone by, I don't know how to undo the lie."

Selena felt sorry for the young man, who was clearly ashamed and distressed. She thought about how Dr. Dalton had "avoided the truth" when they'd met, and why. "It isn't easy to live a lie, Mr. Davis. But I feel certain that Miss Goodwin loves you in return. If you tell her the truth and admit the reasons behind your initial reluctance to share it, I believe she'll find it in her heart to forgive you."

"Do you really think so?"

"I do."

"Thank you, Miss Taylor." Mr. Davis took one of Selena's hands in his and pressed it heartily. "I'll follow your advice. I'll tell her tomorrow. In the meantime, will you keep this between us?"

"I will."

"Thank you," he said again, his eyes dancing with what looked like newfound hope as he hurried off to join his partner.

Selena blew out a long breath. Now, at last, would she find a moment to speak with Dr. Dalton?

A voice called out from behind her. "Miss Taylor. I've been hoping for a moment alone with you all night. Would you care to take a stroll?"

Selena whirled to find Dr. Dalton standing just a couple of feet away. He looked devilishly handsome in his tailcoat and cravat. His wavy hair was neatly combed back from his forehead, revealing the jagged scar that gave him such a roguish appearance, above eyes that sparkled in the moonlight.

Selena's spirits lifted. "I would be delighted." She took Dr. Scott's proffered arm, her body tingling from his nearness as they ventured across the terrace. When they passed Miss Goodwin and Mr. Davis, who were in a tête-à-tête, she whispered, "I'm embarrassed that we suspected them of being Maisie and Joe Webster."

"Don't be. It was a perfectly good theory. You had me convinced that it might be true."

Selena sighed. "The poor Webster siblings. They had nothing whatsoever to do with the murders here at Darkmoor Park. We've never met them, and yet how we've maligned them."

"I'd love to find out what happened to them," Dr. Dalton put in. "Now that we know—or at least heavily suspect—that Mrs. Whitlock was the thief at the hotel that summer, should we tell them?"

Selena considered that. "It would be a kindness to do so, I think. If they believe their brother was a thief, it might restore their faith in his memory." They stopped at a far corner of the veranda railing, where moonlight bathed them in its white glow.

"This has been a strange and extraordinary week," Dr. Dalton commented, gazing up at the canopy of stars.

"It has." Once again, Selena was all too aware that their time together was coming to an end. The notion filled her with a deep, melancholic ache. She longed to admit her feelings for him. But after all the troubles and woe that had existed between them recently, even though they had made peace about it all, she didn't know how to begin.

"Tomorrow is New Year's Day." He held on to the rail, staring down at it. "The other guests will be leaving soon. I have to go as well."

"You don't have to," Selena said quickly. "There's no rush."

"I must," he insisted. "I have no business here any longer.

Unless …"

Hope beat like wings inside her breast. "Unless …?"

He turned and took both of her gloved hands in his. "Selena. When we were at the folly, I wanted to tell you how much you mean to me. But the way things were then, I didn't think I had the right. Now that everything's out in the open, I can't hide it any longer." He took a breath. "I didn't know it was possible to feel so close to a person, and to feel *so much* for a person, in just eight days. But it happened and I can't pretend it didn't. When I think of the future, I can't imagine it without you. You're the smartest, most fascinating, and most courageous person I've ever known. I love you, Selena."

His expression was so filled with affection, it made Selena's heart turn over. "I feel the same way about you. I love you, too."

"You do?" His features glowed with light and hope. But then he hesitated and said quietly, "I'm aware that I am only a doctor and a blacksmith's son. You're a gentleman's daughter, and the heir to Darkmoor Park."

"I'm only here by luck and circumstance," Selena insisted. "I've dreamed of finding the right man with whom to share my life. I believe that man is you."

His lips tilted up in an uncertain smile. "I can't tell you how much that means to me. But I also know how much teaching and your school mean to *you*. I'd never ask you to give that up or to leave Darkmoor Park to move to London."

"My school *has* been everything to me these past few years." Selena's pulse began to pound. She had been thinking this over for the past two days while she'd been lying in bed, and—hoping that the subject might come up—she had ideas to consider. "But Athena could take over as headmistress again if need be. She could run it without me. Mrs. Hillman will live for many long years, I hope, so it will be a while before I'm needed as mistress at Darkmoor Park."

His brows pulled together. "And what would you do in the meantime?"

"Perhaps I could teach at a school in London," she suggested.

"Would that make you happy?"

After having experienced the freedom of running her own school, the idea of being a subordinate at another educational institution didn't really appeal to her. Selena frowned. "I would do it if it meant we could marry."

"No. I wouldn't want that for you. You belong here."

Biting her lip, Selena said, "Well ... Diana and her husband spend a great deal of time apart, for he is away at sea most of the time. They make it work. So could we. We could be together in summer and over the school holidays."

He shook his head. "I admire your sister's and her husband's fortitude and am glad they're happy. But I don't want to spend the greater portion of my life apart from my wife. If you and I were to marry, I'd want to spend every day with you. Enjoy long conversations with you every evening after dinner, sharing the events of our day. I'd want to see my children every day, fall asleep with you in my arms every night, and wake up with you by my side."

His mention of sleeping together and children filled Selena with such intense desire and longing, she found it hard to breathe. "I want that too." She swallowed hard. "But if it's a way for us to be together ..."

"We wouldn't *be* together, that's just it. It's all or nothing for me." He paused and took a step closer. "However, I do have an idea that might work."

"Which is?"

"I believe you said there is no doctor in the village?"

Selena's heart raced even faster; she saw where this was heading. "True."

"I propose that I give up my practice in London, move here, and put up my shingle."

"You would do that for me?"

"I would."

Selena couldn't believe he was offering this—that he would

give up everything for her. "What about the London General Hospital? You have all the money back now. You can build it and manage it."

"The hospital can still go forward. After I pay all the creditors for their work and supplies to date, there will be enough to open the place. I can appoint new people to oversee it."

"But—don't you want to run the hospital yourself?"

His nose wrinkled. "In truth, that enterprise was Clarke's brainchild. I was content running my own practice until Clarke showed up at my door. After everything that's happened, the hospital has lost its appeal for me."

Selena felt a lightness enter her being. "I guess I don't blame you. Still, this is more than I could have ever hoped for."

"I admit, there is another method to my madness." He gazed down at her with hooded eyes.

"Oh? What's that?"

"Although I've been cleared of any wrongdoing by your constable, after that article in *The Times*, it might be more difficult for me to find patients in London. I'll speak to my solicitor about a libel suit and retraction, but even so, my name will have been muddied. It would be prudent to move my practice elsewhere. And what better place than Darkmoor Bridge, a village in need of a doctor … and within walking distance of the woman I love?"

Selena couldn't help but laugh. It seemed that the stars were aligning in their favor. "Your proposal sounds like just what the doctor ordered."

"I hoped you would think so."

The other members of the party began counting down the minutes to midnight. "Ten, nine, eight …"

"I believe another proposal is now in order." Dr. Dalton took one of Selena's hands in his and got down on one knee before her. "I love you, Selena Taylor. Will you make me the happiest of men? Will you marry me and spend the rest of your life with me?"

"I will," Selena answered, her heart full of joy.

"Three, two, one, Happy New Year!" the others chorused.

Dr. Dalton stood and slipped his arms around Selena. "Happy New Year, my darling wife-to-be."

"Happy New Year, my future husband." He pulled her close and they shared a kiss to seal their promise, a delectably intimate kiss that lingered for quite some time. When they broke for air, Selena whispered against his lips, "I can't wait to introduce you to my brother and my sisters and their families. I know they'll adore you."

"I can't wait to meet them." He smiled. "I've just thought of something, my darling. Do you remember the old saying from the Snapdragon game?"

"'Whoever snatches the most raisins out of the flaming brandy will marry their true love within a year.'"

"You may not have snatched the most raisins on Christmas Eve, but you *were* declared the winner."

Selena grinned. "And *you* are my true love."

"And you are mine." He kissed her again.

Selena's heart was so full, she feared it might burst. She had learned so much over the past eight days, about the world and about herself. Although her maxim about charming men had not been disproven, at least all *handsome* men, she now knew, were not untrustworthy—despite what Miss Austen might have portrayed in her novels. (Mr. Darcy notwithstanding.)

Selena no longer felt like the unaccomplished younger sister. She had solved two murders, apprehended a villain, succeeded in finding a hidden treasure, and had the good sense to fall in love with a wonderful man. Dr. Dalton understood and cherished her, she believed, in ways that few men could.

Her knight may not have slain a dragon for her, but together, they would face every obstacle.

Their love may be fresh and new, but that felt right, for this was the start of a brand-new year. Selena knew in her heart that their love would bloom in untold and marvelous ways ... and that it would last forever.

It was such fun to write this novel. I have been a fan of Agatha Christie ever since I can remember. I have a huge collection of her books and plays and adore the clever twists and turns in all her stories. I especially love mysteries set at a secluded place, where all the suspects are contained in that single environment.

Danger at Darkmoor Park is a loving homage to Agatha Christie's most famous play, "The Mousetrap," which has been running on London's West end since 1952 and is the longest-running play in the world. In that story, a group of people are snowbound at a country house during a blizzard, where a guest is murdered and secrets abound. I took that premise and ran with it, inspired by one of the backstories but changing it to suit my own purposes and create something entirely new. Since this novel is not only a snowbound murder mystery at a house party, but also a romance, to keep the hero mysterious, I had him arrive out of the storm, as Agatha Christie's detective does in that play.

Since the novel takes place entirely at Darkmoor Park, I strove to include some intriguing locations and to make the manor house and grounds feel so real so that readers could imagine they were walking its very halls (and catacombs!) in person. I've always wanted to write a story set at Christmas, so this book fulfilled a dream for me.

Another inspiration for this novel was an old family story that my husband told me. I wouldn't want to reveal this to anyone who hasn't read the book, since it's a major plot spoiler! But if you're reading this author's note after having finished this novel, I can share it with you now. My husband said that his grandfather, Robert Haverty, was an attorney at a law firm in Massachusetts in the 1930s, when one of the firm's partners ran off with all the company funds and disappeared, leaving false evidence incriminating Robert, the partner in charge of the finances, as the embezzler. A warrant was issued for his arrest. It was quite a scandal.

Robert, to avoid the possibility of jail and believing it was his duty to repay the stolen funds, gave up his life as he knew it, left his four children in the hands of his wife, moved across the country to Southern California, changed his name, and worked hard as a lawyer for sixteen years until he had earned every penny of that stolen money and repaid the debt. In consequence, his children—my husband's mother among them—grew up without a father.

Once Robert had cleared his name, he moved his family out to join him. My husband's mother, Mary, spent the rest of her life in California, where she married and where, many years later, I met and married one of her seven children—my husband, Bill. So, looking back—if Bill's Grandpa Robert hadn't taken on that life-changing obligation to repay a debt and moved to California, I never would have met my husband, and my life would have been entirely different!

That family story has haunted me for years. It was a thrill to bend and shape it to fit the backstory of my fictional hero, Dr. Andrew Dalton, who finds himself similarly liable for a huge debt. And it enabled me to include a treasure hunt in this novel—another writerly bucket list item for me. Five thousand pounds in 1852 would be worth about $1 million in today's money—a princely sum that would be very tempting to find.

In Books 1 and 2 in the Audacious Sisterhood of Smoke & Fire series, my heroines worked tirelessly to solve murder mysteries despite the objections of the heroes. In this novel, I wanted Selena and the doctor to work together—a sleuthing team like Agatha Christie's Tommy and Tuppence. This gave me the opportunity to have my main characters spend way more time together, to not only showcase their courage and investigative brilliance, but also to develop their burgeoning romance.

I hope you enjoyed *Danger at Darkmoor Park* as much as I enjoyed writing it—and that if you haven't read the first two books in the series, *The Mysteries of Pendowar Hall* and *The Secrets of Thorndale Manor,* you'll check them out! They follow Selena's sisters, Diana and Athena, who are also embroiled in murder, mystery, deadly peril, and romance set at English country houses. Although the books can be read as standalones, the sisters are all mentioned or featured in letters or in person in all the books. If you want to read more about Selena, she's a major character in *The Secrets of Thorndale Manor,* where she and Athena strive to solve two murder mysteries and uncover a host of dark secrets, in their quest to help redeem the reputation of the ancient manor home that houses their school!

ACKNOWLEDGMENTS

I am deeply grateful to the following people who helped to make this book a reality:

Tamar Rydzinski, my wonderful literary agent, for championing my work all these years, and Monica Rodriguez and Celsie Moseley for all your help and efforts behind the scenes at Context Literary Agency—I'm so grateful.

Kathryn Le Veque, for believing in the Audacious Sisterhood of Smoke & Fire series and publishing it at Dragonblade. Thank you so much.

Laurel Ann Nattress, CEO of Great Reads Book Promotion, and marketing guru extraordinaire, for running my book tours and for all your hard work as my author assistant, always going far above and beyond the call of duty and putting in untold hours advising, planning, scheduling, organizing, posting, fixing, writing, graphic designing, and teaching me the mysteries of Instagram and social media. I could not have done this without you.

Amy McNulty, the best editor I have ever worked with, for your genius at copyediting and giving such insightful notes. You make my books so much better, and I am so appreciative.

Natalie Sowa, Shawn Morrison, Evelyn Adams, cover designer Kim Killion, and the entire team at Dragonblade for making this book shine and bringing it to the world.

Ryan James, for your input during the early days of this story's inception, and for helping me figure out how to combine a murder mystery and a treasure hunt along with all the red herrings.

Kasey Arnold Ince, for giving me valuable feedback at a point when I needed it the most. Thank you, my friend—I addressed every single one of your comments.

My cousins Michelle and Adam Rosenberg for educating me about the realities of snowshoeing and the equipment that would have been used in the Victorian era.

Author Cassandra Grafton for confirming the details and reality of a rapid thaw after a Yorkshire snowstorm. Any mistakes I may have made with regard to snow, blizzards, and their aftermath are my own.

My parents, Morton and Joann Astrahan, who left this world at far too young an age, for encouraging my love of reading from early childhood. It's because of you, Dad, (and that box full of the best of children's literature that you bought at a London bookshop, which you brought to me at age seven when we lived in Paris) that I fell in love with books—and it was your insistence that I could "do anything I set my mind to" that gave me the courage to follow my dream and become an author.

And to my readers, you're the best! If you enjoyed this novel, I'd be so grateful if you would post about it, leave a review on Amazon, and tell your friends! Writing is the fire the lights my soul. I can't imagine doing anything else, and I couldn't do it without your support. Thank you from the bottom of my heart! ♥

SYRIE JAMES is the *USA Today*, Amazon, and international bestselling author of sixteen critically acclaimed novels of historical mystery, historical fiction, and historical and contemporary romance. Syrie loves All Things English and is obsessed with the Victorian and Regency eras. (Fabulous gowns! Men in cravats and on horseback! Country manor houses! Tea and finger sandwiches! Sign me up, please!)

Syrie loves to write about strong, brilliant, adventurous women who will stop at nothing to achieve their dreams, and the bold, irresistible men who crash headlong into their lives and turn everything upside down forever. A research and story-structure maven, Syrie is committed to writing page-turning books and taking her characters on challenging journeys of growth and discovery.

After writing a sizzling-hot historical romance trilogy about American Dollar Princesses run wild in late Victorian England (the Dare to Defy series), several romantic novels about Jane Austen and the Brontës (Syrie's favorite classic authors), and a passionate version of *Dracula*, among other books, she has gleefully turned her pen (okay, her computer) to writing historical murder mysteries set in the English countryside. This requires many research trips to England, the best perk on Earth.

A member of the Writers Guild of America, Sisters in Crime, Dramatists Guild, Jane Austen Society of North America, and Historical Novel Society, Syrie has sold numerous scripts to film and television. She is also a published and award-winning playwright and director whose plays have been produced across North America, off-Broadway in New York City, in Canada, and in Australia.

You will often find Syrie dressing up in one of her many Regency or Victorian frocks and dancing the night away at a ball—or performing on stage as Jane Austen herself. When she's not writing or reading, Syrie loves to attend movies and the theatre, design and create historic costumes, play *Scrabble* and *Password*, and spend time with family and friends. Syrie lives in Los Angeles a stone's throw from her grown children and grandson. She loves to hear from readers and can be contacted at www.syriejames. com.

Social media links:
Website: www.syriejames.com
Facebook: facebook.com/syriejames
Facebook Author page: facebook.com/AuthorSyrieJames
Instagram: instagram.com/syriejames
Goodreads: goodreads.com/author/show/806500.Syrie_James